UNDER ORDSHAW

AN ORDSHAW NOVEL

PHIL WILLIAMS

MMXVIII

PART 1:
FRIDAY

1

Pax Kuranes peered over her whisky tumbler at a man in a turquoise vinyl trench coat. At 4am on what she still considered to be Thursday night, the bar was dead, and the only other occupant had approached her with a cheeky smile. A smile like Albie's, when he'd wanted a ride somewhere. This guy had olive skin and long, unwashed hair, but it was the same anxiously innocent smile. He couldn't be more than nineteen, and Pax doubted humouring him would threaten her life, challenge everything she knew or put the entire city in danger. Besides, she was already bored of reading poker news off her phone.

"Rufaizu." The young man held out a hand, the other raised defensively. "Not trying to hit on you, nothing like that. Just curious."

He pointed to his jacket, asking permission to put a hand in a pocket. Pax gave him a slight smile, but folded her arms to conceal her night's earnings in her coat.

"You're having a good time." Rufaizu nodded to the empty glasses on the bar, one hand still up.

"Yeah," she replied. The £3,237 in her pocket was two months' security and more. She'd taken the bulk of it from a pastel-vested finance prick who couldn't believe he'd lost *to a girl*. That arrogance put Pax on a path to join the World Poker Tour's first outing in Ordshaw, right when it had looked like she needed to choose between an entry ticket and paying rent. "It's been a productive night."

"May I?" Rufaizu indicated his pocket again.

Pax let him wait. Good manners were rare in Ordshaw, let alone in the Sticky Tap Sports Bar. Might as well savour the moment. Her eyes tracked to the muted TV crammed between vodka optics. The BBC World News was looping the same images of a bus crash that'd been rolling all night. Pax looked sideways at Rufaizu. He hadn't moved. "Go on then."

He took out a notepad, slowly, as though it might intimidate her. He took out a pen, just as slow.

"What's your problem?" Pax asked.

"No problem!" he replied brightly. "Lookit, I just gather answers." He thumbed through a few crumpled pages for her to see. "My father said you never meet a dull person after 3am. So I have three questions for people after 3am. First –"

"Let me," Pax said, reading a few of the answers upside down. She pulled his hand, and the pad, a little closer, to figure it out for herself.

Petey – payday – all-nighter, shots!

Tyler – been paving roads, beer's the most refreshing.

Luka – girlfriend left him – vodka is like home.

Pax looked from the pad to Rufaizu, then scanned the bar again. It was a weird hobby for a young man, lurking in places like this. Only the lowest people came here. The sort that didn't talk to one another, as Pax liked it. She pushed the pad back towards Rufaizu, concluding, "Name, reason they're out, what they're drinking. All guys, huh?"

Rufaizu whooped with delight, almost jumping. He slapped a hand into the pad and said, "*Damn* right! Damn right! You are *sharp*. I like you." He quickly backed off, face serious. "Not like that. Nothing creepy. I'll just ask the questions and go, okay? Not trying to sleep with you."

"You're making it creepy," Pax warned him. She found herself smiling, though. He was worse than Albie. Her little brother was a dork, but he tried to hide it with dignified quietness. This guy's dorkiness was bubbling out. "Why these questions?"

"Oh, these?" Rufaizu replied, as though surprised at the notepad himself. "I guess they're a start? To tell us if someone's . . . you know . . ."

Pax frowned, but he didn't elaborate.

"Okay. Shall we?" Rufaizu grinned. As quickly as the grin came, it disappeared, as something caught his eye. A suited man stood in the entrance doorway, watching them, coming no further into the bar. With a sharp intake of breath, Rufaizu said, "Lookit, I'll be on my way. Back to my booth, back to my booth."

"You're not gonna ask me my questions?" Pax said, eyeing the newcomer.

Rufaizu lowered his face to hide it. He clicked his pen and spoke rapidly, much quieter. "Um. Sure. Real quick. Can I have your name?"

"Why, you don't like yours?" Pax joked. He paused, not following. She used the momentary lull to sip her whisky.

"He bothering you?"

Pax jumped on her stool, the man in the suit suddenly at their shoulders.

"Son of a . . ." Pax uttered. He'd crossed the bar without a sound. The man's darkly handsome face was lit in the bar's archaic neon, skin like a Latino singer, not a hair out of place, suit freshly pressed. His white teeth shone like headlights in the dim bar and his smile killed Rufaizu's cheer.

"No trouble, friend," Rufaizu said. "Don't want none. Just shooting the breeze."

The suit's eyes stayed fixed on Rufaizu. "He's bothering me."

Pax searched for the barman, but he was nowhere to be seen. No one else in the room.

"The lady's not interested," the suit said.

"Hey," Pax said. "The *lady* can talk for herself."

The man gave her a wink. "Just trying to help."

"I don't need your help."

Rufaizu chipped in, then. "Yeah, man, she don't need –"

The suit pounced, pinning Rufaizu's arm behind his back and slamming his face into the bar. He yanked Rufaizu upright again, the younger man's nose bloody and his free arm snapping around. Pax stepped back, too late, as the two men collided with her and made her stumble, whisky spilling. Rufaizu made incoherent noises of protest as the suit hauled him across the floor. The suit flashed another smile back to Pax and said, "Enjoy your drink, miss."

"Leave it out," Pax replied hotly. "He didn't do anything."

Rufaizu tried to break free, but the man tightened his grip, forcing him still. As he marched Rufaizu to the exit, the suit said, "Trust me, he would've."

Rufaizu gave up struggling and started goading. "Tough guy, I'll set Barton on you, what're you gonna do? He's fought the *minotaur*!"

The door swung shut behind them. Pax stared into their absence.

4am lunacy. An irate office worker taking out his machismo on some mixed-up kid?

"What happened?" The barman's voice snapped Pax's attention back to the bar. He had a tray of clean glasses in his hands as he stared at an overturned stool. Rufaizu's notepad sat on the bar in front of him. Pax grabbed it.

"Fat use you are," she said. He gave her a bored look, said nothing and turned away.

Pax rolled the notepad in her hand. With the cash in her pocket, the Pax Kuranes Beer, Burger and Liveliness Fund was finally in good health. All she had to do was go home, pay the rent and enjoy the tournament starting Thursday. Revel in the memory of her ace-high flush holding up against an opponent's trips.

The notepad felt heavy, though. The handwriting was childish and the paper was warped from being repeatedly wet and dried. Painfully similar to Albie's books of ideas. He wouldn't visit places like this, would he? It might happen anywhere, though. Some suit pounding on some awkward kid for being different. The boy had raved about a minotaur, for crying out loud. Pax huffed. She'd already put one entitled prick in his place that evening. Why stop now?

She downed the whisky, pocketed the notepad and hurried outside.

The road was still, cracked tarmac dancing in the flicker of the Sticky Tap's light. An old air conditioning unit squeaked a few doors down. Pax scanned up and down, nothing moving anywhere nearby. She hadn't heard a car engine. Definitely no sounds of a struggle. They'd been bucking against each other on the way out; surely they couldn't have moved anywhere fast?

Pax frowned, reimagining the men's rapid departure. Rewinding to when the suit had struck. The men had bumped into her. Together. She shot a hand to her coat pocket.

Her fingers closed on empty space. The money was gone. £3,237. Gone.

No wait – there was the hard nugget of a £2 coin in there. Mocking her.

£3,235 gone.

The little bastard.

Pax held her breath. If she opened her mouth her whole venomous vocabulary might fly out. No. Keep calm. Be practical. She had lost more money quicker, in stupider ways, and recovered it – it was a bad beat. She could turn it around. Even if the Poker Tour started in six days. Even if the rent was due.

She took out her phone, bringing up a contact, fingers tapping on autopilot.

"Pax," Bees answered at once. "Heard you cleared up this evening."

"Yeah. The news might've spread faster than I'd have liked."

"Had some trouble?"

A chain-link fence rattled nearby. A black cat pounced to a higher vantage point to watch her. Pax met its green eyes as she answered. "Something like that. Guy called himself Rufaizu. Nineteen or twenty. Looked European, Roma maybe. Long green-blue coat."

"Not much to add to that."

"You know him?" Pax asked.

"Of him. Turned up a few weeks back, held his own in a game or two. Then made off with a chunk of money that wasn't his. The Row Street Rogues are after him. Out of St Alphege's."

She didn't need to be told where the Rogues came from. Some of the worst people from the worst part of town. They wouldn't have sent a suit out to collect. And Rufaizu wouldn't have made a grab for her cash in the middle of a serious confrontation, anyway. They were working together. She'd been robbed, simple as that.

Pax said, "Got a last known location?"

Rufaizu's apartment poked out the top of a red-brick terrace on the edge of the warehouse district, opposite the grimiest station of the K&S Underground. The windows were painted black, lessening the glare of the station's brightly lit sign. Pax drew an impression of the youth from the state of his home: the door locked by a piece of string looped over a nail; *STAY OUT* painted in sloppy red letters; smashed bottles on the floor testifying to the dual triumphs of drinking and hygiene problems. His dirt-encrusted blanket had been shredded, the mattress on the floor ripped apart. The stains and the scent of alcohol, partially masking what Pax feared was a more offensive odour underneath, suggested the place hadn't lost much charm when the guys from St Alphege's had turned it over.

Pax took in the peeling wallpaper, the uneven floorboards and the cracked single light bulb. The cafés in Ten Gardens spent a fortune trying to recreate this shabby look, and here this vagrant had stumbled across the real thing. He probably didn't know it, though; for someone who stole from affluent poker games, Rufaizu was light on luxuries. Pax trod lightly over the floorboards, listening for their creaks. She tugged at the ones that moved, and one came up. There was a crinkled collection of men's magazines in the hollow underneath. A good, albeit disgusting, sign. Rufaizu had hidden stuff here, and the Row Street Rogues had failed to find it.

Pax ran a hand over the walls, checking the cracks and tears. Her finger bumped over a groove. Stopping to look closer, she found the crack ran up in a strangely straight line. She applied pressure, one side and then the other. Part of the wall flexed, a different material to the rest. She jammed a key in the crack and popped it open. The false front came off, a single panel wedged over a cavity in the lath and plaster, apparently containing Rufaizu's most prized possessions.

There were two items in the wall space: a thick leather-bound book and a glass tube trimmed with brass, a lever protruding from one side and a stack of interconnected cogs at one end. The contraption was dented and scratched; it looked like a nerd's desk ornament, but it had been tossed about. A lot. The book was also worn from rough handling. Pax skimmed through it, finding reams of handwritten symbols, with repeated combinations of circles, triangles and lines. The symbols surrounded maniacally etched illustrations and diagrams.

She hummed to herself, closing the tome and reading the title, carved into its cover as though by a knife: *Apothel's Miscellany*.

This would do.

*

It would work out, Pax told herself as she watched the city roll past the bus window. Whether the book's bizarre contents were the product of crazed mania or passionate creativity, the things hidden in the wall had to be important to Rufaizu. Albie protected this sort of creative crap with his life; she had to believe the vagrant kid was similar. If he wanted them back, they could do a deal. If not, they'd give a strong clue as to what he did want. Or at least where she could find him.

She rode the night bus with the items carefully stowed in her backpack, calm. Being calm was everything in a crisis. It was just theft. She was handling it. She had a few days yet, until the World Poker Tour. Eight days before rent was due. There was petty cash in the kitchen drawer. A stale loaf of bread on the counter that was probably still edible.

Everything would be fine.

When she came in sight of her apartment building, however, she gagged on the panic she was fighting to keep down. The man in the suit stood waiting, and everything she had assumed about Rufaizu's simple con, and what it would take to set it right, was shattered.

2

Unreliable people. Say to be somewhere and don't turn up. Unwanted, unreliable, bastard pigs. Give you an invite you want nothing to do with, then screw you. Dragging up the past for no good goddamned reason.

The angry thoughts shot through Darren Barton like a drill sergeant's shouts, encouraging one thick punch after another.

He typically coped with life in one of two ways. Strong enough liquor, drunk quick enough, could help him forget. The next best thing was to beat all hell out of something with his bare hands. He had run out of Johnnie Walker before it dulled the pain, so he was throwing punch after punch into the sack that hung in his garage. The bag swung like a pendulum as the supports shuddered. Half drunk and out of shape in a long-term way, Barton found his punches were glancing off the bag, inaccurate, but his full weight and loathing made each strike matter.

The noise of the impacts, the rattle of the chain and the creaking rafter were all blocked out by his heavy breathing and the sound of blood pumping in his ears. He might have woken up the wife, the kid, but it didn't matter. Their problem.

Another punch. Another animalistic noise to release some of the pressure.

That little scumbag, arranging meetings he couldn't keep.

At this damn hour.

His father's son, another stinking shadow you could trust for nothing more than trouble.

Barton took a step back and his foot caught a can of beer on the floor. Taking a sip from the can in his hand, he slowed down to focus. Catching his breath, he saw three empty cans, now. He blinked to check if it was his vision failing him. Definitely three of them. He must have been going for at least half an hour. His vest clung tight to his chest, skin slick with sweat, hot like a radiator.

Someone cleared their throat, up above.

He ignored it, passing the beer can to his right hand, then flung a stiff haymaker and took another swig.

"Oh for God's sake!" Holly finally erupted.

Barton turned from the bag with a frown, finding his defiant wife staring furiously from the top of the short flight of stairs that led into the house. Too weary from the booze and the boxing to conjure the energy for surprise, he spread his arms in a mock welcoming gesture. He heaved a few deep breaths, then said, "Did I wake you?"

"You think?"

Barton lumbered towards her, swaying on his tired legs. The severity of Holly's disapproving glare cranked up to maximum as he dropped forward to lean on the banister, looking up at her.

"You went out," Holly said.

"I got a message," Barton replied, unapologetic. "Asking me to meet him."

"Darren, it's almost *dawn*. We can't go back to this. I won't go through it again."

"You think I want to?" Barton snapped. Of course he was the one in the wrong. Having been forced to remember and getting stood up. It was his fault, like everything else. He pushed off from the stairs and walked unsteadily back through the garage. He took another swing at the bag as he passed, making it quake. He raised his voice, over his shoulder. "He didn't show. Wasn't there. So don't worry about it."

"Yet you're in this state, all the same."

Barton turned to hold his wife's gaze. She let her arms unfold.

"It's a lapse," Barton said. "I needed this" – he pointed at the punching bag, still swinging from his last blow – "from the moment his name showed on my phone. You think I'm happy?"

"What did he want?"

"Damned if I know." Barton took another swig of beer. "He didn't show."

"Darren." Holly descended a step towards him. That was all the conciliation she was willing to offer, placing a hand on the banister to show it. "For your sake, for our sake, for Grace's sake, it'd better just be a lapse. You told me this was behind us. I believed you."

"He didn't show." He said it one more time. "What else can I say?"

"If he contacts you again?"

Barton grumbled, "I owe it to his dad."

"After all he did for you?"

His face fell at the sarcasm, eyelids drooping. "You never understood."

"I understand" – Holly's voice took on a sharp edge – "that you wouldn't want your daughter to see you like this. Would you?"

Barton said nothing.

"You can sleep on the couch. Then we can talk about it in the morning, or you can let it go. Your call."

With that, she left, and Barton let her.

He put the beer can on the workbench and swayed on the spot. A door closed loudly as Holly made her way through the house. Barton leant on the punching bag, using it to hold himself up, then gave up. He slid down to the floor and sat in an unfocused daze.

His mind was almost blank, but not quite.

Somewhere in the haze, he could still see Apothel's face.

The hole in his head.

Rufaizu screaming.

3

Pax Kuranes lived in Ordshaw's student district, Hanton, the closest spot to the centre with even remotely affordable rent. It was lined with terraced houses, slightly more civilised than the tower-blocks that characterised the other impoverished areas. Pax's apartment was on the top floor of a converted church, and she was surrounded by people a few years younger than her. They rarely disturbed her, as their night-long parties seldom outlasted her night-long poker games. On her return that morning, a banner flapped from a window reading *Lisa's Home!*, but only a single lanky student held vigil on the stoop, hunched over a bottle of cider, red eyes vacant.

It was not the sort of location you found men in smart suits, especially not at the cusp of dawn, yet here one was. His hands in his pockets, he flashed his poster smile at Pax as she kept her distance, a dozen metres down the path to her building.

"I've got something for you," he said, lightly.

He reached into his jacket pocket and Pax took a quick step back. She held off from running, though. Granted, he had assaulted a young man and mysteriously vanished, but if it wasn't a con then maybe he had a genuine grievance with Rufaizu. Was it insane to hope he had her money? She was tired and desperate enough to believe it wasn't, and watched as he took out a piece of folded A4 paper. She caught a glimpse of something else under his lapel. A strap of leather. The unmistakable square of a gun handle.

It was too late to run, now.

He said, "It's a receipt, essentially, for the value of the money. A PO-42c. States that on completion of our investigation the private property that was confiscated will be returned. Assuming it was your money he took."

A dozen questions ran through Pax's mind. She asked the most burning one: "What do you need a gun for?"

"Shooting things," he replied candidly, as though it was obvious. He added, "But I haven't used it on a person in three years."

"Who'd you shoot?" Pax asked.

"An Armenian."

Pax hummed. The answer did not help, and demanded another question. Why had he specified *on a person*?

"There's nothing to worry about," the suit said. He moved a step closer and she took another step back, eyes on the gun bulge. "I'm sorry you had to see that, in the bar. I should've handled it better. He just – his sort irk me. But, please, take this."

He held out the paper. She stood rigidly as he closed the distance to her. She took the paper and unfolded it: a dense block of printed text dotted with legal jargon, headed with an important-looking crest and the title *Public Ordinance Issue 42c – Confiscation of Goods*. In the middle, the amount of money was written in bold: £3,235. At the bottom there was a printed valediction: *Yours Sincerely, Gertrude Gossinger, Acquisitions and Inventory Secretary*.

"What the hell is this?" Pax said. "What's this secretary got to do with my money?"

"It is your money, then?"

Pax gave him a challenging look. "How'd you know where I live?"

"The population of this city gets a lot smaller when you're filtering for nighthawks."

"*Why* are you filtering populations?"

"My name's Cano Casaria," he said, holding out a hand.

Without shaking, Pax rolled on, "Gertrude Gossinger and Cano Casaria? Your friends call you CC? Or KK?"

He let her agitation sit in the air, his hand waiting. His smile wavered slightly when she didn't shake. He said, "You're quick. But I'd imagine something we've got in common is our lack of friends."

"What's that supposed to mean?"

"We're both working unsociable hours when we needn't be. And neither of us, I sense, suffers fools lightly."

"I suffer tons of fools," Pax said. "You attack defenceless boys then stalk women outside their homes. Tell me again we've got something in common."

"I'm just here to do the right thing," Casaria said.

"And what's the right thing that got Cano Casaria out in a dive bar at 4am dressed like he's ready for a meeting, beating on a homeless boy? You want me to believe you're with some kind of government agency? Please – no civil servant has the gall to dye their hair and whiten their teeth. You wouldn't starch a shirt on Her Majesty's account, would you?"

His hand was still waiting to be shaken. The smile had barely faltered. She knew how to needle people, but he, in turn, clearly knew how to take it. Maybe he *was* a civil servant. He said, "I'm a field agent for the Ministry of Environmental Energy. The young man in the bar was a person of interest. And I genuinely thought he might've been bothering you."

Pax ran the unfamiliar Ministry's name through her head, not sure if it was obscure or made up, or if she was just ignorant of government affairs. She said, "And what the hell are you doing here?"

"Two things," Casaria said, finally lowering his unshaken hand. "First, following up on what happened. When I returned to the bar, you were gone. I wanted to ask if you knew that young man. I saw you talking, but –"

"Never seen him before," Pax said. "What's he supposed to have done?"

"You not knowing that will make both our lives a lot easier. Bringing us to the second thing . . ." He nodded to the paper in her hand. "I hoped that my gesture of goodwill might buy me a conversation."

"I don't know what your game is, but I read people for a living and I *know* you've got a game. I don't want your conversation. Just my money."

Casaria paused. "It could take two weeks, maybe more. There's a lot of red tape involved when property gets confiscated in the course of an investigation."

"Two *weeks*?" Pax exclaimed. "That's bullshit – I –"

"You'll get the money back, I can vouch for that. I'd like to know who you are, though."

"Who do you *think* I am?"

"If I'm honest," he said, eyes running from her bulky coat and dark hoodie down to her loose jeans and boots, "seeing a young lady out at that hour, with all that cash, dressed like this, raises some interesting questions."

Pax kept her face neutral, making an effort not to respond to the *young lady* comment, recalling his earlier use of *miss*. He couldn't have been five years older than her. She said, "What's this actually about? The guy you assaulted, the money, or me?"

"Let's talk about it over a coffee."

Pax looked up the road. The nearest café was at least forty minutes from opening, and she had no intention of inviting this stranger into her flat. She was tired, feeling the chill of dawn and wary that if he wasn't a government spook he had to be a psychopath. Either way, being the victim of a theft seemed like a blessing compared to this. "You say you're government. That you just apprehended that guy. Nothing to do with me? How do you explain him picking my pocket while being abducted?"

"He's compulsive," Casaria said. "Not rational. At all."

"Yeah," Pax replied. Shady guy in a suit kidnaps someone unstable because he's about to talk to a stranger. It screamed of a thousand possibilities she wanted nothing to do with. Yet she had to ask. "So why were you after him?"

Casaria held her gaze. There was no chance he was going to tell her, and that, it seemed, was the point. There was something she was not allowed to know. But he still wanted to talk to her.

"I've never heard of your Ministry of Environmental Energy," she said. "And unless you're gonna give me my money, right now, I'd like to go."

She paused, inviting him to respond. He let another smile fill the moment's silence, then said, "Of course, you're free to go. I've got one question, though. Where did you go after leaving the bar?"

"This stinks," Pax said, firmly.

"I get that you might not believe me." The smile escalated to a snigger, like this whole situation was a game to him. "But it *is* a matter of national security."

Pax stared, miffed at the contrast. His unprovoked attack on Rufaizu and his insincere smiles said one thing, while his suit, paperwork and gun said another. As if to punctuate it, he put his hands on his hips in a manner that pulled the jacket back, drawing attention to the pistol. National security was a perfect phrase, wasn't it. Throw national security into the mix and you can get away with murder, that's what he was telling her. Hesitating, Pax considered how best to answer him. She said, "People who work nights look out for each other. I asked my people and got a name, tried to follow it up."

For the first time, Casaria looked concerned. He shifted his weight from one leg to another and asked, "What did you find out?"

The truth, Pax knew, was always the best frame for a lie. "Rufaizu was new in town, knocked over a game in St Alphege's and no one's been able to find him since. I checked the Nothicker Slums, figuring he might have a shack there."

"The Nothicker Slums," Casaria said. Pax nodded. The homeless shanty town was close enough to Rufaizu's place, if he wanted to check her travel route. He said, "What do you mean by a game in St Alphege's?"

"A game," Pax repeated. "Poker."

"Ah." Casaria's face lit up, the penny dropping. "So you –"

"You said one question," Pax cut him off. "You going to leave me alone now?"

"There's more we could discuss."

"I'm going," she said, keeping her eyes on him as she took a cautious step forward. He didn't make a move. She took another step, then another, slow and deliberate. He rolled his eyes, giving up, and waved a hand, "Go on. I slid a card under your door. Call me, any time."

She hurried to her building and took the key from her pocket without looking back. As she let herself in, she sensed he was still watching her.

4

Pax threw off her coat and turned on the radio to try and restore some normalcy to her mood. The early morning presenters were discussing the bus crash. "Twelve dead – twelve – and three of them children. This guy should *not* have been driving, it's as simple as that."

"He wasn't drunk, Marty, he was doing his job same as ever –"

"He fell asleep at the wheel! Unfit – who's regulating these people – who's –"

Marty sounded like he was going to give himself a heart attack. Pax was happy to hear she wasn't the only one having a bad morning. She kicked off her boots and paused to study her thinning left sock. It'd survive a few more washes, but she couldn't wait until Christmas for new underwear. Whatever, socks were way down the list of things she needed that money for.

The radio host decided it was time to play some music, and Pax agreed. Better not to dwell on how shitty life was. Ignore her patchy socks, and the fact that a bad driver had cost a bunch of people their lives. Block out the thought that this apartment needed paying for. A pop song came on about love or dancing, or love of dancing, or some other banality. Much better.

Pax settled onto her sofa and spread *Apothel's Miscellany* out on the cushion. Its coded language had been scrawled with black ink in fits of emotion, surrounding pencil sketches of mechanical devices that combined pipes, tools, blades and arrows: creative ideas for modern medieval weapons. Then there were occasional floor plans of winding tunnels and mazes. There were strange, fantastic creatures. How did a creative kid with interests like this get into the spooks' crosshairs? What would it take for Albie to find himself on the same path? It didn't make sense. Then, this might be something completely different to his board-game miniatures. Maybe if she spoke to him more than once a year, she'd have a better idea.

Pax put that thought out of her mind, to study a creature drawn in different poses. Some sort of biped, the rough shape of a gorilla, with no head and an extra limb rising over one shoulder from its spine. Where the head should have been was a set of mandibles. Patches of alternating scaly and flat rocky textures covered its skin and lines ran between its panelled flesh like veins. The ends of its long arms, which hung just above its flat, elephant-like feet, had three angular claws.

This Apothel was a talented artist, Pax appreciated that. Someone of considerable imagination. It could have been concept artwork for a fantasy comic or a computer game. The annotations gave the same impression, written in that cryptic language. The symbols were a lexicon, repeated frequently and systematically. Occasional notes in the margins, scrawled in handwritten biro, in English, hinted at a translation. Pax ran a finger from one or two of the comments to a few of the underlined symbols.

The monster's name, at the head of the page, appeared to be translated directly.

Glogockle.

The title in symbols had the same number of letters. Another entry at the bottom had a comment, *What?! Seen one OUTRUN A MAN*, next to the number 13 and three symbols. Presumably those three symbols gave a speed: *mph* or *kph*. The word before 13 was five symbols. *Speed?*

Humming along to another irritating tune on the radio, Pax took a pad of paper and a pen from her side table and started to make notes. The cypher was simple, worthy of the man who had tried to lock his door with a piece of string. It substituted English letters with symbols. She made a list of the letters of the alphabet and started matching them to symbols. This was perfect. A mindless task to clear her head, to help her calm down before plotting her next move.

Deciphering the text, Pax ignored the sun rising. When only Q, Z and X eluded her, she started to translate sections of writing, starting at the back where a set of short paragraphs were surrounded by brainstormed words. She'd hoped there might be names or addresses, but the first lines suggested they were more likely to be nonsensical riddles. *The seeping sour flower rests before the needle of two days* . . . Pax flicked away from that nonsense. Back to the glogockle, might as well check something interesting. A series of short instructions annotated the pictures:

Always approach from behind. Soft spot in central abdomen. Feeds on small animals. Max seen speed 13mph. There was the X.

The Miscellany was a colourful and creative project, no doubt about that. A labour of love and the result of painstaking hours of work. And it wasn't Rufaizu's work. His comments in the margin almost offered a conversation with the author. Going back to the beginning, Pax translated the title on the first page, finding the book's name repeated with an epitaph: *Apothel's Miscellany: Essential tips for mastering the Sunken City.* She sat back.

The radio presenter had started raving about something new. A problem with a construction site that people were worried might collapse. He claimed the people of Ordshaw were lazy and cutting corners. They needed a wake-up call. He yawned as he said it, though. Tired of his own vitriol.

Pax turned the radio off.

Checking back through the comments in the margins of the book, she imagined Rufaizu interpreting this nonsense with the same merry enthusiasm Albie had showed when he chattered at her about a race of greenskins when she'd walked him to a model store in London. That must've been over ten years ago. When she was a teenager. She'd ignored him to make mental plans for the £20 her mother had paid her to take him. It seemed Rufaizu had been even more neglected than that.

Pax looked at the odd book with a pang of guilt. When she got this thing turned around, she'd have Albie to stay for a few days. He'd love Ordshaw. Maybe after the tournament. If she could get hold of him without going through Mum or, worse, Dad. Pax shook herself out of it and fixed her eyes back on the book. Focus. There'd be nowhere to invite anyone to if she wasn't careful.

The book had brought her no closer to understanding what Rufaizu was about. What would a government Ministry of Energy want with him? Had he stolen from them, too? The card Casaria had slipped under Pax's door bore the same insignia as the PO-42c, a lion crest with grandiose laurels. Both matched the Ministry of Environmental Energy's website, which she'd checked on her phone. The website said nothing about what they did, though, it merely gave a list of nameless contact emails and stock images of models looking happy and important.

Casaria was troubling, even without this mystery ministry behind him. His wandering eyes, attempts at a charming smile and suggestions of wanting a casual chat all hinted at personal advances. Which was an immediate *no*. He'd dealt with Rufaizu barbarically, for one, and there were things she clearly wasn't supposed to know, for another. To say nothing of his edgy awkwardness, and the gun.

She decided to contact someone else from this Ministry. If they really did have her money, they could tell her when she'd get it back, and what had happened to Rufaizu. Or they could let her know Casaria was nothing to do with them. She pictured the gun again and considered another call to Bees, and as if on cue her phone chirped, making Pax jump.

She fumbled to answer, barely noticing the call came from a withheld number.

"All right bitch-sticks," a rough female voice shouted. "I know who you are and where you live – if I sniff a lie, I'll rain on you harder than a brick bull. You working with them?"

Pax held the phone a foot from her ear, too stunned to respond.

"You hearing me, cock burglar?" the voice snapped. "You working with them or what?"

"Who is this?" Pax replied.

"Are you fucking working with them?" the caller exploded.

"Working with who?" Pax answered almost as hotly, the hostility giving her a rise.

"The suit salesman, the slick prick – we *saw* you."

"The government?"

"Hallelujah, a ray of light in your simple skull."

"Who is this?"

"I'll come down this line and pull your tongue through your ear, you keep this up. Are you or are you not working with him?"

Pax paused. She'd dealt with plenty of angry people at the card table, and the best response was usually no response. But the night's events had her irate. To hell with the best response. She said, forcibly, "One, if you know who I am then you should already know if I'm working with them. Two, if you know where I live, then come say it to my face, instead of making threats through the phone."

Before the mad woman could respond, Pax hung up, as calmly as she could. Her hand was shaking, stung by the intensity of the caller's voice, but she kept her composure. The phone started ringing again, again showing a withheld number. Pax waited three rings, then answered, holding the phone at a distance, expecting more shouting.

The caller was beyond incensed.

"Listen you tall sack of shit, if I tell you to talk you're –"

Pax hung up. Down this road, no rational conversation lay. She moved to the window. Her apartment gave a panoramic view of the sleeping street below. Curtains drawn in the windows, no one lingering in the street. Whoever was calling didn't appear to be in the immediate area.

She stared at the phone. There was someone else involved, apparently opposed to Casaria's lot, and hinting, rather strongly, that he genuinely was from the government. This angry woman had her phone number but had, for some reason, referred to Pax as *tall*. They couldn't actually know who she was, because 5'6" was hardly tall in anyone's books. She was safe, wasn't she? Besides, no one who wanted to hurt her would warn her with a crazed phone call.

Still, it was weird, getting weirder.

Pax returned to the sofa.

The book lay open on a sketch of an Underground train surrounded by what looked like lightning. There were people in the windows, with shaded doubles of themselves lifting from their bodies, as though something was pulling their souls out.

The evocative artwork made her frown. She read Rufaizu's marginal comment: *Minotaur's Grasp. Does this even need explaining?*

"Yes, it needs explaining, you dick," Pax grumbled, turning the page to see if there was any more. He'd said *minotaur* as he was dragged from the bar, clearly a focal point for him. The next few pages showed diagrams of tunnels with no text, though. Crazy people upon crazy people, and somewhere in the middle of all this Pax's livelihood was at risk, along with the life of an odd young man.

The phone vibrated again, once. A text message appeared on the screen.

WITHHELD: You are so fucked.

5

Barton took in Rufaizu's apartment grimly. There were boot-prints in the dust that said someone had visited recently, but they looked too small to have been the young man come home. Whoever it was, they'd raided his hiding places. That left only one option, and Barton hated it. Dr Mandy Rimes. Holly would be furious at him for even contemplating calling her.

It didn't matter.

He'd already breached Holly's trust by coming here. She hadn't cooled off when she woke him from his slumber on the couch, still dressed and smelling like a septic tank. She threw a towel at him and told him to go outside to hose himself down. Deadbeats don't get to use the shower, she'd said. He sat on the sofa for a while longer, rubbing his throbbing temples, while Grace watched him from the adjoining kitchen. Cautious whispers passed between his daughter and wife; he could guess what they were saying.

What's going on? Your father's an arsehole.

The usual sort of thing.

He could feel Grace staring, not venturing any closer. When Barton looked up, she ducked away, shaking her head, adopting the affected child routine. She wasn't a child any more, though, she was at that age where you took pride in hating your parents. It'd bring her kudos: *my dad is the worst.*

Holly got Grace's stuff together for school and huffed that she guessed it was her turn to drive, knowing full well it wasn't. Barton didn't respond. He let them go without any kind of explanation, just sat there staring at the carpet wishing he could stick a spike through his skull to release the pressure.

Holly slammed the door on her way out. Barton took it as a signal to finally get up.

Climbing the stairs to the shower felt like a monumental struggle. Twice he slid to his knees and groaned at the world for being too difficult to live in. Somehow he found it in himself to keep going, and the frosty water partly woke him. He threw on some clean clothes and dragged himself outside.

Struggling to keep his eyes open, swaying in his car seat, Barton suspected he still had more than the legal limit of alcohol in his blood.

It didn't matter.

Rufaizu's apartment was a forty-minute drive away, on the other side of the city, but he managed it in an hour twenty. It was the city's fault, not his; he'd taken the quickest route, using the ring road, but driving around Ordshaw during the day sucked at time like a leech. Damn Rufaizu for forcing him to travel. Barton had moved out to leafy Dalford to pretend he wasn't part of the heaving beast that was Ordshaw. Year by year the city was getting worse; more crowded, spreading into new, more colourfully wretched neighbourhoods that had once been villages in their own right. More like London every day, only less important. Two million people combining to create a monster you couldn't cross in under an hour.

He locked the car six times before he was satisfied that it was secure. If there was ever a place for your car to go missing, this was it. Even his twenty-year-old Scenic was fair game – it'd stopped being scenic a decade ago, but a thief around here could get it started better than he ever could.

Staring at the empty disappointment of Rufaizu's apartment, after the effort it had taken to get there, Barton considered sitting and waiting, but his hangover was getting worse and his ability to concentrate was fading. It wasn't worth it. Rufaizu was gone, not answering his phone, and it didn't look like he'd be here any time soon. It was either leave it all to rear its ugly head at a random point in the future, or call Rimes to try and figure this out.

Barton dialled and hoped, with each passing ring, that the doctor would not answer. It had been so long, maybe she had a new number. Maybe she was dead, who knew. Five rings. Six. Barton's finger hovered, preparing to hang up. The phone clicked.

"Citizen Barton?" Rimes' raspy voice answered, at once tired and surprised.

"Mandy," Barton said quietly. "How are you?"

"I've been expecting your call."

Barton could picture Holly's face. Her mouth and eyes screwing smaller like the narrowing points of intensely focusing lasers. She wouldn't say anything, just burn him with her gaze, letting him know how big a mistake he was making. Silently saying *you've ruined all our lives*. Sometimes she gave him that look when he folded his trousers the wrong way after doing the laundry, mind. It would make a change to receive it for something serious.

Rimes breathed patiently but loudly. Barton knew few people in the world who could so comfortably let a silence hang.

"Expecting me why?" he asked.

"Rufus got in touch. He said he had found something, but wouldn't tell me what."

"For God's sake," Barton groaned. "Did you meet with him?"

"Briefly. He told me to be ready. That your involvement would come first."

"I haven't spoken to him. He wanted to meet with me last night. He didn't show."

"That's not good. Not good at all."

Rimes' tone was completely neutral, but Barton knew well enough that her unemotional words could be taken at face value. He said, "What else did he tell you?"

"Just what I said. He thinks he's found the answer."

"To what?"

"To everything. To kill the beast."

Barton paused, holding back from saying something he might regret. Another question, another sentence, and he might be drawn back in without any way out. If there was a solution, it was not something he could walk away from. No matter what promises he had made to his family. He replied, "Rufaizu's been away so long. He was just a kid. What would he know?"

"I hoped you might tell me."

"Are you still working?"

"Mm."

He could picture Rimes in her laboratory, lights low and blinds down, examining some test-tube of luminous liquid through brass-rimmed goggles, even as they spoke. It was possible that the doctor had never left that unlikely hall of experiments. She might have been born there, for all he knew. It certainly felt like she would make it her grave.

The idea that he could ever have cheated on Holly with her was so far from reality that it wasn't even funny. It was borderline offensive. But Holly hadn't known who the doctor was. Rimes was a lady Barton had visited in the dead of the night. On numerous occasions. In Holly's eyes, those secret visits were a betrayal, no matter their purpose.

Guessing his thoughts, Rimes asked, "Did you tell your wife everything, in the end?"

"Enough to keep her from cutting my throat in my sleep," Barton said. "Not enough that she's any the wiser." Just enough to leave a permanent look of distrust on her face. He sighed. "She got the point that I wasn't having an affair, at least. Mandy, if you see Rufaizu again, let him know I tried to meet him. But it's best he not contact me again."

"Certainly. There's something else you might want to be aware of, though," Rimes said. "I believe he wasn't working alone. He said he had help. Friends."

"Well," Barton said, firming his decision. Apothel had found friends, too, and look where it got him. Rufaizu was his father's son. "Then I definitely want no part of it."

"Aren't you curious, Citizen Barton?" Rimes asked, before he could end the call.

"No," he told her. "I can't afford to be."

On the way home, Barton tried to convince himself that none of it mattered. There was no way to stop the minotaur, Apothel had been clear about that from the start. If he'd found a solution he would've told everyone, not disappeared up his own arse. And for Rufaizu to find something where his own father had failed was unthinkable. The boy was wayward, half mad.

There was no way.

And there were more important things to worry about. Holly's anger. Grace's trust. They needed him. Emotionally and financially. Even this impromptu day off would eat into their small buffer of disposable cash.

When the Scenic sputtered, pulling into the faster-moving traffic of the ring road, Barton pictured their faces on seeing the car he'd been saving for. It was small, the new Civic, but it meant cheaper journeys and fewer breakdowns. More money for holidays. A tour of Scotland. A seaside jaunt. A Christmas market. It was all possible. Holly would soften, at least for a moment. Grace, more importantly, would offer him her smile. She had the most charming smile of any young lady. A heartbreaker. That smile would say her dad was okay. There had been far too many disappointed smiles.

The imagined scenes of his happy family consoled him for the journey, his spirits lifting and the misery of his godforsaken hangover drifting into the background.

Life wasn't so bad.

Rufaizu's lunacy could not be allowed to ruin everything. Barton had the strength to ignore it. He decided he'd go in to work today, after all.

6

Pax had not slept. Years of enduring poker games that stretched into oblivion had taught her you could always find a second wind if you waited long enough. Or a third, or fourth. Rather than struggle to rest, she studied Rufaizu's book while she waited for the Ministry offices to open. After reading about glogockles and surveying tunnel layouts, she decoded notes on other unnatural creatures, taking satisfaction in solving the puzzles. She decoded the headings for *The Drummer Horse, Invisible Proclaimers,* and *Tuckles* before focusing on the entry for the *Sickle* in detail. Its image was a thing of nightmares, a humanoid torso atop four canine legs, with long, curved claws instead of hands. Its face had no eyes, just a jagged-toothed jawline that ran from top to bottom rather than left to right. The short misspelt paragraph curating it gave her the idea that Apothel was not exactly a scholar.

Sickles patrol on set lines. Strongest sense is touch; they look for vibrashans from movement. No eyes, no nose, no ears. Stay still and quiet, they mite not know your there. If cornered by a sickle, get the back legs, they lose balance easy. Sickles are very fast. Teef and claws rip flesh. Avoid – do not fite.

In the margin she found a clue to another person's involvement in this strange enterprise. A triumphant addendum read: *Tell that to Citizen Barton!*

Pax leafed through the book, looking for other names. She reached a long section with no images and a single solitary note in the margin: *Probably inaccurate.* She translated the title, *Layer Fae.* One to come back to. Following that was a list, with pictures of different containers: jars, cylinders and an elaborate flagon that gave Pax a yearning for a medieval banquet. Nothing like the object she'd taken from Rufaizu's place, though.

Continuing, she found a couple of pages stuck together and peeled them apart. She hadn't seen this one before, when she'd been looking for clues to the cypher. The image made Pax pause.

A full-page sketch depicted the insignia from Casaria's

business card. There were symbols around it, passionately thick and underlined. It seemed Rufaizu, if the annotations were really his, wanted whoever found this book to know what this page had to say, because he'd already translated each block of text in small lettering:

Do not trust the Ministry of Environmental Energy. Investigations are baloney. Agents are dangerous. Spies everywhere. Protecting the labyrinth. In with the enemy.

"Jesus Christ," Pax said. She turned the page, but there was no more information. The book devolved into the half-dozen pages of short riddles, then, with their scattered words around them. Apparently Rufaizu had been trying to solve them.

And there ended the book.

Pax sat back and stared at the leather-bound tome. It was pure fantasy, except that it had thrown doubt on her plan of getting in touch with the Ministry. She wasn't sure what else she had hoped to find. More names, an address? There was nothing.

She bit her lip. Whether Rufaizu was half mad or the victim of an overactive imagination, nothing in what she'd seen suggested he deserved to be disappeared. In all likelihood he had no one looking out for him. He'd been squatting there alone, after all. Pestering night-time weirdos and squirrelling away bizarre books and devices.

Pax turned her attention back to the odd cylinder she had stolen.

Half glass, half brass, it looked like part of a Jules Verne machine, waiting to be filled with a magical fuel that could be used to travel through time. For example. Pax turned it over and found a fine set of markings on the underside: a symbol similar to a precious metal's hallmark. It was too small to make out clearly. The mechanisms at one end had cogs finer than a Swiss watch. She thumbed back through the book, searching the sketches for a page that might explain it, but none of the objects resembled this one.

Setting both items aside, she hummed to herself. Her eyes rested on her coat, hanging by the door, with Rufaizu's notepad poking out of a pocket.

That was another piece of the puzzle. Away from the distracting smells of the bar, she caught a whiff of stale sweat on its pages. Pax leafed through the unenlightening pages of notes.

Hundreds of answers to three questions Rufaizu posed to night-dwelling strangers. Pax found herself answering the questions in her head as she read through others' answers.

What is your name? Pax Kuranes. Dad wasn't especially empathetic with that one.

What are you doing out? After-work drinks. I work later than most people.

Why did you choose that drink? To find luxury in at least one area of my life. Another legacy of my father's. Pound for pound, no other drink is as complex or rewarding as a whisky, he said. Always be a connoisseur, even in vice.

Was it any wonder she'd ended up here? Hustling and hiding, separate from the world, refusing to aspire. Was it any wonder that Albie took refuge in fantasy worlds? He'd learnt to escape from their bullshit quicker than her. Had Rufaizu done the same?

Pax grunted and abandoned the questions of life to grab a cubed bottle of cheap bourbon. To hell with being a connoisseur. She drank from the bottle, imagining herself a lowlife in a seedy American carpark. As far as she could get from her dad's House Rules and drink-specific glasses.

As she drank, she flipped through Rufaizu's notepad, reading about other nighthawks' habits. Most of their reasons for drinking were pathetic, either caused by minor tribulations or major personality defects: *My life sucks* or *Because I rock!*

Pax came to the name Darren, though, and saw it had been heavily circled in pencil, with a big tick next to it. Annotated in the same style as the book's margin notes. She realised, then, that the notepad, like the Miscellany, was not the work of one man. Many of the pages were written in slightly different handwriting. Similar, but with smaller letters, more angular. A more reserved, perhaps more mature writer than Rufaizu. Rufaizu had taken over this notebook from someone else, perhaps the Apothel who wrote the journal? With the Miscellany written in symbols, there was no way to be sure, but given how Rufaizu had revisited the original owner's notes here, too, it seemed a safe bet. And given the similar handwriting, were they related?

Rufaizu had celebrated this one name, in particular, with a scrawl alongside the entry: *Citizen Barton! YES!*

The excitement in Rufaizu's writing reminded Pax of his protests as he was being dragged out of the bar. He'd used the name then, too. Barton.

She read Darren's answers:

Darren – sleep wastes the night – strongest and cheapest shit possible.

Now we're getting –

Pax's phone buzzed. She froze for a second, took a breath and held it up. A withheld number again. She answered and said, "I don't find phone calls intimidating, okay?"

"Glad we're on the same page," the woman replied, calmer than before. "I want to be clear on how serious I am. Look behind you."

Pax stood perfectly still, her natural instinct being to not do as she was told, purely because she had been told to do it.

"It's not a trick," the caller assured. "I want to show you something."

Pax turned slowly, away from the kitchen area, back towards the open living room, where her ripped furniture, peeling walls and stacked bookshelves left a lot of untidy surfaces for hiding things. She looked through the window, too, the outside world still asleep.

"Good girl," the voice said.

Pax's skin tingled at the realisation that she was being watched. There was a terraced house across the street, the upper floor visible from here, the blinds in the window down. No sign of life there, but nowhere else for someone to hide.

"Eyes on your wall."

Fighting the urge to resist, Pax looked to the side. In the middle of the wall sat the red pinpoint of a laser. It traced a small circle. Pax looked back to the window, trying to see where it was coming from.

"You won't see us. No one *ever* sees us."

"Congratulations," Pax answered quietly, trying to muster more courage in her tone than she felt. "You've got a laser pen and found out where I live. What's the next step, knock-down ginger and a burning bag of crap on the doorstep?"

"The next step's a bullet through your ovaries, how about that?"

Pax cringed, but wasn't done. "I deal with a lot of talkers –"

There was a crack, and Pax jumped as the red dot exploded into a puff of wallpaper and mortar. She stared in shock for a moment, then slowly turned her gaze to the window. A line ran from the bottom of the pane up to halfway along the side, the glass split in two but still standing. In the middle of the line there was a web of smaller cracks. Pax couldn't so much as blink.

"You like your ovaries, right?" the voice on the phone asked, plainly.

Pax's lips moved for a few moments in silence before any words came out. "What do you want?"

"That's the easy bit," the woman said. "We want the boy you were with last night."

"Casaria?"

"The *boy*. Your boyfriend took him, right?"

Pax swallowed. "Who are you?"

"Just do what we fucking tell you, all right? Find out where he is and get him back."

"You've got the wrong person," Pax said, voice wavering. "I keep out of people's business, they keep out of mine. You want someone found –"

"You seem like a smart girl," the voice interrupted, "so I'll let you figure out what happens if you disappoint us. I'll be in touch."

The phone went dead and the red light disappeared. Pax kept the phone by her ear for a few moments, scarcely able to believe it. Then she ducked out of view of the window, skirted across the room and threw the curtains closed. Plunged into semi-darkness, she sat on the floor, back to the wall, and cursed herself for not going home after last night's game.

7

An hour since being fired at, Pax slumped on a park bench with her face buried in her hands. She had moved as quickly as possible, once she decided to get out of there, and after three Underground trains and a bus she was finally confident that she was not being followed. In the confusion, she'd left everything behind, bar what little cash she had, her keys and her phone.

When she'd calmed down from the chase, she tried to come up with a plan.

Pax liked to think she had friends. Acquaintances, at least. There were more than half a dozen contacts in her phone who could offer protection for a price. Linneman Forsyth, a weak five-card-stud player, could get her a gun in exchange for a commitment to join the working class when his revolution came. But that might get her on some kind of watch-list. And what would she do with a gun? Shoot an innocent bystander, probably. The host of a regular Chinese Poker game, Jack the Tee, could loan her a bodyguard. His thugs could dismember the woman caller. But the Tee was terrifyingly erratic. It was dangerous enough occasionally taking a pot from him in a game.

What else could she do? Contacting the Ministry seemed like a risk in itself, considering Rufaizu's notes and the fact that the lunatic with a gun apparently hated them. Doing as she'd been asked hardly seemed much better – there was no telling what the caller wanted Rufaizu for, let alone what she'd do to Pax if her usefulness ran out.

She had one lead to follow, and that was figuring out who this Barton character was.

In that, she thought of Bees again. Bees claimed to be in imports and exports, which everyone understood to mean drugs. You didn't ask, not unless you wanted to become involved. Bees himself was only a foot soldier, though, for a man of similar standing to Jack the Tee. Bees' apparently limited career aspirations led him to a hobby of collecting knowledge. At the card table, Bees candidly offered opinions on problems that ranged from the innocently simple, such as removing stains from kitchen towels, to the morbidly complex, such as hiding a corpse in plain sight. There was every possibility Bees would track down a person like this Darren Barton, AKA Citizen Barton, for the sheer curiosity of it. He'd probably revel in the mystery in Apothel's book, too, but Pax didn't want him that involved.

Pax texted Barton's name to Bees: *Only got the name and know he likes hard liquor.*

After another half hour, and a café croissant Pax could ill afford, the phone buzzed. Bees said, "Family man, works on IT servers for a blue chip, Raystaten. Wife Holly, kid Grace. If you're thinking he's a mark, you're misinformed. No expendable cash, not on his salary, with a wife and kid and a place in Dalford."

"How do you know it's him?" Pax replied, surprised.

"All hard drinkers end up down the Sticky Tap eventually," Bees explained. "And using a moniker like that, that's a way to get remembered."

"Ralph knows him?" The Sticky Tap's owner hadn't been in last night. Would he have known something about Rufaizu, and nipped all this in the bud, if he had?

"Barton was semi-regular a real long time ago. Ralph said it might've been as much as a decade."

"But he knew where he lived?"

"No. The guy never gave up much about himself in the bar. Just drank. A lot."

So Bees had used some other means to go from a physical description to knowing everything about him. Pax would grill him about it another time. Now, she had the lunatic sniper to consider.

"Send me his address, and his number if you've got it," she said. As an afterthought, she asked, "Do you know anything about the Ministry of Environmental Energy?"

Silence on the line for a moment, before Bees said, "Got involved in something, Pax?"

"Just someone I ran into. There's nothing about them online that I can find. Have you heard it used as part of a con?"

"Let's meet up. Best not to talk about it over the phone."

Pax hesitated. Another bad sign. "I need to find this guy first."

*

Mid-afternoon, Pax found herself on Darren Barton's doorstep, taking in Grace Barton as the slender teenager opened the door. She was fifteen at a push, and a natural beauty, perfect skin, a smile that could sell toothpaste. Her bright eyes regarded Pax with eager friendliness.

"They started you early, didn't they?" Pax commented, erasing that smile.

"Excuse me?" the girl answered.

"Nothing. I'm looking for your dad," Pax told her. "Is he home?"

"He's not back from work yet," Grace replied. "Can I help you with something?"

"Starting to doubt it," Pax said slowly, glancing over Grace's shoulder into the hallway. Clean carpet, wall hung with clinically simple picture frames. Photos of the family. Put it together with the closely trimmed front garden, the dull grey mini-van and the quiet suburban avenue, and nothing about this picture added up to a man involved in psychotic snipers, monster books or shady government ministries. The one positive about coming here was that the low-lying, leafy suburb left nowhere for a gunman to hide, and Pax felt more positive that she'd lost her tail, now. She said, "Can I ask you a strange question?"

"Sure," Grace said, her smile returning.

"Does your dad go out late much?"

"Not any more. Is that how you know him?"

Pax shook her head. "Friend of a friend. Thought he could help me with something."

"You should speak to my mum." Grace turned and called for her mum before Pax could warn her off. Pax suddenly felt very self-conscious. These areas rarely housed people with enough expendable cash to make a card game worthwhile, and the thought of happy families, boxed up in their detached houses with their detached lives, made Pax's skin crawl.

Holly Barton came down the hall asking, "Who is it, honey?"

She stopped and stared at Pax with unashamedly judging eyes as the two women got the measure of each other. Holly had a short bob of blonde hair and a shrewd face, petite but sharply unwelcoming. Objectively, she could be considered good-looking. Alongside her daughter, the bar was raised too high. Holly greeted Pax with raised eyebrows. "Oh, please tell me you're not a drug dealer."

Pax shifted uncomfortably. "I'm not. I was just looking for your husband. I can come back later."

She looked over her shoulder, towards the street. Her own appearance troubled her in the presence of these two. Her boots, her slightly-too-big trousers, and heavy coat all had a practical purpose – hiding her posture from scrutiny, or hiding wads of cash. Above all, they were comfortable. They were not, however, remotely feminine or fashionable. This suddenly seemed important, with a blossoming teenager and her eagle-eyed mum analysing this mess of an outfit, and she wanted to get out of there. Holly stepped aside, though, leaving the doorway wide open, and said, "Fancy coming inside, telling me what it's about?"

Pax stared at the entrance hall carpet, not a spot of dirt on it. She shook her head. "No. Oh no, I don't. Maybe I could leave my number, have him call me."

"Nonsense, you travelled all this way."

The implication was clear. Pax did not belong anywhere near here. Responding to the tone and not the words, Pax said, "You're right. I should just get going."

She spun and thrust her hands deep into her pockets, marching away. Holly called something after her, a half-hearted invitation to stay, but Pax ignored it, out of the driveway in moments. She turned onto the street and saw a boxy Renault approaching, a family vehicle with blotches of rust around the wheel-arches. She slowed down as the driver leant into his window, watching her. A heavyset man in his early 40s, with the slightly disfigured face of a fighter, head shaved. He'd seen her leaving the house.

It had to be Darren Barton.

8

Barton pulled over ten metres from his drive, five metres ahead of the stranger, eyes never leaving her. He had spent enough time in the ugliest hours of night to know a fellow transient when he saw one, and there was no mistaking the fact that she had come from his house. He felt Holly watching, waiting to see what he would do. The darkly clothed young woman had stopped to stare, too.

"Bollocks," Barton muttered, cutting the engine. He emerged from the car and called out, sure to be loud enough for Holly to hear, "Did he send you? What are you thinking, coming to my home?"

She raised her hands. "No idea what you're talking about, mate. I thought –"

"To my *home*?" He raised his voice.

Barton stormed towards her like a bull, for a moment unsure himself if he was going to stop. She didn't move, other than to raise her hands higher and cringe. When he got within striking distance, though, he caught himself, breathing into her face. She averted her eyes and he followed her gaze to the balled-up fist at his side. She took in the cracked skin on his knuckles.

"What the hell were you thinking?" Barton hissed, scanning his head around hers like a posturing animal. From her scruffy appearance there was no doubt she had something to do with Rufaizu.

"I thought you might be able to help me," she answered quietly.

"The others at least knew never to come anywhere near here," Barton snarled. He sensed Holly had wandered out to watch. Had to be convincing. "Who the hell are you?"

The woman squinted, recognition dancing across her eyes. If she knew Rufaizu, surely she knew his situation?

"I'm no one, definitely not who you think," she said, quickly, too softly for the others to hear. "This guy, last night, he took my money and disappeared. I found this book, and someone's put a bullet through my window. I don't know shit, only that your name came up and I need this to stop."

Barton kept glowering at her, but it was hard to maintain the anger looking into her eyes. Big, worried. He said, "You're not helping Rufaizu?"

The young woman shook her head. "Wish I'd never met him." She paused, like she was reconsidering, then added, "But he *does* need help."

Barton shot a quick look to his house. Holly hadn't come any closer; she wouldn't be able to hear them from that distance. "You know where he is?"

"Some guy in a suit got him. I mean, like, beat him out of a bar and took him away without making a sound, and I don't know what. Claimed to be from the government."

"Christ." Barton bit his lip. He ran a hand over his face. "I can't deal with this. I can't. For the sake of my mind," he tapped his temple, "and for the sake of my family. I can't go through it all again."

"I'm not asking you to. I don't even know what this is," the woman said. "But these people are out to get me – and this book said this Ministry is dangerous – and they took my money –"

"You going to introduce me to your friend, Darren?" Holly intervened. She crossed the road towards them as Barton waved at her with a forced smile. Through the side of his mouth, he said, "Forget your money. Don't go looking for Rufaizu. Talk to no one. Trust me."

"Someone *shot* at me!"

"Honey, I've never met her before, I was asking her to leave," Barton said, stepping aside and holding out an explanatory arm towards the girl. She gave him a questioning look as Holly joined them and folded her arms.

"Is that right," Holly said, hardly convinced.

"It's true," she said. "Rufaizu gave me your husband's name."

The name made Holly pause. "What for?"

"He wanted me" – the woman turned her eyes back to Barton – "to invite him back out. It's been too long. I heard your husband used to be the life of the party." Holly raised an eyebrow towards Barton, her suspicions confirmed. Hopefully the less dangerous suspicions, the ones that didn't entertain the thought of him being unfaithful. Before he could add anything to cement that, the girl continued, "We missed him last night. Rufaizu got the idea an invite from a stranger might work."

"I'll say," Holly said, keeping her eyes on Barton. "That family was no good for Darren and I'm sure they're no good for you. I'd appreciate it if you didn't come back here."

The woman nodded, backing off, "Sure. I get it. Sorry to bother you." She turned and went on down the street as Holly and Barton held each other's gaze. Her voice piped back again, though. "One thing. These people who've been calling me. Rufaizu's friends, I guess. Who are they?"

Holly watched Barton carefully, and he didn't dare take his eyes off her as he answered, frankly, "I don't know. But you oughta avoid everyone he knows. And everywhere he's been."

He listened without turning as she made a quiet, awkward sound, like a farewell from someone who wasn't used to it. As the girl's footsteps continued away, Barton put an awkward arm around Holly's shoulders to lead her back towards the house. They walked silently across the road. He slowed down, running the last question through his mind. He took a breath and turned to shout at the girl's retreating back. "This person who threatened you. You see their face?"

"No," the young woman called back. "We spoke over the phone. But they know where I live."

Barton cursed under his breath. Rufaizu might've made a thousand enemies in his life, wherever he'd been, but Barton's instincts pointed to one obvious one. He said, "Take their threats seriously. With the people he knew, if you never see them coming, chances are it's the Layer Fae."

The stranger offered him an empty smile, like it wasn't something she understood or wanted to hear. She waved again, and continued walking.

Holly stared at Barton to ask what he thought he was doing. He avoided her gaze and headed towards their home, leaving the car parked out on the road. She caught up to him and hissed, "Was that for my benefit?" Barton shook his head, aware that the more he said, the more she'd pick at. She said, "If you think I'm going to tell you to go help that girl, I'm not, you know that? It's her problem."

"It's her problem," Barton repeated, in agreement. "Nothing to do with me."

"What did she say to you, before I came over? What's happening?"

"Nothing. She got in with that crowd and wanted my take. I don't know why they're threatening her, probably because she knows Rufaizu." Barton's eyes wandered back down the road. The woman was gone. He said, "God's truth, Holly. I don't know who she is. She wouldn't be the first not to take this seriously, though, and I don't need another death on my conscience."

9

Cano Casaria woke for another night's work, glad to find the sun all but set. Relieved of the ugly innocence and ignorance exposed in the daylight. Only in the shadows did the truth of the world reveal itself. Only in the dark did people really come alive.

Thirteen storeys up, Casaria stood at his window for his daily ritual of watching the daylight ants scurrying back into their holes as the office-block lights blinked off. Making space for the real people to come out. The ones that railed against normalcy, ones who squeezed more from the world than their day jobs gave them. The drunkards, the insomniacs, the smugglers and the thieves. The sex pests and the night workers. Even the tourists who visited in passing; the victims of emergencies, the overnight journeyers, the desperate deadline-makers.

They were the people of his world. They enjoyed empty roads with abandoned shop fronts. With less distractions, they *noticed* one another, noticed every little thing.

From the panorama of his apartment, Casaria went to ground level to hover near the Underground station. He took his dinner in the window of the Indian restaurant opposite, watching the change take place up close. In the early evening, people blindly pushed past one another, pointedly ignoring the man offering free copies of the Ordshaw Evening Standard. As the population thinned, occasional enlightenment slipped in. With two people going for the same door, at night, one might let the other pass. People started to make eye contact with the newspaper vendor, just as he packed it in for the night.

This was the world that mattered to Casaria. Only in these hours could he find people with the two values most cherished by the Ministry, and himself: an acute awareness of, and openness to, the world around them, and the resilience necessary to live in the darkness. Many of these twilight wanderers were less than fully sane, and others could not cope with people, day or night. The ones who had chosen this life when another was possible, though, they were discoveries to be treasured. They were like him. Special.

Like the poker player.

Over dinner, Casaria cut back his people-watching time to think about Pax Kuranes. The Roma boy had seen her potential, no doubt. She was smart, bold and seemingly normal, yet she was drinking in a dive for pleasure. And it didn't hurt that she was easy enough on the eye. Sure, she was no ten, Casaria reflected, but she didn't need to be. A seven would do, combined with her other qualities. He could get tens, if that was all he wanted. It wasn't important, not necessarily.

The Kuranes girl's file had further convinced him of her potential. It had been opened when she crashed her father's car at the age of fourteen. The insurance company suspected her father hadn't been driving, as he claimed he had, because the timing didn't fit with his work schedule. Being an excellent lawyer, he had crushed the case, but the government had already started a file on Pax. Aged eighteen she went to university to study the Classics. Aged nineteen she dropped out. She created two hundred accounts for online casinos and poker rooms, but stopped using them within twelve months. She receded from society. Found work that left no record. Stopped using banks. The only evidence that she was still alive was that she continued to make National Insurance payments and submitted tax returns once a year. Always showing minimal earnings from what she described as consultancy work. For the most part, her gambling winnings went unreported.

As far as the government was concerned, Pax Kuranes became a vagrant who was thankfully keeping herself off the unemployment register.

It was easy to read between the lines. She had been raised by successful parents, was well-educated and had the capacity to do anything she set her mind to. She had run away, playing late-night card games, to avoid the trappings of conventional life. Most telling was that she had snubbed online gambling, too. It wasn't about making money; she was exposing herself to an underworld that held her interest. She played cards face-to-face at undesirable hours, with even less desirable people, for an interesting life. Maybe she enjoyed judging people face-to-face, too. Both concepts made her ideal.

The Rufaizu problem was under control, with no risk of him talking to anyone and no need to process him until Casaria bothered to file the paperwork, so there was plenty of time to concentrate on Pax instead. Get the measure of her. Casaria so rarely got the chance to introduce someone new to his world, and this time he was going to do it right. He wouldn't have a repeat of Sam Ward. Ward had never really belonged out at night; she'd tricked him. She was a day-dweller who'd strayed into his territory, and she'd been drawn right back into the bland conveyor belt of admin drudgery first chance she got. Damn Ward, now settled in a sixteenth-floor office with her five-man Inter-Species Relations Initiative team. Good riddance to her. With Pax Kuranes, Casaria had a fresh chance to draw in a kindred spirit, and he was sure she wouldn't be filing reports on Proper Conduct to wrangle a desk job. As long as he was careful, he could gently ease Pax in, without the attention of the bureaucracy. If it worked out, he'd simply tell the office he'd met her at a later date. He'd return the money in his glove compartment to her himself. Dispose of the forged PO-42c. It would be their little secret.

If it didn't work out, no one would ever need to know, and she certainly wasn't going to be offered promotions and a fast track to management.

But it would work out, wouldn't it?

Imagining a bright future, Casaria finished his curry with a smile.

All he needed to do was show her what he had to offer. Make the possibilities clear to her. And he had a good idea of where he'd find her.

10

"I want it fixed by Monday morning." Hank Cougan's broad Yorkshire accent droned through Pax's voicemail. "Or next Friday's rent doesn't even matter – you hear?"

The last thing Pax needed with a confirmed psycho watching her home was her landlord informing her he'd seen the broken window. That had to be another hundred quid or more down the drain, and if she didn't find *that* money, she wouldn't even be able to negotiate a late rent. If she could survive that long. As she raced to meet Bees, ruing the fact that she hadn't simply called Barton on the number Bees had found, she developed a short-sighted plan of action.

"I'm heading to Frankie's in about half an hour," Pax told Bees, without so much as a hello, slipping into the seat opposite him. She'd scraped together a little under £60 from her apartment that morning. Frankie would front her the rest of his game's £100 buy-in, knowing a female player would loosen up the action. She'd spend the evening making up the cost of the window and a little wriggle room for the rent. Forget the World Poker Tour, that dream was dead. Meanwhile she was counting on the psycho caller thinking she was out doing as she'd been asked. She'd avoid that problem by not going home, while she figured out what to do about Rufaizu's mess.

Bees had chosen a grimy pub to meet in, though his sunken posture, with an empty pint glass alongside his half-finished one, suggested he would have been here anyway.

"Enough time for a pint," he replied. He had a gravelly voice, the sort a man acquired after years of inhaling powdered stone down a mine. His darkly tinged skin and the uniform grey stubble which joined his shaved hair complemented this strange affinity with stone.

"No, I've got to keep my focus," Pax said, shuffling out of her coat. "It's payday at the club and I need the cash."

"Need a stake?" he offered. She didn't reply. Pax had refused a thousand stakes from the likes of Bees. She didn't begrudge criminals their trades at the table, within reason, as they tended to be honourable gamblers with high-stakes games, but she stayed well out of their debt. She wouldn't even take a marker for a hand she had pat. She'd lost sizable pots due to that caution, but she was happy to pay that price. In her silence, Bees nodded understanding. He wouldn't probe. Bankrolls came and went; if explanations weren't offered it was rude to ask. It was enough to know she needed to crash a small game like Frankie's.

"So?" Pax leant towards Bees. "What's so scary you can't talk about it on the phone?"

Bees rolled his eyes to check the pub, with the least amount of effort. He said, "What do you make of this bus crash on the news? One of the kids what died, he stood to inherit a lot from his dad. Divorced. Would've provided for his mum, but she's out on her ear, now. Think there's a connection?"

Pax waited for him to finish the thought, knowing better than to get drawn into it. He took a sip from his beer, foam collecting around his mouth like a second beard. Sure enough, he abandoned that pondering intro to get to the point.

"Ministry of Environmental Energy was created about fifteen years ago. Under the guise of tackling climate change and that sort of shit. But there's already the Department for Environment, see, and there was a Department of Energy and Climate Change until recently. Doing the jobs you'd assume Environmental Energy would."

"You think it's a cover," Pax concluded. Bees nodded.

"The MEE has never submitted any reports or shown any evidence of actually doing anything, see. You've seen their web portal? Nothing there. All records of them are so obscure you won't find anything else, neither. Except I happen to have seen a bit of their mandate. They have national jurisdiction to investigate – I kid you not, these are the words in their founding documents – *any and all circumstances relating to energy and environment*, with *practical powers to disband, restrain and otherwise enforce government policy regarding threats*. No one independently reviewing their work, though, just a few ministers paid a full-time wage to meet twice a year to go over the Ministry's budget."

"Okay," Pax said. "So they're siphoning money into what? Greedy politicians' pockets? Or something covert? Security?"

"They're not lining pockets," Bees said. He took his time to gulp down more beer, breathing deeply to savour the taste. Someone who didn't know him might have thought he had nothing left to say. His eyes were dull, resting on Pax without any particular interest. She waited. He said, "This Ministry, it was set up in 2001. There was a big shuffle in Environment departments, all this hoo-ha with foot and mouth disease. You ask me, it's got nothing to do with climate change, that was only a convenient umbrella to get it through parliament. But they're not doing nothing, the money's being used. I got a few ideas on it."

Pax waited again, sure he would tell her. He took his time, drinking again and staring into the glass as though his beer held the answers. It distracted him instead.

"You know these people have been doing whatever they've been doing longer than we've been allowed to keep pubs open all night? That was 2003. This Ministry had been going two years already, by then. Could be a connection."

"Why would there be a connection?" Pax asked, blunt enough to tell him his wandering thoughts weren't helpful.

"Not as crazy as you might think," Bees said, pointing a stubby finger upwards. "I've looked into the MEE a couple of times, and there's two things I've pegged them on. One's that they only seem to come out at night. Everyone that's met one of these guys has met them at the weirdest hours. I mean, any time after six is weird to meet a civil servant, ain't that right?"

"Tell me they're vampires and I walk," Pax said. Bees smiled. He had a thick, slightly sinister smile that suggested he might be considering punching your face off. His teeth were a little too big for his mouth.

"No, I don't believe they're of the supernatural," Bees replied, "But it's important. Because the other thing I know about them is that they make people disappear. Ronnie Sweet, you remember him?"

"Fat guy who plays at the Ocean Club. Sure."

"Seen him since last October?"

Pax pictured the ever-sweating sporting goods store manager, always late to a game and always eating. He was one of the many people she loved taking money from but hated being around. It was true, he hadn't been at a game for a long time. She shrugged. "Maybe he retired."

"Sweet asked Mr Monroe for some money, around a year ago. Wanted to open another shop. He'd found this nice property under the arches, near the West Quay. Disappeared before it got started. We got curious, found out he'd had a few meetings with someone from the MEE. Then, poof, vanished."

"Could've been discussing regulations," Pax said. "Could be anything. He was meeting with your boss too, you don't blame him for the disappearance."

"No," Bees grinned. "My boss didn't disappear him. Want to ask me how I know?"

Pax shook her head. His boss, Mr Monroe, was a gentleman at the card table, but had an ugly reputation. She had always taken care to distance Bees from the rumours she heard about Monroe, so she could hold conversations with him without a moral crisis.

"Anyway" – Bees' smile left his face – "it's not just him. I found three or four other people with similar stories. People who've had a meeting or two with someone from the MEE then vanished. Also found one or two who *hadn't* vanished, but met someone late at night claiming to be from the Ministry asking odd questions. Like if they'd seen anything strange on the train tracks."

"Right," Pax said. "What's your theory?"

"Clearly," Bees said, "they're hiding some nocturnal work. Seems to be something underground. Could be anything, though: illegal gas lines, sneaking war criminals across borders, who the fuck knows."

"Those are the two things that spring to your mind," Pax noted. "Not stockpiling chemical weapons or conducting experiments on aliens?"

"Could be anything. Nothing seemed to connect these people that disappeared. Maybe they're watering down alcohol on a national scale," Bees said, with an air of finality. "Who. The Fuck. Knows."

"Whatever the case," Pax said, "the point is they're shady and best avoided."

"Bingo. And being that they're government, that means don't talk about them on the phone and don't go searching on the internet. Now." Bees gulped down the last of his beer. "You gonna tell me how you came to meet one of them?"

"In the Sticky Tap. He made someone mysteriously disappear."

"Sounds juicy."

Pax took out her phone and checked the time. She had a moment of relief in seeing no one had tried to call her, but she needed to get to the game. All this was adding up to the simple conclusion that she wasn't likely to see Rufaizu or her money ever again, however much she wanted to end this, and whatever the lunatic caller threatened her with. "I'll tell you about it another time. One more quick question: you ever heard of a group called the Layer Fae?"

Bees shook his head. "Good name for a biker gang. Interesting word, fey. Could relate to magic, could relate to death and doom. Like, this fey guy, he's gonna die. No one says that any more, though."

"Yet you know it."

"Well . . ." Bees' smile returned. "I like to know things."

"Yeah, me too," Pax said. "And this ambiguous shit is starting to bug me."

Circling around thoughts of Rufaizu in a torture chamber and snipers ready to cripple her, Pax raced towards Frankie's game, hoping against hope to simply survive the night. If she could scrape her living costs together, maybe she could give the psycho caller the book and the weird device as a compromise. Barton had suggested the Layer Fae weren't likely to help Rufaizu, but maybe he was wrong – maybe they were his friends, after all. She could give them everything she knew and they could figure it out themselves, couldn't they? It was neater than the thought that no one was looking out for her brother.

No. Not her brother. Rufaizu. Some tramp.

She had to block the madness out, at least for the evening, to play her best and avoid eviction. It'd be easy. The lads at Frankie's club weren't the sort to ask about anything personal, they had their own shit to deal with and would sooner talk about that than worry about her. She could unwind. She could pick up on the hot streak she'd enjoyed the night before.

That was how it worked. You fall down, you recoup.

Her hopes of enjoying that relaxing evening disappeared before Frankie's door, though. She stopped in front of the club building behind its uneven parking area, the sign's wiry lettering and cocktail-glass silhouette flashing first green, then blue, then pink, then red.

"You've got to be kidding," Pax huffed under her breath.

Casaria pushed away from the wall he'd been leaning on to give her a small wave.

11

"Turning up like this," Pax told Casaria, "is stalking."

"Stops people from cancelling," he said.

"Removes the choice," Pax replied.

"Yes. There's something I want to show you. I guarantee you'll find it interesting. You *do* have a choice, though, I want to be clear. You can walk away. No harm done, no strings attached."

"I don't want to see your dick." The response simply jumped out. Casaria grinned, his straight-toothed smile a little too wide, like someone had once told him this is what charm looked like. Pax skirted to the side, trying to move closer to the club doorway without getting nearer to him. "I need to get to this game."

He put a hand into his jacket, making Pax freeze, fearing the gun. He ignored her reaction, taking out a fold of cash. Pax could judge money well enough by sight: a hundred in twenties.

"If that's all you've got, I still need to get to that game."

Casaria smirked again. He put his hand back in the pocket and drew out another, bigger wad of cash. "Let's be realistic. How well would you need to do to recover what you lost last night? How much luck is involved in that? Is that game" – he indicated Frankie's – "even big enough?"

Pax stared at the cash, unconsciously drifting closer like a moth drawn to light. That chunk of notes was definitely more than she could make at Frankie's table, even on the best of nights. And he knew it. Did he know how much she needed that money, too? A government agency might. But would they go around waving cash at people? Her eyes shifted back to Casaria's expectant face and she said, "Seriously. Is this a sex thing?"

Casaria put the money away. "Please. I'd be doing you a favour."

"Ouch," Pax said. He was smiling, of course. Thinking awfully highly of himself. A sex thing would've been simpler. "Rumour is it's best to avoid your Ministry like the plague."

"I'm sure you don't know anywhere near as much as you think."

"I know you beat on an innocent boy. And that you're waving your cash at me like it's . . ." Pax frowned. It was her own money, wasn't it? By rights, she could kick him in the nuts and take it back. "Where's the rest?"

"Safe," Casaria told her. "Like I said, you'll get it all back. I can speed things up, if you'll bear with me. A couple of nights, that should do it."

Pax looked at Frankie's sign, imagining the comfort of a night at the table with a sedate crowd. Going away with a little money and no additional complications beyond the promise of a bullet in the ovaries, and a guilty conscience if she didn't help Rufaizu. She looked back to Casaria's cash and imagined the other possibilities. Disappearing under the auspices of some violent government agency. Learning things she wouldn't be able to unlearn. The images from Apothel's Miscellany sprang to her mind. The fantastic creatures with strange names, capturing Rufaizu's excited attention. His connection to this ministry was a mystery. She said, "Tell me about Rufaizu."

"Huh?" The smile wasn't so permanent after all. Casaria's face was blank.

"What have you done with him? What are you going to do?"

"I thought you didn't know him."

"He took my money. I figured it out. Filtered for nighthawks, isn't that how you put it?"

Casaria's smile came back, apparently impressed that Pax had a memory.

"Where is he?" she pressed.

"Safe. It's our job to keep people safe, Pax."

"Why'd you take him, then?"

"A matter of national security." There was that expression again, telling her nothing. But Casaria elaborated this time. "He's not *innocent*, as you put it. At the very least, he knows something that would be dangerous to share. At the worst, he may have access to things he shouldn't have. He'll be interviewed and we'll take it from there. Is that enough? Will you come with me now?"

Pax kept her eyes on him, feeling something swelling in her chest. How was that supposed to be enough? "I need to see him. I need to see Rufaizu with my own eyes."

Casaria didn't speak for a moment. His blank expression broke, though, and he rolled his eyes away from her. "Fine. You can see the boy – but not until *after* you come with me. By then, though, I think your priorities will have shifted."

Whatever the hell that meant. By then she might be locked up along with Rufaizu, or worse? Disappeared like Ronnie Sweet?

Pax gave Frankie's another glance. She could go in and tell them all about this guy. She could call Bees and insist he come with her. She could run. But if she did any of those things, her money might disappear, and Rufaizu along with it. To say nothing of what these people, and the others, might do if she didn't play ball. Casaria was at least pretending this was an amicable deal, right now.

"You'll give my money back?" Pax asked. Casaria nodded. "All of it?"

"In time," he said. "But you need to give me some time. One evening is never enough."

"How's a statement like that ever lead anywhere good?" Even as she questioned it, though, Pax realised that shitty comment was good in itself. Whatever madness he had planned, Casaria wanted her consent to join him at a later date. He was watching her, waiting for her to reach a conclusion. She shook her head. "I've got bills to pay. I've got a tournament on Thursday."

"Give me until Monday, then."

"Why?" Pax narrowed her eyes. "What *for*?"

"It's something I have to show you, there's no point explaining it."

"Why?" she repeated, more firmly.

He nodded, realising it wasn't the process she was asking about. "Because there's not many people who can handle it, what I want to share with you, and there needs to be more of us. I'm playing a hunch here, but I think you'll be into it."

Pax didn't blink, taking in his squared-off posture, no hint from his body that he wasn't being honest. Unless he knew how to hide his emotions. Pax was good at reading eyes, though, and the way he broke her gaze, just for a second, confirmed her hunch that this was personal. "Three nights, that's what I'll agree to. But we see Rufaizu today. And you give me that cash now."

She held out her hand. Casaria stared at it, hesitating. He took out the hundred again, that was all. "This much. Only this, today." Pax started shaking her head, but he thrust the notes into her palm. "Believe me, seeing the boy is a *big* concession." He let go of the money in her hand, giving her a quick squeeze with his fingers to complete the handshake. The way fifteen-year-old boys give hugs. He immediately moved past her, pointing ahead. "This way. You'll enjoy this, seriously."

Watching him go, Pax told herself this was progress. He might've abducted someone and all but blackmailed her into coming with him, but he liked her. For the first time all day, she felt like she had some kind of leverage.

The icy silence of Letty's dinner was interrupted by her phone ringing. As she finished her mouthful and read Fresko's name off the Caller ID, she was aware that Mix and Gambay had frozen across the table, watching her like they thought she might shout at them for letting the phone ring. She tapped the green icon. "Speak."

"She's going with him," Fresko said. "Asked him about the kid, but nothing concrete. The mug agreed to take her to him after whatever they're up to."

"Finally," Letty said, closing her eyes with relief. "I'm coming to you." She hung up and returned Mix's rigid stare. He could've been a statue set in malice, his masonry block jaw set as squarely as his silver hair. Still pouting over the reams of insults she'd shouted at him earlier. She raised her eyebrows to prompt him to come out and say it.

"We're all going, right?" he said.

"Like shit. The Ministry's on her. I need subtle, not stupid."

Letty could predict Mix's follow-up before it left his lips. He was tough as cheap beef, and old enough to be a father-figure, but tough was all he knew. "We corner Casaria, we can make him talk."

"Spin on it." Letty pushed herself up from the table but kept her hands on it, looming over the others. "You're gonna start thinking now? It was yesterday I needed you. Now you'd just get in the damned way. Casaria's sweet on that girl, he's taking her where we want to go."

Gambay spread his arms across the table with the grace of a prowling lizard, leaning into her plan. "*Then* we ice that Ministry prick!"

"Stop being thick!" Letty commanded. She tossed her can at Gambay. He ducked, too slow, and it caught him on the temple. Toppling off his seat, Gambay turned on Letty with his teeth bared and fists clenched. Letty grabbed a curved knife, making Gambay freeze.

"Give me an excuse," Letty said. "It'd be less than you deserve."

Gambay glowered at her hatefully. He touched a hand to his reddening temple.

"*Please*," Letty said, savagely. He shook his head and sat back down. Letty continued, "Maybe it was good that you arseholes weren't on Rufaizu when you needed to be. The shit you might've done. We need the kid, we don't need a fucking war with the Ministry. Do I really have to spell that out?"

Gambay mumbled something that could have been a no.

"Here's what happens now," Letty said. "Me and Fresko keep on this broad and you two stay sober and wait for my call. Maybe – *maybe* – we put this behind us." She threw an arm to the ill-gotten gains that littered the room. Gold, cash and trinkets in abundance. "We put *all* this behind us. No more mugging pedestrians. Boosting cars. Knocking over card games."

Letty grabbed Mix's can from across the table and gulped down what was left of his drink. She wiped her mouth with her forearm, belched and turned to leave. Neither of the others moved or said anything, but she knew what they'd do in her absence. Gambay would grumble that he had no problem with mugging people and Mix would tell him to grow a pair and stand up to Letty. Then they'd down some vodka to make themselves feel like men. Not too much, though. They wouldn't risk getting blind drunk again after last night. Now that they'd screwed up and she'd chewed them out for it, they'd be ready to make good. They'd tracked down the girl from the bar's cameras in record time, after all, and Fresko had been a trooper trailing her all day. All she needed from the other two was their muscle, if it came to that. Hopefully it wouldn't.

Letty headed out feeling positive. Not great, exactly, but it was the first time in twenty-four hours that she didn't feel like punching her head through a wall with frustration. Rufaizu couldn't have been anywhere that secure. Casaria was promising to take the dumpy barfly to him, and no civilians got inside the fortress that was the Ministry offices. The prick must have put protocol on hold while he trotted after that piece of arse, and that was gonna save them all from an impossible situation.

12

Though visibly pleased with her choice, Casaria became quiet after Pax agreed to come. He led her away from Frankie's, towards an unlit street, and her worries mounted. Flanked by dumpsters and hidden from street lights, the road was a den of shadows. A billboard rose over the area beyond a building, the partly torn image advertising a Dyson vacuum cleaner. It said *The Future's Spotless*, but the image looked two or three decades old. A place that time had forgotten. He could rape her here, murder her. He had a gun, and even if he was unarmed she doubted she'd have the strength to fight him off. The exercise she paid lip-service to in bi-monthly twenty-minute bursts suddenly did not seem enough. She fought the fear, though: *I've handled worse situations.*

Onward they walked, out into the safety of the street lights.

Pax looked over her shoulder, to the passage they'd left behind, and told herself there was nothing to be afraid of. If he hadn't attacked her there, where would he?

As they continued, she decided talk would lighten her mood, and a comment came out unfiltered: "So definitely no rape, then?"

Casaria paused as he gave her an odd look. Common to so many people she'd met, he wasn't quite on board with her sense of humour. She tried an uneasy smile, which didn't help. He said, in a tone that begged to be believed, "Honestly, this isn't about sex."

"All right." Pax took a moment. "Are you gonna tell me where we're going?"

"Underground," he said, showing her his back as he continued.

"What's that mean? We need to get the Tube?"

"No," he answered. "Just its tunnels."

"What have you got to show me in the tunnels of the Tube?"

Casaria did not answer.

They continued to the end of the street and towards Wynbone Station. Its wide open stairs descended in the middle of the pavement, appearing incredibly foreboding. Wynbone was quiet at the best of times, far from the centre of the city, and at this time of night it was deserted.

Pax slowed as Casaria continued. Her earlier question was answered – an Underground tunnel might be a better place to attack her than that street. It could house the many things her father had always feared on her behalf. The nightmares of Ordshaw he brought up every Christmas. A sex dungeon? Human trafficking? Keep working nights, with those people, she could hear him say, and you'll end up chained in a sex dungeon.

She always growled at him that such things never happened.

Maybe they did, though.

Casaria stopped and turned back, realising she was not following. He said, "You'll be safe."

"Give me your gun and I'll believe you," she replied.

"That would make you *less* safe," he said. "I'll explain once you've seen it."

"Maybe you should explain now."

"I've done this before," Casaria told her calmly. "More than a few times. It's better to see it first. Otherwise, you'll just accuse me of making things up. More likely, you won't want to come."

"Now you really need to tell me what it is."

"No. I don't."

Pax watched him continue, towards the steps, and knew it was true. She had to go with him, to pay her rent and look out for that poor kid and to save her ovaries. More than all that, though, now she had a big fat dose of curiosity to satisfy. What could possibly be down there, and was it remotely close to Bees' idiotic ideas? As Casaria reached the station, never looking back, she rushed after him.

"At least tell me where it is," she said. "Give me *something*."

"You've got my word –"

"That's not enough."

"It's beyond the maintenance tunnels. I have a key that takes us to another set of tunnels. We'll go about three minutes into them, not far. Then you'll see it."

Pax kept walking, frowning. "Why are there extra tunnels that you have the keys to?"

"See what's there, then I'll explain. That's the deal."

They reached the bottom of the stairs, the station empty. It was one of the older stations, fading tile walls lined with cracks, steel-rimmed lights caked in so much grime that they gave only the vaguest yellow-green glow. The adverts here belonged in a collection with that Dyson billboard; there was a faded advert for Hooper's Hooch, a *Brand New!* alcoholic lemonade. Didn't that go out of fashion in the late 90s? As Pax tried to recall her alcopops history, Casaria stopped at a maintenance door a short way down the tunnel. He took out a key, opened the door and stepped aside. Pax stared into the darkness beyond.

"Okay." She took a breath. "Tell me one thing before we go another step. Where *exactly* is Rufaizu?"

Casaria shrugged. "I told you he's fine."

She folded her arms. He stared at her.

"All right. He's in St Alphege's. In a safe house. Waiting for me to process him. At that point he's going to the MEE building in central Ordshaw, which you would *not* be allowed into. Okay?"

Pax read his face, trying to judge how far to trust this. "Does anyone else know he's there?"

Casaria's silence gave her the answer.

"You're not on the level, are you?" Pax said. "You shouldn't be attacking suspects or imprisoning them in the sticks. Or bringing girls down here, for whatever this is . . ."

His smile came back crookedly. Pax was starting to notice the difference – straight and toothy was his show smile. This cock-eyed smirk betrayed genuine amusement. He said, "The Ministry has a great deal of rules and regulations. Forms to fill in. I like to keep things casual until it's absolutely necessary to go through the red tape. If I didn't, your money would be lost in the system. You should be thanking me, really."

He waited as though expecting her to say thanks.

"What'd he do?" Pax asked. "Exactly."

"It's connected to this." He indicated the doorway. "Again. The explanation will be so much easier after you see what's down there."

Pax shot him a fierce look, to say this was not cool. Acknowledging that didn't help, though. She walked on past him into whatever hell lay beyond.

"There's, what, three safe houses in St Alphege's?" Letty shouted at Fresko as they sped through the city. "Send the others to the east one, we'll cover the near two. We've got time to recover from this before he seals the deal with that vacant cow."

Fresko had his phone out, and quickly relayed her commands to Mix. He looked like a bloody banker, as always, in his shirt and suspenders, tie flapping over a shoulder. He hung up without waiting for a response and put the phone away, then shouted to Letty, "We could get more people, do this quicker. I don't like going to their places alone."

"Don't be a fucking pussy," Lett snapped. "We're fine on our own, even if you prats keep trying to prove otherwise. We'll find him in a half hour, tops."

"We gotta do more than find him."

Letty stopped suddenly, Fresko almost crashing into her. He was sharper than the others in every way, with his Wall Street wardrobe and selective vocabulary, but when she gave him an inch he was still an insubordinate arse. She told him, firmly, "We're doing this ourselves. *I'm* doing this. We haven't needed anyone in nine years, we don't need them now."

They continued in silence, side by side, before stopping at an intersection at the edge of St Alphege's. Fresko stared at Letty like he had something more to say, but her eyes warned him off. This was a time for everyone to do as they were told.

"Any problems, shout," she said.

"You too," Fresko replied.

"I'd rather shoot my own face off than admit to needing *your* help."

With that, she sped away from him, flipping a middle finger in his direction.

The idiots were cocky, never guessing that the Fae knew their safe house locations. Letty's target building stood three storeys high at the end of a terrace of derelict homes, with all the windows but the top one boarded up. That neglected one was Letty's way in. It was only open a crack, but that was enough for her.

Starting from the top floor, she searched her way down. Most of the rooms were empty, bar dust and the randomness of those occasional bricks that always appeared on the floors of abandoned properties. Complementing the beams of street light coming through the boarded windows, Letty scanned the walls and floors with a torch, looking for hidden rooms.

She made a quick circuit of the ground floor and discovered a single armchair with a magazine by it. Letty snorted at the cover, a half-naked man with his fists raised, every muscle on his torso tensed and bulging. *Martial Arts Illustrated*. She muttered to herself, "Christ, get out of the closet."

She continued to the kitchen, where the refrigerator hummed and emitted a dull blue light around its edges. A single washed glass sat by the sink. The place was in use, at least.

Letty spiralled around the bottom floor again. There was no other furniture and she doubted the whole building was dedicated to someone reading a magazine. Frustrated, she rested on the kitchen counter and took her phone out. A message from Fresko blinked up onto the screen: *Nothing but rats. Come to you?*

Letty replied: *Empty, too. Join the boys.*

As she put the phone away, she took another look at the fridge. It was a hulking ceramic model, like in a 1950s movie, and it looked like it would take three men to move it.

"Makes sense," she said, and dropped to the floor next to it, peering under. The glow wasn't coming from inside the fridge, but behind it. She rose and searched the wall around the fridge. Nothing there. Rushed back along the counter, searching the few empty cupboards, but still nothing. She headed back into the front room, where the armchair sat, and checked underneath it. Then under the magazine. Finally, she paused and saw another of those random bricks, on the floor, up against the wall.

"Why not," she said, and shifted it out of the way.

She stopped triumphantly. Behind the brick was what could have been a light switch, if it wasn't level with the floor and hidden. She flicked it and heard the fridge move, then raced back into the kitchen and found the blue glow expanding. A cellar door.

Fuck them *all*, she was about to save the day. Save everything and everyone.

She went through the opening and down a set of dimly illuminated stairs. At the bottom, there was a corridor that opened onto two closed doors. One of them had an electronic lock by its handle, lit with a red LED. She allowed herself a fist pump of success and approached it.

Something clicked.

She froze, eyes darting to all corners of the corridor. The walls were bare, besides the single fluorescent tube light.

Something hissed.

She spun and saw it. In the shadow above the stairs, a waft of almost invisible gas.

"Oh crap," Letty gasped and flung herself towards the stairs. She tried to keep low, to avoid the gas, but it was already too late. She smelt it and reeled away, back to the corridor. Gagging and coughing, she tore her phone from her pocket, but her vision blurred. She dropped the phone and it clattered across the floor. Unable to focus, she fell to the ground and bounced, once, before coming to a halt.

As she used her last strength to lift her head, her eyelids became too heavy to hold open.

She slumped onto the floor, into darkness.

13

Casaria stopped in the tight tunnel. He lowered his electric lantern to one side, its unnatural blue light stretching deep shadows across his face from below. "This'll do," he said.

Pax folded her arms again, hoping the lantern would give her expression the same campfire ghost-story effect. She had trained herself to hide or show emotions at the card table. She was determined to keep her posture rigid, defiant, to hide the anticipation she was starting to feel as they got closer to their goal. In this case, her scowl was to tell Casaria to cut the theatrics.

He smiled, another flash of perfect teeth. He leaned closer, lowering his voice, and said, "I need to insist that however you feel about what you are about to see, you must not react. That's something you're trained in, isn't it?"

"All right," she said. "Whatever you've hidden in this rape tunnel, I won't react."

"What is it with you and that word?" Casaria replied. "Besides, a rapist coming down here would be doing society a favour. Now stand as still as you can. See up ahead? Where the tunnels join? Something will be along any minute. Don't move, don't speak, don't freak out."

He lifted the lantern to light the tunnel. Ten metres ahead of them, the tunnel split into two, right and left. Pax narrowed her eyes, trying to pick out any details in the shadows that weren't just the lines of stacked brickwork. The place was empty, not a pipe or cable on the floor, walls or ceilings, only the occasional shells of old lights that might never have worked.

They waited in silence, Casaria's breath seemingly non-existent and Pax instinctively slowing and lowering hers. They waited long enough for her to start running his words back through her mind, as she wondered what indescribable thing could possibly be down here. She thought of the weird and wonderful creatures in Apothel's Miscellany. The creatures of nightmares with their bizarre rules. As she thought over some of them, Casaria whispered, almost inaudibly, "It's coming. What you're about to see senses things by touch. Vibrations. So if you don't move, and don't make a sound, it won't know we're here."

Pax screwed up her face. That sounded familiar.

"You're kidding," she replied, loudly enough for him to shoot her a warning look. She was surprised into quiet by his severity, and kept her eyes on the tunnel.

A scratching noise came from somewhere up ahead. Something was moving there. As the scrapes got louder, Pax picked out the distinct sound of two separate taps, almost at the same time. A creature on four legs. She stared hard, willing her first conclusion to be wrong.

It couldn't possibly be.

But it made sense. The book, the Roma boy being taken away before he could spread the secret. The government agency, covering something up.

The noise became louder, the creature getting closer.

It took all of Pax's willpower not to demand an answer from Casaria there and then, not to blurt out what she was afraid she was about to see.

Its shadow came across the tunnel intersection first, lancing over the floor as the creature jerked into the light. Then the claws. They looked like the curved blades of a farmyard tool; black, jagged shapes, stretching into the light. As they came further into view, it became clear they were attached to limbs. Arms that rose to a shoulder. A shoulder that sat below a head with no eyes. A bare head that bounced the light back towards them. A head that turned slightly to the side and revealed a set of teeth, running from the chin to the forehead like a zip.

Pax held her breath, digging her fingers into her palms to stop herself from moving. She couldn't take her eyes away, transfixed by how bizarre and fearsome it looked.

It stood over five foot tall and its legs were inhuman. The torso joined a lower body the size and shape of a large dog's, like a centaur. It wasn't furry, though; it was smooth, too smooth for human flesh. The creature had the same bare flesh all over, except for its terrifying claws, which had hardened into something like metal.

Its head turned in their direction, and for all the world Pax wanted to do nothing but run. She was rooted to the spot, though.

All the panicked thoughts punching through her head had no command over her body. She stood staring, horrified, as it looked at her, as though about to pounce, and her heart pounded against her ribs, blood thumping in her ears.

It would hear her, she was sure.

It would charge.

It moved.

Out of the tunnel, through the intersection and into the next passage.

Its footfalls moved away, becoming quieter, as Pax quaked. She pulled her gaze away to find Casaria looking at her. He had been watching her the whole time, and as she caught his eye his lips spread into his overfamiliar smile.

"A sickle," she uttered, finally finding the presence of mind to say it. "It's real."

Casaria's smile was gone. "How'd you know that name?"

They drove in silence, Casaria shooting furtive glances at Pax as she stared out the window without focus. She hadn't been able to speak as they left the Underground, variously tackling the two conflicting thoughts that kept repeating in her mind: *It can't be real. It is real.* Casaria had asked if she was okay and she had said yes, he had asked if she wanted to leave and she had agreed. They had walked to the car and he had described where they were going next but it was all just noise. She was trying to process the creature, trying to figure out what it meant. If the sickle was real . . .

She didn't dare complete the thought.

"It wasn't a trick," Casaria said, after ten minutes on the road. "That thing could tear a person apart, if it knew you were there. That's where I come in."

Pax turned with the vague recollection that he existed.

"What was it?" she asked, quietly, and knew, as the words left her mouth, that this was her admission that it was true. It brought her back to reality with all the worried thoughts and confused images of the beast in the tunnel. She had seen something otherworldly. And this man could explain it.

"You knew its common name, apparently," Casaria replied, a touch irritated.

Pax stared at the side of his face, his indignation unbelievable at a time like this. She said, "Where did it come from?"

"How did you know its name?" Casaria shot her a look.

"What?" Pax gaped. "Who *cares*?"

"I saw him greet you," Casaria said. "You made a joke about him asking your name, remember? You didn't know each other. At what point did he tell you anything?"

"Who gives a shit?" she said. "After seeing that thing –"

"It's important. How did you know it was a sickle?"

Pax paused. The book was evidently every bit as valuable as she had suspected, and if he knew about it he would want it. She lied, "There was a sketch. In the notepad he left on the bar."

Casaria shot her more glances, trying to read her face in brief moments between looking at the road. He echoed her: "The notepad he left on the bar."

"You might've noticed if you hadn't been busy hurting him."

"A sketch." They were statements, not questions. Sceptical statements.

"Yes, a sketch – you want me to go home and get it for you? Let's dwell on that, after seeing that shit! Jesus Christ, did you see what I just saw?"

Casaria nodded, slowing down as he concentrated on what to say next. Pax looked out of the window again, distracting herself with the city. They were passing through Ten Gardens, her old neighbourhood, streets of tall townhouses and warehouses repurposed from working-class slums to chic middle-class hangouts. The next neighbourhood would be the warehouse district, mostly derelict and as good a place as any to kill someone who knew too much.

"Where are we going?" Pax asked, expecting a cryptic answer.

"Someplace safe," Casaria told her, and immediately continued. "I know what you're going through. Eight years ago, I had the same experience. When I'd calmed down, the guy who showed me a sickle gave me the same information I'll give you. The same choice that I am going to give you."

Here it comes. Trapped in a tight space with nowhere to run. Pax had certainly seen too much, and wondered if it was the same for Ronnie Sweet and the others. Sweet had wanted to open a shop under the arches; had he trespassed into their tunnels? Were they all people who had seen too much and decided not to go along with whatever Casaria proposed?

The car turned into the warehouse district. They were travelling east, between the ruins of former industrial plants. The docks wouldn't be much further. Better and better locations to dispose of a body.

"The Ministry has a number of safe locations across Ordshaw," Casaria said. "Places where we can do things in private."

"Things?" Pax spat the word back at him.

Casaria rolled his eyes. "In this case, talking."

"I think I've had enough for one night. Can you take me home?"

He didn't answer, didn't look at her. She had little hope it would work, but it was worth a try. He finally shook his head. "We had a deal. And we're going to talk. Somewhere secure."

"Where no one can hear me scream."

This made him smile again, for the first time since the sickle had appeared. He turned down another road, into another residential area. Old brick houses that didn't look lived in. Pax tried to follow the route, to figure out where they had ended up. She knew the city, and had visited all sorts of difficult locations for games, but she was not familiar with this place. That made it one of the neighbourhoods she actively avoided. The other side of the warehouse district, it had to be St Alphege's.

Casaria pulled over and lifted a hand towards the building next to them, a brick terrace that looked like it should be scheduled for demolition. Pax gave him a nasty glare and he said, "I like your attitude, Pax. It could take you far."

He got out of the car but she stayed, giving the house a hard look. This was it. The perfect place to commit a murder. Willingly travelled to.

Casaria waited patiently at the side of the road.

She could lock the door, start the car somehow. Crack the ignition and spin a few wires together, that's how it worked in the movies, right? But he could shoot her through the glass before she got it going. Unless, being a government agent, he had bulletproof windows . . .

His patience ran out while she considered the full scenario.

"This way," he said, and started towards the building.

She watched him. If his intention was silencing her, he had a nonchalant way of making it happen. Then, wouldn't building her trust in this way make the job easier?

Guessing and second-guessing people was one of Pax's specialities. Bluffs, double-bluffs, triple-bluffs, it was all about thinking a few moves ahead. It was also, after a degree, impossible to truly know what was going on in other people's minds. This wasn't fair, that she had to figure it all out herself. It wasn't fair that she'd seen a dog-centaur with blades for arms, and the only person she could talk to about it was this inherently untrustworthy spook. No. That wasn't good enough. She took out her phone.

Damn Darren Barton and his happy family life, he was gonna tell her something about all this or she'd bring her world crashing into his. She tapped out a message quickly while Casaria had his back to her. Pressed Send. At the least, he would know she'd got more deeply involved in this. Shove that up his conscience. In case she didn't make it back.

Casaria stopped at the door and turned back to her. His face crossed with annoyance when he clocked her still sitting there. "What are you waiting for? *You* asked to come here."

Huh?

Pax checked the surroundings again. Run down. A rough part of town. St Alphege's, he'd said that before. A safe house. They'd come to where he was keeping Rufaizu. She closed her eyes. He'd taken her to the boy. This might work out, yet. She regretted thinking it, the moment the words entered her head.

14

The building was as lavish on the inside as it promised to be from the outside: a desolate shack of dust and decay. Unfurnished, unlit, forgotten. Casaria didn't give Pax a tour, he just walked ahead of her, through to the kitchen, talking as they entered. "The first thing to tell you is that those tunnels spread all across Ordshaw. Further than that, even. The network was built –"

Casaria paused in the doorway to the kitchen, his blue-lit face fixed in steely focus. Pax came up behind him and looked over his shoulder, into a kitchen as grim and bare as the rest of the ground floor, with the exception of its vast fridge. That had been pivoted to one side, revealing a passageway that descended into a luminescent glow.

"Is that a secret entrance?" Pax asked, taking the opportunity to disrupt Casaria in a moment of discomfort. "Who *are* you guys, the Thunderbirds?"

He did not respond, but took out his gun. Before Pax could make a sound, he descended the steps. She listened to his footsteps going down to whatever lay below.

Silence.

Then a loud exhale, and his voice came, almost merry. "Come here. It's your lucky day."

Pax crept through the kitchen and peered down the steps. They ended in a bland corridor below, where the blue glow was brighter. Casaria was barely in view, looking further in. Pax ventured down the stairs slowly, and when she reached the bottom she didn't immediately clock what he was looking at. There were doors leading off the corridor, to the sides, and a single light on the wall, but nothing else.

"Here," Casaria said, pointing at the floor.

Pax followed his gaze to a small object near his shoe. A bug?

She took a step closer and squinted at it. It had wings, and was hardly bigger than a house spider, but it wasn't a bug. Spread out on the floor, it had humanoid limbs. Pax imagined a child dragged down here, dropping their action figure on the way into one of these torture chambers. When Casaria crouched and picked up the figure, however, she saw that it was limp, hanging from the arm he lifted it by.

Pax shifted closer, to get a proper look.

A tiny woman, two inches tall, with lacy wings like a butterfly's. She had fantastically detailed clothing; a white t-shirt with a pattern too small to make out, and small denim shorts with a relatively thick leather belt. Strands of hair in various shades of pink and blue hung across her face. Strapped around her thigh was a minuscule holster, the handle of a pistol sticking out. It was an incredibly detailed and stunningly lifelike action figure.

One of her wings was suddenly snapped from her, jerking her torso as it was ripped out. Pax started in alarm, eyes wide as she looked at Casaria.

"In case it wakes up," he said, holding the freshly plucked wing between the thumb and forefinger of his other hand. He ground the lacy material between his fingers and it split apart and crumbled into the air. "Get one of these things flying around, you'll never catch it."

Pax returned her attention to the tiny woman, still immobile despite the brutal mutilation. Her other wing hung limply to the side, and she wasn't bleeding, the extraction done as freely as it would be with an insect. Pax caught herself thinking – why would a toy bleed?

"What do you mean wakes up?" she said.

"Take it." He held the little woman out and Pax raised her hands without thinking. He dropped the body into her cupped palms. It flopped like a rag doll, making her tense. The little lady weighed roughly the same as a plastic figurine, but Pax could feel the textures of clothing and flesh, and the soft hair.

"This place was only recently rigged to detect things like this," Casaria said, pointing to the ceiling. "Releases a gas that they're highly sensitive to. It could be out for the better part of a day. We'll be rid of it before then, though." With that, he turned to open one of the doors. As Pax stared dumbly at the miniature figure in her hands, Casaria moved into a room and flipped a light switch. He raised his voice as he got further away. "Haven't seen one in maybe nine months, myself. They're masters at staying hidden. But dangerous as all hell. No matter how cute you think it looks, you do *not* want to see one of those things alive, let alone awake."

He reappeared in the doorway, noticing Pax hadn't moved. She said, "What's it doing here?"

"Well, it's no coincidence, that's for sure."

Pax looked up at him, not following, but he didn't elaborate.

"It's good we came across it," Casaria told her. "It's another thing I doubt you'd believe without seeing. There's a plague of these things in the city, but we've never found their source. It's because of their sort that the Ministry does what it does."

"Does what it does . . ." Pax echoed, barely following.

Casaria pointed through the doorway. "Come in."

Holding the small figure out ahead of her, as carefully as if it were a baby bird, never taking her eyes off it, Pax walked after him. In the room, there was a table, a set of filing cabinets, a computer and three office chairs. Casaria indicated one of the chairs, but Pax remained standing, transfixed by what she was holding. He passed her and pointed at a map of the city on the wall. It was overlaid with thick lines, like a maze.

"There's something under Ordshaw, Pax," Casaria said. "A force that makes this city special. I need to get this across to you, straight away, because it's vital. It makes great things possible, but this force comes at a price. Things like the sickle. Things like this abomination." He pointed loosely at the small figure. "They're the price. We keep them in check. *I* do. I protect ordinary people from this extraordinary world. And I protect that extraordinary world, too." Pax eyed him, sure that he'd said these grandiose words before. Maybe practised them in a mirror. He gestured to her hands. "These things are, as a rule, disruptive and violent creatures. They'd do harm to anything and everything down there."

"So what's it doing *here*?" Pax asked again.

"You want my guess? They're thinking if they get the boy, they make amends for what his father did. His dad got in with them, a long time back, and there's tales he stole something of theirs that could harm everything we seek to protect. It got him killed, but whatever he took never surfaced."

Pax looked from the figure to Casaria, then back to the figure. She swallowed her thoughts. There was a *thing* in this mix-up. He'd said it before, that Rufaizu might have access to things he shouldn't. Things like that weird object she'd taken from his apartment.

Apparently reading her troubled face, Casaria said, "You've always known there's something more than the ordinary world, haven't you?"

"Not like this."

"The details aren't important. You have the right attitude, I knew it when I first saw you."

"The details are a little important." Pax looked up at him again, feeling like she hadn't blinked in a day. "I have a tiny woman in my hands. A . . . fairy?"

"No, don't make that mistake." Casaria quickly shook his head. "That's not a person, and it's certainly not anything magical. That's a vicious little monster. A pest."

Pax took a defensive step back, holding the small figure closer to her. "What are you going to do with her?"

"Not *her*," he insisted. "*It*. It needs to be disposed of. We've got an incinerator not far away."

"No," Pax said, hearing the word come out on instinct.

"What?" Casaria replied.

"No," she repeated, slower, forming her thoughts as she spoke. "You can't burn her."

"Right." He put his hands on his hips. "I told you I'd offer you a choice, Pax, and this is as good a way to do it as any. I can show you a whole new world. Involve you in something that really matters. In order for you to join me, though, you have to be able to accept what needs to be done."

The figure in her hands looked so peaceful, like a sleeping doll. It had impossibly small fingers, tiny boots on its feet.

"You're thinking too much," Casaria said. "Imagine it's a locust."

"Let me take her," Pax said. "I'll take care of her myself. Humanely."

"Not a chance," Casaria replied with a short, sharp laugh. "I have to be sure there's no trace of it. Pax, you have potential, but you've given me no reason to trust you."

"Then . . ." Pax hesitated. The drive to flee she'd felt before, all her fears, were now transferred to the little life in her hands. She could run, bolt for the door and maybe make it back to the car. She could try and push him down, wrestle the gun from him. What other option did she have? She couldn't just let him kill this beautiful creature. She tried to distract him as her mind raced. "You can't burn it. That's horrible. There's got to be a better way."

"Smother it first, then, what do I care? It's already drugged."

"No, let me –"

"There's no way that thing gets out of my sight. For everyone's safety. And now we're on it, you should come with me to the incinerator. We'll do it while the thing's still breathing to be sure this is something you can go through with. In its extreme."

"If I refuse?"

Casaria gave her a firm look. "This is important, Ms Kuranes." He'd brought out the surname. Full sincerity. "There are necessary evils we have to live with, for the good of this world. Hand it back to me, we'll deal with it together."

To hand the small figure back would be as good as committing murder herself. But he wouldn't stop. Wouldn't let it out of his sight. She said, "Hold on, just hold on . . ."

"It's a lot to process, I get that," Casaria told her plainly. "But I'm hoping you won't disappoint me. I thought you had the right temperament for this work. You understood about the Roma boy, after all."

She kept her face straight as that sank in. What did he think she understood about Rufaizu? That she hadn't wanted to help him?

Her only option, she saw, was to play up to this odd impression Casaria had formed of her since he first laid eyes on her. Whatever she had done to convince him of whatever he thought she was capable of, she could use that. If she wanted to avoid being disappeared herself, she had to at least make him believe she was still capable of being who he thought she was. Pax thought out loud: "Okay. I can do it. Not the incinerator, though. Not like that. I could . . ."

It was so small, she could pretend to squash it. Just like palming a card. It wouldn't be hard to slip the figure into her pocket and have him believe she had crushed it. But there would be no remains. He would never believe it. Had to remove all trace.

"I knew I was right about you." Casaria was smiling, confirming Pax's suspicions. "But you'd better let me –"

Pax flung a hand up to her mouth, thrusting the little figure in. It was barely a mouthful, but she made a show of her bulging cheek, holding Casaria's gaze as he started, "What the hell are you –"

She quickly positioned the creature in her mouth, cringing at the feel of the small human on her tongue. Then she swallowed as Casaria yelled in alarm. She gagged, keeling forwards and putting a hand to her mouth, and he rushed to her side, hopping about frantically.

"What the hell!" he repeated, escalating almost to a scream. "What was that? What's wrong with you? Why would you do that?"

Pax rose to standing with tears in her eyes. She let out a little whimper.

"Jesus Christ," Casaria continued. "I've seen some sick stuff – that takes it. Who the hell does that? Are you out of your mind? Why?"

"I –" Pax went to speak, then swallowed again, putting a hand to her throat and making a show of another little gag. She cringed and said, "I think her gun scratched me."

He stared at her in sheer disbelief.

"I've got the right temperament," Pax croaked. "I . . . couldn't let you burn her."

"That was your solution?" Casaria gaped, incredulous. "Jesus Christ! That's *worse*! That's so much worse!"

Pax bit her lip at him, affecting her best innocent look. He ran a hand through his hair, muttering obscenities. She suggested weakly, "Maybe we should call it a night."

He stopped and stared at her, looking utterly exasperated. Then he shook his head. "No."

She froze. He took a deep breath. It wasn't going to be this easy.

"We had a deal. You won't get another chance."

Pax frowned at the ominous comment, and flinched as he walked past. He ignored her, though, back on his own track, seemingly not bothered if she followed or not. He went along the corridor to next doorway, then took out a key and unlocked the door. Pax crept slowly up behind him as he opened it, just a crack. Just enough for her to see Rufaizu. He was slumped in a chair, like he'd been drugged too, but the sound of the door stirred him. His eyes shot open and Pax shot towards him, but the door slammed shut again.

"He won't be here tomorrow," Casaria said, as he turned the

lock again and whatever the young man called out was muffled. "I shouldn't even be showing him to you here. That's got to be enough. You're satisfied?"

Pax's eyes were wide open but she had no idea what to focus on. In the confusion of the tiny lady she'd forgotten why she was even there, and that brief glimpse had given her no idea whether Rufaizu was hurt or not. He was alive, at least, and Casaria had, for his faults, kept his word to show her so. He was looking at her, even, with an expression of hopefulness.

She nodded and muttered appreciation, and his shoulders slumped with some kind of relief.

"Good," he said, lighter. "Great. What a night, huh? What a start."

Pax nodded again, not trusting herself to say anything, letting him form his own ideas. All that mattered now was to get out of there before he realised the fairy was still alive. And now she'd seen Rufaizu, she might have something to fend off the psycho caller.

15

Fresko watched the pair exit the safe house through the scope of his rifle. The stiff suit and the rough-looking girl, both the worse for wear on the way out. Something had happened and there was still no sign of Letty. He adjusted the scope, tuning his microphone as the pair moved around the car. The man stopped and said something over the car to the girl. Fresko missed it, but got a clear read on the lady's response: "I saw a dog human claw creature and swallowed a fairy, I'll need some time to process."

Fresko sat back in surprise. *What?*

The humans looked at each other gravely enough to suggest it was true. Flashing in anger, Fresko trained the rifle sights on the girl's temple. Finger on the trigger, he gave a second glance to the man. He was behind the car. By the time the shot hit her he'd be behind cover. Fresko couldn't get them both.

The man opened the driver's side door and gestured to the lady to get in. Fresko squeezed the trigger, slightly. Testing it.

Letty always said there were two ways to do things: the right way and the dumb way. It usually followed a suggestion from one of the others. Shooting that girl would be a dumb thing to do, Fresko didn't need anyone to tell him that. He would expose himself and might get caught. It'd inspire the wrath of the Ministry, and do a whole lot more damage to rest of the Fae. But if what that girl had said was true, something had to be done.

Letty was a handful, an uncompromising badass, but she was *their* badass. For all their faults, she had never given up on any of them.

And he'd let her go in there alone.

Let those monsters get hold of her.

Fresko's finger shook against the trigger.

The lady twisted to his direction before ducking into the car, and he got a good, hard look at her face. Big round eyes, big nose. Big fucking idiot in general, gonna eat a bullet.

Maybe not tonight, but some day soon.

A flutter of wings announced the arrival of Mix and Gambay, swooping onto the ledge next to Fresko. The car doors slammed shut and the engine started.

"What's happening?" Mix asked.

Fresko sat back as the car pulled away. He said, "They were in there. The suit and the girl. Letty was in there, too."

"Where is she now?"

The sniper gave him a cold, don't-ask look.

"If they did anything –" Gambay started, but Fresko cut him off.

"She's toast. We go down there looking, whatever got her will get us too. Listen. Them congregating on this place, with something that trapped her there, it's gotta be where the boy is. There's no way we're getting him out of there alone, though."

"So let's punch a hole in that car and get some human assistance," Mix growled.

"We should be cutting his balls out already," Gambay said.

"That'd be the dumb thing to do," Fresko warned, the car already all but out of view. "This is the Ministry. He's not exactly gonna do something because we ask, no matter how we ask it."

"We need that boy," Mix said.

"We need more men," Fresko said.

Mix stared at the safe house. The other two waited, Gambay grinding his teeth in anticipation. Mix said, "If Letty got in there, then this place is burnt. The girl's new to this, so your man will be getting her out of the way before coming back here to move Rufaizu. We get him then, outside the defences. Get him out the way and take his car."

"He's a Ministry agent," Fresko reaffirmed sternly.

"Who fucked with Letty," Mix snarled. "We don't need to kill him, anyway, just scare him off. Spring the boy, get the Dispenser back. Finish what Letty started. We're supposed to roll over because he wears a goddamned government suit?"

"It could start a war," Fresko stated.

"Not a war," Gambay answered. "A massacre. Long overdue."

Mix nodded agreement. "Yeah. Might be exactly what we need."

The drive to Pax's apartment was even more awkward than the drive to the safe house had been. Casaria chastised her, but tried to stay positive and practical, insisting she check her stool to leave no trace of the bug. She barely responded. He wasn't upset with her; it was tough to be introduced to this world, and she had done better than most when faced with the sickle. Hard-case Sam Ward hadn't been any better on her first outing, vomiting in the gutter, though no one would believe it now. A few hours, maybe a night to sleep it off, and Casaria was confident Pax would be able to see this with the calm and logic it deserved.

Her swallowing that thing was a part of her fear and confusion, that was all. Pax must have had her reasons. Some aversion to fire, a serious need not to drag out what they were doing, *something*. Whatever it was, it must have made sense in her mind in the moment, maybe like jumping into the sea rather than slowly lowering yourself in. She took an extreme course because she was overwhelmed by the choice he'd forced on her. Yes – that made sense.

Her mind was ticking over this new reality, he could see that. She was no longer fighting the urge to run and seemed to have quickly got over any sense of denial. She had also demonstrated some very lateral thinking. He would never have considered such an action, in trying to get rid of a body. It was sick, and strange, but he couldn't deny it was a solution. No, better than fear and confusion, it was a sign that she'd roll up her sleeves and get involved in the dirty work, with gusto and innovation.

The problem was, it left a niggle of doubt that he really didn't want to entertain. It was possible – he couldn't deny it – that it might have been some kind of trick to save the wretched creature. It wouldn't be the first time a woman had lied to him. He took the long route back, driving slowly, to make sure she had enough time to digest the creature, or at least kill it, before they parted ways, in case she planned to throw it up the first chance she got. At least he was certain she'd swallowed it. He had seen the thing in her mouth. He had faith in himself for spotting that kind of detail.

When they reached her apartment, he stayed in the car. As she was leaving, he told her again that she needed to be sure the evidence was gone, and she told him to fuck off.

"I'll check on you tomorrow," he said. "We'll see what we can do about your money, then."

She didn't reply. That aspect of her deal, it seemed, had lost all importance.

Casaria made the return journey in a third of the time, blotting out the thought of Pax Kuranes as his mind shifted back to business. Their safe house had been breached, though the defences had worked. It was one of the more secure ones, totally secluded – that's why he had chosen it. Now it was useless.

Had they been following him? No, then they would have found the place sooner. Were they following the girl? No, the thing had got there before them. Maybe they were just doing a blind sweep of known safe houses in their desperation to find the Roma boy.

Casaria scolded himself: *idiot*. Believing in coincidences was a sure route to failure.

Back at the safe house, he kept an eye on the monitor in his pocket – no sign of any Fae nearby. He headed to the cellar. Rufaizu stirred again at the sound of the door opening, groggy and barely able to speak but conscious enough to move without Casaria having to carry him. Not giving the boy a chance to gather his senses, Casaria hustled him through the house.

He was pushing Rufaizu's head down, a moment from safety, when the monitor beeped. He reacted instantly, shoving the Roma into the car, drawing his gun and dropping to the ground at the same time. The first bullet caught the top of his shoulder; it ripped cloth and drew blood but the sting was no more than a flesh wound. The second shot went clear over his head, splintering the door-frame behind him. The monitor beeped more violently – at least two separate pulses, getting closer.

He fired back without aiming, over the car, into the air, gun emitting fast, wide balls of light. Another shot shattered a window on the far side of the car. The sniper was on the other side of the road.

Shaken awake by the noise, Rufaizu kicked out of the car as Casaria searched the night sky. The Roma screamed, struggling to his feet, but Casaria pulled him to the ground, shouting, "Stay down, you moron!"

Then came a series of gunshots above the safe house, with the volume of firecrackers. Bullets pattered onto the roof of the car and the pavement around Casaria as he rolled out of the way. He returned fire, his gun erupting in a blinding flash, the projectiles fading into the air above. He pushed off with his feet, dragging Rufaizu's flapping body partially under the car as the barrage continued. The attackers were either terrible shots or were aiming to miss.

Casaria reached up to the handle of the car and a bullet struck the back of his hand. He yelled, but kept going, clenching onto the handle and wrenching the door open. As he did, another shot passed his ear. He fired back, this time seeing a shape in the air swerving for cover.

There was a moment of quiet as the attackers regrouped. Casaria grabbed a canister from a compartment in the footwell of the car and hit a button to activate it. Rufaizu rolled out from under the car and half rose. Casaria pulled him back as the gunshots started again, then he threw the canister high above his head.

It made a rumbling noise, and a shockwave spread through the air like a heat shimmer. The wave shot through Casaria with an electric jolt. The canister dropped back to the ground a few feet away, the gunshots silenced.

Rufaizu was gasping, feet randomly kicking. Casaria got a better grip on him, finding the young man bleeding from the neck, eyes wide with panic and mouth voicelessly moving.

Mix rose from the gutter of the safe house roof as the grenade's pulse shot subsided, barely having missed him. He spotted Gambay, falling into a grass patch the next house down; he hadn't been so lucky. Then Mix spotted the blood, streaming out of the Roma boy as the suit scrambled out from under him and put a hand on the wound to stop the bleeding.

"Gambay's down," Fresko said over the radio, factually.

The suit pulled the bleeding boy into the car and pulled the door shut.

"So's Rufaizu," Mix said. Equally business-like. "We're gonna need a new plan."

16

Barton writhed in bed as Holly somehow slept through it.

She always slept through it. He could snore, he could toss and turn, he could watch TV or sing to music, none of it disturbed her once she'd slipped into a slumber. That was what had made it all possible. She was such a deep sleeper he was able to live another life at night without her ever knowing he was gone. It gave him alone time, certainly, but it also meant he had zero support in the darkest hours. He sometimes wondered how different it might all be, if he'd married a lighter sleeper.

He was haunted by imagination and memory, thinking of the things that lurked in the Sunken City and the consequences of their actions. He saw Apothel's face, over and over. Sometimes smiling, laughing and drinking. Sometimes crying, shouting, screaming. Always, in any mood, with that hole in his head. Blood streaming across his eyes. Apothel. He had been so alone at the end.

He saw Rufaizu's face, too, no better. That cheeky child. Full of heart, in heavy supply of smiles. He could only imagine the trials that Rufaizu had been through in his naïve enthusiasm, after he had disappeared from all their lives. Who had raised him? Where had he gone? An orphan at nine on the streets of Ordshaw. Half his lifetime spent without parents, cut off even from Barton, perhaps the only person who knew where he'd come from.

And when he finally resurfaced, what had happened? Barton pictured his face beaten, bruised. The boy tied to a chair in some dark basement, electric probes tied to his bare flesh. Water thrown across his face. Barton spun on the bed, not sure if he was experiencing visions of the truth or nightmares of what might be.

Between the distressed faces of father and son he saw the creatures.

The glogockle's dragging knuckles and clucking cry.

The sickle's gnashing jaws that split its head in two.

The turnbold's tongues as they lashed from under its turtle-like shell.

The wormbird's slashing talons.

All scraping in and out of shadows, one erupting from another and blending back into darkness in the kaleidoscope of his frenzied mind. And behind them all the colour blue. Blue in large, distinct rectangles. Over and over, spinning, splitting, merging and expanding.

Blue screens.

Blue screens everywhere.

He saw the glo, swilling from tankards, rolling off a boat by the barrel-load, disappearing down hungry gullets. Luminescent liquid that opened eyes wider than they were meant to open.

Apothel laughing like a lumberjack, the first time they drank together. Tree-thick arms pointing down the tunnel as he curated new discoveries. Barton swaying on his feet, not sure if he was hallucinating when the helluvian hound appeared. They tackled it together, without explanation; it simply had to be done. They clamped its jaws shut as fire lanced out the edges, and they bound it with fireproof fish leather before thrusting it into a pit. Only after the excitement, after the thrill of the fight and the chase, after the laughter, did they stop to talk. It was almost dawn and the explanation scarcely mattered, then.

The explanation never really mattered. Not once Barton had tasted the thrill.

There were reasons, very good reasons, but they weren't important. What was important was that he was there, involved, doing it because it felt right. He had never needed to explain that feeling to himself. That's what made it so hard to stay away. The logic behind abandoning that life was sound, the emotion was not.

He saw Rufaizu dying, stabbed in the heart and bleeding onto the floor, alone, crying. He saw Apothel's face, blood leaking into the eyes as he tried to blink it out. And what? Wingless hawks flooding out of the rafters like a hail of bats, clawing at them, flying back carrying his family.

His family.

Grace being torn from his arms. Holly screaming.

He thrashed in the bed.

"Take him!" He grabbed Rufaizu's body, throwing it to the hawks. "Take him, not them! Give me back my daughter!"

Barton shook awake, soaked through with sweat, sticking to the bed. He pushed up onto his elbows and looked around. The curtains were open and the sun was up. He was alone, Holly apparently long gone. The house sounded still. He dragged himself to the window and looked out.

Dalford glowed in the morning light, yellow sun bouncing off green leaves. The road wide and clear of cars. As far as you could get from the tight grimy inner-city. Except for one thing. He looked at it, the manhole cover, down the road, like nothing more than a regular sewer entrance. His breathing slowed. He had never been sure why it had been so important to move here, above two houses that needed less work. To be close to that thing. Holly had bought his idea that he wanted a house he could fix up, but that wasn't it. That manhole cover had drawn him here, stronger than anything. There was nothing down there, not this far from the centre, but it was an option, in case he needed it.

No. It was a reminder. A warning that the temptation was close to home; giving in was not an option. Something he could never let himself forget.

He turned away from the window and saw the clock on Holly's side of the bed.

10am.

He scrambled for his clothes. Had to get to work. He flung himself into the bathroom and splashed water over his face, threw on a crumpled white shirt and ran down the stairs as he crookedly buttoned up. He skidded into the kitchen and paused to see his wife perched on a stool, eating a piece of toast. She raised a quizzical eyebrow and said, "Going somewhere?"

"Why didn't you wake me?" he demanded, flicking on the kettle and grabbing a piece of toast from her pile.

She snatched it back at once. "Because it's Saturday. And frankly, you looked like you needed the rest."

Barton stopped, catching his breath. It took a moment to sink in, then his whole body slumped with relief. "Oh thank God."

"Don't thank Him quite yet," Holly said, placing a hand on the kitchen counter. She had his phone. "You're going to wish you were at work in a minute."

He stared at the phone, the possibilities flooding his mind. Had Dr Rimes called him back? He started forming a defence. "Whatever you're thinking, you know I haven't been out."

"I know," Holly sighed. "It doesn't stop it from being a problem."

She passed him the phone and he snatched it, desperate to get it over with. The most recent message was from a new number. From the first line, he realised a call from Rimes would have been better.

Holly said the words out loud as he read them, apparently having studied it enough to know the message by heart. "*I see why you don't want your family involved – but I saw a sickle. You need to talk to me.*"

Barton looked from the phone to her.

"You said you didn't know her."

"I *don't*," Barton insisted, picturing the thousand things his wife was going to attack him with. "She knew our address, you think she couldn't find my number, too? It's not –"

"Tell me again," Holly said, "about the Layer Fae."

"Don't do this," he answered weakly.

"No, I want to hear it again."

He closed his eyes, preparing the words he'd said to her a dozen times, the story he knew she never truly believed. A story filled with half-truths that she must've been questioning again. He said, "The Layer Fae were a gang, the sort we ran into when everyone else was sleeping. They were the worst of a bad bunch. We avoided them. I don't know why, I don't know exactly when, even, but Apothel started talking with them. He said or did something they didn't like, or maybe they just had a bad day, I don't know. He had a bullet in his head. No trace of who did it. The Layer Fae being who they were, everyone was too scared to go after them for it. Not on account of a bum like Apothel."

"The police turned a blind eye."

"Yeah," Barton nodded. "They said it was suicide. A bullet in his forehead." His voice wavered somewhere between anger and sadness. "Rufaizu was there. He was just a boy. Never should've seen it."

Holly stared at him, letting the weight of his tale fill the room. It had taken three months of degenerate drinking and wallowing, with dozens of fights and accusations and intrigues in between, before she had first drawn this painful explanation from him. She had accepted it, finally, his story that he had only been spending time with drug dealers and gangs, not cheating on her. That he had been partying at night with, essentially, a homeless man. She always seemed to suspect there was more to it than that, though, and he feared one day she would start asking again. For nine years he had been waiting for the probing questions to come back. It had been inevitable, with Rufaizu reappearing.

But she didn't ask any more.

She said "Don't you think you should meet with this girl? Don't let the same thing happen to her."

PART 2:
SATURDAY

1

Grace Barton, at 14 (almost 15), believed she had life more or less figured out. The important thing, which a lot of people seemed to miss, was that you needed to stay positive. No one likes a complainer. A lot of girls bitched about people, and their lives, to be heard. But then you had to think of new things to complain about and new ways to be nasty about other people, to keep things fresh. In the long run, it was easier to be positive about things, and people noticed that instead. Like when Kylie Taylor told the group she was mad at her dad because he'd come home drunk, falling over all the furniture in the house, and she hadn't got any sleep. Grace could've offered a similar sob story. She'd seen worse than knocked-over furniture. But she put a positive spin on it, instead. Alcohol was cool, after all. So when Kylie complained about her bumbling dad, Grace asked if he had any alcohol to share. The girls all laughed, and it was better than complaining. Maybe Kylie's dad didn't do it so well, though. It was easy with Grace's dad, because he was an expert, of sorts, rather than a problem drinker.

"Drink half a litre of water, half a litre of beer and half a litre of whisky," she had heard him say to her mum once, a few years ago, "and see which one changes your life most."

She was not privy to the context of the conversation, or exactly what point he had been making, but Grace liked it. That's why she made a point of sneaking some of his whisky in a flask when the other girls were experimenting with sugary bottled drinks. Kylie had said "You're so classy!", and she wasn't totally kidding. And someone had told Luke Merrick about it, and apparently he'd said Grace was a *legend*.

That was where looking at the bright side of life got you. Grace knew her mum had been upset with Dad about how he used to go out too much, but she just hadn't been looking at it the right way. Mum didn't get that Dad needed a particular kind of stimulation. He loved her, with all his heart, there was no hiding that. You could see it in the way he couldn't leave a room without touching her on the way out, even when he went for something small, like to get a drink. It was a bit gross, but also kind of sweet. And he even seemed to enjoy being told what to do by her, at least a little. But Mum hadn't given him enough of that – enough attention – that's why he went out so much. Once she started caring more, and gave him real specific instructions, he was happy. Sure, he complained a bit, and there had been some pretty big arguments a while back, but he genuinely seemed to enjoy being home, and the most annoyed he got now was when he couldn't do something for them, like buy Grace the best bike in a shop. He just cared, a whole lot, and that was over little things. Grace often thought he must've been sad, like, beyond belief, when his friend died.

No one ever brought that up, now. Even in her head, Grace couldn't put a positive spin on *that*. It was too long ago for her to remember what really happened. When she'd asked him about it, once, all he had replied with was: "Bad choices got him killed. Remember that. He didn't know when to stop."

She did remember it. Like when she drank herself sick in the park once, and she moved on to weak cider for Lonnie's party the next night. And she had a long-term plan. She would cut back around her mid-20s, maybe early 30s. That would give her more time to recover than her dad had, and he was doing fine. With a bit of sensible planning and positive thinking, life didn't need to stop being fun. Not completely. That was Mum's problem. That was most adults' problem. They thought that at a certain age you weren't allowed fun any more. It was like children going to playgrounds. At 14, it was wrong to go on slides and swings and roundabouts, but Grace loved rounding up her friends to raid the parks with the enthusiasm of kids. Fun's for whoever wants it, she said. Adults should go on swings and slides and roundabouts, they'd still enjoy it.

If Mum understood that, Dad would be happier. He was good and settled, sure, but he got a bit vacant at times, didn't he? There was still a little room for more, if Mum only let him loose.

That street lady showing up on their doorstep was a reminder. Grace knew, from the moment she opened the door, that any adult woman dressed in boys' clothes, with almost no make-up, spelt fun. Grace wanted to ask her a hundred questions at once, like what she did for a living and what music she liked, but there was no time. She didn't even get to compliment her on her coat – which was really retro.

Mum was angry, obviously. She'd been angry before the lady showed up, after Dad had been drinking again. The lady obviously wasn't the cause of the anger, and even more obviously wasn't having an affair with her dad, so Grace saw an opportunity where Mum saw a problem. When she found her mum on Saturday morning, stewing over Dad's phone, writing something in a notepad, like she was plotting murder, Grace knew she needed to calm Mum down. Her mum said she didn't understand. Grace said she understood pretty well, actually. Whoever that woman was, she came from a place that her dad knew. He hadn't been back, for a long time, and he was at least a bit unhappy about it. Maybe it was time he got some closure?

The problem was Mum didn't know about it, before. She didn't realise he needed a little something extra in his life. They'd talked it out, sure, and Dad was doing okay – but there'd been fights and arguments and probably ultimatums. What if they looked at it together, now, a bit more relaxed? Couldn't she do that for him?

Mum hadn't said anything. That was a good thing, Grace thought. It meant she was considering it and not just telling her to mind her own business. And with that on her mind, Mum was more positive than before, and didn't grill Grace about the million things she had planned that day. Grace left the house pleased with herself, on her way to the Ten Gardens Arndale.

It was going to be a good day.

2

Pax woke up feeling strangely rested, yawning and stretching her arms. She stood and rubbed her eyes with the backs of her fists, calmly noticing the light creeping in under the curtains. Lit like that, the sun was on the east side of the building. Early morning. She must've had something approaching a normal night's sleep for once. She dragged herself lazily to the window and drew the curtains. She thrust them shut again.

The crack.

She spun to the bullet hole in the wall.

Jesus Christ, she wasn't supposed to be here, with them watching – it wasn't safe. She shook herself wider awake, whipping past the bed to sweep up her keys, her wallet, her phone. She jammed on her boots, scrambled into her coat. Burst out the door and vaulted the stairs, cursing herself. Stupid. What'd she been thinking, letting Casaria drive her home – should've given him an excuse – a late-night game or something – anything to avoid coming back here.

She ran out of the block and down the road, almost knocking a young man off his bike. Squinting her eyes against the sunlight, she shot looks at the nearby windows. They could be hiding anywhere. She hurried into an alleyway between buildings, concealed by high walls, and cut through to the next street. She looked back. No one was following. The Tube station was a block away, she could lose a tail there, for sure.

She paused before exiting the alley.

Why *had* she come back here?

Her mind flashed back to the night before.

Bollocks.

There was a shoebox in her closet with a tiny woman trapped in it. She'd come back because protecting a fairy – *a real life fairy* – had put any thoughts of her unsafe apartment out of her mind. More than that, what with all the frantic energy she'd expended pacing about in despair at what the hell this little woman was, she'd finally just collapsed into sleep, still dressed. She must've been lying around for hours at risk. Idiot – *idiot*.

But wait. She'd been lying around for hours. Nothing had happened.

Was the lunatic caller no longer watching?

She took out her phone. No messages or missed calls. Maybe they were giving her time. And she'd seen where Rufaizu was – when the lady called back, they might be able to work something out. Things might not be so bad, at least as far as being shot in her ovaries was concerned.

On the other hand . . . she was outside, now, she could skip across town to be sure she wasn't being followed, then figure out a proper plan of action. Though that small person would wake up trapped in the dark with only the padded comfort of a scrunched-up t-shirt and a small thimbleful of water. She'd made a prisoner of this small miracle and now she'd abandoned her without an explanation. Could she explain it? Did little insect women speak, or understand, English?

What else could she do? Take the fairy with her, risk dropping it or accidentally sitting on it or something? Take it to a vet? She should find her a bed or a dollhouse or something, at least . . .

Pax's phone vibrated in her hand, the surprise almost making her drop it. After taking a calming moment, she read the message. Barton's number.

I'll meet you. But somewhere safe. Don't come to Dalford again.

She reread her own message above his, remembering her desperate idea of dragging this family man back into her mess. She looked back towards her road one last time. Casaria had said the fairy might be knocked out for a day. Maybe it wouldn't even notice she was gone. Shoving her hands in her pockets and pulling up her hood to hide her face, she slunk away towards the Underground.

Weirway Park rose over the city of Ordshaw in the north-west, the peak of its green hill offering a panorama that encompassed industrial warehouses, brick terraces, shimmering skyscrapers and, to the east, leafy suburbs. The River Gader snaked around the base of the hill, in earnest to the north and in gentle tributaries to the south. In the autumn, the trees of the park were a mix of gold and red, and the breeze from the sea was brisk without being outright cold. The hill's peak, wide enough for everyone to spread out and feel alone, felt personal, even with its all-encompassing view. Pax had used it as a thinking spot ever since she moved to Ordshaw. She basked in the quietness of nature while looking over the chaotic city beneath. Apart from it all, but connected at the same time.

"You alone?" Barton asked from behind. She turned and took him in. His scruffy shirt and trousers looked as if they might have been his old work clothes. He had a builder's face, with heavy features, untamed stubble and a few incongruous marks that could have been old wounds or natural defects. He had a big gut, and big arms; probably used to work out but got tired of it.

"Yeah. I mostly am," Pax said. She held out her hand. "We didn't get a proper introduction before. Pax Kuranes."

"Darren Barton." He gave her a short but firm shake, his beefy hand dwarfing hers. He looked around, checking that no one could hear them. The nearest person was an elderly man preparing a toy plane for flight, well out of earshot. Pax was about to start, to reel out everything she'd gone through, but Barton's expression turned serious as he spoke first. "Let's start at the top. What do you know about the Blue Angel? You tried glo yet?"

Pax's hopes for simple answers exploded. She said, "That's the top, is it?"

"Pretty much," Barton nodded, not noticing her lack of understanding. "You met someone from the Ministry, he wouldn't tell you about that stuff. Chances are he doesn't know it. But you need to."

"Shit." Pax's voice fell. She closed her eyes, hit by a wave of exhaustion. She hadn't slept as well as her brief waking ignorance had suggested.

"You come here on the Tube?"

She nodded without opening her eyes.

"No wonder you're tired."

"No," she said, looking at him again. His serious expression had softened, replaced by concern. "I'm not used to being up this early, and I'm kind of up against it right now."

"What happened?"

Pax paused. Barton's eyes told a whole story. They had been mad like a frenzied dog's the day before, but now they had the

softness of a worried puppy. The sympathy in his expression was
genuine. He was deeply driven by his emotions. Would fiercely
protect anyone in need, whether it was his family or a stranger. He
had actually come here to help her.

"Let's sit." He swung a hand to a bench down the hill. As they
walked, he said, "You didn't run, after what I said?"

"I got curious," Pax said. "Same time the Ministry guy got
friendly."

"So you went with him." Barton sounded disappointed. "I told
you not to."

"Yeah. I've never liked doing what I'm told. I saw a monster,
you know?" As they sat on the bench, she said it again: "I saw a
monster. Under the city. Casaria said there's a whole network
down there, and it's all fucked up. What am I supposed to do with
that?"

"That's up to you," Barton said, not at all surprised. He'd been
through this himself, somehow. "You want to get away from it,
now?"

"Would they let me?"

"I doubt it," Barton said. "They never approached me. I've
never knowingly seen or talked to one of the Ministry myself, but
I know people who have. They tend to go missing."

"I heard that too," Pax said.

"Keep them onside if you can. But if you want answers, and
don't want to be a pawn in their game, you need to contact the
Blue Angel. You got family, friends?"

"No one close. I see my folks, my brother, maybe once a year.
That's how I like it."

Barton didn't ask why, and Pax was thankful. He lived in
Dalford, he wouldn't get it. "That gives you options, at least. I got
involved for my family. I was trying to protect the city, because
that meant protecting them, too. Then I realised my kid needed me
more than she needed this city."

"I've never felt a special need to protect anyone, or anything,
other than myself," Pax said, but his eyes looked doubtful.
Rightfully so; even as she said it she imagined Rufaizu strapped to
that chair.

"You don't want to walk away, do you?" Barton asked.

"I don't want to get torn up by a monster or shot in the ovaries,
that's for sure." She ignored his questioning look. "Look, first off,

I lost a big chunk of cash, which is crazy bad timing – I've got rent due and there's this poker tournament – and these people, the things they're doing – I mean . . ." She trailed off, seeing that Barton wasn't entirely following her, and she turned her toe against the ground.

He said, "It's all become background detail, hasn't it? You want to help. You're not even sure why. But trust your instincts. Rufaizu's heart's in the right place. The creatures down there, they're bad news. They've got one big, ugly purpose, hiding a bigger threat. A force that drains people, feeds off this city. Me, Apothel, the others, we wanted to stop it."

"Casaria said there's something good down there."

"What would he know? The Ministry never listened to the Blue Angel, they're clueless."

"What is that? Someone's lofty codename, right?"

This made Barton stop. He said, "I'm not sure if you'll believe me."

"I'm about ready to believe in unicorns, Darren," Pax replied.

"It's a little harder to understand than that. The Blue Angel is someone who told us all we needed to know about the Sunken City. They communicate through blue screens that appear on walls, like projections. Maybe one person, maybe more, I don't know, but they helped us. To a degree. It was never actually enough."

Pax slid down into the bench, legs shifting forward until she was almost hanging off the edge, head lolling into the back. She rolled her eyes to the sky and took her time to release a loud groan. Indulging herself in the frustration of a petulant child. She said, "Fuck me. What do I have to do to go home and forget about all this?"

"You tell me," Barton said.

She met his gaze, maintaining her slouch of discontent. Rather than answer that, citing the kidnapped fairy, an imprisoned youth, the Ministry stalker or her sniper friend, Pax decided to move on to what he knew. "What'd you learn from this Blue Angel?"

Barton continued, "It shared some specifics about the creatures down there, but mostly it pointed us towards glo. Drink glo and you can see everything more clearly. Literally, the Sunken City makes more sense. Most importantly, you can see the minotaur."

"Oh piss off!" Pax sat back up like a shot – that word again.

"There's *not* a minotaur down there."

Barton shook his head. "That's what we called it, the thing that sucks the energy out of people. It appeared as something we could see and understand, when we were on glo, but it's made of light, or energy, I don't know." Pax gave him a blank expression and he went on. "I can't describe it well, I'm no poet. It's why I asked about the Tube. It sucks energy from above, but especially from people down there. They blame travelling, don't even know it's feeding on them. What we'd do, we'd go down there and find the beast, and we'd communicate through these blue panels with the Blue Angel, and it'd help move it away from the more populous parts of the city. That's the best we could do. Damage limitation, if not prevention."

"Hold on," Pax said. "How'd this Blue Angel move it? Who's behind these blue screens?"

Barton hesitated, as if he didn't like to admit the next bit. "We never found out. The blue screens were weird."

"Compared to the nightmare monsters?"

He shrugged that off. "To get hold of the Blue Angel, you scratch words into walls. It has to be scratching – don't ask why. We tried pens and other stuff, no good. The answers come back in scratches. We communicated through these screens for years."

"Leaving a trail of love notes on public walls?" Pax said.

"No, these screens cleared up after themselves. Someone, somewhere out there, wanted to help us, but kept it totally secret. And like I said, that help was never quite enough. Sometimes the directions led us to empty glo stashes. Sometimes we'd find the minotaur and it wouldn't get moved. And the Blue Angel never contacted the Ministry, or never got through to them, near as we knew – never persuaded them of the truth of what was going on down there. But still, it was the best we had. I could give you an address where you might be able to find a blue screen, if you want. It's been a long time, might not work."

Pax could see this was a bad start. Barton was a few cards short of the full deck, and his unreliable, anonymous source hardly sounded like a solution. "Who else was into all this?" she said. "You, Rufaizu, and Apothel, right?"

"Not Rufaizu, he was too young. We had a few friends, though. It was stupid, like an adventure club. Some mates get together for a pub quiz once a week, or a game of poker; we got bladdered and picked fights with monsters. We had a scientist helping us, Mandy Rimes. And the filmmaker Rik Greivous. Heard of him?"

Pax shook her head.

"He shot weird stuff. He was trying to get glo to work with his cameras, to record it all. The scientist, she tried to figure out what these creatures were made of, so we could hurt them. The Ministry turned a blind eye as long as we never got near the minotaur. They needed the other stuff culled anyway. I took down glogockles, sickles, the things that they didn't want late-night drunks stumbling across. The minotaur's not like the other creatures, though. It's massive, and not exactly . . . I dunno, physical. Nothing we tried hurt it. No way to record it or study it. You can't even see it properly without glo. Apothel always had some new idea, though, so we kept at it. Until there was an incident with the kids, and I got into it with the wife. Rik disappeared, he had other things going on. Apothel started to run around on his own. We lost touch and he started talking to the Layer Fae. It was bound to go south from there. The Fae hate everything that's not Fae, they're psychotic. I never crossed paths with the little bastards myself, thank God. You wouldn't see them coming if you did."

Mystery psychos you never saw coming. That had been important before, hadn't it, when he gave her that name? You didn't actually *see* the Fae. Little bastards. Pax closed her eyes. The caller had called her "tall". The tiny woman had had a pistol she'd plucked out of the holster with tweezers. Fae. The word was literal. She said, "The Layer Fae aren't people, are they?"

Barton laughed, bitterly, devoid of humour. "They'd have you think they were. But no, they're not. Again, you won't believe it. They're . . ."

"Fairies."

Barton paused. He was surprised she'd guessed it, but he didn't care to ask how. "Yeah. Nasty, gun-toting little shits. The Blue Angel warned us about them, said they had a long-term interest in the Sunken City."

Pax swallowed. She suddenly didn't feel so guilty about the shoebox. Nor so worried about going back to her apartment, now it was possible it really *wasn't* being watched. She said, "Are there a lot of them?"

"Oh, I think so," Barton nodded. "But they don't work

together. Antisocial, aggressive things."

That was the caller all right. That was the lady Pax had trapped. She snapped in another piece of the puzzle. "Apothel had something they wanted, right? Now Rufaizu has it? Or had it."

Barton paused. "Possibly. I knew Apothel was into something with them, and Rufaizu seemed to follow that up, but every plan Apothel came up with was a dead cert, you know? This is the big one, he'd always say. The thing that'll kill the minotaur. You couldn't take it seriously." Barton sighed. "It was me who found him, you know? Apothel. I hadn't seen him in months when Mandy called up, worried he was missing. I had a kid of my own and began to worry about Rufaizu. I found the boy in one of Apothel's half-dozen hiding places. Alone. He'd been locked in a room for days, no food. Piss and shit in a corner."

"My God . . ."

"Finding him was the good news. Apothel was in the loft space above. Rufaizu followed me up there and saw everything. He ran. He ran and I couldn't stop him. I spent weeks trying to find him, chasing up leads with Mandy, to the point that my wife was all but ready to kick me to the curb. The kid had vanished, though, carrying this image of his dead dad with him."

"I'm so sorry," was all Pax could say.

"Still not the worst of it. No one did a damn thing. Police barely opened a report. Said it was just another vagrant gone. The Ministry were covering it up. They got in touch with Mandy and told her to drop it. It wasn't a friendly suggestion. You starting to understand what you're dealing with?"

Pax nodded grimly. "So was it the Fae or the Ministry that killed him?"

"The bullet was a millimetre wide."

Pax tried to picture her wall, back home. The bullet hole. How big had that been? The window was hardly shattered, it was definitely possible it had been a tiny shot. Her thoughts were interrupted when she noticed how Barton's face had fallen. She hovered a hand over his for a second, not sure if this was the appropriate move. She braced herself and took the plunge – placed that hand on top of his. He didn't react. She was left unsure, and after a consolatory pat she took the hand back. She said, quietly, "Thank you, Darren. I know it's not easy."

"I've got a daughter," he replied. Pax hummed appreciation. It was explanation enough. He turned his sad dog eyes to her. "I prayed Rufaizu had escaped it all, and ended up in a normal city, with a good life. But wherever he's been, he's stepped right back into his dad's footsteps. Maybe it's a blessing the Ministry took him, though. That's what I'm telling myself. If they lock him away, at least they'll keep him from getting hurt."

Pax nodded, for his sake, but she knew it was nonsense. There were at least two sides to this thing, and if Rufaizu had picked up where his father left off, then he was in danger from both of them.

3

Letty woke with a dull pain in her back, face buried in material. She pushed herself up with a groan and felt behind her for the source of the pain. The groan turned to cursing when she felt the uneven stump where her wing was supposed to be. She blinked a few times to clear her eyes. It didn't help. The shards of light coming through the holes in the wall barely lit the room. With effort, she moved off the soft bedding, getting momentarily tangled in its folds, and kicked back at it as she broke free. The ground felt soft. Card. The walls, she now saw, looking at the holes, were card too.

There was good news and bad news, she decided. Somehow, the Ministry hadn't got her. They wouldn't have put her in a shoebox. The bad news was that she didn't know where the fuck she was.

She strained to see anything through one of the holes. The box was near a wall. In a closet, perhaps, barely lit outside. She tugged the hole; the card was thick, too strong to rip. Cursing again, she checked the rest of her surroundings.

A small thimble of water. That might work.

She threw the water at the card around one of the holes. It soaked in, a splatter perhaps an inch wide, and she tried to get a fresh grip on the soggy surface. It wasn't enough – the card held firm. She looked at the thimble and considered her other options. She needed a piss, but if that didn't work she'd be stuck in here with the stench of urine.

Huffing, Letty threw the thimble down and looked to the ceiling. The lid. Way out of reach and probably hard to shift. She tried her remaining wing, which flapped, still functioning, but when she tried to fly it spun her out, like stumbling on a bad leg. She hit the wall and rested. Cursed one more time.

Pax resisted the urge to give Barton a hug when they parted ways. The large man spoke with great sadness, and looked at her with such kindness, that she felt an affinity towards him. She could tell by the way he talked that he had lost a dear friend in Apothel and he missed going into what he'd called the Sunken City. But she could also see that he had forcibly put it behind him. The rest of the answers lay with Rufaizu or the Blue Angel. He was done.

The address he had given her for one of these blue screens was on her way home, but she didn't feel ready to engage with that weirdness. If the thing was even still active. Barton and his friends might have drunkenly trusted the anonymous stranger's wall messages, but it hardly sounded like the best contact to her, and the last thing she needed was a third (or fourth? she was losing count) party mixing up matters. Besides, she already had a potentially better source of information in her apartment.

Wary of using the Underground, she rode the bus home, a journey that took twice as long but gave her a rare glimpse of the city during the day. People dressed for the weekend, dipping in and out of shops with bags of junk. Pub tables overflowing into the streets, even this early, with young people laughing over pints. Market stalls with loud vendors offering deals on bananas. She reached her flat with the feeling that she wasn't missing much. Ordshaw was still a vacuous hole of pointless lives, like everywhere else, but it was *her* vacuous hole, all the same. And she liked to believe that she wasn't the only one here who'd step up and do something if they discovered an intangible minotaur was draining the city's energy, or that demonic creatures threatened to rise to the surface if left unchecked.

She returned to the apartment, scanning the surrounding windows. There was no one watching her. It was safe, it had to be. She climbed the stairs, entered her flat and went to the curtains. She stopped there with her hands on the material.

Maybe it was better not to tempt fate.

Leaving the curtains drawn, she went to the cupboard instead. With her hands on the doors, she told herself things were about to get better. She had Apothel's book, and possibly the thing he'd been killed for. She hadn't heard from Casaria today, so he was giving her space. Rufaizu was taken in because he knew about this device, not for knowing about the Sunken City itself, so Pax wasn't necessarily in danger from the Ministry, as long as Casaria thought he was in control of what she learnt. She had enough money to repair the window, as icing on the cake. There was every chance the only serious threat in this whole affair was trapped in that shoebox.

All considered, she was ready to take control.

Letty stirred at the sound of a door slamming. The box shook with the thumps of footfalls. A female sigh. Letty pictured it: a bedroom, a closet.

No prizes for figuring out where she was now.

With the girl not approaching, Letty quickly became impatient. She shouted, "Hey! How about some water! You fucking lummox!"

It took a few more shouts before the footfalls came tentatively closer. Letty got louder, roaring, "Yeah, get down here you giant fucker, I got something for you!"

The cupboard creaked open, and the floorboards flexed as the girl crouched in front of the box. The shoebox walls relaxed from a strain, puffing out as a weight was removed from above. Then stillness, as the girl hesitated.

"It's you, isn't it?" Letty shouted. "The dumpy tomboy?"

"You the one who acts tough on the phone?" Pax's voice rumbled through the shoebox.

"Open up and I'll show you an act!"

"You've lost a wing," Pax reminded her. "I've got your gun. And you're two inches tall. What are you going to do?"

"Fuck you up!" Letty snapped.

The ceiling creaked as a weight rested on it. The girl's hand, staying there a moment, not sure what to do. Letty crouched in preparation.

"Don't try anything, okay?" Pax said. "I want to talk."

The lid opened, slowly, light pouring in, and Letty shot up for the gap. Her single wing was not enough. It buzzed and spun her out, sending her rolling across the floor, unable to steer, let alone fly. She buzzed it again, flapping from one side to another, as the lid was completely removed and Pax stared down at her. Letty came to a halt, punching both fists into the floor with an angry shout. She sat up and swore at the top of her voice.

"It wasn't me," Pax told her. "Before you start."

Letty looked up at her hatefully. Her giant captor's face filled the sky, dark hair brushed back over her shoulder to stop it falling in the way. Letty held up a hand, extended her middle finger.

Pax's expression remained blank. She sat back slightly, then her hand descended into the box. Letty rolled aside, yelling, "Oh hell no!", and she tried to crawl away. There was nowhere to go, and no time to get there. Enormous fingers fell around her and as she lunged to escape Pax rolled her into a fist. Feeling the ascent in her gut, Letty kept fighting as the grip tightened.

Pax sat back onto her heels, bringing her hand up in front of her as the fairy used her last remaining weapon, clamping her teeth down onto an exposed bit of flesh. Pax flinched and opened her hand. Letty dropped and started flapping the wing again. She spiralled gracelessly to the floor, hitting the carpet hard and bouncing. Winded, she saw the shadow of the hand descending again and tried to run. Pax closed her thumb and forefinger over her waist and lifted her back up, kicking and screaming.

Letty thrashed violently, but she could no longer get the angle to do any damage. Pax held her in front of her face, staring with fascination, as Letty swung fists in the direction of her nose and demanded, "Put me down, you prick! You've got no idea the pain you're gonna be in!"

"Right," Pax answered. "You need to stop. Calm down."

"Go to hell! You want calm? I'll rip out your heart, show you calm when that stops beating!"

"Jesus," Pax said. "What's wrong with you?"

"Where's my gun? Where's my fucking gun?"

Letty continued to thrash, searching the room for a weapon, even with no chance of reaching one. Pax's apartment was untidy, books across the floor and on the shelves, clothing on the floor. There it was – the pistol barely visible on top of a wooden crate that passed for a bedside table. Pax saw the fairy spy it and lifted her to the side, drawing her attention back to her face.

"You're not getting it," Pax told her. "And you're not going anywhere till we talk."

Letty slumped, at last, energy spent, arms and legs hanging loosely from Pax's grip. She used her last reserves to look furiously into Pax's eye.

"Put me down," Letty said, calmer. "And I'll maybe go easier on you."

Pax twisted on the floor, turning to the bed and sweeping Letty through the air with her. She lowered the fairy onto the bed and let her go. Letty fell onto the duvet with a huff, stood up and patted her clothes down to remove the filth of Pax's grip. She was a long distance from the end of the bed where the pistol was, and there was a big jump if she was going to get it. But fuck it, why not.

Letty sprinted headlong into Pax's palm. She fell back on her arse and rolled aside, tried again, moving to skirt the hand that had fallen in front of her. The hand shifted in an instant and blocked her again, this time joined by the other hand, cupping over her like a dome. Letty punched at Pax, shouting in frustration, but it was no use.

"You're crazy, you know that?"

Letty roared.

4

Cano Casaria had had a long night. His arm needed stitches, his hand was bandaged and painful to use, and the Roma boy was barely clinging to life. He was angry at himself for not having slaughtered all his attackers and that made waiting in the Ministry infirmary harder. He was in no mood to be confronted by two fellow agents this early in the morning. Landon was a portly man who looked like he spent more time eating than breathing. Wisps of grey hair highlighted the unkempt black mop on his head, and the bags under his eyes had folded into bags of their own. The other man was slighter, younger, with patchwork facial hair and pale, blotchy skin that had seen little sun. He wore a leather jacket and a shirt; Landon, a suit, faded, loose around the shoulders and tight at the belly, probably from a charity store. In their own unique ways, the pair of them had tried and failed to comprehend the concept of respectable clothes.

These were the sort of people that gave field agents a bad name. Though Landon had been with the Ministry for decades, Casaria had reached the same level within a year of arriving in Ordshaw. This leather-jacket whelp was Landon's protégé. And they were Casaria's supposed backup.

"Got word from Deputy Director Mathers," Landon said. "You're to stay put, keep an eye on the boy."

"If he needs babysitting, that's a job for you," Casaria said. "I've got real work to do."

"He said you'd say that," Landon replied blandly. "And said to tell you that's why you need to stay here and keep watch."

Casaria imagined Mathers saying it. Another dry husk in this vast bureaucratic machine.

"We've got our best people looking for the suspects," the younger man said. He'd introduced himself earlier. Gum, Gung, Gong maybe? Casaria actively tried to forget his name and gave him the least favourable option.

"The Ministry's best people, *Gumg*," Casaria replied, "are

clerks who skim online databases all day. Not fighters. Not *me*."

"The decision's been made," Landon said. "You're grounded."

"They shot at me," Casaria said, standing and wincing as the pain from his shoulder cut through him. He closed his eyes and swallowed. "The Fae are dangerous. We need to act."

He hated himself for letting them get the drop on him. He hated himself for letting the prisoner get hurt and he hated himself for letting them get away. He was fairly sure he had hurt at least one of the monsters, but they hadn't confirmed a single kill.

"What were you doing there, Cano? Your IO-3 was still pending."

Casaria cringed at the mention of the permission slip required to interrogate their prisoner. "Call it a hunch. I thought Rufaizu might have friends looking for him and I wanted to check everything was okay. Rightly so, considering what I found."

They didn't need to know about Pax. Definitely not that he had taken her there to ease her nerves. Looking at these two made him all the more confident that he needed to persist with her. Amateurs and sociopaths, the lot of them. Whatever else had come of the abortive evening, it had felt good to let himself believe, even for a short while, that someone as bright and normal as her might join him. Someone he could talk to without wanting to shoot his own brains out. Someone who wouldn't gravitate naturally to hiding in this office following the whims of stuffy Mathers.

But Pax was hesitant. And possibly crazy. And the Roma boy had got to her, somehow, without Casaria realising. His gut still said she knew more than she'd let on. Casaria asked Landon, "Is it possible Apothel spoke to people we don't know about?"

Landon gave Casaria a disapproving look, then shook his head as slowly as humanly possible. He said, "This was the Fae, and we are on it. You need to stay here, okay?"

The younger man chimed in, in some twisted way hoping to lighten the tension. "I'm sure we'll find a peaceful resolution to all this."

Casaria locked on him, and told him sincerely, "I don't like you."

Gumg's face fell and Landon stepped in front of him. The big guy said, "Take a break, Cano. You obviously need it."

"Shove it up your arse, Landon," Casaria replied frankly. "I think you need that."

Landon chose not to respond, and led Gumg away. Casaria watched them go and looked up at the security cameras. If he so much as stepped out for a cigarette he'd probably get a call from Mathers.

It was three hours before the doctors announced that Rufaizu was stable, another hour before Casaria got a call from Landon saying he was being relieved and it was time to go home. Preliminary reports from the Fae Transitional City were saying that the attack had not been sanctioned. It was a group of rogue Fae, acting without orders. It was unclear what they wanted; the Ministry's Fae contacts denied all knowledge of the group. Casaria left the building sullenly. Just the thought that the Ministry *had* Fae contacts made him miserable. His initial passion had waned, though, replaced by nagging anger at the thought that Deputy Director Mathers had deliberately trapped him there to cool him off. Had Mathers consulted with Sam Ward on that? It was the sort of dirty trick she would endorse. The sort of information and suggestions she'd fed them in her field reports.

Cowards. We don't need cool. We need results.

The Fae *would* deny it, of course. And the Ministry would buy their denial. The cowards in charge would use any excuse not to get into a fight with the FTC. A few lightning balls and a canister of gas and they could exterminate the lot of them, if they were only willing to commit. The inactivity made Casaria sick. As he told them, again and again. But there were fears that the fairies had devastation technology, comparable to nuclear warheads, which no one had ever proven.

It was nearly 8am when he got out of the infirmary, making it too late for his usual recreations. He would have to wait to properly vent his frustrations. Instead, he drove for hours staring at the city, his monitor checking for any hint of the Fae. It was fruitless, though; the insects knew well enough how to avoid people like him. Finally, he went home and sat in the car, hands clenched over the steering wheel as he stared at the parking garage wall.

He considered calling Pax.

The more he thought about it, the more convinced he became that she had actually swallowed that bug. He wanted to believe it. It meant she'd be willing to do whatever it took to get this job done. That she was better than sane. She was like him.

He could imagine the pair of them hunting together. He'd make a comment and she'd reply with something witty. Funny. He wouldn't laugh at first; he'd say they had a job to do. But it would lighten the mood. Make it enjoyable, as it should be. After they tracked and killed some fiend, he would take her to a cocktail bar and they'd share stories about their misshapen backgrounds. How he'd been too busy staying up at nights to ace his exams, though he knew he could've, and how he'd been asked to leave Southampton Uni after hurting that yuppie who'd made fun of his mother. He hadn't wanted to be there anyway; who ever changed the world after graduating from Southampton? Maybe he could open up to Pax about school, too, and how he played trumpet. She'd joke, sarcastically, but deep down she'd understand.

Maybe their hands would touch over the table.

Not straight away. They'd be very professional, they'd make an excellent team, and raise the whole standard of the Ministry. He'd put her off, because he could do better.

But eventually she'd wear him down.

Their hands would touch and she'd tell him everything was okay.

He was okay.

Casaria did not smile at his imagined future. He picked up the phone to make it happen. He caught himself and stopped. This was wrong.

He should go see her in person.

5

Pax knelt by the bed, with the fairy slumped in a seated position on the duvet. Letty had exhausted herself running and fighting and had very well established flying was not an option. Her chest rose and fell with deep breaths, her single wing occasionally fluttering. Vulgar and violent as she was, it was incredible to watch her. Her voice was quiet but easily audible, like a distant TV set. Her fingers were minuscule but slender and fully functioning. There was a subtle beauty in the way her hair flowed. Pax could sit and stare at this marvel for hours. Letty would not let her, though, not for a moment, even finding one last ounce of energy to snarl, "What the fuck are you looking at?"

"I saved you, you know."

Letty glowered at her. Impossibly mustering more strength for insults, the fairy pushed herself to her feet and made a show of curtsying, speaking with bitter sarcasm, "Oh thank you! My hero!"

"You're a dick," Pax concluded.

"Don't like suffering giant pricks, that's all."

"Well, you're here now, and you're not going anywhere. So are you ready to talk?"

Letty slumped back onto the duvet and folded her arms. "Ain't got a thing to say to you."

"Did you kill Apothel?" Pax got straight to the point.

Letty gave her a vicious look, then said, "What's it to you?"

"Casaria says you're trouble," Pax said. "Talking to you seems likely to get someone killed. But when you told me you wanted Rufaizu, it was to get him away from them, right? Am I wrong?"

"Like I said, what's it to you?"

Pax leant in, bringing her face close to Letty, and the fairy backed off slightly in surprise. Pax said, more firmly, "You threatened me, that's what it is to me. You shot a bullet through my window. So how about you answer my questions or I'll crush you?"

Letty did not move. Pax raised a hand, balled into a fist, demonstratively, and put on her meanest face. Rolling her eyes, Letty lay back onto her elbows.

Pax sat back, humming in disappointment.

"Yeah, thought so," Letty laughed.

"Well," Pax said, "I don't have to hurt you."

She lifted her hand again and Letty scrambled back across the duvet, waving frantically and shouting, "No no no, you fuck off with that grabby bullshit."

Pax paused. "Tell me what's going on. What do you want with Rufaizu?"

"He has something we've been after for a long time," Letty said. "Okay?"

"Yeah?" Pax said. "A weapon, right? Something that could be used in the Sunken City?"

Letty paused. She replied slowly, "What do you know about it?" She pointed towards the head of the bed, where Apothel's book sat. "Did he write it up in there? Who the fuck *are* you, anyway?"

"How about I ask the questions? You're after Apothel's son because of that weapon?"

Letty eyed her carefully, then started scanning the room. The fairy seemed to read the book spines she could see, then looked into the cupboard, where the odd brass canister sat. She took a few steps towards it suddenly, trying to see around Pax.

"Holy shit, you've got it?" she said.

Pax looked over her shoulder, then fell back to close the door and hide the contraption. She paused, blocking the cupboard, and looked down at the fairy. Both of them were well aware it had been far too late to hide anything.

"Sweet gangrene." Letty stood staring, strangely calmer. Almost in awe of having seen the device. "You know how long . . . how long I've been looking . . ." She shot Pax another look. "Rufaizu gave it to you?"

Pax answered with a question of her own. "How'd he get mixed up in this?"

"You oughta know. You've got the Dispenser. His daddy's book. What else do you need?"

"An explanation!" Pax insisted, shifting away from the cupboard again. "*Please*. I don't trust this Ministry and I don't like that they've got Rufaizu – but everyone says it's *your people* that are dangerous. Even though you're the only one that's shown an interest in freeing him."

Letty kept staring at her, weighing up her options. She said, "Okay. So you're not all the way on their side, maybe you need some schooling. What's in it for me?"

"I saved your life!"

"Think that makes you hot shit, huh?"

Pax gaped at her. She shook herself out of it and tried another point. "You talked to Apothel before you killed him, didn't you?"

Letty's tiny eyes narrowed. "I didn't kill him." She paced aside, throwing angry looks at Pax, then over to the cupboard. Pax waited. The fairy huffed. "You want to get yourself killed too, is that it?"

"One," Pax held up a finger, "I want to pick the right side in this quagmire. Two," a second finger, "I don't think Rufaizu deserves whatever's coming for him."

Letty kept eyeing her, considering whether or not to believe her.

"Three," Pax leant closer, "Casaria has offered me money – my own money, which I desperately need right now – and my instincts, in saving you, have potentially burnt that bridge. Give me something."

The fairy finally let out an annoyed breath and threw up her arms. "That's a bridge you want burnt! Burnt, ground down and shat on! The Ministry are the vilest, most self-serving, pathetic gaggle of shits this world's ever seen."

"And your people are better, are they? Apothel was shot –"

"Not by me! I told him our weapons would make his dumb prancing around meaningless. All he had to do was wait. I tried to *save* him, from those that thought he needed removing. He went off half-cocked developing his own plan, though. He pleaded – *begged* – me to set up an audience with our great leader, Valoria." Letty spat aside at the use of the name. "They said no, but he'd already gone off, before I told him that. He never gave my people a chance, not really. He snuck in and stole exactly the weapon I'd told him about. I'm blamed. Thank you very fucking much you stupid shit, last time I trust a human. Some prick I thought might be a friend."

Letty stopped and stared at Pax, letting this hang in the air. Pax said nothing, and she continued.

"He turned up dead after *that*. But it sure as shit wasn't me. It was an amateur – didn't even know about the kid. Rufaizu vanished before anyone started looking for him. Meanwhile my crew and I are all exiled. And between then and now, which has been a shitting long time, I've been trying to find that weapon – that thing *you* have apparently just stumbled upon."

Pax crouched in front of her. "You wanted to work with Rufaizu when he came back?"

"I *was* working with him," Letty said. "He resurfaced out of thin air, and told us he'd got the Dispenser. Rats knows where he'd been all these years, we didn't have time to get chummy. We held off flat out handing him over to the FTC, and let him hang onto the device, because he said it needs a very specific fuel – something that can only be found underground. The weapon's no use without it."

"What's the FTC?" Pax asked.

Letty rolled her eyes. "The Fae Transitional City, *obviously*. The great fucking refugee camp we got forced into when the Sunken City got overrun by the myriads."

Pax opened her mouth to ask another question, but Letty bowled on. Now her tongue was loose, she suddenly seemed a lot more comfortable spilling information.

"So, Rufaizu convinces us to go after the fuel before anything else. It makes sense – you need something from the Sunken City to fight whatever's down there – and it goes a ways to explaining why no one's ever made another Dispenser. Except it turns out the fuel is some kind of electric weed, and it's harder to get than you think. Needs someone with serious balls, like Citizen Barton. So Rufaizu tries to persuade the lummox, only my boys get drunk when they should be watching him, and he gets nabbed and here I am. Captured by a giant loser." Letty turned aside and scuffed her boot across the duvet with frustration.

Pax let the fairy stew for a moment as it all sank in. There was much more going on than she'd appreciated, but the bottom line was simple. It all pivoted on the device stashed amongst her dirty laundry. The question was, what could she do about it?

A loud knock interrupted her thoughts, the door shaking with the force of an impatient visitor.

Pax and Letty shared a look of equal alarm.

"Don't you put me back in that box," Letty hissed.

"Pax, you with someone?" Casaria called from the hallway. "It's only me."

"Only me?" Pax mouthed, as though his presence was supposed to be reassuring. Pax shot forward and grabbed the fairy, shoving her into a pocket before Letty had time to complain. Feeling the small lady punching and kicking, Pax closed her hand over her and warned, "He wants you dead!"

Feeling Letty go limp, Pax moved her down into the deeper recesses of the pocket. Pax straightened her crumpled top, pushed her hair from her face, then opened the door.

Casaria immediately strode in, scanning the apartment past Pax.

"Come right in, why don't you?" she said, testily.

"Who were you talking to?" Casaria asked.

"This is my home," Pax snapped. "You don't just barge in here, and I sure as shit don't owe you an explanation as to who I talk to in here."

Casaria stopped in the middle of the room. His jacket was beeping. A low, regular beep, like a quiet Geiger counter. He took out a small device, the size and shape of an electronic guitar tuner. Holding it up, unapologetic, he said, "This detects things from the Sunken City. Fae, among others."

"You checking if I'm one of them?" Pax folded her arms. He came back towards her. The beeping increased the closer he got. She noticed the bandage on his hand and a graze near his right temple. "What happened to you?"

"I'm going to ask you plainly," he said, inches from her face, "do you still have that creature?"

"You saw what I did," Pax answered through gritted teeth. "Think it was a party trick?"

"This doesn't lie." He held the device higher. She stood her ground.

"So you want to frisk me? Or do you think maybe swallowing her got whatever that thing detects into my bloodstream? *Maybe*?"

Casaria paused. He looked from her to the machine, the beeping continuing into the terse standoff. He lowered the device, frowning. Switched it off.

Pax threw a hand towards the door. "Now could you kindly get the fuck out of my home?"

"I..." Casaria hesitated. He ran a hand through his hair,

averting his gaze. "This wasn't why I came. I've been searching for them and I came to – not for this – it started beeping."

"You interrupted a call to my mum, you paranoid moron."

Casaria nodded, distractedly backing out. "Not paranoid. They came at me. The little bastards are ready to go to war, I swear."

"The fairies?" Pax questioned. Thinking quickly, she shifted to block his vision, making sure he wouldn't see the bullet mark in her wall. She said, "And what, you thought if they came for you they'd come for me, too?"

This got a smile. His tension faded as he apparently recalled the innocent woman he was dealing with. Arrogant twat. "I wouldn't let that happen. They were after the boy. Trying to silence him, no doubt, seeing as they couldn't spring him. They did a bad job. I'm sorry to worry you."

The danger of the situation caught in Pax's throat. She thought back to Rufaizu, witness to his father's death, kidnapped by the government for trying to talk to her. Not, as Barton had hoped, safe in custody. She asked, "Is he hurt?"

"He'll live," Casaria sighed. "I told you those little shits were dangerous, didn't I? Hence my concern that you did actually do . . . what you . . . you know."

"Yeah. Let's not talk about it, okay?"

"Okay. No. I didn't come about that – I wanted to ask you to join me again this evening. I wanted to give you more warning, after last night. Some time to prepare. I'm going on patrol near one of the Sunken City exits. It could be educational. And, of course, financially rewarding."

"Yes, please, offer me my own money again," Pax said. "Keep forcing shit on me."

Casaria stared at her. The awkwardness of his apology was gone, now, his face serious. He said, "You don't have to come. But it would be in your interests."

Pax did not ask why. There was a thinly veiled threat in his tone.

"I'll be back at 8pm. How's that sound?"

"Sounds like you should go get some sleep," Pax replied flatly.

"So you'll come?"

She nodded. He smiled, genuinely pleased, and apologised once more before going out into the hall. He stopped to say something else, but she closed the door in his face. She rested there with her hand on the handle. Silence beyond. Then footsteps as he left. Descending the stairs.

Pax looked through the spyhole. The corridor was empty. She took a breath and went to the window. She waited in silence. Finally, Casaria emerged in the street below, walking towards his car.

Pax let out a breath of relief, thumping onto the bed and burying her face in her hands. She could feel the adrenaline now. She could act as well as a Hollywood star at the poker table, but the consequences of being caught out in a game seldom invoked the wrath of madmen with guns.

Letty crawled out of her pocket and pulled herself up onto Pax's thigh. She straightened out her t-shirt with a few irritated tuts as Pax parted her fingers to look down at her.

"I think you need to explain to me," Letty said, her voice quietly angry, "what you meant by *swallowing her*." Pax shook her head, biting her lips closed, but the fairy was nodding, "Yeah, that sounds like something I need to know."

6

Fresko leant against the wall with a hand on his upturned rifle, watching Mix across the room. The grizzled veteran was searching through a pile of tools and weapons, discarding handfuls of metal and leather contraptions that didn't match what he was looking for. He'd said he had an idea, so Fresko waited it out. It gave him a moment, at least, to reflect on having left Gambay in the ground, and Letty somewhere far worse. That pair had been a thousand miles apart, a manic liability and their scheming leader, but they were both good Fae, in their own ways. They deserved a vigil, but Mix was racing forwards. Always a man of action.

Probably better that way. Move on, take the next step, avoid dwelling on the dark hanging over them. It'd been bad enough just the four of them, all these years. Just the two of them promised to be worse. Whatever idea Mix was concocting, Fresko was happy to give it a go if it meant taking them that much closer to rejoining the wider Fae community in the FTC.

"You're sure there's nothing we could do for Letty?" Mix asked. There was little genuine query in his voice, but he clearly wanted it repeated, to shirk the responsibility.

"I know what I heard," Fresko said firmly. "There's not many reasons a person would say they swallowed a fairy, is there?"

"Fucking animal," Mix spat into the disparate pile of crap. He'd said it before and he'd say it again. "That's what it's come to, is it? Fucking animals."

"I know where she lives." Fresko had thought about it already, and that was an option, too. "I could plug her from across the road. Didn't look like she's got any friends, no one would find her for weeks, most likely."

"She can wait. We lost Gambay being bull-headed, now we do things the smart way." Mix turned to Fresko like he was expecting a comment. Some allusion to Letty's ideas of what was smart and dumb, no doubt. If she were there, she'd never call whatever idea Mix had smart. The sniper shrugged, so Mix continued, "The way you and me know is smart. You know what Letty's problem was? She thought too much."

"Reckon I think as much as her."

"Yeah but you think about killing. That's smart thinking. She thought about how to please people. How to get Val and the FTC back on side without offending anyone. We never should've cared. Should've been doing what made sense to us – not worrying about wider bloody consequences. Should've been doing shit like this," Mix pulled back from the pile triumphantly, lifting up the device he'd been looking for. It was the sawed-off tip of a human-sized pistol barrel, only 10mm thick but as wide as his chest, suspended in a contraption of shoulder harnesses and spring-loaded levers. He heaved it up with a grin. "She got soft – was scared to let us use this bad boy."

Fresko watched with a neutral expression, still stuck on a response to the reductive summary of his intelligence as being solely focused on killing. He knew about strategy, too; coming at things from different directions. Knew how to make a good rat stew, with the right spices. Knew how to dress so people took him seriously, and all; how to keep a shirt white and uncreased.

Mix tested the weight of the gun-tip as he lifted the device's straps over his shoulders. He pulled a lever and the springs pressed the gun barrel forwards rigidly, supported against his body. A classic Fae device, used to fool a human into thinking they had a gun jammed in them, if they believed someone was standing out of their view. Fresko said, "A guy like Barton knows our tricks, doesn't he? And he's stubborn as a mule besides. You think he'll do anything at gunpoint?"

"You see." Mix pointed a finger his way. "That's thinking too much. You're jumping right into the problems, like Letty did, before considering the possibilities."

"What else are we gonna do?" Fresko said. "The goal's still that fuel, isn't it? And that means persuading Barton."

Mix was nodding. "Sure it does. But we'll do it the way Gambay would've done it."

"Kids?" Fresko frowned, recalling their late partner's frequent insistence that human kids were easy targets. Letty had never liked that suggestion, snarling about how erratic kids were, and how stupid Gambay was. That was their whole relationship right there; cautious and calculating versus brash and mad. Didn't matter now that either was right or wrong. A day had passed and both of them were dead.

"One kid," Mix said, tightening the straps. "Citizen Barton caved for the sake of his dear darling girl before, he'll cave again, won't he?"

Fresko shifted away from the wall as he put together Mix's plan. It was a new angle, one they hadn't needed to consider before. Not when they had Rufaizu to win Barton over. It made sense, though. "Threaten the kid, force the Citizen to harvest some electric weed."

"Damn straight."

Fresko weighed it up, watching Mix scanning the archaic tool. This would definitely put them on the dumb side of Letty's scale, but Mix was right. Plans like this had worked before, and sneaking about talking with humans evidently hadn't. And they needed that weed. Letty had been a bitch, but she'd known where they stood. A thanks-fucking-much for returning the weapon alone wouldn't get them back in. A functioning weapon, maybe the means to make more, that'd set them up. A choice of positions in the FTC, enough wealth to sack off ever working for or with anyone else. Renewed access to the best Fae tailors and cuisine, at least.

"You're worried about going back, aren't you?" Mix asked, into his silence.

"No," Fresko said, but the old mercenary gave a deep laugh.

"Sure you are. It's been a pipe dream for so long. Letty making promises that none of us thought would amount to anything. Now there's a chance we can get back in and you don't know what you'll do when we get there. See women again, real women. Eat proper food. Think it'll be hard?" Mix laughed again, even louder, and grabbed his crotch as he boomed, "Yeah, it'll be hard!"

As his companion kept laughing, Fresko sighed and pushed off from the wall.

"Never bothered me too much, being away," he said. "I just want the choice."

"And this is how we do it!" Mix slapped the gun contraption. "Not through sweet-talking and negotiating. Honest to goodness brute force, that's our way."

Fresko couldn't help but smirk. He said, "Letty never sweet-talked anyone in her life."

"No," Mix agreed. "She wouldn't have loved this, though."

Fresko nodded at the device. "That's because you're half-cocked, like always. How'd you see that playing out?"

"Get her scared, dictate a call to daddy, all done," Mix said, plainly.

"We need more than that. The lummox is a brute, he'd answer a plain threat with anger. We want to put the fear in him, we need to take her away, completely, at least for a while."

Mix's face glazed over with confusion, like there was no other plan possible than simply threatening one of the lummoxes. Fresko checked the room, searching for something among their piles of treasure. Near a wall, a hefty chunk of plastic served as a table for a pile of precious stones, pried from jewellery. It was an electronic device, a souvenir from one of their more ambitious pranks against the humans. Mix followed his gaze and frowned.

"What're you thinking?"

"Daylight robbery," Fresko said, the plan forming even as he said it. "No one's gonna see us, holding that gun to her neck. We lead her to a car, she gets in willingly, we move her right across town and get her hidden. Just need a car that we can control."

"Last time you drove, you hit a damned lamppost."

"Yeah," Fresko shrugged. "But this time I'm sober. All we need is the right motor. We've got an inflatable Joe, don't we?"

Mix looked from the electronic key back to Fresko. As he let the plan sink in, his rough jaw twisted into a leer. He started filling in the blanks, thinking out loud. "Gotta be a recent model, something super fancy, with those electronic controls. Gotta have those dark windows, too."

"Yeah."

"And we'll need gas. Knock-out gas."

"Yeah."

"You see, my man…" Mix walked past Fresko, towards the door. "We put our minds to something, it gets done. We'll get it done damn well. Val and the FTC are gonna squeal when they hear what we've done." He patted Fresko's shoulder, moving out. Fresko followed with his eyes.

Gambay would've loved this, but he would've gone wild with excitement and blown the whole operation. Letty wouldn't have let them anywhere near the idea of kidnapping a lummox, she would've axed the plan before it was one. The pair of them were gone, though, weren't they? It was just them left, and maybe, just maybe, they had a better balance of balls and brains between the pair of them than there had been before.

Fresko followed Mix out of the lair, calling after him, "When we're done, I'm going back for that girl. We'll plug that Ministry man, too. It's what I'd want you to do for me."

"Sure," Mix laughed from up ahead. "We'll slaughter whoever the fuck we have to."

After two hours prowling the Ten Gardens Arndale and a light lunch in a rooftop bistro, with the sun out and a party to go to in the evening, Grace couldn't imagine a better Saturday. She and Kylie Taylor and Jenni With An I had laughed themselves stupid watching a bin-man trying to fend off a seagull. They had raided vintage clothes stores for bargains. They had tossed a bottle of water at a cute street-side coffee clerk and *run*. Grace felt like she was getting wrinkles from smiling too much.

By mid-afternoon, they were languishing in one of Ten Gardens' many parks, a place packed with up-and-coming artists in multicoloured clothing, strumming acoustic guitars. Kylie had persuaded a man coming out of the supermarket to get them a bottle of cider, and they had quickly become merry, rolling on the grass and heckling buskers to take their tops off. A young guitarist did as they asked, to uproarious laughter and cheers.

When the cider rushed through Grace, she excused herself to go to the public toilet. Normally they would've gone together, but Katie was busy chatting with the busker and Jenni was half asleep. It didn't matter – the park's green-tiled outhouse was too small, anyway. Grace squeezed in, sat down and read lewd graffiti as she peed. Guys had snuck in and written nasty sexual stuff, which made her giggle.

Finishing up, she left the cubicle, ran her hands under murky water and gave herself a look in the grimy mirror. The reflection was a metallic blur, but she guessed she looked good. She turned to leave, eager to rejoin the sunny day, and felt the barrel of a gun press hard into the nape of her neck.

Grace gasped as a rough male voice snarled near her ear, "Don't move a fucking muscle."

Sober terror hit her like a slap. She couldn't move if she wanted to.

"We're going for a walk. Don't make a sound. Don't even *think* about running."

Some life came back. Grace trembled, her extremities shaking. Run? Could she run? Just bolt out the door? But it was a gun. What did he want? She blubbed, "I don't have any money –"

"Shut up," the voice said. "Out the door, to the right. Walk real slow, to the gate."

She hesitated, desperate for a solution. If she stalled, someone might come in, save her. She couldn't die – not here – not like this. That happened to *other* people. Oh Christ was it going to happen to her? Was this her life? She'd be a face on the news. Dead in a public toilet because she had been dumb and gone in alone. Everything wasted.

"*Now.*"

She did as she was told, focusing hard on moving one foot after the other, away from the toilet, between the hedges. The people of the park joked and played games together, none looking her way. She pleaded with her eyes, notice me, do something. Don't let them take me, don't let me die. No one saw there was anything wrong, though. Surely they didn't think this sicko was with her? Tears streamed down her face. Another step and she was out of view, almost at the gate.

"Good girl. See that car? Get in."

"No," she whimpered. "No no no please – please – you've got the wrong person –"

"Real slow, calm, how about a smile?"

"Please please I'm only fourteen!"

"Got a lot to live for then, don't ya?" the man growled. "Do as you're told."

She walked to the car, glancing from side to side, this corner of the park opening onto a dead road.

"Open the door."

"Please –"

"Make me repeat myself again and I'm gonna cut your kidney out. Understood?"

She nodded and opened the door. She paused, looking over the car, across the road, as a man turned the corner, walking his dog her way.

"Get in."

"Oh God," she cowered, trying to catch the man's eye. He looked her way, a disinterested glance, then looked away again. Hadn't he seen what was happening? Why wasn't he doing anything? There was a man behind her with a gun!

"*Now.*"

She squeezed her eyes closed and ducked into the car. The gun pulled away.

"Close the door."

She looked out. There was no one there. The engine started and her eyes darted to the front. Her eyes rested on the driver, sat rigidly at the wheel. His skin was shiny and bulbous, like plastic. Unreal. She looked back to the door. There was no one *there*. Where had the man with the gun gone? Had she even heard footsteps behind her? Was it –

Something dropped over her head and the world went black. Material smothered her face – a cloth sack, tugging back. It muffled her responsive cry, then the gun barrel pressed into her neck from the side. The man was back. "Close the door."

She felt sideways, groped for the handle and pulled it shut.

"Good girl. Now go to sleep."

As the man finished his sentence she could already feel wooziness overtaking her. Her body was numb, blending into the car seat beneath her. The car engine was a distant sound, like she was hearing it through water. She slumped down, into sleep.

7

. . . Fae society used to be just unconnected family units and raiding parties. In the middle of the 20th century, the Fae were driven together, maybe by humans coming into their territory, digging underground. In Ordshaw, around the start of World War 2, the Fae built the first Transishional City, an above-ground community. They fite a lot, but have an elected counsel with one main leader. Currently Valoria Magnus, who took over from Retcho.

"Retcho?" Pax commented, looking up from her translation of Apothel's text. The dense pages covering the Layer Fae provided a brief history alongside the basic characteristics of their people: small, winged and difficult to spot. She'd already learnt they were uniformly addicted to a powder substance dubbed *dust*, which had psychotropic effects on nearby people. When Pax asked Letty for clarification on that, the fairy told her to spin on it.

Letty had otherwise been quiet since Pax had tried to explain what had happened in the safe house. The fairy had glared furiously and said nothing, her anger reaching a silent zenith. She barely even protested when Pax lifted her back into the box, though she did later snap that a toilet would be nice. The best Pax could come up with was the plastic lid from a jar of hot sauce. It stopped the complaints, though Pax decided not to check on the results for the time being, instead trying to find something in the book that she could use to relate to the diminutive woman.

Stood over the open shoebox, holding the book, Pax said, "You really had a leader called Retcho?"

"It sounds as stupid to us as it does to you," Letty said. "Big whoop."

"This is incredible." Pax knelt down. "A whole civilisation – a community – right under our noses, and no one knows about it? With your own politics, history, culture?"

Letty gave her a bored look.

"I'm not your enemy," Pax told her.

"You're a dead bitch, is what you are," Letty told her, more factual than insulting. "My boys came for him, they know what happened. They'll know to come for you next."

"So why haven't they?" Pax countered. Letty had no answer for that. Casaria had made it clear Letty wasn't alone in this, and the bullet hole in the wall was a constant reminder of what the Fae were capable of, but it had been the better part of a day and Letty's people hadn't come. "Either they don't know you're here or they don't care?"

Letty glared at her. From the attitude this fairy was giving her, Pax suspected it was the latter. If they were anything like her, their focus would be Casaria. Now that they had apparently tracked Rufaizu, what did they need her for? Pax said, "Well, either they'll come and it won't matter if you talk to me, or they won't and you might give me a better idea of how I can help you." She tapped the book. "There's a comment here, from Rufaizu I think. He says this is inaccurate. Why?"

The fairy couldn't resist snapping an answer. "Because no fucking human should be talking to a Fae, and anyone that writes shit about us is probably making it up."

"But Retcho was real? And the Transitional City exists?"

"Of course it exists," Letty spat. "Nice and above ground where it doesn't belong."

"And your people would prefer the Sunken City for your home?"

"It *is* our home. Those monsters drove us out."

"It didn't look like much of a home to me."

This gave Letty pause. "What do you know about it? Casaria took you down a couple of entrance halls?"

"I saw bare tunnels," Pax said. "Nothing down there but bare walls. Human-sized tunnels, at that. What's so special about it?"

"It's a whole other world," Letty said. "A place where we're hidden from the prying gaze of people like you. A network that takes us everywhere with total freedom of movement – where we don't have to rely on *dust* to stay hidden. The halls are empty because it all got taken from us. Those creatures came in and ruined *everything*. But if you'd seen it in its prime…" Her voice softened, with the fond recollection of a childhood fantasy. "There were vistas of Fae buildings – the sort of architecture that'd make you curl up and weep. Fucking *vistas*. All we've got now is prefab huts and towers that can be dismantled for moving at a moment's notice. They even built 'transitional' into its name."

Pax didn't think it'd help to say the Fae might be equally disappointed with the tunnels she'd seen, so she asked, "Why kill Apothel, then? Even if he stole from you, he did it to fight those creatures."

"What would I know?" Letty said. "He didn't let me in on his plan, did he?"

"But it *was* your people that killed him, right?"

Letty gave her another harsh, uncooperative look. That was a question too far.

"Okay. You've got guns, you built this weapon, what's stopping you from taking the place back?"

"There a section in there on wormbirds?" Letty replied.

Pax sat back to leaf through the book. The monsters got more horrible and unlikely the more she read. She paused on the page about the griffix, which stripped the flesh off its victims while they were still alive. Taken by its disgusting visage, she wondered what she would do if faced with one in the flesh.

Perhaps kneel down quietly and cry.

She continued until she found pictures of winged creatures with tendrils hanging from their abdomens. She showed the fairy to confirm. Letty said, "They lay eggs under the skin of living prey."

Apparently a lot of these creatures fed on living flesh. The wormbird had maggoty offspring, the glogockles fed on flesh where the blood still pumped, the tuckles boiled your unblinking eyes. That was, it seemed, the uneasy truth Letty was highlighting.

"Those things sound bad enough to a knuckle-dragging human," Letty said. "Ten times worse for us. And they come at us ten times quicker. Like they can smell Fae. Guns ain't enough for that shit. The weapons we did develop never got used – we'd need . . ." She trailed off, not wanting to go there. Pax was about to prompt her when she angrily said, "You gonna feed me some time, you crater of filth?"

Pax stared in silence for a moment. She said, "I give you some food, you gonna talk to me? Properly? Without the insults?"

"Oh, poor baby. Didn't realise I'd upset you with my mean words. Here, let me sing it better. Fae are fantastic singers, you know?" Letty began a warbling shout that sounded a little like a tiny dog barking. Pax sat back, waiting for it to stop.

It did not.

When she leant back over the shoebox, her captive was marching in a circle, throwing her arms up and down as she squawked.

"All right," Pax said. "Enough."

Letty started hopping on the spot, though, picking up volume, lost in the moment like a wild child jumping on a bed. Pax gave the shoebox a small push. The movement tripped Letty onto her back. She rolled, grimacing and touching the point where her wing had been severed. Pax shifted with concern, raising a protective hand, but Letty cursed anew: "You goddamned fat stick, I'll cut off your ears!"

"Does it hurt?" Pax asked. "Where your wing . . . I mean . . ."

"What do you think?" Letty snapped. "It's like a dog ice-skating down my back."

Not sure how to picture that, Pax sat back again. She asked, "What do you eat?"

"Human babies."

"That's not –"

"What? You can eat us, we can't eat you? Fuck off. Get me a baby."

"I did it to get you out of there. *Thanks* would do."

"Centuries of coexistence" – Letty waved a hand – "no one gets this sick idea. Then you come along, now people will be wanting to eat Fae all over the shop. I feel so violated."

"Oh, bullshit," Pax said. "You'd have been burnt alive."

"It's a smoking gun, whatever it's called – that thing, where you see a gun in the theatre, someone's gonna get shot. That's what it is. You've said it, now it'll happen."

"Chekhov's gun?" Pax replied with surprise. "You read our literature? I used to study –"

"Look at the space between my fingers and calculate how much I care," the fairy instructed, holding up a middle finger again. The perfect Letty Action Figure pose.

Pax left the fairy to check her kitchen. She had protein bars, cereals, old pasta and some leftover Chinese. Nothing seemed appropriate for such a small person. She broke off a piece of protein bar and placed it in the shoebox. Letty stared at the lump of date and nut, bigger than her head, and said, "Did you literally just hand me a nugget of shit?"

"Take it or leave it," Pax said. Letty did not look up, investigating the food and raising her middle finger once more.

Pax finished the bowl of Chinese, which was close to being too old to consume, then left the abusive fairy sealed in the box while she freshened up in the shower. The sun had gone down by the time she was done, and Letty had gone quiet again. After a few more fruitless questions, Pax settled back onto her bed to continue reading Apothel's book.

She read about munfle, a toxic fungus that grew in the tunnels. Touching it could cause you to shit and vomit for two days straight. Somewhat paradoxically, it could also be boiled for a nutritious soup which could supply your whole day's energy in one bowl. How that worked, and how Apothel had come by that information, was not explained. Perhaps just rumours from the inexplicable Blue Angel.

Pax returned to the large chunk of Layer Fae text. There was a little more about Retcho, the previous Fae leader, who had been a titan of Fae industry as well as a benevolent dictator. His dethroning had led to the closure of many manufacturing plants, and many Fae technologists had been killed. Pax carried the book to the closet and looked at the canister from Rufaizu's apartment. She said, "That's why this is so important? The means of production were lost when Retcho was overthrown."

Letty did not answer. The fairy was lying in the folds of the t-shirt, eyes closed. Asleep and uncombative, she looked harmless, almost sweet. She may have been difficult and foul-mouthed, but however you looked at it there was nothing right in killing her.

Casaria would want to finish the job, though, given the chance.

Pax needed to squash his suspicions and placate him long enough to figure this thing out.

8

Casaria was waiting outside Pax's converted church long before 8pm. He had nowhere else to be, so he parked there and sat motionless. Her curtains were drawn, cutting off any hope of seeing what she was up to, so he occupied himself thinking over the things he could do to the Fae when he caught up to them. Burn their city, crush them, chop them in two. Nothing would be too harsh, not when they'd had the audacity to come after him, one of Her Majesty's finest agents. He was so engrossed in imagining his vengeance that he didn't notice Pax approach. She rapped on his window, snapping him out of the trance. She got in and said, "Looked like you were off chasing bears."

"Huh?"

"Nothing." She held up a hand. "Got something for you."

Casaria frowned, not seeing anything, but put out his hand anyway. She opened her fingers and a metal object a few millimetres wide dropped into his palm. A pistol.

"From my bowels with love," Pax said, and Casaria cringed, almost dropping it. He took a tissue from his jacket and placed the pistol in it, then stuffed it in the cup-holder.

"Can't be good for you," he muttered. "Did you check . . .?"

"I'm not talking about it."

"As far as anyone else is concerned, it never happened, okay? We incinerated that body."

Pax grunted agreement. She said, "You look like warmed up crap. Sure you want to go out?"

"I've got responsibilities," he told her, and started the car. As he pulled out, she started checking the vehicle over, and Casaria sneaked glances at her, hoping she'd be impressed. It was government issue, the Mercedes, but he treated it like his own, washed it and polished it once a week, carpets spotless, nothing she could – oh no. Her eyes fell on an empty can of Monster Energy in the passenger side door and his heart sank a little. He said, in all but a whisper, "Sorry about the mess."

Pax raised an eyebrow at him and he looked away, not sure if she was judging his tatty car, his choice in energy drink or the fact that he'd apologised. To stop her reading too much into it, he quickly took an envelope from his pocket. "This is for you. We didn't discuss any terms last night, so I want to be clear. Three evenings, we agreed to that much – leaving today and tomorrow. You can have half now."

Pax took the cash and flicked through the notes without a word. There was close to £1,200 in there and she barely blinked at it. She really was like him, wasn't she? The money didn't matter – not now. Casaria smiled. She wiped that smile off with a question: "How's Rufaizu?"

Casaria mumbled the answer. "Fine. Recovering. You're not going to ask to see him again, are you? You know that was a one-off. I shouldn't have brought you there."

Pax didn't respond, and looked away from him.

There was still work to do, he could see. He said, "He was lucky I was there, you know. He's unstable, he would've run right into the gunfire. If he'd been out on the streets alone, he'd be in a gutter right now. People like him, they have no idea how much we do for them."

She didn't say anything to that either, but he imagined she was starting to get the idea.

They'd been driving for half an hour with no conversation, which suited Pax fine. Casaria made a few false starts, like he wanted to say something and failed, and she preferred to let him stew in that awkwardness than give him a hand. It was the least she could do to soften her bitterness at having her own money doled back to her in instalments, to say nothing of how far she felt from being able to do anything for Rufaizu. Casaria had given her enough to fix that window and pay rent, though, so she consoled herself that getting through this night might at least keep a roof over her head. The rest was the difference between her getting into the World Poker Tour or not, which didn't seem so important now. Given the mess of the night before and the promise of increasingly threatening monsters, she might even be willing to let that final payment go if the opportunity presented itself. There'd be more tournaments in the future, and anyway skipping it would keep her name from getting too well known.

Casaria pulled up at a derelict building complex with a faded sign, only a few letters remaining of the original *FRITZ DRYERS*. There were massive ventilation ducts rising from one of the low buildings, and dented metal sheet doors closing off a wall, corroded and discoloured from years of neglect. Casaria cut the engine and pointed past a handful of abandoned cars.

"Over there," he said, "is an entrance to the Sunken City. When they built this place, they put in an underground storage room and knocked through to the tunnels. The site was fined for encroaching on government property, a PO-13 violation, and the storage room made off limits."

"Did you close the place down?" Pax asked, imagining Fritz, a plucky business owner with a simple dream of industrial-scale laundry services, thwarted by government fines and regulations. Where was he now, stacking shelves in Aldi?

"This business is still open," Casaria told her. "Contrary to what you imagine, Pax, we're here to help, not ruin, this city. There are dozens of entrances like this across Ordshaw, surrounded by fully functioning civilian operations. We monitor them 24/7, mostly through motion detectors and cameras, but it pays to have people on the ground too. Especially when there've been recent vibrations."

"Which you've had here," Pax concluded.

"Yes," Casaria said. "Something has been circling around this entrance. We might get a glimpse."

"What'd happen if it got out?"

"We'd deal with it."

"Right. And *it* is?" Pax pressed.

"Something medium-sized," Casaria said. "And fast. Could be a hound; it had a strong heat signature last time it came close."

"Like, a stray dog?"

"No, a helluvian hound. They set fire to things."

"Charming." It wasn't one she'd come across in the book. She had been hoping that some of them would turn out to be fictitious, that maybe it was just the sickle Apothel had got right. But no, the opposite was true: there were nightmarish things she hadn't even heard of yet.

Casaria leant over to open the glove compartment and Pax shrank back into the seat to avoid him. He took out a gun with a half-exposed cartridge, filled with long-needled darts. "This neutralises helluvian fire glands. Stops them destroying everything."

"Noted."

"But this will knock it out." He patted the pistol under his jacket. "Permanently."

"And you're allowed to shoot it?"

"Not with bullets. It would explode. No, this has a projectile that's more reliable."

Pax glared at the bulge of his pistol. "A projectile of what? Wizard cum?"

"You can joke," Casaria said simply. She waited for more, but it seemed that was his full response. He indicated the tissue containing the fairy's gun and said, "Before we begin, I want to thank you for this. I didn't like to pressure you, but you understand why it was necessary."

Pax shrugged, not wanting to say anything to suggest she condoned his behaviour.

"I knew you could handle it. The rewards will be great, you'll see. This work gives meaning to this meaningless world. Makes you feel like you have a purpose." He picked up speed, rushing it out like he'd been waiting to say this throughout their quiet journey. "It helps you understand the ignorance of the people around us. Those that walk blindly through life during the day. How could they be anything more than they are, without even knowing there are things they don't know? People like you and me, we know there's more, we know the importance of living that experience. I've had recruits who didn't get it, who wanted to study this like it was some academic project – but I can see you're different. We herd the beasts, and we protect the populace, because they don't understand."

Pax barely took in his soliloquy. From the first words she got the overall gist: *we're better than other people, and fighting these monsters proves it.* However he'd ended up in this position, as a glorified night watchman, he seemed to have gone to great lengths to convince himself it was by choice.

"It's us, the ones who dare to get close, who form the front line of defence for the *praelucente*," he finished, piquing her attention again.

Pax deliberately misinterpreted: "Sorry, did you say something about a placenta?"

Casaria gave her a sideways look. Serious. "The *praelucente*. The force down there. The power base I told you about. Maybe a natural phenomenon, might be a little bit of God, no one knows. Whatever it is, it helps us. The aberrations it creates are necessary for a greater good."

"A *fuck the estates to bolster the banks* kind of thing?"

Casaria gave Pax a sympathetic grin. She gave him an insincere smile in return. He said, "The *praelucente* doesn't discriminate. It moves, constantly, affecting a few blocks at a time."

"You know how nuts this sounds?"

"After what you saw yesterday, you're not willing to open your mind?" Casaria paused. "No, that's a good thing. You think for yourself, I respect that. The *praelucente* is real, though. Look at any great achievement in the city, say an inspired sporting event, or a day that a composer produced a masterpiece. The data *around* that event will show reports of tiredness, weariness, declines in work. But the focal point, the epicentre, that's where the real difference is made. Great things are achieved through this power, even if people suffer on the peripheries."

"If I'm honest," Pax said, "that sounds like an unreliable source of energy."

"We need it." Staring ahead into the unmoving night, Casaria wrung his hands over the steering wheel. "This city is rotten. All the world is. The *praelucente* gives us hope. Gives us something worth fighting for. You'll see."

He rose from the car, swung the door shut and started pacing away. He was not waiting, not even looking back, with his usual tactic of leaving her to make her own choice. It was basic reverse psychology, acting like he didn't care, and she had no desire to play his game. But he still seemed determinedly on Team Pax. He'd given her some space, and returned some of her money; he might be trusted to give back the rest and leave her alone. As if. His interest at least kept the Ministry part of this equation from destroying her life, though, and might take her closer to understanding how to get out from under all this.

Pax caught up to Casaria as he rounded the rusted husk of an old van. Behind it was a knee high structure with doors on the top, like the outside entrance to a cellar. A chain ran through the door handles, locked with ancient padlocks. Casaria took a set of keys from a pocket and started trying one after another. The pause gave

Pax a chance to inspect the shadows. She thought back to the sickle. There were tuckles and wormbirds and God knew what else down there, weren't there? Actual, real monsters. Pax said, "How long are we going down for?"

"As long as it takes," Casaria said. "Believe me, this thing will be worth seeing."

Pax bit her lip. "Is it sensible, going down there? Aren't you supposed to be an observer?"

"I never said that."

"Is it really necessary?" Pax continued, warily, "Maybe you could just tell me more about this stuff, I don't actually have to *see* it, now, do I?" Casaria paused with a look of worry. She'd hit a chord, so before he could dwell on it Pax hurriedly continued, "I mean, what if – what if there's still Fae in me? You said the things down there could sense them? Isn't this risky?"

His worry turned to confusion as he tried to recall if he'd actually said that. He shook his head. "I've got the detector on, Pax. You're clean. And we're going in."

9

After a day spent fighting down the memories of the Sunken City, blocking out thoughts of the dangers Rufaizu and Pax might be facing, Barton became gripped with anxiety when he realised his daughter had not come home for dinner. No flying visit to stock up on food, no hour in front of the bathroom mirror. She was a growing girl, increasingly independent, and he'd allowed her to spend a whole day out with a party in the night in the past, once or twice, but they always at least caught sight of her, or received a message. She always replied to messages.

She was off the radar, and, though he was staving off panicking, he sensed that the minotaur and its myriad creatures were responsible. Staring into empty space, he imagined her being dragged into a government vehicle for ruthless interrogation. Worse, being tricked into entering one of the Sunken City's gateways. He had no rational explanation for it, but somehow, something had happened. Rufaizu had come stumbling back into his life. That roguish girl was creating waves, too. His family weren't safe.

During dinner, he sensed Holly watching him coldly, neither of them talking beyond monosyllabic courtesies. She hadn't been satisfied when he told her he had tied things off with Pax, and her face said she was waiting for him to slip up again. Trying to detect his longing to return to his night-time activities. He was careful not to show her where his mind was going, and waited until she was taking a shower to put his fears about Grace to rest. She had lost her phone, or run out of battery, and was eating dinner at a friend's, that had to be it. He called Kylie Taylor. She answered chirpily, "Hi, Mr Barton!"

After a few pleasantries, striving to sound casual, he said, "I was wondering if Grace is with you? She didn't answer her phone."

"Oh? We thought she'd gone home?" Kylie replied with a hint of worry. "I haven't seen her since the park, she left without telling us. She hasn't messaged me – do you think she's upset with me?"

Barton swallowed his tension. What was wrong with her, she'd just let Grace disappear? "When was that?"

"Just after lunch."

"Where?"

"Ten Gardens. Heenway Park, I think. The one with the little fountain, you know?"

"Did you see where she went?"

"No, sorry Mr Barton – we were hanging out on the grass. We – I'm sorry Mr Barton – I wasn't totally –"

"Sober?" Barton asked, carefully. Of course. They were kids, it was so easy to accept random shit when you were drinking for the first time.

"She's not in trouble, is she?" Kylie asked it meaning in trouble with her parents. Oblivious to the idea that some other trouble might exist. "Does it mean she's not coming to the party? I don't want to go with Jenni With An I on my own."

"I'll get her to call you," Barton told her, then hung up. He ran a hand over his head and tried another number. Pax's phone went straight to voicemail.

Barton grabbed his coat and headed to the car, not letting himself think until he was sat with the engine purring. Looking at the road ahead, deciding between turning left or right, he realised he had no plan. It could be the Ministry, it could be Rufaizu's people, it could be something completely unrelated. Maybe Grace lost her phone and was with another friend. Maybe she met a boy and they were making out behind a carwash. Was that any better?

Maybe Pax was a plant. She'd used what he'd told her to get in favour with some other group. Some group that wanted Grace. Or him.

It didn't make any sense.

He punched the steering wheel.

There was one option. He hated it, but he couldn't waste time if his fears were true. He had to get in touch with the Blue Angel. He braced himself and, about to pull out, checked his mirrors. A shape was quickly approaching. His wife. There was still time, she was a few metres away, he could pull out and pretend he hadn't seen her. He hesitated, picturing how mad it would make her, then she was upon him, no way to make it look accidental now.

"Wherever you're going" – Holly dropped into the passenger seat – "I'm coming too."

Her eyes burnt with bottled fury. Barton was speechless.

"So what is it?" Holly snapped. "A pub? A gang meeting? A park rendezvous? Where are we going?"

"I can't tell you," Barton muttered.

Her expression faltered. The sternness and anger weren't enough to hide her strongest emotion: fear. Barton saw it in her trembling eyes, desperately trying to stay strong, to believe he was in control.

"I love you, Diz," she said weakly. "I always will. And I've tried so hard. But there's a line. I'm telling you, this is it."

"Please," Barton said to her. "Trust me. I just need to get some answers."

"Answers to what?"

He couldn't say he feared Grace was missing. That Rufaizu or the girl were somehow responsible. He didn't even know if it was true. "Give me one night, I'll make all this go away. Forever."

"No." Holly shook her head. "You don't get to leave me behind again. You don't get to have secrets. We share this life, that's what you promised me. I don't care what you think's dangerous, there's nothing that can be worse than you not sharing it with me. Nothing."

Barton saw desperation in her eyes, her voice quivering on the brink of sobs. He took a breath. "If I show it to you . . . you'll see why I didn't want you to know. But you have to see it for yourself."

10

The tunnels Pax entered from the empty storage room were eerily similar to the ones from the night before, half a city away. Equally bare and unused, of an almost identical size, with the same occasional faded light boxes, none of which were lit. Equally unlikely as a paradise for fairies.

They travelled along straight paths, intersecting and turning at right angles, occasionally sloping up or down. It was impossible to tell where they were going, or if they had at some point turned in a circle. Pax walked behind Casaria as he lit the way with his blue lantern, checking his monitors for signs of the things that dwelt down there. There were sickles a few blocks away, he said, but it was a distant signal and they weren't of interest. He was tracking something else.

As they descended a set of stairs, onto another unending stretch of tunnel, Pax grew weary of the monotony of their footfalls and the seriousness of the hunt, and she broke the silence. "Are there special laws for your prisoners? Can you legitimately hold Rufaizu for something? Suspicion of possessing a weapon is pretty weak grounds for arrest, isn't it?"

Casaria looked over his shoulder at her, his expression disapproving. "If it was Fae technology, it could do a lot of damage. Unlikely as that is. But yes, we have special jurisdictions. You have no idea of the trouble idle talk could do."

"Who'd take him seriously? My brother used to play fantasy games, you know, and he –"

"This *isn't* a game," Casaria replied shortly, continuing down the tunnel. "Rufaizu stirred those Fae assassins out of their nest, for one."

"You're sure that's what they were? Assassins?"

"What else would they be," he scoffed. Not a question. "You've no idea the complications people have introduced, trying to argue the rights of different animals down here."

"How do you –"

"It used to be simple," Casaria cut in with annoyance. "Fighting these monsters, creating a firm line between the city above and below, preserving the things that mattered. Then people started asking questions, creating absurd diplomatic initiatives for clerks who prefer to sit behind desks than do anything active. Suddenly there's specific words we ought to use, specific protocols to follow when engaging with our enemies, countless regulations they've invented to create meaningless jobs for people enforcing them. There's a lot of ugly ambition in the Ministry, I'm sorry to tell you that. But you stick with me, I'll show you how we can get around it."

They continued in a terser silence, his shoulders stiff ahead. Pax kept quiet, trying to put together the exact issues this loon was dealing with. He cleared his throat and rolled his shoulders to loosen up. Trying to think of something to say, wanting to redirect the conversation. Without looking back, he said, "I used to play the trumpet. When I was a kid."

Pax frowned. Why not. "Yeah? You don't strike me as the type."

"Gave it up when I lost a tooth."

"Was that somehow related?"

"Yeah," he said, but didn't explain. Instead, he said, "I often wonder if I should've got a gold tooth, instead of the white one."

"Would've looked badass. But, like an ex-con. Not really respectable."

"Not like a badass who hunts monsters for the government?"

"No," Pax said. "You'd want a tattoo for that. A coat of arms. Like the SAS."

She could see from his cheeks that Casaria was smiling. Hopefully this nonsense would help when she asked him not to kill her for wanting nothing more to do with the Ministry.

He looked at his monitor and stopped dead. Pax almost bumped into him as he swore.

She spun around, looking back, left, right, above her. "What? Where is it?"

He drew his pistol. "Got behind us. Keep calm, I'll handle it."

They turned and Casaria moved in front of Pax. As he did, the lantern lit up something on the floor that scuttled up the wall, back into the shadow. The alien thing moved with the many legs of a spider or crab. Its claws clicked against the concrete, little green eyes twinkling briefly in the light. Pax froze as Casaria held the lantern higher and revealed it again. It was about a foot wide, five wiry legs joined in a central, round body, which hung under the joints. The body was spiky like a sea anemone, and had a square, toothed mouth in its centre.

The creature paused, seeming to look straight at them, then scuttled into the shadows again, and started moving rapidly away, its otherworldly patter making Pax shudder. Casaria thrust the lantern into Pax's hands and flicked a switch on his pistol, lighting a torch. He ran, gun raised. Pax ran after him.

They caught up to the creature as it turned a corner, two of its queer legs folding as they lifted. Casaria skidded into the open, aimed and fired. A few metres back, Pax flinched as a ball of lightning erupted from the gun like an electric meteor. She turned the corner and saw what was left of the creature charred into the wall, bits of leg sticking out of a smoking black smear.

"That," Casaria said, holstering his gun, "was an Item 13. Scientifically called a *crus adsecula*. Crusad for short."

"It was a giant fucking spider!" Pax exclaimed.

Casaria let out a short laugh. "Oh no. Much worse."

He prodded one of the legs with his shoe. Nothing more than a burnt stick now. He turned back to Pax with a smile, but his eyes widened and his hand fell back to the holster. She followed his gaze to above her shoulder, where a second creature had appeared. Its beady eyes focused on her as it bared its teeth like a dog.

She shrieked and fell sideways as it pounced. She felt the weight of its horrible little body on her shoulder as the talons pinched into her. She shook her shoulder violently and held her arms up and out, trying not to touch it. As she spun, Casaria swore and ran closer. He batted the thing off her. It thumped into a wall, then another thump as it hit the floor. Finally another blinding electric blast and it was gone.

Pax was panting as Casaria helped her to her feet. She looked at the half-incinerated mess of the thing with horror. The shot had torn through it on one side, this time, leaving behind a half-mutilated, twitching monstrosity.

"Holy *fuck*," Pax said. "It was trying to bite my throat out!"

"No," Casaria replied, calm. "Crusads don't eat flesh. It probably just saw you as an easily reachable object to get to the other side of the tunnel."

"Fuck off – it was trying to kill me!"

"If it wanted to kill you it would've used its stinger. You're not hurt, are you?"

Pax quickly looked herself over. She was too pumped with adrenaline to sense any pain, but didn't see any marks. She shook her head. Casaria nodded in approval, then took out his sensors to check for other targets in the vicinity. He said, "Crusads are open season, they need culling. They keep the turnbold population down, but there's a shortage of turnbolds right now."

"That's all right then," Pax muttered, stunned at how this man could talk about hunting an alien spider as casually as if it were chicken farming. Something jarred him out of that calmness, though.

"We need to leave," Casaria said, putting his gun and monitors away. He grabbed the lantern from Pax. She frowned, but he was already striding away. "Right now."

She rushed to match his brisk walk, and asked, "What now? Boar with a chainsaw?"

"Save your energy," he shot back. As he picked up his pace to a jog, Pax's worries grew, aware that serious cardio was beyond her. She tried to keep up without exerting too much energy. Watching his monitor, he cursed once more. His jog turned to a run.

Pax chased after him. He ran and skidded around a corner, and she struggled to keep up, to keep sight of his guiding light. They came to some steps, and as Casaria cleared two or three at a time Pax hit one of the first ones and tripped, falling onto her hand. She cried out and he stopped to look back. As she shoved herself to her feet, he yelled, "Hurry!"

She gave a quick look back to see what it was they were running from, and in that moment was too awestruck to move. Creeping around the corner of the tunnel they'd come down was a branch of effervescent light. It flaked into view like a climbing but crumbling vine, its extremities breaking free with the flutter of autumn leaves. All around the strangely spreading shape was a glow of electric blue.

Casaria's hand clamped on to Pax's upper arm and hauled her up the stairs. He shouted, "Move your damned feet!"

She did as she was told. He dragged her as he ran, and as they reached the top of the stairs she looked back. The glow was floating up after them. Casaria kept going, taking her with him. He was running as though his life depended on it, spurring her into doing the same, charging for the next set of steps, back up into the empty storage room.

They powered through the last stretch together, bursting out into the room, and Casaria slammed the door shut behind them. He rammed the bolt in and brought the barrier down, firmly securing the door. He leant against it, almost as out of breath as Pax.

Breathing so heavily she felt like she was going to swallow her tongue, lungs burning and legs aching, Pax turned to retch. The exertion, the panic and the fear brought up part of her dinner. As she spluttered, she demanded answers, flapping a hand in the direction they'd come. "What the hell was that?"

"The *praelucente*. Part of it, anyway. It shouldn't have been there. The scanners –"

"You said it was a good thing!"

"I *said*," Casaria replied, "it serves a *greater* good. That doesn't mean it's safe."

She glared at him as he walked by.

"We're done here."

It was only when she asked that Casaria really thought about how he'd been testing Pax. She wanted to know what came next, and he told her she should rest and think about what had already come. He had established well enough that he could talk to her and that she could behave herself, and she hadn't baulked at the strangeness of it all, or shown any particular need to expose and undermine the Ministry. Or to climb its convoluted ladder. She had also shown enough independent spirit for him to feel he could respect her. He respected so few people. She would be a valuable companion, with a little conditioning. She just needed more exercise and at least a general awareness of how to handle herself in a physical confrontation. If he filed the D7-RRb he was putting off, to make her involvement official, the first step would be a full medical exam.

Running this assessment through his mind, he decided on the next step. Before dropping her off, he said he would see what he could do about getting her some firearms training. She stared at him as though she had just been told he would organise a sex change for her. Nevertheless, she mumbled thanks.

She lingered by the car as he waited for her to leave, clearly keen to ask questions quicker than they mounted in her mind. There was just one point he hoped she wouldn't touch on, and of course, she did: "What's next for Rufaizu?"

She wasn't ready to drop it yet. Watching her reaction carefully, he told her, "It's not up to me now." He held up his bandaged hand. "After the attack last night, the pencil-pushers will take over. In all likelihood, those idiots will turn him loose rather than risk creating ripples."

Another question was clearly forthcoming, but instead Pax held her mouth as though something had risen in her stomach. She retched again, with a nasty cough, but nothing came out except the rancid smell of bad Chinese. Casaria marvelled at how much she'd suffered from such a short run. Perhaps the fairy was repeating on her. "Try and get some rest," he told her.

Waving an irritated hand at him, she spat noisily, then pointed to his bandages. "What about those Fae that came at you? Are they still out there?"

Casaria shrugged. "I might have got one or two of them in the fight, we're not sure. But I'll deal with the others, don't worry."

She nodded.

As Pax left for her apartment, Casaria pulled away and checked his phone for any reports of incidents across the city. Nothing of note. There was no way the administration would actually let him join the Fae hunt, anyway. They resented his enthusiasm for practical activities. Handing over the severed head of a glogockle for examination had once cost him a week of writing reports in a windowless room. Meanwhile Sam Ward got a promotion for conducting a demographic survey. *That* was considered research?

Bastards.

He slowed down at an intersection and saw a man resting against a wall, behind a piece of cardboard declaring his sob story. Young, not yet 30, still strong, though with the vacant look of one who'd lost his intelligence to drugs. If he'd ever had it to begin with.

Casaria pulled over behind a warehouse, sheltered from cameras. He wove back through alleys on foot until he got to the main street, then approached the homeless man with a smile. "You want to make some money?"

The young man looked up at him, eyes half-closed. He didn't appear to have heard.

Casaria took out a note. "I've got £20 with your name on it. Meet me around the corner. But take that path, don't follow me. It's not a sex thing. And it'll be fair."

The bum couldn't take his eyes off the money. He nodded slowly, not entirely following or caring, then Casaria walked away. The homeless man stood with great effort, then ambled in the opposite direction. The CCTV footage would show this pedestrian in a suit taking pity on the vagrant, leaving him enough money to set him prowling through the alleys for a fix. The homeless man disappeared into an area with no other cameras, where he would be found bloody and bruised late the next day.

When asked who did it, he would refuse to give details.

He'd mumble through his broken teeth that it had been a fair fight. Couldn't fault that.

11

Pax couldn't focus as she tried to find the section in Apothel's book on the *crus adsecula*. It was unlikely to be the name Apothel had used, given the pattern of the others, but it should have been recognisable from the pictures. Her eyes blurred, the detail of the pages hard to make out, and her head started swimming. She felt nauseous, cursing herself for being so out of shape, and twice since she'd left Casaria she felt like she was going to vomit again. It never came, though.

She drank a glass of water, took a few aspirins and sat on the bed waiting for the feeling to pass. She felt the room expanding and contracting like the breathing of some great beast. How long had the fairy been shouting for? The words only vaguely sifted into her ears, and for a moment she didn't understand where they were coming from. She stared across the room to the closed cupboard.

Oh yes.

The fairy.

She closed her eyes, but that made things worse, like she was about to roll off the bed despite sitting still. The shouting continued and she grunted, pushing off the bed and lurching towards the closet. She tried to speak: "Like having a damned pet I never asked for." The words came out like the cries of a dying goat, her tongue barely moving. She opened the cupboard and lifted the lid off the shoebox. Her focus lasted long enough to see the tiny lady looking up.

"You look like shit."

She fell, with just enough time to realise something was seriously wrong.

Letty had pretended to sleep when Pax left, conserving her energy. She had done a good enough job of hiding the tiring effects the Ministry gas had had on her, she felt, but needed to recover in anticipation of a rescue operation. If one came. When the lummox had made a snide comment about no one having come to save her, Letty held her tongue, but there was truth in what the girl said. The boys had not come, and she didn't know why. They had Pax's address, they should have at least followed up on threatening her. But nothing. Letty was alone, out on her arse. Betrayed by those useless pricks.

She was fuming on that when the girl returned. Deciding to vent some anger, Letty started shouting, until the shoebox was finally opened and the girl collapsed with a great crash. Letty took advantage at once.

Using her full weight, Letty shoved the giant t-shirt into the corner of the box, balling it up enough to clamber to freedom. With the lumbering giant felled like a tree, it was a free ride out. Letty jumped onto the cupboard shelf and landed next to Pax's twitching hand. The girl's forearm flopped into the cupboard, her body slumped against it. Her head lolled against the cupboard door, barely conscious, half-open mouth drooling. The arm was a perfect ramp down, which Letty pounced onto, running over the long sleeve of Pax's hooded top. She stopped as she reached the shoulder, though, seeing erratic rips in the terrain, a hole close to the neck. The skin beneath the cloth looked completely wrong.

Letty continued down Pax's back, throwing a few glances back to the wound. She reached the floor and jumped off. As she started across the carpet, its weaves up to her ankles, the fairy slowed down, considering the girl's chances.

Not good, she thought, approaching the looming door. There was a draught excluder at its base, but enough space was left to squeeze through. Letty stopped as the girl let out a groan. She looked like a semi-comatose drunk. Standard human affair on a Saturday night. But there was nothing alcohol-related in Pax's condition. The wound, festering with a bubbling, slightly green tinge, was unmistakably the work of caustic venom. The sort caused by pentanids. It would start with dizziness and nausea, immobilising her and leaving her numb, then the bite would spread through her system, decaying her organs, corroding her bones. The anaesthetic would wear off by the time that happened, when it was too late to do anything about it. She'd suffer a lot.

Which was good, Letty told herself, staring at the massive doomed girl. Teach her a lesson for sympathising with the Ministry and for kidnapping her and tossing her about like a toy.

Pax's whole body shuddered, her upturned hand flapping into the air, and she rolled over onto her back, giving a kick as she lay flat on the floor.

She stank, too, Letty decided. The scent of stagnant sweat all over her.

Pax's foot twitched, near Letty, and the groaning changed to a quiet whimper. Almost no energy left to resist it now.

Letty lifted the draught excluder to form a gap so she could squeeze through. She paused.

There was a problem. Leaving this place, unable to fly and without her gun, she would have difficulty getting back across town. She had no dust on her, so her chances of going unnoticed were slim.

The twitching girl was clearly not well in with the Ministry if they'd allowed her to get in this state. Which made it possible that all her dumb questions were actually geared towards choosing the right side, and she really had saved Letty. Disgusting as the giant's methods were, Letty should never have woken up after taking a dose of that gas.

But it was still a dumb human getting what she deserved.

Letty gritted her teeth.

She swore and marched back across the room. As she got close to Pax, a foot jerked suddenly and the fairy ducked and rolled, barely avoiding the heel crashing into the carpet behind her. "Fuck this," she grunted, and pulled herself forcibly up Pax's trouser leg, to avoid the risk of being squashed. She picked up her pace, running up Pax's body to her neck. Taking a breather, Letty leant against Pax's upturned jaw and surveyed the damage. The toxic green had spread up over the front of the neck, veins coming to the surface in angry colours. Small sounds gargled from Pax's throat. Letty crouched, put a hand to Pax's skin and felt it pulsing with unnatural warmth. She cleared her throat, hoping it wasn't too late, and spat gutturally into her hands.

12

The Whistler Bridge site was not always the most active or helpful spot to visit, but it was one of the closest to Barton's home, so it was his usual port of call when he wanted some quick, simple answers. It was on the remnants of a disused railway, an overgrown ditch that was used by runners during the day and youths smoking pot during the night. A road crossed over the original bridge, and a tight path snaked down its side, through nettles and brambles, to the nineteenth-century brickwork tunnel. Low and concealed, with its surface made fragile by time, this was an ideal spot to write messages.

Barton used his phone light to lead the way, then handed it to Holly so he could concentrate on the writing. Despite insisting that he didn't need to explain as long as she could come and see, she had voiced a dozen barbed questions about where on earth they were going and what on earth they were doing. The first few times, Barton had repeated that she needed to wait and see. Then he stopped replying. He had other concerns. It had been so many years, maybe this site wouldn't work any more. Maybe the Blue Angel was long gone.

He took a lock knife from his pocket, unclipped it and chipped at the brick.

"Oh, you're not serious!" Holly said. "Diz, I swear if you scratch our names into that wall I'm going to slap you."

Barton did not respond, scratching in the two words he needed. His lettering was efficient, a series of quick, sharp lines in block capitals. Holly frowned, reading it as he went.

Where . . .

Impatient, she stirred a foot, checking the old railway. She shone the torch into the tunnel, revealing weeds, empty beer cans and an abandoned tyre.

"On me," Barton instructed. She turned the light back to him as he finished.

. . . Fae?

"Is this some kind of Boy Scout nonsense?" Holly scoffed, and again Barton ignored her. He stood back and waited. "You're right. I wouldn't have believed you if you told me."

It wasn't going to work. It had been too long.

"Honestly, scratching on –"

When the blue screen appeared, Holly clamped her mouth shut.

The wall around the writing changed colour, blending into a foot-wide square, centred on the writing, glowing blue. The deeply etched lines in the brickwork folded in as Barton let out a breath of relief. The mortar reformed, the surface smoothing out. Then new etches appeared, the surface sinking as it created words.

Barton. Why?

Holly took a step back and almost dropped the phone. She pointed with her free hand, finger shaking. "What is that? What did you do? How did you do that?"

As she spoke, the words faded from the brick again, its original surface restored. Holly looked over her shoulder, flashing the torch high and low.

"There's a projection or something? A hologram?"

"It doesn't matter," Barton replied quietly, more interested in continuing the conversation. He used his knife to scratch into the brick again, in the centre of the blue patch.

"What are you doing? Why are you doing that? What is this, Diz? Would you stop that!" She raised her voice sternly. "Stop it at once and tell me what's going on!"

Barton told her, "I am finding out where I need to go. This is what we did. Someone out there wanted to help us, this is how we communicate – they told us where to go."

"Go for what?" Holly cried.

"That comes later," Barton said. He continued scratching. Holly took a few steps around him, looking closer at what he was writing.

Stop them.

"Who's writing that?" Holly asked as Barton's letters faded into the blue. He waited for a response as she continued, "Diz? Who's answering these questions? Where are they writing from?"

"I don't know!" Barton snapped impatiently. He felt ready to hit something, but forced himself to keep calm. "I've never known, but whoever's behind it, that" – Barton pointed at the blue screen – "is the best option we've got."

Holly shook her head. "Don't mess with me. What's going on?"

"Right now," Barton said carefully, "I'm trying to find out where we need to go."

She almost shouted at him, confusion turning to anger. "Why are you asking a bloody brick?"

Barton cringed. The Blue Angel's answer appeared on the brickwork.

Anders Ave.

He took a moment to stare at the address, a little stunned by the importance of what had just been shared with him. Holly must have sensed his surprise, as she asked quietly, "What does it mean? What's wrong?"

"That's where they are. That's where they're hiding," Barton said.

"Who? Jesus, Diz, when are you going to tell me what this is?"

"The Fae. That's where we're going next."

13

Pax opened her eyes slowly, feeling the pain in her shoulder before she saw anything. She winced and blinked to clear her blurred vision. Her throat was dry, and a searing ache ran from her neck down to her left side. She rolled her head to the side and saw the shape of a tiny woman, sitting on a book on the floor, just about eye level. Letty had her arms folded. Her expression said she'd been waiting a while.

"What –" Pax tried to speak, but her voice came out in a rasp. She cleared her throat and went rigid as the pain surged through her anew. She reached for a glass by the bed and took a few gulps of stagnant water, then slumped back onto the carpet. She looked at Letty again, the fairy still motionless. "What happened?"

"You're in a bad way," Letty told her. "Caustic venom in your shoulder. Some nasty fucker in some nasty place gave you a toxic bite."

"I wasn't bitten," Pax whispered.

"You may actually be thicker than you look," Letty told her.

Pax closed her eyes, picturing the encounter in the tunnel. With the prickling of that disgusting creature's many legs, it was possible that one of the touches had been a bite or a sting. In the panic of running away she hadn't noticed a wound. She opened her eyes and said, "You're still here?"

"What can I say, I'm a sucker for a bitch in need," Letty said, less than sympathetic. She pointed at Pax's neck. "That will bore through you, dissolve your insides. I can help, but I'll need assurances."

Pax hesitated. She could move just well enough to call someone. Casaria would know what it was, but he'd see the book, maybe the device. Barton might be able to help. He knew a doctor, didn't he?

"Whoever you think's gonna come, they're not gonna be here quick enough to save your sorry arse," Letty said. "You don't have long."

"What . . ." Pax took in a pained breath. "What can you do?"

"Heal it. It's well within my skillset."

"How?" Pax frowned at the thought of the tiny fairy operating on her wound.

"After I've got your word."

"On what?"

"This thing…" Letty threw a hand around her head, gesturing to the room, the world, the situation, whatever. "This is over. You'll take me out of here. Back to my boys. And you'll keep me safe. And fed. And you'll get me a drink. And I want half your money."

Pax rolled onto her back and looked up at the ceiling. She wheezed, "Your boys . . . they'll shoot me."

"Not if I say not to. I'll be counting on your word, I guess you'll have to count on mine, huh?"

Pax closed her eyes again. Can't get beholden to the psychotic miniature person that everyone says is dangerous. Avoided so many unhealthy attachments, this one has to be the worst. But the pain was real, enough to stop her moving. It burnt, all around her shoulder, as though she were silently on fire.

"Tick tock," Letty said. "It's a good fucking deal."

"You can really heal me?"

"You want to find out? Or just die?"

Pax could feel it moving inside her, spreading down her arm, creeping over her. As though acid was seeping through her veins. Her heart was beating faster, body panicking.

"Do it," she said quietly.

"What's that?"

"Do it!"

"I got your word?"

Pax rolled her head towards Letty, eyes urgent. "I promise. Save me, I'll let you go. I'll take you back. Anything."

"Great." Letty grinned, then held out a tiny hand. "Shake on it?"

Pax stared, unbelieving for a moment, and the fairy started laughing.

"I'm kidding. You're good. Now the first thing to do is go back to sleep. Trust me on that one."

"How are you . . ." Pax started to ask, as the fairy reclined onto the book.

Letty called out in a singsong voice, "Go back to sleep, you big lummox. When you wake up you'll feel a hell of a lot better."

Pax winced as a breath caught her off guard. She held the agony down, clamping her teeth shut, and closed her eyes again.

Think happy thoughts.

Think of staying alive.

Think of all this going away.

14

In the hollow carcass of a once proud building, the walls towering five storeys high, with no floors left to divide them, Barton and Holly scanned their surroundings with phone torches. It was as devoid of life as any place Holly had been, the only structure left standing amongst the rubble of Anders Avenue, in the heart of the warehouse district. The word "avenue" had been used rather liberally, as Holly told Darren.

Still unclear on what they were doing or on whose orders they had come to this impossibly desolate place, Holly secretly let herself enjoy seeing this side of the city. She knew of the warehouse district, populated by these odd relics to bygone industries, from what she had read about the decline of the region, but she had never had any call to actually visit. She imagined, as they crept in through a truck-sized hole in the wall, that very few people did. Even the derelicts of the city didn't camp here, so far from valuables to steal and honest citizens to irritate.

Barton had stayed quiet throughout the journey, ever since seeing the address. It was his *I've got money on this game* face; the one that said all outside influences would be met with wrath until his current obsession was out of the way. She had asked, "Has something happened to that woman?"

"What?" Barton shot back quickly, on edge. He hurriedly shook his head. "No, why would it have? Of course not, she's fine."

He was too insistent, making Holly suspicious, but she took it at face value, at least, that the strange girl wasn't in immediate danger. There wasn't much else worth worrying about, so she decided to let him worry, for a change.

When they'd arrived, he told her to stay in the car. Not on your life, she had told him, and he had, once more, conceded. It made it impossible for her to stay behind, though, when he took the tyre iron from the boot. If there was no immediate danger, he might create some. She considered scolding him for even thinking about violence, especially with her around, but it didn't seem like the right time.

And so they walked through the middle of the vast building, exploring empty corners, looking for God-knows-what, with it more than clear that there had been no people around for the longest time. They traipsed about the bizarre location for a quarter of an hour. Barton studied bricks, stuck his nose in tight cracks, checked behind creeping ivy, all as though he had dropped something very small.

He even shouted a few times, his voice echoing back at them, "Anyone here? We need to talk!"

He finally came to the centre of the enormous space and squatted, thinking things through. Holly tutted. She wasn't sure exactly what had gone wrong, but she was fairly sure he could be held to blame, so she employed a chiding tone to say, "Are you quite done?"

"This has to be the place," he murmured.

"Maybe they were here before," Holly said. She could imagine it would be a good place for burning oil cans, rough sleeping-bag beds, and propped-up Harleys, but she'd seen no sign of a biker gang's footprint.

Barton stood, face fixed in concern.

"It's getting late, Diz," Holly reminded him.

A drum sounded from beyond the walls. A flat, heavy thump. Then another. Holly's superior calm faded.

"What's that?"

The beat picked up tempo, thump thump, thump thump, like a tribal signal. It was getting closer. Coming towards a gap in the wall. Behind the drum was something else – a heavy tapping sound, someone playing coconuts. Holly watched the empty space, dreading the chain-swinging ruffians who might step out.

What stepped into view, though, was a seven-foot-tall, immaculately white horse, thick-limbed and gracefully groomed with a flowing silken mane. It walked into the frame of the gap in the wall, a stick held firmly in its mouth, and as it moved it swung its head in a full, majestic arc, from left to right. The stick slammed into two huge barrel drums, one hanging on each of the creature's flanks.

"Now it makes sense," Holly gasped, taking in the incredible sight. "I'm dreaming. Is that right? I'm dreaming."

The horse stopped in the clearing, letting its head hang for a moment's rest. Then, from above its back, with no apparent source, a muted trumpet let out a few gentle toots. The horse resumed drumming and continued walking. As Holly stared with her mouth wide open, the horse clopped out of view. The sound of its drums diminished as it got further away.

Holly darted forward to get another glimpse of the incredible beast. She leapt over remnants of wall, out into the open, turning towards the horse's departure.

It was gone. She swung her torch around, finding nothing but an empty dirt patch with dry weeds clinging to occasional chunks of discarded machinery. As the thrill of the moment subsided, replaced with disappointment, Barton approached her. He slumped past her, heading the way the horse had come.

"Did you see it?" Holly said. "Tell me you saw that too! I didn't imagine it!"

"It was a drummer horse," Barton said, irritably. He followed the line of the building, scanning the bricks with reduced urgency and purpose.

"A drummer horse?" Holly cried. "As though it's as common as a house fly? That sound – it played that music – and the trumpet. Where did the trumpet sound come from?"

"Invisible proclaimer," Barton said. He stopped next to a small tree that had partly embedded itself into the wall. He brushed the branches aside, reaching through the thicket.

"What are you doing?" Holly ran up to him, giving a few more looks in the direction of the horse's disappearance. "Where did it go? How did it get here?"

"They come when they're needed," he said distantly, "with one simple purpose."

"What? What purpose?"

"To show us where these are stored." He pulled back from the tree, taking something from a hidden recess. Holly lit him with the torch, revealing a metal cylinder in his hand. "This is what got me started. This is what I've been avoiding, since before the Fae caught up to Apothel. Someone's taking the piss, leading me here."

"What is it?" Holly took it from him and he let her. She unscrewed the lid. A liquid rolled around inside, glowing luminescent green. Holly said, "Is it radioactive?"

"Taking the piss!" Barton shouted, almost making her drop the canister. He surged forwards, throwing a punch that clipped the wall. The brick shattered from the force. Holly stared in startled silence as her husband's big shoulders heaved up and down. He looked mad, ready to tear the whole building down.

"Diz . . ." Holly said carefully. "What is this?"

"I don't know," he grunted back.

"Why are we here?"

He slowed his breathing, pushing the anger deep down inside of him so he could look up and meet her eye. He admitted, bitterly, "I haven't heard from Grace. I'm worried something's happened."

The sound of a slap rang down the road, Holly's hand suddenly stinging.

She hadn't realised it was happening until it was done. She stared at his reddening face, holding her open palm out to the side as though considering hitting him again. Barton didn't move. He held her gaze with tired eyes.

"Diz," Holly said through gritted teeth. "If you've done something . . ."

"I haven't done a damned thing," he said, though he accepted the blow as though he deserved it. "I just don't know where she is and it's no coincidence. And this bastard" – he raised his voice, taking the canister from Holly and shaking it to the air – "this bastard is messing with me!"

He was so furious himself that Holly's own anger seemed pointless. She could hear her breathing increasing in speed, not for the first time realising that her husband might be more animal than man. She kept quiet, kept staring. She hadn't heard from Grace either, had she? She'd assumed – she'd just assumed. She squeezed her eyes shut.

"What now, then?" she asked.

Barton didn't have an answer. He just started broadly striding back to the car.

Barton's mind was ticking over the possibilities for the journey home. Holly's eyes were fixed on him, so he avoided looking at her. He needed a solution. Maybe the Blue Angel had hidden Grace to trick him into coming back. Maybe Rufaizu was involved too, maybe Pax. It had worked, after all. Got him riled up blindly following their directions. Exposed once again to the glo, drawn to it like an insect to light. Grace would be safe, though, if it was all a trick. Or she might be with a friend after all. Or she might be genuinely missing, abducted by some other psycho, and the Blue Angel had simply taken advantage of it.

That possibility was the worst.

When they pulled into their drive, he could feel Holly's intake of breath and knew what was coming next. She was going to ask what he was going to do. He hadn't come up with a good answer yet.

But she didn't. She said, "What's that?"

A white envelope sat by the front door.

He knew, the moment it caught his eye, exactly what it was. He rushed out of the car before Holly, hurrying to grab the envelope. He'd torn it open before he had stood up straight.

A simple note, on a small piece of paper, written in large, untrained letters.

We have your daughter. Safe. We'll be in touch.

15

Pax groggily opened her eyes and stared at the horrendous criss-cross of plastering in the ceiling. She blinked a few times, focusing on the pain in her shoulder and arm. It seemed to have subsided to a slight ache, where there had previously been burning agony. She sat up, seeing she was on the floor. She rolled her shoulder. Nothing.

She took off her hooded sweatshirt, heavy with sweat, and threw it aside. She pulled back her t-shirt and looked at her shoulder. A wide bruise surrounded an indentation like a dog's bite mark, which had already scabbed over. Whatever it was, the danger had passed and left a rancid urine-like smell.

Pax scanned the permanent mess of her room. Everything still. The shoebox was open and askew. The fairy had gone. Rather than tempt contact, Pax lumbered to the toilet. She relieved herself at length, with a greatly satisfied sigh, and rinsed her wound with soap and water, before returning to the doorway. There were plenty of places for a two-inch person to hide. She said, "You still here?"

There was a quiet shuffle, a waking curse. She followed the sound to the base of the bed. One of her spotless Nike shoes. Letty pulled herself up over the ankle of the shoe and looked around like a mouse poking from a burrow. She yawned loudly. "You pulled through, huh?"

Pax crouched in front of the shoe and said, "What happened?"

"Saved your dumb life, didn't I?"

Pax picked up the shoe before Letty could complain. She lifted it to her face, the movement knocking the fairy back inside. Letty shot back up the wall of the shoe's ankle and angrily said, "This shit stops, we agreed. You think for a minute to welsh on our deal –"

"Please," Pax said quietly. "It's easier to hear you." She shifted onto the floor and leant against the bed before lifting the shoe and Letty up to eye level. "You slept here?"

"Seemed safe, looks like it's never been used," Letty said. Pax shrugged; it was a fair observation. "Now, you're up. Time to take me to my boys."

"Do you ever let up?" Pax murmured back. "What time is it?"

Pax searched the floor for her phone and picked it up with her free hand. 3.03am. Two missed calls from Darren Barton. She closed her eyes for a moment. It was too late to call him back, wasn't it?

"Hey! Focus!" Letty shouted. "Time *is* an issue here. You heard that prick yesterday, didn't you? Considering my idiot boys never came for me, they're no doubt doing something monumentally stupid right now. And you, you lunatic, you have that thing." Letty pointed back towards the cupboard. Pax followed the small gesture to the odd contraption of Rufaizu's. Apothel's? The Fae's – whoever. "Which means whatever stupid thing my boys are doing is not going to go well."

"Why not?" Pax asked quietly.

"Because my people want the goddamned Dispenser back!"

Pax stared at her silently.

"Thick-shit, it's time to get moving!"

"Give me a *minute*. Are you at least gonna explain what happened to me?"

Letty smiled, proud of what was about to come. "You got bit. I saved you."

"The *crus adsecula*."

"Oh get out. Don't speak Ministry around me, okay? It was a pentanid. They've got a toxic bite with one cure. Similar cure to a lot of the shit in the Sunken City, as it happens. Fae fluid."

Pax blinked and responded slowly, "What fluid?"

"I pissed in the wound, okay?"

Pax kept staring. Not sure if there was a correct way to respond.

Letty prompted her: "Thank you is enough."

"It was spreading through my body, you said – how could you –"

"Oh I'd already done it by then," Letty said. "You gotta get it quick."

"You what? Then that deal –"

"Fucking stands," Letty said quickly. "Don't you dare."

Pax paused, then said, "If I let you go, are we even? I can walk away from the Fae, at least?"

Letty's face hardened. She shook her head. "I can bury a

grudge, but you've definitely seen too much. That's your problem, though. Mine is that you get off your arse and take me where I gotta go."

Pax glanced at her phone again, then to the kitchen. "We're not going anywhere, not yet. I'm beat. A drink was part of the deal, wasn't it? We can talk, seeing as you're no longer plotting to kill me."

Letty watched her warily. "You trying to change my mind?"

By way of answer, Pax placed the shoe on the bed and got up. She walked to the kitchen as Letty climbed out of the shoe and watched. Pax grabbed a bottle of beer from the fridge and popped the cap. She turned and held it up for Letty to see. "This do?"

Letty hesitated, clearly not wanting to condone the distraction. She had a thirsty look about her, though, drawn to alcohol. She said, "Got any spirits?"

Pax opened up a cupboard and took out her selection of bottles, one after another, until Letty chose one with a thumbs up. Pax poured a small measure of rum into the cap and returned to the bed. Letty took it in both hands, the cap spanning her shoulders' width. Pax knelt in front of her and raised the beer bottle. "Cheers."

Letty took a big swig of rum, made an appreciative gulp and let out a fearsome belch. Pax cracked a smile. She said, "How are you so loud when you're so small?"

"Fuck you, I'm tall for a Fae," Letty said, failing to answer the question. "This is good. Good rum's rare. Maybe you're not a total idiot."

"I won it," Pax said. "Collateral from a rich guy who ran out of cash."

"Okay." Letty lowered the bottle cap. "I've endured this shit for a full day, so I guess I gotta ask. What's your deal?"

"Huh?"

"This." Letty pointed to the room. "Who the fuck are you? Clearly you don't work or have a life, just dirty boys' clothes and a collection of gambling books. What are you, the thinking man's degenerate?"

Pax reconsidered her surroundings from the fairy's perspective. The clothing, partially strewn about the room and, in many cases, unclean. Then there were the books on poker and psychology, dog-eared from rereading. Plain, bare walls. A stack of empty beer bottles by the sink. There was, at least, one point she could make: "They're all women's clothers, actually."

"You work nights, right?" the fairy said. "Too poor for drugs and no way you're a hooker."

Pax pointed at the books. "Figure it out."

"Card games? Can't be much good, needing to read all these books about it."

"I do all right." Pax caught the defensive note in her own voice and frowned. She looked at the books: the psychology tomes of Herman Lakers and Dutch McRory's *Cash Game Analysis* were genius literature that she treasured. Piotr Venk's *Lockpicking Masterclass* was harder to justify, but everyone needed hobbies. She said, "I'm good enough to have a chance in the WPT next week. I wouldn't expect a psychotic elf to know what that means, though."

"Elf?" Letty laughed without mirth. "Good one. Miss WPT, I could teach you things you can't learn in books. You've only ever played against humans. I'd destroy you."

Pax raised an eyebrow, curious. She said, "How? Physically, I mean. You can't –"

"Oh, we can," Letty said. "Online, for starters."

"You have the internet? On what? Miniature computers? Phones? With apps?"

"Yeah," Letty answered harshly. "We wipe our arses with toilet paper, too."

Pax let out a little snort of a laugh, almost choking on her beer. As she wiped her mouth she commented, "There's an image." She paused, then said, "I don't play online."

"So we use a Fae deck. I can deal and tell you what your cards say," Letty said.

"Thanks but I'll pass."

"You're no fun. Where's your three Fs?"

"What?"

"The things any Fae needs. Fighting, fucking and funnies. You've got none of them."

"Funnies?"

"Shitting with people. Having a laugh."

"I have a laugh," Pax insisted. "My work isn't exactly ordinary."

"Oh yawn. Do you have," Letty asked slowly, giving the

question the full weight that it deserved, "any friends?"

Pax drank for a moment, rather than replying. Why was she having to justify herself? "Do you?"

Letty went quiet. She seemed to consider the question seriously. "I played a game with Apothel, you know, where I convinced him to use our cards. He was an idiot. And he raised an idiot kid."

Pax shifted a knee up under her chin. "You were friends once, weren't you?"

Letty hesitated, then said, "Who gives a shit." She took a big swig of the rum. "Good riddance to him. The lot of them."

"Hey." Pax tapped the duvet next to her, drawing her full attention. "What happened between him and your people? Why the theft and why the murder when you all wanted the same thing?"

Letty shook her head. "I told you – he cut me out of that part, didn't he?"

"But you never wanted to know –"

"Forget it. We've talked enough." Letty flung the bottle cap back and chugged down the rest of the rum. The cap finished, Letty threw it aside and stood up. "Time to go."

Pax stared at her. It was a big question mark, and something the fairy either didn't know or didn't want to face.

"We have a deal," Letty snapped.

"You have my word," Pax said, "I'll do what you ask. But the moment I let you go, I'm in the shit, aren't I? And if that's how it's gonna be, I want to be informed and I want to be rested. So I'll give you a choice. Keep talking, let me know everything, or clam up and we get some sleep. Either way, we're not leaving, not yet."

Letty stood silent for a moment. She took a breath and let it out with a loud groan, looking skyward. "Ugh. This had better not be an elaborate Ministry set-up. I swear, I'll cut out your tongue."

The threat made Pax smile. The fairy's tone had changed, no longer fully serious or angry. Letty was ready to work with her.

16

Grace Barton stirred with a splitting headache, groggy and confused. The ground around her was hard and damp, cold. She pushed herself up, blinking and trying to make sense of the murky grey. She looked up, into a wall of eroded brick. Concrete floor. Dust. She murmured to herself, "What the hell . . ."

She rose wearily, back onto her haunches. The only illumination was a sliver of artificial light creeping in through a high window. The ceiling was twenty feet up, rising into corrugated iron, but the room itself was maybe fifteen feet square. There was a single metal door. It was completely quiet, completely still.

"Hello?" Grace called out, afraid of who, or what, might answer.

Nothing.

She put a hand to her head and moaned, trying to figure out what had happened. The last thing she remembered was drinking in the park. No. There had been voices. The press of metal against her skin. Going somewhere by car. A clumsy bit of blind walking. Sitting on a cold floor. Peeing awkwardly into a bucket. She spun around. It was there in the corner shadows. The metal bucket, her only luxury in this room.

They had taken her. *Kidnapped* her. But it was hazy, like she had been only half awake. Which bits were a bad dream?

"Oh, Christ." She put a hand to her head. "How much did I *drink*?"

She took out her phone and saw a number of missed calls and a handful of upset messages from her dad. She tried to call him back, but the phone buzzed off. No signal. She struggled to her feet and swayed on the spot, then noticed the chill for the first time.

It had been ambitious to head out on an autumn day in shorts. Now it was the dead of night and this creep's warehouse had no heating. She wrapped her arms around herself and rubbed them to try and keep warm.

Whimpering, fears starting to fill her mind, she uttered, "Daddy . . . please . . ."

"Oughta have some fun with her, while we can," Mix commented to Fresko on a rafter, as they watched the girl stir. He took out a cigar and lit it with a generous inhale.

"Don't want anything more to do with them than we have to," Fresko replied. "Big ugly beasts, makes me sick that we need them."

Mix allowed himself a small laugh at his friend's negativity. He pointed the cigar down. "At a distance she's not so bad. Imagine she was our size, you'd do her."

Fresko gave him a look. "She's a kid."

"Lighten up," Mix sighed. "This is gonna come together. You make sure her shit of a father does as he's told and I'll tell Val all what we've done. Get some extra hands together to collect the weed and the Dispenser."

"You wanna talk to Val alone?" Fresko couldn't keep the aggravation from his voice. It had been bad enough taking orders from Letty, but at least she thought things through. Mix was a walking heap of hormones, only interested in how best to cause damage. Fresko needed to plan all the details. The simple concepts of bringing the girl round to walk herself inside, of leaving her a bucket to piss in, the idea of leaving a note for her thick-skulled father. Left to his own devices, Mix probably would've knocked the girl out before getting her in the car, even. There was no telling how he'd screw things up during a chat with the leader of the FTC.

"Got a better idea?" Mix sneered. "Think one of us needs to stay and watch her? She's not going anywhere. Or you want me to manage the dad?"

"No," Fresko said. There was no way around it: whatever task Mix was left with, it'd be a risk. "Once we're done with the dad, and done with her, we go to Val together."

Mix went quiet as he eyed Fresko, taking the comment as a criticism. Rightly so.

"Please!" The girl's voice rose from the room. Maybe she'd heard them. She turned on the spot, searching the shadows. The low light bounced back off the tears on her cheeks. "Someone! Anyone! You can't leave me here!"

"All right. Go on ahead," Mix said. "I'll shut her up."

Fresko shot him a look and said, "We might need her."

"Relax. I've dealt with her sort before."

"She doesn't *need* dealing with."

"She will. One way or another. You know that, right? Her, the dad, whoever else. We're not leaving a trail."

Fresko looked down at the girl. She was crying. "My family don't have any money, if that's what this is. And . . . and . . ."

"Leave her be," Fresko said, trying to keep the situation manageable, "until we're done. We don't need complications right now. We need leverage."

Mix let a moment pass.

"We good?" Fresko asked carefully.

Mix nodded, his smile anything but warm. "Sure. But when this is done we need to talk, don't we? A crew of two don't work, does it?"

"No," Fresko said. "All the more reason we need to pull this off."

The girl thumped a balled-up fist into her thigh. "You can't keep me here!"

Mix shouted, his voice booming through the room, "We'll do what we want with you, bitch – get used to it."

Grace went silent, staring up at the rafters, unable to see them. As Fresko watched her eyes quiver with fear, he had to hand it to Mix. The guy had a voice that could contend with the humans.

PART 3:
SUNDAY

1

"Apothel didn't need to die," Letty explained. "There's countless dumb lummoxes that've got in our way before and lived. Draws too much attention to kill them all. It's on me, that. Totally on me."

Pax crossed her legs on the bed, trying to get comfortable as she sat over the small woman, a fresh beer in hand and more rum in Letty's cap. Letty was looking away from her, staring into the memory. She continued, "There was a power struggle going on in the FTC around then, which lasted years. The big leadership contenders were Valoria Magnus and her brother-in-law, your mate Retcho."

"Ah ha."

"Retcho and his followers were developing weapons. They wanted to wage war on the myriad creatures and anyone associated with them. Val had a more academic approach. Believed in improving the Fae supply of dust and laying low, building up the whole community's strength to reclaim the Sunken City later. She also spread word that Retcho wanted to use his weapons on his own people, that his work needed to be stopped. Things swung her way in the end, but it came out, after her big coup, that Retcho *had* been close to completing something that might destroy the berserker."

"That being your name for Rufaizu's minotaur? The *praelucente*."

"Yes." Letty drew this out at length, demonstrating annoyance.

"Our name for whatever stupid shit other people call it. It's the beating heart of the Sunken City's disease. Everything else follows it around down there – and that thing, more than anything else, senses Fae presence in the tunnels. Everyone wanted to know about the Dispenser, then. What if it really could secure the Sunken City? A lot of Fae were dead and the functioning of this thing wasn't clear, so Val set the boffins in FTC Uni to studying –"

"There's a university?"

"Crispy geckos, is everything in our fully functioning and technologically advanced society surprising?"

"Crispy geckos?"

"Shut up. Where was I? These boffins were studying this machine, and starting up new studies into the berserker. They realised Apothel's crew of prats could be matched to the movements of the berserker. We'd known about them before, bums bumbling about Sunken City entrances – but now it seemed this merry band of idiots had graduated from drinking funny juice to actively tracking the berserker. And half the time they got near it, the thing moved."

Pax nodded. "Barton said they got instructions through blue screens – they were trying to stop it, but whoever was talking to them was only able to move it around. Somehow."

"Yeah. I learnt that, too, eventually," Letty said. "Most people were pretty heavily against Apothel from the outset. It's a known fact that any human working underground with the Ministry of Environmental Energy's permission is bad for us. And every human underground has to have the Ministry's permission, official or not. The Ministry guard that place like a shrine, and they hate all we stand for. When Val took charge, the FTC had been moved like three times in four years on account of them hunting us. Part of her mandate was keeping that from happening again. Whatever she was up to, developing new tech, sending out scouts, whatever – it worked – the MEE didn't come close to us again. But whatever Apothel was up to, the feeling was that the Ministry benefited, so his people needed to be stopped. My team were sent to do it, and we started with Barton, him being the muscle of the group. Organised a little accident with his kid to scare him out of the game."

"You what?" Pax's jaw dropped open.

"It was nothing, just enough to shit him up. He backed off, and without him the others started to lose their bottle, too. Apothel, though, you weren't scaring that guy off, he was too crazy to worry about his own safety. I came up with the idea of drawing him away; tell him fairies exist and we've got a pot of gold waiting in some far-off country. He seemed the sort to buy it – he was a goofy fucker, acted like everything was a big game – a burly animal with a thick beard like birds could nest in. You saw him in the street, you'd peg him for a circus strongman who'd let himself go. The pair of them, him and his son, first got on our radar when they did over a mansion we were casing, on Friedrich Boulevard, so I knew he had a bit of Fae sentiment in him."

"Wait," Pax said. "A mansion you were casing? A human one? Why?"

Letty stared at Pax as though the answer was obvious. "Anyway. I couldn't help myself, I got curious about this guy. We talked. Drank, too. He tells me how he got started in the Sunken City, after stumbling across this juice that made him see things. He'd found it after burgling some corrupt local governor. Apothel being the sort who'd huff glue, he downed the lot."

"That was glo?"

"Sure, whatever. High as a crow, he started seeing the myriad creatures. He ventured into the Sunken City, found himself a continuing supply. He'd started producing this manual –" Letty nodded to the book "– full of wacky names he'd come up with for creatures we barely knew about. I'd never spoken to anyone who'd been down there, see, and he was eager to share. Then he tells me all about this Blue Angel of his and I realise that all this time Apothel's been thinking he's fighting the monsters. That, if anything, he's on our side. So I come clean with him – I tell him whatever he's doing, it's not working, but if he lays off for a while we can put the Dispenser to use.

"It takes a bit of persuading. He was the opposite of patient, but I got him to calm down while I ran it by Val. Her and her council, they were angry that I'd got familiar with him, but mostly said it was pointless talking to him if we still didn't know how to use the Dispenser. It was too soon, even if we wanted to take that kind of step. Except then it was too late. You know the rest. I didn't kill Apothel, but I *got* him killed, right? All I needed to do was persuade him to leave town. Instead I got him to stay. Gave him the stupid idea to cross the Fae."

"It's not that simple, though, is it?" Pax said. She moved forwards onto her knees, to get closer, and Letty scrambled back quickly, raising her fists. Pax froze. "Sorry. I didn't mean to –"

"Yeah, didn't mean to," Letty hissed. "Story of humans' fucking lives, isn't it?"

"But listen for a second. Apothel followed instructions from an unknown stranger for years, thinking fighting that minotaur was what was best for the city – why didn't he stick to your plan?"

"Because he was an idiot."

"He must've somehow got the idea that he needed to take things into his own hands with the Dispenser. And it sounds like he was partway right – your people weren't ready to work with him."

"He didn't know that."

"He knew something, though, didn't he?"

"Apothel was nuts! You don't get into a vocation of hunting monsters while high on hallucinogenics without being a few bullets short of a full clip. He got his own ideas, he got dead."

"The details are important," Pax insisted. "He died and Rufaizu escaped – and in the time since, nothing's been done to cure the city of what's down there. You're not seeing what I'm seeing?"

Letty stared, refusing to play along.

"Is there any chance that your people didn't intend to use that weapon? And Apothel somehow knew that when he stole it?"

The fairy laughed, nastily, and paced aside. She threw a hand in the air, raising her voice. "Oh, that's rich! Real fucking rich! You have no idea!" She pointed a stern finger. "You, who the hell are you anyway? Fancy yourself smart, sticking your friendless nose in damn books, *talking* your way round things? You're thick as the rest of them – you have *no* idea."

"I can see the way things add up – and the only –"

"I hunted for that device for nine years!" Letty snapped. "I was cast out – and my boys with me, with the whole FTC spitting on everything I'd done! If you could've seen the hate I've seen – the attitude from the Fae – *didn't intend to use it*? Even if Val said I could come back, I wouldn't, not with what my *whole society* think of me – not until I make it right. It's on me, you don't get that? It's all on me."

"Well, it's sprayed me too, now," Pax said, keeping cool. "And for what it's worth, I think you did the right thing. Even if it didn't work out. What I'm trying to say is –"

"You're trying to say shit," Letty said. "Apothel's dead and that weapon's laid dormant when it might've been used a decade ago. The Fae's home might have been reclaimed if I'd stayed the hell out of it all."

"I'm saying," Pax said, more firmly, "it's *not* your fault."

"Well, you're wrong. How'd you think Rufaizu feels now, after he came back to me? And now we've had a chat, you think you'll even survive the day? You're gonna learn, don't you worry – it doesn't pay to be my mate."

Pax didn't respond for a moment. She said, "You can have your Dispenser, and I can help you get that fuel – we can get people outside the Ministry onto Rufaizu's case. But it all starts with deciding who we can trust, doesn't it?"

"There's no *we*, all right? This" – Letty held up the cap of rum – "gets you a little closer to not being dead, but it doesn't make us friends. All *we* are going to do is find my boys, hopefully before they do something catastrophic."

Pax placed her empty bottle down. She said, carefully, "Thanks, anyway. I'm glad you talked to me, even if you've got a habit of getting people killed."

Letty went quiet, staring like she was trying to figure Pax out. The usual look. Pax smiled at her, then pushed herself up off the bed with such force that the mattress bounced and Letty was knocked off her feet. As the fairy threw insults, Pax went towards the washroom, holding up her middle finger.

2

Come to Galley Road station now or she hurts.

That was all the confirmation Barton needed that the Fae were behind Grace's disappearance. He knew enough about them to know they couldn't explore that nest themselves. It wasn't where they had taken Grace – there was something there they wanted, which they needed him to get.

Galley Road connected the heart of Ordshaw with the docks, but the Underground station of the same name sat in cold neglect halfway along it, a long way from anything useful. The station was notable for having four platforms serving a single train line, the spares allegedly built to serve a line that was never completed. The empty platforms were sealed behind temporary metal walls that had sat chained and bolted for over thirty years. People had heard and seen things moving in the shadows behind the barriers, and Galley Road station frequently made lists of Ordshaw's most haunted places.

Darren Barton and Apothel had known better. Galley Road station was actually near a nest of glogockles. They lurked close to the abandoned platforms, drawn to the lights, and sniffed around the edges of the barriers looking for a way in. They retreated at the sound of people, though. The superstitious station workers avoided the area, but Barton and Apothel had seen a dozen of the sickly creatures lurking there.

Barton drove there alone, with the sun rising. Whoever had left the second note had to be nearby, but he knew better than to waste time looking for them.

He hated doing as he was told. He hated that he had a cylinder of glo in his hands again, tempting him towards the bitter unreality of its influence. He hated that the Blue Angel had led him to it, instead of helping him. The only positive he'd had was that in her nervous exhaustion Holly had fallen asleep shortly before the second note had been delivered. She would wake up and find him gone, and she would know why, but she would not be able to

follow. By the time he got home, he'd either have saved Grace or
had something truly terrible happen, and whatever that meant to
Holly now was a very minor concern.

The hate helped. Barton knew that when he reached Galley
Road, whatever else was going on, he'd have a few glogockles to
use his hate on.

Barton stopped at the corner as he walked the final distance to the
station. It hadn't changed in fifty years, an arch of concrete with
basic, faded lettering chipped into the header. The metal shutters
obscured half the entrance, where they got stuck on opening.
Barton walked in, down the steps into the green glow of the
station's belly. A few men in shirts were hovering around, waiting
for what must have been the first train of the day. They were
yawning and stretching, barely keeping their eyes open. On a
Sunday morning, they must have been going to church or coming
home from a bad night. It had to be a bad night if it had ended
anywhere near here.

Barton passed them, went into the dividing corridor and made
his way to the dead end of two of the metal walls, ready to punch
something. The makeshift door in the barrier, a smaller bit of
metal that had been hung on hinges, had its chains hanging loose.
There was a padlock on the floor. Someone had come here before
him. He pushed the door aside, creating an opening big enough to
get through. Beyond the metal, there were no lights, only a dark
cavern. There was a piece of paper hanging on the door. He took it
off and found the same abrasive writing that had been on the
previous notes.

Bring us the electric weed and you get her back.

Barton frowned. He looked into the darkness. They'd come
down here, and the place wasn't crawling with monsters, so the
station itself must've been safe from the minotaur. The little
bastards must still be hanging around to watch him.

"Face me like a man," he growled. "I'm not doing shit until I
know she's safe."

There was no answer. He looked around: no movement in the
tunnel behind him and nothing in the darkness ahead.

"Forget it." He turned away. He was halfway back to the other
platform when a whistle caught his attention. He turned back but
there was still no one there.

"Up here, numbnuts," a sharp voice said, and he looked to the ceiling. Near the metal barrier, a tiny figure sat on the edge of a luminescent light. The rifle in his hands targeted Barton. The man, in the white shirt and suspenders of an '80s financier, had one eye fixed to his scope, hands not moving as he said, "Need me to explain what happens now?"

"Where is she?" Barton snarled.

"Safely waiting for daddy to do as he's told."

"If you've touched her –"

"Get to work. Or you join Apothel, and your sweet little daughter takes your place."

Barton fought the urge to charge at the fairy. He'd never clear the distance, and probably couldn't reach the light anyway, but he wanted to hurt him, bad. The sniper told him, "I know, I know. Now be a good boy."

All he could do to show his discontent was to walk by very slowly, glaring at the little man all the while. The thing was wearing a tie, even. What kind of fairy was it? Barton stopped at the entrance to the platform, then went in. It was colder on the other side, as though the darkness had sucked the heat away.

"What am I looking for?" he called back through the door.

"Electric weed. You'll know when you see it," the tiny man said.

Barton resisted the urge to make more idle threats. He'd learnt long ago to save his energy for when it was needed. He walked over the empty platform until his feet touched the rippled edge. He took out his phone and lit it up. The unevenness of the floor was apparent in the pit ahead, but there were no tracks. This part of the station wasn't even half-finished.

He climbed down and checked in either direction, then started walking. The tunnel to his sides and above was too vast for his torchlight to reach its edges. The sounds of his footfalls rolled back towards him. A sound ahead told him he was close. A stone knocked loose or a claw scratching the ground, indicating one of the myriad creatures lurking in the shadows. He slowed down, searching for all the precious little detail he could make out.

Another scuffle, like a fox picking through junk, and his eyes fixed on its location. He shone the torch at it and the creature shied away – slightly. It crouched into the shadow, then rose out of it, pincer-jaws snapping in his direction. Though it was a foot shorter than him, it was still a big one, its rocky flesh lighting up

as the veins that ran through it glowed peculiar green. Its gangly
arms flopped to the sides then drew in, tensing, the claws clicking
together. An extra appendage sprang forward over its left shoulder
like a scorpion's tail.

Barton stared it down, unafraid.

"Come on you bastard," he said, putting his phone away.

It thumped a flat stump of a foot towards him. Then the other
one. Each step sent vibrations through the room to help it sense
where he was. Its edges lit up enough to create a pool of light
around it, giving Barton all the visibility he needed. He raised his
fists defensively, preparing for its charge.

The glogockle clicked like an oversized beetle, gnashed its
mandibles, then ran at him. It was an ungainly creature, listing
from side to side as it moved, but its power was unmistakable, a
wall bearing down upon him. Barton let it approach, not moving
until the last second. It swung both clawed arms towards him in a
windmill arc. He ducked, the grab going over his head, and he
jabbed the thing's gut. Its flesh cracked and erupted around his
punch, green light spilling out of it as the glogockle howled. Not
finished, it slashed its claws at him. Barton lunged aside and threw
a flurry of punches into its side, finishing with a punch to where
its kidneys would be, if it had any. The glogockle could not turn
quickly enough, the strength of the punches and the force of its
own momentum making it trip over itself and roll into the wall. It
crashed to a stop, twitching, a pool of luminescent blood spilling
out around its legs.

Barton stood over it, shaking his hands off at his sides,
breathing deeply.

Not quite fit enough for this.

A series of clucks chattered behind him. He turned and saw the
rest of them, thumping into the tunnel, claws pinching and jaws
clicking. The flank of glogockles shunted into each other as they
formed a mob of brightly lit monsters. To the left, where the first
one had been sniffing around, he saw what the fairies were after.
A patch of moss with a neon blue light sparking around its tips.

Barton stared at the monsters, unflinching. He reached into his
pocket for the cylinder of glo. He opened the cap. The smell, the
flavour and the burning brought back memories of another life, a
decade past.

At least he could tell Holly he didn't have a choice, this time.

3

Rufaizu woke with a tube down his throat. Teeth clamped onto a chunk of plastic, mouth forced open and impossible to move. He gagged, panicking, but gagging did nothing. He tried to sit up, but his arms were bound, giving only an inch of movement. He shook the shackles, arms and feet, then threw his head from side to side to see where he was. The tube ended in a large machine with some kind of artificial lung, its accordion plastic slowly rising up then falling down, each breath met with a muted beep.

On the other side of him, a man sat staring.

Another suited cog in the Ministry machine.

This one had been more volatile than the others Rufaizu had encountered. His eyes were fiery, and vanity seeped from his pressed suit and well-groomed hair. He had the aura of a hunter who did it for sport.

Rufaizu grunted, tried to demand he take the tube out, release him, anything. The man took the maximum amount of time possible to fold away the newspaper he was reading. He watched Rufaizu buck, and said, "Don't waste your energy."

The man scraped his chair closer, leaning in.

"You won't be able to breathe for yourself for a while. What with where the bullet hit you. You're lucky to be alive."

Rufaizu glowered back at him.

"What everyone's asking," the man said, "is why you'd come back here, and reconnect with the Fae, considering their history with your family? I mean, surely you saw this coming?"

Rufaizu tried to snarl, baring his teeth. The man sat back, offering a pitying look.

"You really are animals, aren't you." It wasn't a question. "You couldn't pose a threat to anyone. But here we are, the biggest news in a decade. A feral boy scrapping with the fairies." The man glanced to the door, checking they were still alone. He lowered his voice. "You can nod, or shake your head, so you can answer me. Do you even know why the Fae tried to kill you?"

Rufaizu fixed his eyes on the man, making every effort not to move.

"They *did* try to kill you, you realise that? They sure weren't shooting at me. I was in the open, wasn't I? An easy target, really. No, they were 100% on you, didn't particularly want to hurt someone from the Ministry. You need protection. Without my help, they could still finish the job."

Rufaizu narrowed his eyes in what he hoped was a piercing look, to say: *you're wrong.*

The man's mouth twisted with satisfaction. "You're genuinely not afraid of them? They must've convinced you they were your friends. Maybe you had something they wanted? You know your dad thought they were his friends, too."

Rufaizu twisted away from the man, trying to hide his face.

"The thing is, the FTC say that the Fae you were involved with were known deviants. Bad eggs. Yeah, we've had word from them. These creatures you were dealing with are the sort of Fae" – the man held up his left hand, bandaged around the middle – "who would risk crossing the Ministry. I can only hope you're smarter than the facts suggest – that you'd know better than to talk to the sort of maniacs that killed your dad. You were running a con with them, weren't you? Looking for revenge?"

Rufaizu looked back at the man, then, and shook his head.

"Oh please. Kid somehow returns from hiding after his father's murdered, what else is he gonna have on his mind? Hell, *I* would go after whoever killed my dad, and I didn't even like my dad." The man placed a friendly hand on Rufaizu's shoulder. "I want justice, the same as you. Help me help you."

Rufaizu looked at the man's cracked knuckles, oddly blemished compared to the rest of his smooth skin.

"You know where I can find them," the man said. "Just give me an address."

Rufaizu kept staring. Even if a word this guy said was true, he was still a suit in the system. If the Fae couldn't be trusted, he was no better. Silence hung between them for a moment, then the man closed his grip on Rufaizu's shoulder and the boy tensed, pain shooting through his body. There was a wound there he hadn't noticed before; it lit up with fury. The man held on tight as Rufaizu squirmed, screams muffled by the tube in his mouth.

"They did this to you," the man told him. "This and the one in your neck."

Rufaizu dug his teeth into the tube, as his eyes streamed. The bonds that held him dug into his wrists and ankles as he struggled.

The man released his grip suddenly. "Are you gonna help me help you? You want me to stop those animals, once and for all?"

Rufaizu nodded quickly, urgently, his body forcing the answer out even as his mind tried to resist. The man sat back. Rufaizu slumped, shuddering, fighting back sobs.

"See, we can cooperate. You're gonna write down their address, aren't you?"

Rufaizu eyed him again, regretting his moment's weakness. But he remembered, now, they were shooting at him. Those *were* Fae gunshots. They could've shot the suit and they didn't. And the implication was clear enough. If he defended them, after what they did, he was going to suffer, one way or another.

The man spoke softly: "These creatures want you dead, Rufaizu. They're a menace. You're going to give me an address, and you'll be doing the whole world a favour."

Rufaizu closed his eyes, preparing himself for it. It wouldn't matter anyway, would it? There was no way Letty and the others would've stayed in their hideout after firing on a Ministry agent.

Casaria straightened his jacket and tie as he left the prisoner's room. Just being close to that homeless urchin made him feel dirty. He paused as the door swung shut behind him, finding Landon and Gumg waiting for him in the corridor.

"You got something from the asset?" Landon asked.

"The asset?" Casaria scoffed at the attempted sincerity. "He's got a tube in his mouth, what could I get from him?"

"Wherever he sent you, we're going with you."

"He didn't send me anywhere. Go in and ask him yourselves – I'm going out on patrol."

"I've been doing this job a long time, Cano. I know you want the Fae. The Ministry know it. You can pretend to patrol for a few hours, and we can watch while you do it, or you can cut straight to the chase."

"That's a go-ahead, is it? I can do my job as long as you come along to stop me from doing it?"

"We'll make sure," Landon said plainly, "that whatever is done is done right."

"You don't have a choice," Gumg said, confirming the initial dislike that Casaria had felt for him. Casaria shook his head dismissively at the pale man. Gumg wasn't deterred. "We've got our orders."

"All right," Casaria said. "Come along. Give the Fae someone else to shoot at. Maybe I'll get lucky and see them castrate you."

"We're not looking for a fight," Landon warned.

"Don't be naïve. Whether these Fae were under FTC orders or not, the fight's already begun."

4

Pax took in Riley's Bettor Off with a mixture of awe and disgust. It cut a fine example of everything that was wrong with West Farling: a betting shop for the middle classes, taking all the grittiness and danger out of gambling to make it safe, bright and friendly. The shopfront of beech wood and clear glass looked in on low armchairs and coffee tables. Its flat-screen televisions were framed like antique pictures, and the tout's counters had been fashioned in the style of an early-20th-century bank. This sort of innocuous spectacle of vice made West Farling an area Pax despised, even as she used it regularly for games. The rich businessmen around here enjoyed hosting her crowd as a challenge, when their games weren't being done via the safety of the internet or as part of an off-limits millionaire's club.

She watched a young man in a two-tone shirt ask a patient teller for the odds on some race or another. Letty was up above in the eaves, a perch that Pax had barely been able to reach. Pax was not sure if the fairy was coming back, and was even less sure she should want her to. They might return in a whole pack, after all. With guns. She was confident she'd made progress with the tiny lunatic, though, and that there was a solution they could work out together. In the meantime, she was content to watch the affluent losers placing bets on a Sunday morning, and told herself this calm was awaiting her when she was done with the Sunken City. Letty would be free, the threats cancelled, and she could tell Casaria to stuff it. Rufaizu's release would be a more long-term, administrative interest, which could wait until after she'd turned the money she had recovered into something workable.

Her phone started ringing. She took it out quickly, hoping to see Barton returning her call.

It was Casaria.

"What?" she answered abruptly.

"Where are you?" he replied, equally blunt.

"Somewhere I'm supposed to be?"

"You're not home."

"And you're not welcome to go looking for me there," Pax said. "Do you even get what I do for a living? *Why* I do it?"

"Of course I do. The same as me. And you can have all the time and space you need to do whatever you want. *After* we know we can trust each other."

"So..." Pax felt her patience wearing to breaking point. "I need your *permission* to go out now? Can't go to the shops? Visit a friend? I didn't ask for any of this."

"Is that what you're doing? What friend?"

Pax barely paused. "You want me to put her on? She can tell you to fuck off, too."

There was a sharp intake of breath on the other end of the line, Casaria biting back his irritation. "I wanted you to join me for something. It's important." His tone sounded forced through his nose, his jaw clamped shut.

"Take a day off."

"That won't work."

"Make it. Look, I'm busy –"

"I really think you should tell me where you are."

"And I really think you should back off. We had a messed-up night last night, that's two nights running. I need a break. If you don't give me some space, I'll snap, I swear."

Casaria was quiet. Hopefully feeling admonished. "I'll give you today. Tomorrow, we'll pick up where we left off. No fooling around."

Before she could respond, he hung up. Pax looked at the phone for a moment, rolled her eyes and put it away. As she did, another unwelcome man came towards her. Curly locks of hair, unnaturally broad shoulders, a gleaming white grin that drew attention to how narrow his mouth was. Milton Tran was an insufferable card player who wore suits in an impossibly unlikeable array of colours. Today's choice was the off-mauve of a pensioner's hair overdue for dyeing.

"Pax? I thought it was you!" Tran went in for a strong, uninvited hug, the sort that had probably been practised to show off his firm chest. It made Pax wince. She didn't return the hug, and he didn't notice, letting go with a look of satisfaction. He said, "What are you doing here? At this time of day? I thought you only came out at night."

"Catching some Vitamin D," Pax said. "You live here?"

"Two blocks over, you know that," Tran laughed. She had no idea where he lived; if he had ever told her, she hadn't listened. "Come to bet on the nags. Got a sure thing, want in?"

"Not my thing," Pax replied.

"With this tip, you should make it your thing. Say, though, what are the chances – we've got a game this evening, if you're up for it. I'd pay money to see my alphas lose a hand to a girl."

Pax frowned, not sure whether to be offended or flattered. "How much?"

Tran laughed. "Oh not literally. You'd do well though, I'm sure. Bankers from the city."

"As opposed to rural ones."

He laughed again. "Shoot. How long's it been? Three months, at least. I've missed you, Pax. You hanging around? I'll buy you lunch."

"Already eaten," Pax said.

"Coffee, then."

"How about you place your bet, and we can talk at this game of yours later?"

The rebuttal made Tran stop, losing some of his cheer. He said, "Okay. Guess you've been up all night again, am I right?"

"Yeah," Pax replied without conviction. "You have fun now."

"I'll message you the deets. If you change your mind about the coffee, I'll be here."

He ducked into the shop, looking back at her, a little wary now. Pax gave him a one-handed wave, basically telling him to piss off. He turned away, and Letty called from above, "If you're done flirting, can we go?"

Pax looked up to the tiny lady standing directly above her, on the edge of the shop's sign. She had a bag over one shoulder, and was clearly alone.

"You gonna catch me?"

Pax nodded and the fairy jumped without warning. Pax quickly raised her hands. With Letty's weight, the fall was gentle, and she landed in Pax's cupped palms with a little thump. Pax immediately closed her fingers over her as she took a step back, looking into the shop to see that one of the punters was watching and frowning. Tran, beyond the man, noticed the strange look and stared at Pax himself.

"Where are your guys?" Pax asked quietly, backing off.

"Gone," Letty replied. "Taken their stuff, which means they're already trying to pull off a scheme. Which means they've entered a world of shit. There's half a dozen places they might've gone. We can start by heading to Hanton."

"As a random option?" Pax said. "How about we start by you thinking a bit more clearly about where we *need* to go, rather than keeping us moving out in the open where someone might notice us?"

"Someone being . . ."

"Who do you think?"

Letty went quiet, staring at Pax while apparently considering her options. Pax turned on the spot, though, checking up and down the road.

"Take your time," she said. "We're getting a coffee, at least."

5

Mix and Fresko had never had much use for ceremony. When Valoria Magnus approached them and the nearby Fae guards stiffened to attention, the pair merely stared, unimpressed. She was a large lady, prone to indulgence and inactivity, and the act of travelling out of the Transitional City to meet them appeared to tire her. Her expression said she was angry before she had said a word, her footfalls shaking the corridor as she approached.

"Where's Letty? She has a lot to answer for."

"Letty's gone," Mix replied.

Fresko added, "So's Gambay, before you ask."

Valoria slowed down at this news. She settled her attention on Mix, deciding he was the leader. "What happened?"

"The Ministry," Fresko said coldly. "Some new girl, they got her to do it. Don't like to say how."

Valoria kept her eyes on Mix. "Was this before or after you imbeciles tried to start a war?"

"Letty was trying to make things right," Mix said. "It got her killed. Since then, we've done things our way, and got results."

"Results!" Valoria let out a humourless laugh, a sound that came from the bottom of her gut. "You got the MEE hunting for us. The FTC is on high alert, ready to evacuate."

"It'll be worth it," Fresko said. She still did not look at him, eyes boring into Mix.

"I'm aware that you failed to release, or silence, the boy. The popular feeling is that the Fae responsible should be executed. That the Ministry should be placated. Tell me what you could possibly have that would make me even consider letting you go."

"We needed the boy to get fuel for the Dispenser," Mix said. "He was gonna persuade Citizen Barton to help. We found another way to persuade him." Mix left a meaningful pause, savouring the surprise in Valoria's face. "So, you want to make idle threats or you want our results?"

Valoria checked around her, the half-dozen guards appearing

completely disengaged from the conversation. All of them had to be listening, though.

"Yeah." Fresko followed her thoughts. "Maybe we should talk in private?"

The pair of mercenaries escorted Valoria and her single most trusted bodyguard down the steps of the emergency tunnel and out to the widening cavern of a human room. There, on the floor of the empty room, lay a large plastic bag, filled with what looked like a pile of dirt lit in blue highlights by occasional lightning sparks. Overcoming her initial surprise, Valoria flitted over to the bag with a few beats of her powerful wings. She landed next to it, hands greedily running over the moss. The men followed at a slower pace.

"Where did you find this?" she asked.

"Where Apothel said it was," Mix said.

She turned back to them, face steely. "And what do you expect us to do with it?"

"Use it, what else? The boy *found* the Dispenser. We know where he left it." Mix walked past her, throwing a hand up towards the bag. "But we knew better than to bring it back without power. It's worth at least a big fucking thank you, maybe a sorry or two along that road."

Valoria stepped back, taking in the crackling pile of dirt for a moment longer. "Do you have any idea what this means?"

"Yeah," Mix said. "It's means we're back in FTC favour, ain't that right?"

Valoria held his gaze. "Did the boy talk to you about it? Did *he* know what it was?"

"He knew," Fresko said. "We also know it was worth killing humans for before, so we figured you'd forgive a few casualties now."

This finally drew her to look at Fresko, her voice becoming more severe. "You need to learn your place. I never much liked Letty, but she at least had more sense than to antagonise the MEE. So don't think you are entirely in the clear. This is merely a step in the right direction. I'll send a team with you to collect the device."

"Tell us what it's worth, first," Mix said.

"And demonstrate that gratitude," Fresko added.

"I will arrange for your pardons," Valoria said. "Believe me, that is more than generous."

"We can take this to Retcho," Fresko warned. "See how he defines generous."

Valoria's face turned to stone. "You people bring shame to our society. To even suggest such a thing."

"We're businessmen. Same as you."

Valoria grunted, looking from Mix back to him. Mix looked no better than a thug for hire, but Fresko saw Valoria's eyes, scanning his shirt, his tie. Now she'd deigned to look, she knew he was something else. She said, "Very well. There are other rewards we can arrange." She stepped back from the moss as it sparked again. She frowned. "How did you get Barton to do this?"

"We didn't exactly negotiate," Mix said.

"Then I assume you cleared up after yourselves?"

"We left him to rot. The daughter, too. No sign of Fae interference."

Valoria raised an eyebrow. Without asking for details, she said, "That sounds far too vague. I don't want them *left* to do anything. I want the job finished. I don't reward incomplete work."

"With respect, he might still have his uses," Fresko said, though Mix gave him a look that disagreed. "How else are we gonna put the Dispenser to use?"

"That's not your concern," Valoria said. "All I need from you right now is their silence."

6

There was a ferocious knock at Dr Mandy Rimes' door. Any knock was usually enough to startle her into dropping whatever was in her hands, given the infrequency of visitors, but this was a particularly severe knock, causing her to scatter a project all over the worktop. She fussed towards the door with tuts, pushing her welding goggles onto her forehead, and called out, "Who's there?"

"Me," came the gruff reply.

She opened the door. It was just as well she'd recognised his voice, because she wasn't sure she would have recognised his face in that state.

"Oh heavens!" she cried, reaching towards Darren Barton, then taking her hands back. She stepped back, then out towards him, utterly at a loss for how best to respond.

"Water," Barton said, one shoulder digging into the wall for support. "Please."

Rimes scurried away with mild curses, knocking over a pile of metal on the way. She stopped to pick up a piece, then left it be, and spiralled back towards the tap to get water. In the time it took her to find a glass, Barton had managed to drag himself to one of her many cluttered work surfaces and had sat on a high stool. He leaned to one side, blood dripping from his forehead onto a gutted watch mechanism.

"What happened?" Rimes asked, forcing the glass of water into his hands.

"The Fae," Barton said. Cracked blood ran down one side of his face, while the other had swollen like a balloon. One of his eyes was halfway closed, and his sodden ear was out of shape. Perhaps there was a piece missing. The rest of his body was little better, but it was so dark with blood that it was hard to see where the injuries lay. "It's their technology."

"What is?" Rimes replied.

"The plans you said Rufaizu had. It was a Fae device. That's what Apothel stole. And it's got them after me, got Grace . . . Grace kidnapped. You need to tell me how I can find them."

Rimes blinked behind her thick glasses. "Darren, you need medical help –"

"So give it to me," Barton said. "Then point me to the FTC."

Rimes gave a quick hum, hesitating between questioning him and helping. She chose the latter, scurrying to a small medical kit at the side of the room. She rummaged through the supplies, saying, "Are you sure they have Grace?"

"Sure enough."

"They did this to you?"

Barton shifted with effort and pain. "More or less. They needed electric weed. Needed me to get it. From a glogockle nest. There was . . . ten of them, maybe."

"It's a miracle you're alive."

"No miracle, just a necessity. They came in. Took the weed from me and drew the myriad towards me. But I got out. They didn't give me enough credit. You know where they are, don't you?"

Rimes paused, holding a gauze pad to a gash on his forehead. "No. But I have been testing a device that might help. It's a bad idea, though. The Ministry –"

"Can rot," Barton rumbled. "I'm getting my damned daughter back, and I'm burning them all to the ground."

Rimes backed off, too chilled by his rage to argue. As he calmed, Barton fished in his pockets for something. He said, "There's something else. Tell me what you know about this."

He pulled out a crumpled sandwich bag, faded in parts as though plucked from the gutter. He placed it on the table, its contents partly spilling out. It looked like a clump of earth. Rimes frowned, coming closer to it. The dirt suddenly glistened, bright blue in places, as though sparking energy, making Rimes jump back in surprise.

"You held some back?" she asked.

"Seemed damned important. What do you know about it?"

"I only know *of* it. I've never seen electric weed in the flesh. As it were. I'm not sure anyone has. Darren. It's a very strange power source. What did you say it was for?"

Holly was barely surprised to see her husband was not home when she woke up, late. She was mad at herself for letting it happen.

She was no kind of mother, being able to sleep at a time like that. But they had called all Grace's friends, they had notified the police, they had driven through the streets, what else was there? Barton had done it all convinced this was no ordinary disappearance, and now he had gone, leaving Holly, in the new day, to think of her own solution. Fighting down the anger and the fear and the confusion, she forced herself to be calm. Told herself, in no uncertain terms, that this was a time to think rationally. The best way forward was to write a list of problems and possible steps she could take to overcome them.

Daughter missing.

Husband missing.

Possible supernatural creatures responsible.

Police no use?

Each point seemed to present an impossible task, so instead of solutions she started to come up with more problems.

Husband still lying.

Possible relapse to radioactive drink.

Horse playing a drum.

He had taken whatever that infernal liquid was with him and buggered off back into his mystical world, alone, but she at least had a firmer grip on what it was she should be annoyed at him for. And that was partly satisfying. No more fears for his unfaithful gallivanting, though the fear that he was involved with unruly gangs was heightened. How could he have got Grace mixed up in it?

The thought of Grace distracted Holly from her useless list of problems. She picked up a photo album she had created when Grace had been young. She smiled at how healthy and happy they had all looked. It was easy to create that impression in front of the camera. The memories were less than perfect. There were photos of Grace in Darren's car. A photo of her sitting amid a pile of cables from some computing project he'd clearly botched. Then one with her grinning happily at the filthy bandage around the top of her head. She'd even looked happy then, after the accident. Daddy's tough little girl. Darren hadn't been so happy. Holly had been positively livid.

That was the last time Holly had felt so afraid, she realised. Not just for Grace's safety, but for her own. She had known, when Darren had told her their daughter was hurt, that his attention had been divided. He had somehow let it happen. He could not be trusted to be left alone with her.

Holly looked at the injury in the photo and Grace's unflappable spirit, and realised that she didn't know the truth of what had happened that day. Darren said she had fallen off a stool. From what Holly had seen the night before, though, anything was possible. Had she been trampled by a riderless horse? Slipped on poisonous goo? What?

Holly slammed the photo album and huffed.

There *was* something she could do. She had always been vigilant, and kept careful note of the new numbers in Darren's phone. She said it was in case of an emergency; there was no telling exactly who she might need to call, if something terrible should happen. But there were lots of types of emergencies, and that included the sort that required her to keep track of strange ladies Barton be in touch with.

It was a line to cross, though. He had gone out with a plan, surely. He might come back, before she opened this particular Pandora's box.

Taking a rueful glance at the clock, gone 11am, she poured a glass of red wine to help make the decision. People were out of church by now, and *they* must have had a drink, so screw it. After the first few sips, she was already confident in moving forward.

She scrolled through to the number she had resisted calling for years. She had contemplated deleting it so many times, but she'd kept it for the extra special days when she thought nothing would cheer her up more than shouting at someone who truly deserved it. Now, though, she hoped that the lady on the other end of the line might be able to help her. The one whose name she had cursed like a voodoo doll. She dialled Dr Mandy Rimes' number.

A mousey-voiced woman answered. "Mrs Barton. How can I help you?"

Holly paused a beat. She'd expected at least some surprise. "Have you seen my husband?"

A pause. "No." Rimes answered too carefully. She clearly wasn't used to lying.

"Is he there now?" Holly demanded, firmly.

"He is not."

"Then where is he?"

"I don't know. He's trying to save your daughter."

Holly froze. So it was real, then. The doctor knew about the threat. Darren was out there fighting. Something, somehow. Holly squeezed her eyes closed. "Tell me you know something. Tell me there's a solution."

Rimes paused again. "Your husband is possibly the strongest man I know. If anyone can get your daughter back, he can."

Holly caught the trailing off of the final word, and prompted, "But . . ."

"Strength alone is rarely enough."

7

Pax sat on the upper floor of a minimalist café with cheap plastic seats and coffees the price of a meal. No wonder it was empty. Her back shielded her from the room so Letty could sit on the table in front of her, unseen. The wide window had a good view of the street, opposite Riley's Bettor Off, from the junction to the right to the Tube station to the left. The pair watched pedestrians as Letty mused over locations they could go to, spread across the city.

"There's a water tower near the river," she said. "Good place to hide a human. But you'd have to get them up the ladder." The fairy muttered something else, dismissing the idea.

"You honestly think they'd try and take Barton?"

"Try and fail, probably. Yeah. But it's gotta be somewhere they could hide him."

Pax inhaled deeply over her coffee. Alcohol would've been better, but it'd do. She took another bite of croissant as Letty mumbled random curses to herself. Pax broke a bit of pastry off and put it down next to her, saying, "You eat pastry?"

Letty gave the croissant a glance, then twisted to look up at Pax, ready to come out with another insult. She resisted, though. She tore off a flake and took a bite. Chewing with her mouth open, she said, "Better than nothing."

"You're welcome," Pax said. Watching a local walk by, she tried to lighten the fairy's mood. "Were you guys out here enjoying the company of high society? I made a grand playing a game run by a dentist out here once. He told me his shirt was worth more than the pot on the table. I won it off him. The shirt off his back."

Letty gave Pax a look like she wasn't sure why she was being told this. She swallowed another mouthful of croissant and asked, "Was it?"

"Huh?"

"Worth more than the pot?"

"No idea," Pax shrugged. "Even if it was, who was I gonna sell it to? I gave it to Bees as a thank you for getting me in on another game. Never saw him wear it."

"Bees," Letty echoed thoughtfully. She looked back out the window. "Yeah, we didn't camp out here by chance. We took these pricks for everything they were worth."

"How?"

"Every way you can think of. It's a whole neighbourhood full of marks."

Pax smiled at the thought of these violent fairies somehow mugging the oblivious rich fools. "My mum, she used to send me property suggestions for out here. *If you've got to live in that god-awful city, you could at least move to a nice area.* My dad told her to stop encouraging me, though."

"Your dad. Was he a bit of a prick?"

"Still is."

"Wears a suit and has a number-plate with something vaguely close to his initials?"

Pax laughed. "That's about right."

"Dumb fucking humans."

"Yeah?" Pax shifted over Letty, getting more comfortable. "Your parents were perfect? Assuming you're not hatched from eggs or something?"

"Ha ha," Letty replied dryly. "My dad was a lunatic. He got in fights with literally every person he spoke to, like other people being alive just pissed him off." She trailed off into the memory, her voice almost fond. Pax smiled at the fairy again.

"I'm Pax, by the way. Since you never asked. Pax Kuranes."

"Jesus," Letty laughed. "Your dad didn't give you a chance, huh?"

"It comes from the Roman goddess of peace."

"Except that's not where *you* got it from. It's not enough of a prick move for your dad."

Pax raised her eyebrows. "You're good, you know? No, he took it from his university motto. *Pax et Lux.* You know the worst part? They weren't even the first to use it. They copied it from a research centre in America."

Letty laughed harder, coughing out some croissant. "Classic. All right. Let's do this. I'm Letty." She held up her hand and Pax stared for a second. Minuscule as it was, the gesture was important – she took the tiny hand between her thumb and forefinger, as gently as possible, to shake it. Letty seemed satisfied, twisting away. "That doesn't make us mates, though. You know, with the whole eating and kidnapping shit."

"I'd call it rescuing," Pax said. "And don't knock it yet. In other circumstances, I think we'd get along."

"In other circumstances?" Letty straightened her face, giving Pax a mock scolding look. "In other circumstances, I'd have taken you for everything you were worth."

"Sure," Pax said.

Letty flapped a dismissive hand at her, turning back to the window. She paused, though, a thought hitting her. "The research centre. That's a possibility."

"What?"

"For my boys. We've got a big room there. A good place for dealing with humans. But we haven't used it for ages because . . ." Letty gave Pax a serious look. ". . . it's not far from the FTC. In the circumstances, and being a dumb bunch of fucks, the boys might think that's a good thing."

"Near the Fae city, whose location is a fiercely protected secret?"

"Yeah, there."

"The sort of place the Fae might consider shooting a person for getting too close to?"

Letty nodded.

Pax was about to suggest trying the water tower first when a movement below caught her attention. She hunched down suddenly, slamming her hand down in front of Letty to create a barrier before the window. Letty shot to her feet, shouting, "Are you fucking –"

"Quiet!" Pax hissed. "They've seen me."

Casaria disliked West Farling. It was full of people who had graduated from the bohemian seeds of Ten Gardens into thriving better-than-thou wretches, looming over their inferiors with roots dug deep into the city. In the shiny SUVs and cashmere-scarved dog-walkers of West Farling, Casaria saw people immune to speeding tickets, who walked away from charges of sexual assault by virtue of importance.

Sam Ward lived somewhere in the neighbourhood. When he'd

dropped her off after work one night, he'd asked why she didn't live in Central, like him, in the action. She'd given him a pitying look, and hadn't even bothered to answer.

That said it all, didn't it?

Casaria wished he could fight these people, knuckle-to-knuckle out on the street. But there were cameras on every street corner and Neighbourhood Watch everywhere. He had devised a thousand plans passing through here, from a staged road rage assault to a simple balaclava mugging, but there were always flaws. The best he could do, instead, was to make sure any assignments he had in West Farling were taken slowly, to maximise the opportunity for the side effects of the Sunken City to deliver some damage to the area. With the help of an able partner, he mused, maybe he could come up with a better plan. Pax was bound to hate these people as much as he did; they clearly represented everything she opposed. But then, she was hardly full of enthusiasm for continuing their training.

He put it out of his mind as he swung the car onto a high street's overly high curb, across double-yellow lines. There were enough people here that if there was trouble with the Fae, he might be able to draw a few bystanders into the fray. Discretion was the Ministry's principal watchword, but if it was a matter of national security, it might be possible that someone would get shot, or at least punched, for being in the wrong place at the right time.

He was smiling at the fantasy as he got out and surveyed the betting shop, not listening to Landon's complaints about the antagonistic parking job. Rufaizu had given Casaria an accurate address, as far as the shop name and street went, and there was the Underground station he'd indicated in the childish map he'd scrawled. The boy hadn't taken much persuading. Maybe it was an old Fae hangout and he thought it wouldn't do any harm. It was a start, though.

Landon gave up huffing and ambled away to check the area.

"Mr Casaria!" Gumg shouted over the roof of the car.

Casaria turned to him with a severe look.

"I asked if I should check over there." He was pointing across the road, to a hair salon, a café and a clothes shop that looked like an art gallery.

"Considering the boy gave me the exact address of this betting shop," Casaria said, "what would you hope to achieve by volunteering to search a different location?"

Gumg shrank in shame, but Casaria froze, spotting a flash of movement in the window above the café. Gumg and Landon followed his gaze. Too late to duck out of view, Pax merely stared back.

Pax tucked Letty into her inside coat pocket and hurried down the stairs to find Casaria and his two goons in the door. Casaria stopped rigidly, the leather jacket and tatty suit pair behind him forming an impassable wall. The clerk behind the counter opened his mouth to welcome the men but said nothing as the strangeness of the scene grabbed him.

"It's more than a little worrying to find you here, Pax," Casaria said.

"You've got to be kidding," Pax started indignantly. Her instincts took over. "You came looking for me after what I said? Seriously?" She pulled towards him, fists clenched, every bit the victim of a stalker. "I told you to leave me alone. How'd you find me? Have you been tracking my phone?"

"Please, Pax," Casaria answered. "They might buy it, but I'm no idiot. Meeting a friend, were you?"

"You need to step the fuck back." Pax raised her voice. "And what's this?" She gestured to the two men, aware of the counter clerk watching them. "Backup, in case I didn't want to come with you?"

"Excuse me…" The clerk tried to intervene, his voice cracking at a high pitch, as though he'd chosen that moment to hit puberty.

Casaria glanced at him, affecting a forced smile. "She's unstable. We'll take care of this."

"What is this, Casaria?" said the bigger man, in the threadbare suit. "Who is she?"

"Apparently she's our ticket to the Fae."

"Am I shit," Pax snarled. She took a step towards them, making for the door. "You need to leave me alone." The two men instinctively stepped aside, but Casaria stood his ground, and moved to grab her shoulder. She jumped back, raising a fist. "Don't touch me, you prick!"

"Where's this friend of yours?" Casaria said confidently. "Too small for us to see?"

Pax kept her fist raised.

"Landon," Casaria said. "Got your faeometer on you?"

"Over there." Pax pointed past Casaria's shoulder.

"Huh?"

"My friend. *He* is over there. In the betting shop."

The others followed her gesture, but Casaria stayed fixed on Pax. "I thought you'd be better at bluffing, given your –"

"Tran!" Pax shouted, waving. Casaria turned, spotting the man leaving the shop on the other side of the road. Tran waved heartily back as he ventured into the street, his golden hair flopping about his face. With Casaria momentarily dumbstruck, Pax pushed past and ran out.

"You're still here," Tran said merrily, approaching her.

"Yeah," Pax said. "Ran into some acquaintances." She lowered her voice. "Not exactly welcome." Tran frowned slightly.

Casaria and the other two edged out onto the pavement behind her, Landon rummaging in his pockets. Casaria was sizing the man up. "Good friend of Pax's, are you?"

"Sure." Tran grinned, showing his bleached teeth. "And you are . . . ?"

"I really do need to go." Pax smiled sweetly at him, the sort of smile that crossed her face only when she was working. "Send me that address and I'll see you later."

"Definitely, most definitely. You run along."

"You start to get the idea," Landon said in a disgruntled tone, shuffling around the group, "that this is why you needed help, Casaria."

Casaria looked from his colleague back to Pax, his eyes saying he hated every inch of human fibre that surrounded him. "Pax, you can't just –"

"Leave me the hell alone, all right?" Pax snapped, and moved to leave. The moment Casaria took a step after her, Tran stepped in the way and placed a hand on his chest. Pax kept going, giving them a backwards glance to make sure this played out.

"There a problem, pal?" Tran asked. He was taller than Casaria by a head, wider by a shoulder, and open to dealing with troublesome squirts. Casaria was grinning, though, like he welcomed the challenge.

"It doesn't concern you."

"Leave them alone, for Christ's sake," Landon said, starting to cross the road. He had a tracking device out, like Casaria's from the day before, and he was shaking it to get it to work.

Pax continued, heading for the Underground station. She heard Casaria move, and Tran moving in step with him. The guy in leathers suggested, in a nasal tone, "Maybe we should get back to it, huh?"

The tracking device beeped.

Pax stopped in the middle of the road, everyone going quiet behind her.

It beeped again.

Pax didn't look back. They'd be exchanging concerned looks. It beeped again and she took a step away. Careful. Then another. A gap in the beeps this time. Slower.

"I knew it," Casaria said quietly. "She has it on her."

Pax ran.

"Stop her!"

Hearing the footfalls of Landon close behind her, she flung a fist back without looking and connected with his face. He stumbled and grunted a curse as she broke away. Pounding over the pavement towards the Underground, she heard the leather jacket shout, "I got her!" She threw a quick look back and ducked as she saw the gun, the man's legs spread ready to shoot. Someone screamed. Casaria bowled into him from the side, throwing his aim off. The shot went high and wide, the noise sending bystanders diving for cover. Pax watched in shock as Casaria chopped the leather jacket's neck. The man fell down in splutters.

Pax was all but at the Underground station now. Landon was steadying himself in the middle of the road, clutching a bloody nose, any semblance of giving chase gone, and Tran was next to Casaria, startled still. Casaria gave Tran a sideways look, then his eyes rested on her again. He raised a pointing finger. "Pax! Stop!"

"No, you stop!" Tran shouted stupidly, leaping at him. Casaria ducked the hulking man's grasp and swung a punch into his temple. The blow knocked Tran onto his delicately chiselled teeth. Pax winced as he rocked back onto his knees, upright just in time for Casaria to catch him with a punch square to the other temple. This one toppled him.

Pax bolted, all but diving down the Underground steps. She shoved through a gathering of people hiding from the sound of the gunshot. She vaulted the barriers and glanced back as she sprinted onto the platform. A train was rolling into the station, and Casaria hadn't caught up.

8

Pax struggled to breathe as the train moved, sinking deep into the seat and closing her eyes as she panted. Sweat dripped down the back of her neck. No chance of showering that off any time soon. Letty shifted in her pocket, and Pax quickly checked for fellow passengers: an older couple stared unashamedly her way; a young man was listening to a stereo a few seats down; a man in a shirt was checking out a girl standing further down the aisle, over his magazine. Pax opened her coat and whispered, "Not here . . . too many people."

Letty shoved the pocket opening outwards slightly so she could see up, her face stern. "Get off this fucking train," she hissed. "Right now."

Pax covered her mouth and ducked. "They'll catch up at the next station."

"You brought a Fae underground, we've got bigger problems than those arseholes!"

Pax pulled her coat closed again, putting a hand to her chest to hold Letty closer to her, muffling her protests. She looked up and around. The next stop was a five-minute drive for the others, at most. How dangerous could it be to keep going? As she thought it, the train slowed. The lights dimmed, then came back brighter. They dimmed again, almost to darkness, as the train screeched to a halt.

The other passengers looked around, more curious than concerned. The older couple turned their attention away as the man mumbled about forgetting to water a hydrangea.

Pax stood and walked down the carriage, brushing past magazine man and moving close to the door. Looking back, she saw the other passengers starting to yawn. The lights came back up, a little brighter, and there was a spark of blue light somewhere outside. The sort that railways randomly throw out, she told herself. She flinched as part of Letty's tiny form jabbed at her through the pocket, punching or kicking at her.

Blue light flickered at the end of the train carriage with a cackle of sparks. Pax jumped back, remembering the thing that had chased her and Casaria, earning a disapproving look from the magazine man. The other passengers had slumped, eyelids drooping. The young man with the stereo rolled his head back against the seat. The lights went out.

"Oh bollocks," Pax uttered.

"Happens all the time," the magazine man said. Was that supposed to be comforting or scolding? The lights came back up as she glared at him; he caught her eye and looked away.

The train started moving as the blue lights flickered around it again. It continued rattling along the tracks, too slow for Pax's tastes. It rolled into the next station, the platform opening up in light. The moment the doors opened, Pax charged out, glancing back only briefly to see the tunnel flickering as though lit by vast blue candlelight. No one else noticed or cared.

She sprinted out of the station, up the stairs, through the barriers and out onto the street, a carbon copy of the place she'd left behind. Checking for Casaria's car, Pax turned away from the road to run down a side street. She went on for two more blocks before turning again, into an alley that cut towards an open green area, then she finally stopped.

She leant forward, gagging on her own saliva, put her hands on her knees and cursed. As she hung in exhausted relief, the fairy in her pocket started shoving at her again. Pax half walked, half swayed to a bench and slumped down. There was no one else in the park, but Pax wasn't sure she cared anyway. She lifted Letty out of her pocket and opened her hand in front of her face. Letty clambered to her feet and steadied herself in the middle of Pax's palm. Her fists were balled tight and her eyes bulged with anger.

"Don't you ever do something like that again," the fairy said.

Pax spat out some phlegm. "What? Save you from those nutters?"

"What'd I tell you about the Sunken City? We go down there, the creatures come at us in an instant. The berserker could've travelled the full length of Ordshaw to get to us just there."

"It didn't though, did it," Pax said. Letty folded her arms. "Get us, I mean."

"They knew where we were," Letty huffed.

"But they weren't expecting us," Pax noted, before the fairy could blame her.

Letty nodded. "Rufaizu gave the place up. Guess I should've expected it, given how much of a louse his father was."

Pax took that in. At least that meant Rufaizu was okay, if he'd been able to tip off the Ministry to the Fae's location. He was alive, anyway. He was safer than her. She said, "They know where I live, too. That makes me homeless right now. Homeless and an enemy of the state. Fuck. My cash is in the apartment, what am I supposed to do?" In her frustration, she shifted on the bench and Letty had to steady herself on Pax's hand.

"Oi! Settle down!" Letty said. "You're gonna take me to my boys, that's what you're gonna do. Figure yourself out after."

"Figure myself out?" Pax gaped at her. "That's all you've got?"

"Sorry I don't have plans for hiding humans from the Ministry. In case you didn't notice, I'm out on my arse with a wing missing, which gives me bigger problems of my own."

"I'm in this mess because of you!"

"Oh please. You'd be *dead* if not for me. Here's what's gonna happen. You're gonna jump on a *bus* to the warehouse district, I'm gonna tell you where to get off, and we're gonna check the abandoned research centre building."

"And then?"

"We part ways. Most likely, you start hightailing it as far from Ordshaw as possible."

"Hightailing it?" Pax shot back. "All right. Counter-offer, we go back to mine and you sneak in to get my cash for me. Then we figure out a plan *together*."

"Not going to happen. They're looking for me the same as you."

"Except you're decidedly less conspicuous. And seeing that I'm your ride around this city, I don't see you having much choice."

Letty held her gaze, testing her, seeing how serious she was. She nodded slowly and crouched down, opening the bag that she had taken from the betting shop. As she delved in, she said, "Okay. Here's my final offer." She drew back holding a chunky metal pistol. Chunky compared to her, at least; it was the size and shape of a plug fuse. "You take me to where I've got to go and I don't scatter your brains."

Pax didn't respond at once. It was hard to feel threatened by such a diminutive figure with such an insignificant weapon, even with the strength of Letty's conviction. "You realise you're standing in my hand, right? I could squash you like a bug."

"Bet you all the cash in Ordshaw you're not quicker than a bullet."

Pax paused again. "And I'm supposed to believe that thing works?"

"You believe Apothel's dead, don't you?"

"Right." Pax tried to think quickly. "So shoot me, where does that leave you?"

"Without having to worry about loose ends, for starters." Letty toed the bag at her feet. "I got all I needed at our stop. Even if I can't fly, I've got dust, I can stay hidden. I don't *need* you, Pax. But if your life's worth something, you *can* still help me."

"Just like that?" Pax said.

"Just like that," Letty replied coldly.

So much for bonding. Pax said, "And when you get to where you're going . . ."

"I'm good for my word, same as you. You can walk. But that's where this ends. Now get moving. I'll have this on you every step of the way."

Pax took a deep breath, eyes fixed on the fairy. She said, finally, "For such a small person you're a massive bitch, you know that?"

Along the quiet journey, on more than one occasion Pax considered taking her chances. With Letty in her pocket, she could slap a hand against her and potentially incapacitate her. But all the fairy had to do was pull the trigger. And Pax also suspected that Fae people were stronger than they looked. Their small size did not necessarily make them frail; it didn't seem to have the expected effect on the volume of her voice, after all.

Having spent most of her physical energy running from Casaria, and her mental energy on fresh feelings of animosity towards her companion, the effort of sparking a new fight with Letty didn't seem worth it. A few bus rides and she would be rid of her, no more fuss. With that resolved in her head, she tried to plan her next course of action.

They would definitely be monitoring her apartment, but whatever she wanted to do she needed her money. And her passport, if it came to that. Why couldn't they be like all the other government agencies she knew of – slow and ineffective? The government agents she crossed had to be the ones who carried guns and shot people to solve problems. Whatever happened to receiving a strongly worded letter in the post ten weeks after an infraction?

Her mind was wandering. She looked out the window and saw that they were passing through Ten Gardens. It wouldn't be far from here.

The most sensible option was her original plan, which she resented Letty for not going along with. If an inconspicuous patsy could get into her apartment for her, she could avoid the Ministry and get away safely. And go where? Back to London? Abroad? Home for a thick slice of humble pie? She sighed. Home might not be so bad after all this. At least she'd see Albie again. He'd appreciate what she'd been through. He might even believe it.

Passing the ivy-dotted facades of renovated townhouses, where a group of eclectic adults were making music from pots, pans and a guitar, Pax swallowed those thoughts. She didn't want to leave Ordshaw. It had been her home for long enough that she felt she owned a piece of the city. It was hers. From the abandoned industrial behemoths to the allotment shacks, part of it belonged to her, and part of her belonged to it. It didn't matter that she woke as the rest of the city slept, or that she followed her own path while they slaved within the system, she was still a part of it all, in her own way. She wanted to stay a part of it. And she wanted to protect it, if that's what it came to. The words slipped out of her mouth: "I don't want to leave."

She felt Letty shift in her pocket, but the fairy said nothing.

The bus passed a street vendor trying to convince a smartly dressed couple to buy a ceramic pig. They didn't look interested, but he was giving it everything he had, hands waving and mouth flapping.

There was another option. The money in her apartment wouldn't get her far, but the device that the Ministry and the Fae were willing to kill for might.

Pax took her phone from her pocket. A present from Bees' friend, Howling Jowls Jones, who'd insisted it was untraceable. That had been important to her once, probably for imaginary reasons; it was a godsend now. It was unregistered, contained none of her personal details and used a series of masking programs to access calls and the internet. She brought up Bees' number and hesitated before ringing.

Was it safe?

"Letty?" she said quietly, not caring that there was a handful of other passengers who might or might not be able to hear. It would look like she was making a call, and given the fairy's small voice, it would sound like her responses came from the phone. Letty didn't answer. "Letty? It's okay to talk."

"Is it fuck."

"I'm on my phone."

"They can trace that shit, you idiot."

"That's my question. How did you get my phone number?" Silence from the pocket. Pax kept staring at the phone. "It's not registered."

"We followed you home. After that prick took Rufaizu. Then we used a scanner on your building. Yours was the third number we tried."

Pax imagined the fairies threatening two strangers before getting to her. She said, "A scanner gave you my number?"

"Quick tip," Letty said. "Assume, at all times, that Fae technology is at least a few years ahead of yours. We know everything you've got, we deconstruct that crap and make use of it when we need to. Only we've got our own stuff, too. So, yeah, we did that. With a cheap bit of kit."

"There's a lot we could do, working together . . ."

"No. There's a lot we could teach you. What would *you* offer *us*? Ignorance and idiocy?"

Pax went quiet again. They were back to this. She kept staring at the phone.

It could wait.

They alighted near an anonymous series of buildings that could once have housed entire businesses, with a look from the driver that said no one ever got off here. The surrounding streets appeared to have lost their names, and many of the buildings were without roofs. Pax waited until the bus was out of sight, then crouched and took Letty out of her pocket. She held her up and asked, "This it?"

"Over there." Letty pointed. "The hexagonal building."

Pax walked towards it, taking in the strange complex. The paint was cracked around it, some of the windows were missing, and someone had scrawled graffiti on another wall. *COCKS.* A faded sign on a wall read *Innovation Centre.*

"Holds a certain subtle irony, doesn't it?" Pax commented. Letty didn't answer.

The glass entrance door was open, the building inside abandoned. Pax followed Letty's instructions through a network of halls to a corridor that left the offices behind. Past a few more doors, Pax came to a metal bulkhead with a five-inch metal contraption over its lock, blinking with a red light. Some kind of electronic lock.

"Fucking knew it," Letty commented as Pax came to a stop.

Holding the fairy in her fist, as Letty took in the door, Pax considered her options again. The gun was still there, vaguely pointing in her direction, but Letty was distracted. A quick squeeze might –

Letty's gun went off. Pax flinched, tightening her grip, and Letty spun to her. "Watch it, fuckwit!"

Pax loosened her grip as Letty shoved against her fingers. The fairy gave her a mean look, gun raised, and Pax took a moment to figure out what had happened. Letty had shot the lock. The red light was now dead and the metal box gently smoking.

"Open her up," the fairy instructed.

"Yes, master." Pax rolled her eyes. She pulled the door towards them and looked in. Then she froze. "You've got to be kidding."

"Fuck," Letty snarled. "Worse than I thought. Useless fucking morons."

They both stared in silence as Grace Barton kicked away into a corner, too scared at their entrance to say anything. She had one arm raised defensively, covering her face.

"Close the door," Letty hissed. "Close it now."

"Are you serious – we can't – "

"Close the fucking door!" Letty snapped, rattling her gun. Pax did as she was told, not arguing now she'd seen what the pistol was capable of. Grace found her voice as the door was sealed. "No, don't leave me in here!" It was a dry, desperate plea, accompanied by the scuffling of her feet. She was cut off by the door thunking into place.

"Right, to the FTC, then," Letty said.

"Your men are clearly –"

"They're not here. They would've made it known if they were. Back the way we came."

"We can't just leave her here."

"Why the hell not?"

Pax raised Letty to her face. "Because I'm not a monster!"

"Look like one to me." The pistol was aimed right between her eyes.

"You're not either, I don't believe that," Pax said, undeterred. "You never would have talked to Apothel if you were. Never would've shared a thing with him if you didn't think there was some hope in it. And you wouldn't have spent all these years trying to get that Dispenser back if all you cared about was yourself. You never would've talked to *me*."

"Bullshit, you don't know me. And this is *not* a discussion. You oughta be thankful I don't involve you in this, because in all likelihood that girl's gotta go now."

"I'm not letting that happen."

"Well *I* am, so get the hell out of here."

Pax flexed her fingers on the fairy. Letty's eyes dared her to make a move, the pistol unwavering.

"This doesn't have to end badly for you, Pax," Letty told her. "Just walk away. I can have my people take back the Dispenser before you get home, and you can forget any of this ever happened. That's what you wanted from the start, isn't it?"

Pax growled, finding words failed her. She couldn't argue with the pistol. She turned from the metal door, striding back the way they'd come. Letty told her to walk carefully, but Pax only moved more quickly through the building, up the road and along the block. Away from the offices and on towards the empty warehouses. She came to a half-crumbled wall and thrust Letty down onto it, the fairy stumbling to regain her balance on a dislodged brick. Letty spun back and aimed her gun at Pax, but Pax had already stepped away, hands on her hips. "This far enough for you?"

Letty checked her surroundings. She eyed Pax, but didn't complain. "I suggest you walk that way. Steer well clear of where I'm going. Don't even look my way. Twenty minutes or so you'll hit the edge of Ten Gardens."

Pax followed her gesture. It all looked the same, brick walls after brick walls. She said, "Do what the hell you want, I'm not leaving that girl behind."

"Well. Good luck with surviving the day."

"And you know what, I would've taken you back here. Whatever else we did, I was gonna keep my word. You didn't have to pull a gun on me."

This gave Letty the briefest pause. "Yeah, well, you're still a fucking human."

Pax shoved her hands deep in her pockets and started back towards the Innovation Centre, Letty's directions be damned.

"Hey!"

Pax turned, the tiny person barely visible. "What?" Letty hesitated, couldn't bring herself to say what was on her mind. Pax huffed. "Whatever. Have a nice life."

She kept walking, not looking back this time. She took out her phone and dialled Bees. He answered on the second ring. "So they didn't disappear you."

"Not yet," Pax said. "But they tried. I need some help."

"Thought you'd never ask," Bees answered brightly.

9

Barton pulled his car to a stop at the edge of the warehouse district, swaying in his seat like a drunk. Rimes' vague hunch to come here was hardly the most inspiring start to a city-wide search, but her hunches tended to be better than most. If the Fae city was anywhere in the sprawl of Ordshaw, it made sense that they'd use the abandoned warehouses. And maybe the Blue Angel hadn't been entirely wrong before, maybe there'd just been a mix-up.

He stared at the decayed industrial buildings. Big enough to hide whole streets, tall enough to build rockets in. Wonders of human engineering rendered useless, now that born labourers like him spent their days pining over numbers and computer servers. If he'd had a life in the factories, however hard it might've been, maybe it would've satisfied that part of him that always wanted to get out and do something physical. He reflected only as long as it took to recover enough energy to get out of the vehicle. Light-headed, he almost sat straight back down.

Barton took out the device Rimes had given him: a scanner with an archaic black and green display and two pointed antennas. He was sure she'd designed it for kitsch value as much as practicality, such was her way. He switched it on and held it high. It made a slight buzzing noise, hard at work, but that was it. No change on the display, no sign of life.

He walked away from the car, turning on the spot to scan the area. He moved in and out of a few derelict buildings. Finally, returning to his car, he took out his phone and cringed at the number of missed calls it showed. They weren't all from Holly, but at this point he couldn't see Pax being anything better than a distraction. He brought up Rimes' number. She answered straight away.

"It's not doing anything," he said.

"No beeps?"

"No."

"No blinking light?"

"Nothing."

"Then they're not there."

Barton looked at the canister of glo on the passenger seat. "Any chance it just doesn't work?"

"It should work. In theory."

"You ever actually tested it?"

"The Ministry wouldn't allow it. They hold the Fae's privacy in high regard, Darren. I've been trying to tell you – it's complicated. There have been discussions. Agreements. Diplomacy."

"Give it a rest," Barton told her roughly. "My daughter's out here somewhere."

"I don't know what to suggest."

Silence as Rimes waited for Barton to come to a decision. He studied the green liquid in the canister. Its thick warmth would comfort his throat. His angry thoughts would dissolve in the liquid. It had all happened too fast in the tunnel. He didn't get to enjoy it. "If they're nearby, I can pick up the trail."

"Darren? If you mean glo, that's not a good idea. The medicine I gave you –"

"Mandy. I know what I'm doing."

The doctor hesitated. "Of course."

A few moments later, Barton had his phone in one hand and the glo in the other, as he toyed with the idea of taking the drink. He dreaded pressing Call just as much. The nastiest creatures of the underworld couldn't make him shake like this. He gritted his teeth and did it.

The phone rang. A painful series of beeps with no answer. He closed his eyes and realised the one thing worse than having to explain himself was the thought that she might not answer. Holly's voice interrupted his fears. "Darren?"

"Holly," he said, voice hoarse.

"My *God* Darren, you bastard, you tell me you're safe. Tell me Grace is safe."

"I'm fine," Barton lied. "And I'm close to her. But there's something I have to do."

"Where have you been?" Holly's voice rose. "You tell me where on earth you've been!"

"There was another note. I did what they said, now I'm following them."

"Call the police! Get someone else involved! Are you out of your goddamned mind?"

"There's no one else who can do what I need to," Barton told her.

"Is there hell! This is our daughter –"

"I need to go . . . back down the hole. I wanted to talk to you. Wanted to let you know. I've hidden it all for too long. And this time . . ."

"Darren . . ." Holly's anger was subsiding, replaced by fear.

"Holly," Barton said, "it'll be okay. This is just something I need to do."

"Where are you? Let me come and help. Let me do something."

"The best thing you can do" – he took a breath – "is stay safe. Don't worry. Don't . . ."

He trailed off, looking into the drink. Holly waited only a moment before starting up again. "Darren Barton, you listen to me. I am not impressed. I am not happy at all. You tell me where you are this instant, and I will come and I will –"

"I love you, Holly," he said, quietly. The quiet *I love you* of a man who was afraid he might not get to say it again. Holly's voice quivered in reply.

"I love you too, Darren," she said. "You come back to me. You bring our daughter back, with you, or I'll never forgive you, you hear me?"

"I hear you," he said, then hung up.

He lifted the canister and took a hearty swig. This sweet, vile drink had taken him many places in the past. It was time it took him to the one that had got his friend killed.

10

Pax was relieved to find Grace where she had left her. The poor girl hadn't even tried the door since they'd gone. Checking the rafters to make sure there was no one else around, as though she could even see the tiny people, Pax raced to Grace's side. She put an arm around her and Grace flinched away. "Please don't hurt me please don't hurt me!"

"Everything's going to be okay," Pax whispered, more to herself than Grace.

Hearing her voice, Grace lowered her arms and looked into Pax's face. She was stuck halfway between relief and renewed fear. "You? Did you . . . are you . . .?"

"Oh God, no!" Pax waved a hand towards the door. "I'm not a part of this. I'm getting you out of here. Taking you home."

Grace nodded quickly, and Pax helped her up. Grace asked, "Is my dad here?"

"I've got no idea where your dad is," Pax said, taking stock of the girl. Her bare legs were turning blue. She'd suffered the night in this place. "It's okay. I know someone else who can help us."

The steel door slid open a few inches with a piercing screech. Bees poked his head out and stared at Pax as though her presence was a complete surprise. Then he saw Grace and his eyes relaxed. He was wearing a white apron and face mask, sprayed up and down by barely dried blood. His neutral voice betrayed nothing as he said, "It's cold, you shouldn't be out dressed like that."

Grace merely lowered her gaze, meekly, as Pax led her into the building. Bees closed the door behind them.

"Got any food?" Pax asked, rubbing her hands together.

"Yeah." Bees pointed. "Got a blanket in the office too, for the little one. Do us a favour and don't look into the main room. Save you asking questions and save me giving answers." He regarded Grace. "You sure she should be here?"

"No choice right now, no time to piss about," Pax said, and

Bees nodded. That was that. He walked ahead down the corridor, and Grace gave Pax a nervous look. A mechanical drill, or a saw, or something, whirred somewhere in the building. Pax fought the urge to turn in the direction of the sound, to where the building opened up to some kind of factory floor. In her line of work, avoiding seeing certain things might help you live longer. A tip, she realised, which she should have given herself a few days ago.

Bees led them up some stairs and into an office. After Pax and Grace entered, he closed the door and went to the fridge. He gestured to a dusty couch, and they planted themselves down as he took out a tray of sandwiches: a variety of flavoured triangles, such as might be found at an academic conference. He tossed the tray onto the coffee table, then threw a heavy blanket to Grace and took out a can of beer. Pax turned down a beer herself, but started shovelling small sandwiches into her mouth. Grace was more hesitant, but once she got her first bite she quickly overtook Pax, famished.

Bees watched the pair patiently.

"I think my apartment's burnt," Pax started explaining, finishing a messy mouthful. "The Ministry guys chased me out of West Farling, and they know where I live. But I need to get something out of there. Fast."

"Who's the girl?" Bees nodded to Grace. Grace paused mid-bite, frightened.

"Separate problem," Pax said. "Kind of. I'm taking her home."

"What happened?"

"Basically…" Pax sat back. "I saw too much."

"Think they're gonna kill you?" Bees asked, as though asking about the weather.

"I think they'd like to question and torture me first." Pax saw Grace hadn't moved, shocked still. Bees nodded, though, like that was a good thing. "I've got nowhere else to go, Bees."

"It's just the MEE. We can put feelers, see what it'd take to get them off your back."

Pax stared at him for a moment. Of course, Bees would come to her rescue, digging in the hooks of debts. She took another sandwich while she chewed the prospect over. He looked like he could wait a decade for an answer. Grace still hadn't moved.

"I've got no intention of owing you," Pax said. "Or your boss."

"Didn't think you would," Bees said. "There's options, though.

You want money, we could stake you for a cut, no debt involved. I can vouch for you. But you're not *that* good, so you're not going to find the terms favourable."

"It's not money I want right now."

"Indeed. Option two would be more interesting to both of us." Bees took a deliberate sip of beer. The drill in the factory below got louder, then skipped a beat, followed by a loud curse. He ignored it. "I value information. As does my boss and as, I'm sure, do you. You've got information people might kill you for. See to sharing that and we can make other arrangements."

"They'd come after you, too," Pax replied.

"I can handle myself," Bees said, and she didn't doubt it.

"Right." Pax took another moment. Faced with the prospect of sharing the secrets of the Sunken City, she realised again how important that information was. She studied the office, appreciating exactly where they had ended up. The desk was thick with dust, likely never used for paperwork. The real work was done below. Work involving aprons and masks and blood. Bees and his associates were the least responsible people she could involve in this. But she needed help.

She cursed Letty for abandoning her. Just when it seemed like she had an ally. However vicious the little woman was, Pax felt there was something good in her. Or at least some affinity with hers. But she was gone now. And this was her backup option. The fruition of friendlessness.

 If she could keep Bees just far enough from the truth, she could work it out. Letty and the Fae couldn't be trusted to do anything good; even if they put an end to the minotaur, which she doubted the would, they weren't saving Rufaizu. They weren't looking out for Ordshaw. The sole means to turn the whole situation around sat in Pax's apartment, in her cupboard. She frowned, uncomfortably acknowledging these weren't thoughts that would get her free and clear.

"I trust you, Pax," Bees said, seeming to respond to her uncertain face. "Enough that I'd tell you what's going on downstairs and know that information would be safe. You can trust me just the same. You want us to help you, we need to know what we're dealing with."

Pax bit her lip. There'd be no going back from it.

There was a shout below. A door slammed and heavy footfalls

rang through the building. Bees' companion burst into the office, announcing his presence loudly. "Snapped the bloody saw head. That's two this morning. This guy must've –"

Howling Jowls Jones was halfway across the office, headed straight for the fridge, before he noticed Pax and Grace. He paused as Pax gave him a light, nervous wave. Dressed in overalls like Bees, he also wore plastic gloves and a hairnet. There was little white showing around his bloodstains, though his cheekbones were sharp and high enough that Pax could make out his smile behind the mask.

"Good to see you, Pax – to what do we owe this pleasure? And who's this young dear?"

"She's in trouble with the MEE," Bees explained.

"The MEE?" Howling Jowls let out his trademark whoop; it was a wolfish sound that Pax suspected he practised. He turned to the fridge to get a beer, pulling his mask down. "So that's why Bees has been waxing lyrical about them. Chewing my ear off about this theory and that theory – why there's no methane in the sewer system, why the skyscrapers in the CC1 postcode have green antenna lights, cover-ups and conspiracy on a national level. Ain't that right? I've heard it all and it all sounds like shit, but here you are." He opened the can. "It's you that's been digging up dirt about them."

"Something like that," Pax said.

"I was telling her," Bees said, "we might find a way to get her clear of a predicament, if she happened to let us in on the details."

"Now there's a proposition," Jones swung his beer can around. "I'd be game just to shut him up. There's no aliens in Ordshaw, are there? Or is it a water supply scandal? Give me *strength*." He spun away from Pax, letting out another whoop. He was going to keep talking, that's what these guys did. But time was an issue. "It'd be fun if I didn't already know no government ministry ever did anything more interesting than filing shifty budgets. The MEE. Give me *strength*."

"They're hiding a secret network of tunnels." Pax rushed it out. Jones froze with his eyes and mouth equally wide open.

Bees placed his beer can aside. "What kind of tunnels?"

"Ones that run all over the city. They're extremely dangerous."

"Dangerous structurally, or some other way?" Bees asked.

"Some other way."

Jones turned to Bees and they exchanged a look. Jones cleared his throat. "Pax, you're bright, we all know that. If you're talking about a network of tunnels that might get us from A to B unseen, you'd be talking about something our boss would take a *real* strong interest in. You'd know that, wouldn't you, before bringing up a thing like that? You'd need to be thinking that this is something you *really* want to share."

"I think it could get you in a lot of trouble," Pax said, "but if you can help me out, you're welcome to the problem."

"You got a map?" Bees asked.

Pax shook her head. "I know where a couple of entrances are."

"Monitored by the MEE?"

"Yeah," Pax said. "They're not so interested in the tunnels as in what's down there."

Jones let out a loud, heartfelt laugh. "Stop being dramatic. What's down there?"

"That's as much as I'll give you right now. Here's the cut." Pax stood up, to firm her point. "There's stuff I need from my apartment and I don't feel safe going back there. I need it yesterday, because there's other people after it. Not the Ministry – they might be watching the place, but they don't know what's there. You help me and I'll tell you where to find an entrance to these tunnels. I'll give you some idea of what's down there, but you need to see it for yourself. And I want to be 100%, before we start this, in saying I think you should *not* go down there. Got it?"

"All right," Bees replied carefully. "What's this stuff you need?"

As they walked away from their factory, Pax let out a breath of relief, freed from the stress of being in the same room as the two bloodied men. Grace asked, quietly, "Who were they?"

"Just friends."

Pax didn't like the answer herself. Too many of her suspicions about them were being confirmed, a step beyond imagining she lived in a dangerous world to knowing it for sure. Contrary to what they had said, she did not know exactly why their boss would be interested in the tunnels, but the best case scenario involved contraband. The very best case. She might have just contributed to a criminal enterprise, but it had to be better than whatever was already down there.

"I'd really like to go home now," Grace said.

Pax gave her a smile. "That's exactly what we're doing." The teenager did not look convinced. This detour probably had her questioning whether she had even been freed. Pax's smile faded. "I'm not a part of the bad stuff. Honest. I need those guys to help me the same as I'm helping you, that's all. You'll be fine."

Grace nodded, clearly filled with doubt.

Pax sighed and kept on walking. She checked her phone and saw a missed call from an unknown number. It gave her pause. Had Letty changed her mind and wanted to get back in touch? Maybe she would help out after all, and she could call off Bees and protect the secret of the Sunken City. But the voice she heard when the voicemail clicked on was not Letty's. It was a woman who sounded equally hostile.

"This is Holly Barton. You spoke with my husband. I'd like to speak with you myself. Call me back."

Pax turned to Grace. "See. That was your mum. She's waiting for us."

11

Letty was received without the flanking honour guard that typically shielded the Fae leader; Valoria had chosen discretion above safety now, and only her bodyguard Hearlon attended their meeting. The brick-headed goon strode into the dugout room, a cavity in the concrete walls, and all but pressed into Letty in the tight space. When he moved to frisk her, she raised a warning finger.

"You fucking dare."

Every time they met, he backed down with an expression that said he'd like nothing more than to punch her face off. The feeling was mutual. Hearlon stepped aside, settling for the threat of resting his hand on the handle of a pistol, holstered at his shoulder.

Valoria squeezed into the room and looked Letty up and down. "There were reports of your death."

"Guess they exaggerated," Letty replied dryly.

"You were in a Ministry compound," Valoria continued. "You know our thoughts on Fae that leave Ministry compounds alive. My council would have you shot on sight."

"Good thing you know better, huh?" Letty replied, sarcasm dripping off the ceiling. "Guess you're just too damned curious about that Dispenser, aren't you?"

The governor kept calm, making a clear effort to tune out Letty's attitude. "Of all the Fae I know, I'd imagine you to be the least likely to be turned by the Ministry. But yet, I must ask." She didn't.

"The fuck do you think?" Letty said. "As to what they got from Rufaizu, though, I couldn't say. Your people haven't taken care of that, have they?"

"The Roma's fate is uncertain."

"I can certain it," Letty said coldly. "He's alive enough to have ratted on me."

"That's disappointing. But your team hardly helped matters."

"No? Seems to me they've made some kind of progress. Seems

to me it's something we need to discuss. In pretty serious terms. Things are moving forward, Val. At long last. You know what we've uncovered, right?"

Valoria fixed her with an icy stare, designed to make Letty uncomfortable. Letty didn't get uncomfortable about people's looks. She stared right back.

"Do you expect me to be impressed?" Valoria said, each word thick with bitterness.

"Are you on the cusp of getting the Dispenser back or what?"

"No thanks to you."

"No thanks to – are you fucking serious? I'm the one that got Rufaizu onside. It was me that organised to have –"

"It was *you* who got it stolen in the first place. And from what I can gather, your men used their own initiative to get it back, not yours."

Letty could feel the colour rushing to her cheeks. "If they had followed through with my plan, you wouldn't have had this human collateral to deal with right now."

"Nevertheless, the Dispenser is all but secure. And your . . . boys' . . . security has already been negotiated. It did not involve you."

Letty's eyes bulged with hate. "You know it was my project, those are my –"

"You dealt with humans without our go-ahead, you led an attack on a Ministry compound, you got yourself injured, if not caught – there is nothing in any of this that suggests you deserve a reward, Letty. Your team performed better, and quicker, without you."

"This is bullshit and you know it."

"This was *inevitable* and you know it. Your back-street diplomacy got you nowhere and your half-measure violence threatened us all. So here you are, where you belong. Outcast."

Valoria turned on her heel, as though that was all there was to say. As she moved away, Letty surged forwards to curse and throw fists and shoot if necessary. Hearlon moved faster, though, pistol drawn and aimed at her chest. Letty stopped, but wasn't done.

"This is *bullshit*!" she repeated, louder. "You're bullshit! How are you gonna use the Dispenser without human help? You need me if you want the Citizen onside, at the very least! You can't keep forcing a brute like that!"

"It's time you left," Hearlon told her.

"You can't keep me out!" Letty roared at Valoria's retreating back. "I know how to make things work with the humans! I've got friends!"

Valoria paused. All but out of view, she turned back but kept her distance. "We don't need human friends, Letty. Why did you never understand that? Your *friends* give us all the more reason to keep you away."

"You honestly think we can reclaim the Sunken City without at least a little human help?" Letty growled, but as she said it she saw that there was no question in Valoria's eyes. Letty frowned, thinking of the dumb questions Pax had raised. Was there a chance the Fae didn't want to use the weapon? Did Apothel know something she didn't, when he stole it? "Do you even want to take it back?"

Valoria gave her a slight smile, not deigning to answer. Letty saw what it meant, with such surprise she had to look to Hearlon to share it, no one else to turn to. "You know what's going on here?"

Hearlon said nothing, trained to lack emotions.

"You never belonged here, Letty," Valoria concluded. "You never understood. Our relationships are nuanced, our place in this world layered – you cannot shoot your way through everything."

"What the *fuck* are you saying?" Letty snapped. "You've got the whole of the FTC waiting to reclaim what's ours, who gives a shit about nuance?"

"I'm being incredibly generous not punishing you for what you've already done," Valoria said, the first strains of impatience entering her tone. "Keep talking and you'll leave me no choice. Walk away, Letty. Let it go. It's probably better that our people still think you're dead."

Letty bared her teeth. "Where are my boys?"

"They won't want to see you," Hearlon answered.

"Who the fuck asked you?" Letty shouted. "Are they in the city? Are they still working? Fucking give me something! I'm out here with one goddamned wing!"

"They're putting everything you started to rest."

Letty looked from Hearlon to Valoria, neither giving anything else away. She shook her head, saying, "Out of order. You're bang out of order."

"This is the first and only lesson you need to learn, Letty," Valoria said. "They're only humans."

Letty backed off, still eyeballing them both. Without another word, she turned and ran.

Mix and Fresko were, at that moment, standing side by side in the rafters at the Innovation Centre. Both regarding the emptiness of the room. The lock had been shot by a Fae gun, but there was no sign of violence. Mix lit his cigar, speaking through the side of his mouth. "What do you make of it?"

"I don't get the why," Fresko said. "Must've been Fae, someone who knew we'd been here. Don't see what they'd gain from boosting her. Or why they'd do our job for us. Doesn't make sense. But we need to be sure, don't we?"

"How's that?" Mix took a deep puff, blew smoke in Fresko's direction.

"We go to her house and check she hasn't escaped."

"To her house," Mix repeated.

"Yeah." Fresko shouldered his rifle. "Either someone already did away with her, and we got nothing to worry about, or someone helped her out. And took her home."

"One of our own?" Mix raised an eyebrow.

"We can figure out the why of it later," Fresko said. "Right now, let's finish the job."

Mix grinned and slapped Fresko's back. "Now you're talking my language."

12

Pax and Grace had made it to a street corner in Ten Gardens by the time Holly caught up to them. Though her energy was waning, Pax wanted to keep moving as long as it took to put a distance between herself and the Fae, and the sight of clean streets and stoop flowerpots was welcome. As they waited for Holly, Grace struggled to make conversation, with meek questions about how Pax was feeling and how far they had to walk, too tired for anything else. When Holly skidded her car up next to them, Grace's energy barely came back. She mustered a smile and a hug for her fussing mother, but that was all. She crept into the back seat and all but fell asleep.

Holly stayed out of the car, halfway between scolds and blessings. "Oh thank God you're all right. You had me so worried! What were you thinking? I'm so glad you're safe!" She turned on Pax. "What happened? Where's she been?"

Pax took a moment before responding, partly from the force of this sharp woman, partly from confusion at her attire. Holly was dressed in jeans and a t-shirt with an important-looking crest and the words *Professional Wine Taster – Free Consultations Offered*. Not taking Holly for one with a sense of humour, Pax took a moment to realise that the t-shirt was a joke, by which time Holly was ranting on. "Speak, would you? You don't think I'm owed an explanation?"

During their walk, Pax had thought about what she might say or do when Holly arrived, and now it was time to put it into action. Rescuing Grace wasn't just a means to do good; it presented an opportunity. She needed somewhere to lay low while Bees did his bit, and no one was likely to go looking for her in the suburbs. She said, "I'll explain what I can, if you take me with you. I'd like to make sure Grace is okay. And . . . to see your husband."

Holly gave her an uncertain look. She quickly made the decision, though. "Get in." She rushed back to the driver's seat.

Pax scanned the road, as though they might be under surveillance already, then she got into the car. Holly spun the tyres pulling out, and started throwing looks back to Grace, who was curled up like a child trying to sleep on the sofa.

"Young lady. You tell me what's going on."

"Someone with a gun," was the best Grace could offer. "A man. I never saw him."

"Where? How?" Holly asked urgently, but her questions came too quick to answer. She turned on Pax. "You know who it was?"

"Kind of," Pax said.

"Kind of? My daughter's been kidnapped and the best you can do is *kind of*? That's not good enough. We're going to the police."

"No!" Pax said firmly, imagining the police handing them straight over to the MEE. "They'll only get worse people involved. Trust me – the best thing for us right now is to get you both home."

"Are you out of your mind?" Holly thumped a hand into the steering wheel. Pax gave her a moment to calm down. Holly took a deep breath, in through the mouth and out through the nose, as though she had been trained to do it. She said, "I just think that when a teenager has been abducted by a man with a gun, the police are the logical people to get involved. Don't you?"

"I would," Pax agreed, "if it was a man that did it. They weren't men, though. Not as you understand the term."

Holly glared at Pax, doubt in her eyes. She knew there was more to this. Yet she ventured, hopefully, "Transvestites?"

Pax shook her head. "Is your husband home?"

"He went looking for Grace. You haven't seen him?"

"No. I tried to call him."

"I'm going to give him such a talking to when he gets back, don't you worry. Damn all of this." Holly frowned. "How did you find Grace?"

"It's a long story," Pax said, quietly.

"You'll tell me, though. Someone has to tell me something or I'm going to do something terrible. I'll drive this car straight off a bridge, or I don't know what. He is going to get *such* a talking to!"

Pax stared at the side of her head. There was no way for Holly to cope. Raise your family, live your happy life, get your ducks in a row and finally have your daughter kidnapped by something that wasn't a man. Suddenly you have no reasonable way to deal with it.

Holly gave Pax another questioning look. "Who *are* you?"

"No one," Pax sighed. "A card player." It was an answer that never failed to pique people's interest, and even Holly's hard façade softened in surprise.

"That's . . . all you do? I mean – your work?"

"Yeah. Pretty much."

"And . . . Darren plays?"

"No," Pax said. "He doesn't know me. Honestly."

Holly concentrated on driving for a minute longer, apparently deciding how to continue. "My husband has told me very little about all this. I need to know more. Why was my daughter taken? Why on earth won't the police do something about these maniacs?"

"I can't pretend I know everything. But what I do know is hard to believe."

"I saw a horse playing a drum, with an invisible horn, and I saw a blue square writing things on a wall. I'm willing to give you the benefit of the doubt." Pax frowned. The descriptions sounded familiar. Things from the Miscellany. In her pause, Holly bowled on. "I can pay you."

"Excuse me?"

"Cash." Holly offered it quickly, as though the thought was dirty. "I can pay you to tell me, just say how much."

"I don't want your money."

"Then what *do* you want?" Holly's voice rose. "Why are you here? Who *are* you?"

Pax stared ahead, looking through the world as she asked herself the same questions. The answer seemed obvious, though, now that she was delivering this innocent girl back to her family. Now that she had sent gangsters to square off against the Ministry, and liberated a fairy who wanted, in her own way, to fight the monsters. Now that she seemed further than ever from being able to help Rufaizu. She wanted her part in this madness to mean something. "I fell into this the same way your husband did. I avoided an ordinary life long enough for the extraordinary to corner me. Now I'm trying to do something about it."

"About *what*?" Holly implored. "My daughter was kidnapped. My husband ran off after Grace with a vile liquid that looked like something a cartoon villain would use to kill rabbits. He's been talking with that blasted woman again and he's been running off talking to this" – Holly threw a hand towards Pax, suddenly speaking as though she wasn't there – "this younger, mysterious woman, and I don't know if I should hate him, and I'm scared." Holly took small, sharp breaths. "I'm scared, for myself, for him, and for my daughter, and I don't want to lose them."

Without saying anything, Grace sat up and shifted forward, apparently having been listening. She put an arm around her mother and rested her head on her seat. Holly fought back a tear, and in a flash, on and off, offered a thin smile. She took one hand off the wheel to pat Grace's arm and whispered, "Thank you, dear."

"It's okay," Grace said softly. "I wasn't hurt. Just frightened."

"That's hardly the point," Holly huffed, coldness returning. "Honestly, you've been missing for a day and all you have to say is you weren't hurt? I despair, Grace, I do. Now, please…" She turned to Pax. "Tell me what you know."

Pax took a breath and began.

Holly listened to the account of Rufaizu, and Apothel's book, and the notes that pointed to Barton. Of the Ministry, and then the tunnels, and the monsters that Holly had no reason to believe in. She responded by mentioning what she had seen herself. The horse and the blue square again, writing on the walls – something Pax realised she understood now. The Blue Angel, communicating as Barton had described it. And it had misled them, only confirming her initial instinct, and Letty's insistence, that whoever was sending those messages was not to be trusted.

Finally came the fateful question. "Who, exactly, took my daughter? What kind of gang are the Fae? Is it something to do with that liquid? Drugs?"

"They're not a gang," Pax said. "Not exactly. And there's a good reason Grace never saw them, even if I don't quite get how they pulled it off."

Holly slowed down as they turned into a familiar street. Pax went quiet as the green of the Bartons' neighbourhood glided into view. Grace pressed towards the window, smiling at her home, no doubt sensing the nightmare was over.

"Don't worry dear," Holly assured her. "You're safe now. We just need to figure out where your father got to." She turned to Pax. "You'll stay with us, won't you? You'll help bring this to an end?"

Pax nodded. Let's settle into this paradise, she thought. Have a cup of tea, put on the gas fire and wait for Barton to come home. Wait for the bad men to finish whatever needed to be done across town. Worry about how she was going to use the Dispenser when it was back in her possession. In the meantime, she could try and explain why the Barton family were in the crosshairs of two-inch-tall psychopaths.

Why not.

13

Casaria split his attention between watching Pax Kuranes' church apartment block and flashing nasty looks into the rear-view mirror at Gumg. The younger agent's face had swollen where he had been struck, taking on a satisfying tinge of purple, and every time he met Casaria's eye he looked away. It was a good way to pass the time, Casaria had discovered, inciting unease by staring at this subordinate clown. He needed the entertainment to take his mind off Pax's betrayal. She had promised so much but, like him, she was too rebellious. Quite the opposite of Sam Ward's stuffy ministerial ambitions, Pax was actually showing loyalty to the monsters. She might still see the error of her ways, but it was unlikely. The damage was done and he'd have to take care of her. To save the thought, he distracted himself by glowering at the moron in the back of the car. Landon was handling the real work, after all, by motionlessly watching the building's entrance. He was built for this kind of job, silently fixing his eyes on a point and doing the sweet sum total of piss all.

"What?" Gumg snapped, at last.

"Huh?" Casaria feigned innocence. "Something wrong?"

"What's your problem?" Gumg shifted in his seat.

"Easy," Landon warned in a monotone, not looking back. "We're here to do a job."

"No," Gumg insisted. "He's messing with me. Trying to get a rise, dammit!"

"Looks like it's working," Landon answered tiredly.

"He oughta be sent home," Gumg continued. "You saw what he did. He's mad."

"Have you taken him down the tunnels yet?" Casaria asked Landon.

"Hey, I'm talking – you hear me?" Gumg said. "You're a lunatic! This is assault, I'll –"

"Have you?" Casaria pressed. Landon turned slowly to him, then gave a disinterested glance back to Gumg. "Didn't think so.

You can see it in him. Green as the grass."

"Green?" Gumg protested. "You think anyone *needs* to go down there? We've got databases – hotlines – diplomacy for crying out loud. You're a gatekeeper, man – that kind of attitude – that – it's no wonder you're still out on street patrols, instead of doing things that matter."

Landon raised an eyebrow, making Casaria smirk. This hotshot thought he was on the fast track to a better position in the Ministry, didn't he? Like all their worst recruits. Landon didn't say anything, but Gumg caught the look and cooled off. He said, "Are you gonna report him? Because I will."

"Oh, I'd love that," Casaria said. "Tell Mathers exactly what happened. How are you gonna make firing a gun across a crowded street sound like something that *doesn't* warrant quick preventative action?"

Gumg glared back. He gritted his teeth. "What about the man you beat up?"

"Beat *down*." Casaria grinned, entirely unapologetic. "Have you ever seen a sickle?"

"Stop avoiding the question."

"Hesitate with a sickle and it'll tear your arms off," Casaria said. "I've seen it. I know how to avoid that sort of thing. Whether it's a sickle or a man on the street. The Ministry respects that kind of decisive action more than your ability to file reports."

"The Ministry would prefer to keep things calm," Landon said, though his attention remained on the church. "For whatever reason you think they let you get away with this stuff, it's only because we're understaffed."

"Like hell. I've got a specialist skillset."

"Disparaging as this recruit may be," Landon said, too dry to even bother looking at Gumg, "he's right. You're not supposed to go into the tunnels. You don't need to fight a thing. Quite the opposite. You should be more discreet."

"It's people like you that let the Fae get the drop on us, that let this happen." Casaria held up his bandaged hand.

"As far as I'm aware," Landon droned, "you poked that hornet's nest yourself."

Casaria met his eyes with contempt. He left it there, deciding this waste of fat was not worth convincing. Gumg was right about one thing: *these* agents were nothing more than glorified zookeepers. One with aspirations to follow in Sam Ward's desk-bound footsteps, the other with no aspirations at all. They didn't understand that there was a delicate balance that could only be maintained on the ground level. That the Ministry needed the likes of Casaria to do the unthinkable in times when no other option remained. Landon and Gumg didn't understand the Sunken City. Rufaizu probably knew more than they ever would.

Landon nodded towards a white van. "There's two men over there, waiting to go in. Recognise them?"

Casaria followed his gesture. It was a rusty Vauxhall, no windows at the rear. Both men were larger than average, one darkened by stubble, the other sporting greasy golden curls. They looked like people you might regret hiring to evict squatters, when they accidentally crippled a harmless student.

"Couldn't see Pax hanging with their sort," Casaria decided.

"They're looking at us like we should be looking at them," Landon said.

"How long have they been there?"

"About as long as you've been patting yourself on the back for being a loose cannon," Landon replied, without any humour. Casaria wondered, in that moment, if he could contrive a way to cut his heart out. "Looks like they've had enough."

The van doors opened and the two men got out. They were both easily over six foot four, burly though neither in especially good shape. In their workmen's boots, ragged dungarees and shirts patterned by incongruous stains, they belonged at a roadside diner. They stared at Casaria's car as they walked purposefully towards Pax's apartment building. Their unblinking looks were a challenge, daring the agents to follow them in.

"Here's what's going to happen," Casaria said. "We're going up to her apartment, and when they give us trouble, we're going to give them trouble back. If either of you has a problem with that, I'll do it alone. But say it now, because I'm not having you get in the way."

"Maybe they're not connected to her," Gumg suggested, anxious.

"They bloody well are, and they *are* going to cause trouble," Casaria replied firmly.

"We should call for backup," Landon suggested warily. "Or just follow them."

"*You're* the backup," Casaria hissed. "Come or don't, but don't get in my way."

*

"It was on the radio," Bees said, climbing the stairs as he continued the conversation from the van. "Back in the '80s, a sewage worker found it. He was curious about this smell from the drains, see. Knew how the system worked, so looked into it himself, and what did he find? A whole bloody tunnel that wasn't on the maps."

"You're confusing it with the Fallout Train," Howling Jowls Jones replied. "There's a system in the south-east of the city that allegedly connected directly to London, they set it up during the Cold War. That was what the sewage worker tapped into, and they blocked it all up because it wasn't safe. I took that to Mr Monroe once. He said his people already tried it, but it didn't go under the city, just touched the south-east corner."

"*I'm* his people that told him that," Bees said as they reached the third floor landing. He lumbered towards Pax's door and took out her key. "I'm not talking about the Fallout Train, this was something else. Listen, see, on the radio, when they interviewed this guy –"

Bees stopped, key in the lock, and turned around, with great deliberation, towards the movement he'd seen from the corner of his eye. Jones turned with him, folding his arms as he stared at the man in the suit that had followed them up. Leaning against the wall, Casaria smiled, pearly white, straight-cut teeth.

"Not subtle, are you?" Bees said.

"Look who's talking," Casaria replied.

"We're picking up some things for a friend. No business of yours."

"We all know that's not true."

"Whatever," Bees said, turning back to the door. He opened it and looked into the apartment, then back at Casaria. The suited man hadn't moved. Bees said to Jones, "Wait here, yeah?"

"Yeah," Jones replied, eyes locked on Casaria. As Bees went inside, Casaria moved to follow him and Jones stepped in the way, a mass that almost filled the door. "Invitation only."

"I'm sorry," Casaria said. "You don't know what you're getting involved with here. I've no doubt you're not close enough to Pax that you'd risk your lives for her."

"Who's risking their life?"

Bees only vaguely listened as he opened up the cupboard and

scanned for the things Pax had wanted. The little money safe, the book too. The mechanical device was strange. He'd have a think about that later.

"You're not taking anything away from here," the guy in the hall was saying.

Bees took a moment to give the apartment one last look. He wasn't sure if the spare clothes he'd collected were clean or not, but that didn't really matter. It might be an idea to discuss a few matters of personal hygiene with Pax, anyway. She'd seemed to have been keeping a pet in a shoebox lacking amenities, and all. As he lumbered back to the door, he found two newcomers standing in the stairway entrance, behind Casaria, both hesitant to move into the corridor.

Casaria stepped back, smiling wider than ever, and his jacket fell open to reveal a pistol.

"He's got a gun, Bees," Jones commented. "Says he can't let us leave."

"That's a shame," Bees replied. He drew his own pistol from the back of his trousers and held it up. It was a large revolver, the sort that looked too heavy for the average man to lift. Usually enough to convince people to rethink their life choices just by looking at it. He twisted it from side to side as the two new arrivals backed into the wall, stunned. Yeah, these weren't the sort that were used to having someone tell them *no*. To drive his point home, Bees said, "I've got this, see, and I don't think I want to let him stop us."

"You poor, clueless morons," Casaria said, the smile still fixed on his face but the humour gone. Bees' gun was out while the agent's was still deep in its holster. The suit had balls, you had to give him that.

"Ministry of Environmental Energy?" Bees said, looking from one man to another.

Jones commented, "Seems to me civil servants shouldn't be threatening the public on matters of picking up things from a friend's apartment."

"Maybe you fancy yourselves as special kinds of civil servants?" Bees said.

"Casaria," the bigger man warned, as close to the stairs as he could get without moving down them. He had the right idea. "Perhaps we should let the gentlemen –"

"Don't be a damned coward, Landon," Casaria replied. "We're not going anywhere until I see what's in that bag."

Bees shrugged. "You're welcome to stay."

"Here's what I suggest," Casaria said. "You leave the bag and go on your way, with the knowledge that you're still intact and did the right thing. No one needs to get hurt on Pax's account."

"Oh, that sounds lovely," Bees replied, his gravelly tone suggesting the opposite. "Only we already told Mr Monroe we were coming, and he'd be very disappointed if our deal fell through. Unless you yourselves wanted to give us what she offered us?"

"What did she offer you?" Landon asked suddenly, concerned.

"We're not giving you anything," Casaria said. "And neither is she."

"Awful shame," Bees said, turning the gun in his hand again. "Awful shame."

Bees lifted the revolver, but before he could make any further threat Casaria sprang forward. For a relatively slight man, he moved with tremendous speed and force, his full weight meeting Bees' chin headfirst as the gun went off. Bees snapped back into the wall and flopped to the floor, eyes losing all focus. As Jones tried to draw a weapon of his own, Casaria drove an elbow into his ribs.

Jones stumbled aside but was not down. With a few feet between himself and Casaria, he raised both hands in guarded fists. Bees blinked heavily, trying to clear his head, his own hands limp against the floor. The scuffle before him was a hazy blur; Casaria skated around the hallway, light on his feet, laughing excitedly. Jones took a swing, missed. Casaria swung back and connected. With Jones momentarily stunned, the smaller man started pounding at his body, but Jones recovered and returned the punches. It was like watching a fox attack a bear. They scuffled around each other, exchanging short, nasty strikes, before separating and stumbling apart.

Bees pushed himself back against the wall and up to his feet, checking the floor for his pistol. He looked up as Casaria moved away from Jones, touching a hand to a bleeding lip, head shaking.

Jones flexed, rolling his muscles, inviting another bout.

"Don't move!" Landon shouted from beyond them. Jones looked sideways, finding the agent's pistol trained on him.

Landon was nervous, hands shaking even with both of them clamped on the gun. It was the sort of nervous that could see a gun going off.

Casaria deflated, saying, "Seriously? *Now* you do something?"

"That's enough, Casaria, you damned lunatic," Landon snapped. "Just get the bag."

Casaria glared at Landon, apparently upset about taking orders.

Bees spotted his gun, way over in a doorway. He exchanged a glance with Jones, who was shaking his head. They were covered. These guys were too erratic to test. A more professional bunch of spooks would've been easier to take down. Bees glowered at Casaria.

"We'll come after you," he said. "Mr Monroe doesn't like to be disappointed."

"Mr Monroe can sit on a rusty dildo," Casaria snorted. He picked up the bag from the middle of the hall and looked inside, frowning at the contents. He pulled out the mechanical device, regarding it with an expression that said it was a mystery to him. As he put it back in the bag, he gave Bees and Jones one last, questioning look. He didn't ask, though, and went towards the stairs. "Let's go."

"What about them?" Landon said. "They attacked an officer of the –"

"You want to arrest them?" Casaria called back, already halfway down the stairs. "Be my guest!"

Bees glared at the overweight man as he and his young, terrified colleague gave them worried looks. The older one shook his head, backing off after Casaria, and offered a moronic parting comment. "You boys stay out of trouble."

14

Barton scanned the red-brick wasteland, holding up the useless instrument Rimes had given him and still getting nothing that resembled a response. It didn't matter. He was confident that it didn't work, now that he could see the trails of colourful light hanging in the air. The pain from his injuries had gone. His niggling doubts and fears, too. The drink gave him focus: a narrow, sharp mind to follow the trail and do what needed to be done.

Destroy them all.

He had picked up the trail easily after swigging from the canister of glo. He could sense the flutter of wings and muted voices from half a mile away. He blundered towards them. Then he saw them emerge from between the abandoned buildings, talking in hurried tones. "Let the FTC sort it out, we take care of ourselves first."

They flew between the buildings like a pair of dragonflies, black shapes against the sky that would not usually have warranted a second look. Barton was used to the tricks of the Sunken City, though, and knew not to trust his eyes. When he squinted he could see through the mirage. The insects flickered like a heat ray, not entirely solid, though he couldn't see what was hidden underneath. There was no doubt they were fairies. They darted off through the sky, leaving a trail behind, fresh and thicker than the others. The clear glint of gold in the air gradually faded to the pink he had followed to get there. He watched them go, high above the buildings, making a beeline towards the city.

Barton did not follow them. He turned in the opposite direction, continuing along their earlier trails, the ones that were slowly dissipating. They didn't lead to the FTC, he could sense that. He continued until it took him back to the dusty remnants of an office complex. The trail led into a building, and back out. They had made a stop here. He crept inside.

There, in the back room, he found a very different energy. The dull grey cloud that glo revealed as human. Someone had been here. More than one person. It was hard to make out, much less distinct than the trails that fairies left. Frustrated, Barton picked out the pink of the fairies again and followed them back out into the road. From here they might have gone to their camp. Maybe the FTC itself.

The trails ahead were fading. He picked up his pace and clambered over half-fallen walls for the quickest route, and less than a block away he started to see more colours in the sky. Different paths crossed over the pink, some stronger, some weaker. Greens, blues, yellows. Other fairies, heading to a central location somewhere behind the buildings ahead. Was this the hub? The Fae Transitional City itself, up ahead? He dropped Rimes' device and cracked his knuckles. No idea what he would do when he got in there, only that someone was going to answer to him. He took a heavy step forward. A female voice came from somewhere up above.

"Wouldn't do it if I were you."

It had taken Letty longer than she'd have liked to get mobile again, and the result was hardly impressive. After a decade operating outside the FTC, it was little difficulty for her to locate a mechanic in the periphery of the city, but it was another matter to trade for the specific and expensive piece of machinery she needed. Fae disabilities were a niche market that demanded high prices; while alternatives to wings and limbs were available, sometimes even superior to the originals, the funds she had taken from their Bettor Off hideout were scarcely enough. Only through her fiercest haggling was she able to get the minimum equipment required to puff through the sky, with a tractor-engine hum. The fan stabiliser on her back was the flying equivalent of a leg crutch.

At least she was able to move again. She needed to concentrate on matching her surviving wing to the erratic stop-start of the artificial engine, but she could still cross the city quicker than any human.

She headed straight for the Innovation Centre, hoping to catch her boys returning to the hostage before they discovered Pax had screwed up their plan. Assuming they hadn't already done the unthinkable and gone after Barton. Had her leadership really been all that was keeping them from murderous idiocy? Mix, she could understand, he liked to solve things with his guns, but Fresko was at least a little brighter than that. The pair of them must have known that Barton, even if he was a dumb lummox, was not their enemy.

She flew to the research centre and found it empty, the girl long gone and no sign of Pax or her boys. That meant going to the Barton household. On her way out, though, she spotted a suspiciously human shape leaning around a wall, looking in the direction of the city. Given his attempt to hide and his focus on the sky, he was searching for something particular.

Letty floated towards him with a sigh of relief.

Finally, she told herself, some good fortune.

Barton slowly looked up at the voice, fists ready.

"You're incorrigible, aren't you? Gonna punch the sky?" The fairy settled on a windowsill above his head. Barton put a hand over his brow to block out the sun's glare, trying to get a better look at her as she studied him. He could see this one alright. Maybe because she was closer, maybe just not as well masked. She rested the pistol in her hand on a knee. "Shit, what happened to you?"

Barton hadn't got any cleaner since the morning. He had seen his reflection on the way over, skin caked with dried blood and coloured by bruises. So what, he had no desire to speak to this little nightmare creature. He stepped out, preparing to launch at her.

"You wouldn't stand a chance," Letty said. "And what the hell were you thinking to do in *there*?" She screwed a thumb in the direction he had been heading.

"Improvise," Barton said, barely opening his mouth beyond a snarl. The fairy smiled.

"Well, now you don't have to. You can thank whatever God you jizz over that you ran into me. I knew Apothel, lummox. And I know you. We can help each other."

"You *killed* Apothel."

"No. He betrayed me, actually, if you care."

"I don't. Should've come for you people years ago. You've crossed a line now. My daughter. My goddamned *daughter*. Where is she?"

"Last I saw," Letty said, "she was safe. If you're lucky, she's on her way home. We have a mutual friend that was trying to help her."

Barton frowned. "Who? Why?"

"The card player. Except going to your home does not mean safe, right now. The bitch in charge has given orders for a clean-up. That means you, your family, whoever else has touched this."

Barton's face brimmed with anger, his eyes running from the fairy to the direction of their city. "Not if I tear your whole world apart first."

"If I hadn't seen you," Letty told him flatly, "you'd have been shot the moment a scout spotted your face. Still a long way from the FTC. I'd rather keep you alive."

"What's it to you?"

"You know what Apothel was killed for, right? You know why Rufaizu came back?"

Barton glowered at her, echoing the words. "What he was killed for? What *your people* killed him for? Trying to *help* you?"

"Something like that. I just had a very interesting conversation that might've shed some light on that. Some people…" The fairy looked aside, seeming to reflect on her distant, hidden home. "*My* people, have an idea of what's possible. What the device Apothel took can do. And they don't all want to do it."

"What's it matter now," Barton snarled. "You went after my family, you're all –"

"Are you listening to me?" Letty snapped. His response had angered her, causing her to swoop down towards him, and he took a step back as she buzzed in his face. "You want to help your family, you need to do as I say!" He looked at the odd contraption slung over her shoulder, as a single wing flapped at the other side. She wasn't normal, this Fae. "Your family are in the firing line now – Pax too – all because there's people that don't want us to succeed in the Sunken City. Actively fucking sabotaging it. *Listen to me* and we can take them out *together*."

Barton took a breath. He asked, slowly, "Like I said. What's it to you?"

"They fucking cheated me. They're cheating them-fucking-selves. Now, you're gonna take out your damned phone and make a call."

Watching through his scope, Fresko could see activity in the house, but it came to a halt in the living room area. They were exchanging pleasantries or something when the roughly dressed one received a phone call. The others stopped when she held up a hand for quiet.

"Something's wrong," Fresko said.

The one on the phone waved at the others. The mum rushed to the window and drew the curtains, cutting off their view.

"Shit." Fresko sat back from the gun.

"They're going for the blinds," Mix said, pointing. "Take them out."

"I'd get one of them, maybe, then the others go to ground and we have to go in there. No. They think they're keeping safe in there right now. Means we can still do this slow and simple."

"No, numbnuts," Mix said, "it means Barton's alive and he's coming back."

"Can still make it look like an accident." Fresko checked through the scope as the younger lady pulled a blind down over another window. "Set some charges."

"Why bother?" Mix snarled, drawing his pistol. "Let's do this the old-fashioned way."

Fresko hesitated. It was unlikely that Barton could stop them if he did come back, but he added an element of uncertainty. If it was even him they were waiting for. It was the card player who'd taken the call, and she had to have her own plans. She'd found the girl somehow, after all. Fresko thought out loud: "It'd take us five minutes to set the charges."

"And it'd take us ten seconds to shoot the pigs."

"The Ministry can't know it was us."

"Fuck the Ministry," Mix grunted. "Let Val worry about them. Come on, are we Fae or what?"

All the windows of the house had been covered, now. The women inside had to be hunkering down in fear as they waited for their slovenly hero to return. Idiots and cowards. "All right," said Fresko. "It's not every day we get to have some fun. Let's go in."

"Yes!" Mix let out a booming laugh. "I knew you hadn't gone soft!"

15

"What did he say, *exactly*?" Holly demanded as they pulled the last blinds closed.

Pax was moving in a flurry, running from one room to another, checking the walls for holes, any ways for the smallest of creatures to get in. She replied, without looking at Holly, "Lock the doors, close the windows, he's coming back soon and he's got help."

"What help could he have? That mad scientist woman?"

"I don't know, I just know we're not safe," Pax said. "Do you have a chimney?"

"A what?"

"A fireplace, somewhere Santa could drop in!"

"No, we have gas –"

"Vents? Extractor fans? Any gaps in the walls at all?"

"This isn't a country pub, for heaven's sake!" Holly said. "What exactly are you expecting? Rats? Snakes?"

"Worse." Pax stopped and gave her a level look. "Fairies with guns."

Holly held the look for a moment. Grace, hovering at her shoulder, paused too. After processing the word, the mum let out a shrill laugh. "You have got to be joking."

"I said you wouldn't believe it." Pax turned away to keep checking the house, scanning the awnings, the corners. Her urgency, she felt, made Holly pause and take note. "Block any holes you can. Nothing so big as a mouse can get in here. And don't worry, as long as we can keep them out we can work through this. My people are going to bring me something we can use to negotiate."

"Negotiate with fairies?" Holly laughed again, this time without humour.

"Believe me, we need to."

"In there, the toilet." Grace pointed helpfully. "There's a fan above the mirror."

"Thanks." Pax hurried through to the opening. She took off the extractor fan's grate and shoved a hand towel in, blocking it tightly.

"Grace, don't listen to this nonsense," Holly said.

"It's not *nonsense*, mum!" Grace protested. "You don't have a better explanation!" Holly went quiet as Grace dogged Pax's heels. As Pax backed off from the toilet, she bumped into the younger girl, and Grace whispered, "I love your coat."

Pax paused, taken off guard, and checked her tatty fleece-lined jacket. She couldn't help but feel a little warmth at being validated by the teenager. As she muttered, "Thanks," a window smashed.

They all froze, locking eyes as the sound came again, in the living room, followed by glass shattering against the floor. Grabbing Holly by the wrist, Pax pulled her into the bathroom with Grace and shut the door.

"What on earth –" Holly spun back, but Pax kept hold of her, shooting a finger to her lips for quiet. They all listened in deathly stillness. Something moved into the corridor, with the flutter of a tiny bird.

"All right," a man's voice said. "Light up the closet."

"Get down *get down!*" Pax shouted, pulling Holly and Grace to the ground, with not a moment to spare before an eruption of gunshots. The door burst apart in miniature explosions of splintering wood. The sink cracked as though hit by a lightning-fast ball bearing. Grace screamed.

Pax kicked the door out, counting on catching the fairies in the tight space of the corridor. The gunshots paused as she caught the blur of one of them flying to the ceiling, the other twisting around the door.

"Move, quick!" Pax yelled, sprinting for the front door. The two fairies quickly recovered and started shooting as she crashed a shoulder through the plate glass of the door and rolled outside, the wooden frame exploding around her in tiny gunshots. Holly and Grace came out shrieking under the gunfire, ducking the shots that were meant for Pax, and before the fairies could adjust their aim they were outside, too. On her way through the door, Holly dragged the coat rack down and a mess of jackets flapped behind them, bullets tearing through the down of a winter coat.

Pax tried to stand and winced, something stinging her leg. She rolled aside with a cry and landed on the grass, both hands grabbing at her calf where something had gone through. It was at the very rear, her jeans lightly ripped; close to the surface, but a bastard all the same. Warm blood rushed over her hands as she clutched the wound.

"Son of a bitch!" Pax screamed back at the doorway.

"To the car, the car!" Holly cried, taking Grace by the hand. She skidded next to the vehicle, patting her pockets. No keys.

All three of them looked to the front door, as the tiny attackers navigated their way through the mess of coats. Grace let out another scream and picked up the nearest object she could find, a ceramic plant pot. She hurled it.

"Back!" one of the men shouted, as the plant exploded over the entrance. In the mess of shattered pot and scattering earth, one of the shapes appeared to spin out of control and hit a wall.

"More, more!" Holly encouraged her daughter, picking up another pot and throwing it. A short barrage of plant pots followed as mother and daughter threw every unfixed piece of the front garden back at their unseen attackers, creating a cloud of debris.

Pax pushed herself up and limped away from the house. In the momentary respite from the gunshots, Holly took out her phone and started dialling. Pax bowled into Grace and Holly together and pointed down the road, shouting, "Keep moving! Head for the manhole!"

Without questioning her, the two women sprinted. Holly was already shouting into her handset, "Yes! Police! I need the police!"

"No!" Pax yelled, slapping the phone out of her hand. "Just run!"

The gunshots started up again from the doorway. They were more than a building's length away from the door now, though, and the first shots went wide.

"Stay low, Grace!" Pax warned, as she raced past the teenager to the manhole cover in the road. She threaded her fingers into the holes and hauled for all her worth as the gunshots stopped, the fairies either reloading or repositioning.

"What do we do, what do we do?" Grace pleaded.

"Help me!" Pax commanded, and suddenly Grace and Holly were at her side, all three of them taking a grip on the cover and heaving at it.

As the metal shifted, Holly demanded, "How is this going to help?"

An immediate answer came as Pax pivoted the cover behind them and a bullet twanged off it, the makeshift shield protecting her chest. She gave herself only a moment of surprise, then pointed into the opening. "Get in there, now!"

"The *sewer*?" Holly exclaimed.

The gunshots picked up again, another bullet hitting the manhole cover, one scratching the tarmac nearby. Grace and Holly threw themselves into the dark hole. Pax dropped down after them, hearing the man's voice as she fell. "You done preening, get after them!"

Pax's feet found the slippery rungs of a ladder and she dug her heels in as she put all her strength into hauling the manhole cover back over the hole. It shifted and almost swung onto her, making her let go and drop. She fell ten feet onto hard concrete, with a thump and a light splash of surface water. Looking back up, she could see the light of day through a crack in the cover – it hadn't quite fallen into place.

Holly and Grace came to her, trying to help her up, as the small silhouette of a man appeared at the cover's edge. He had a pistol in his hand, which he aimed down at them.

Pax rolled aside, just as the gun went off, its sound echoing through the arched chamber. The three women sprang up and started running again, Holly directing this time. "Over there!"

They ducked around a buttress, falling into shadow. The sound of their deep breathing filled the void, guns quiet.

"Did you see that?" Holly hissed. "It was a – he was small – you'd think the detail to mention was the fact that they're the size of doorknobs, wouldn't you?"

"Not that they've got fucking *guns*?" Pax snapped back at her.

The men's voices filtered down. "Get in there."

"It's no sewer," a second voice said, a higher-pitched one.

"You think I'm stupid?"

There was a pause, and Holly looked questioningly at Pax as they held their breath. Pax crouched slightly, touching a hand to the wound on her leg and flinching at the pain.

"My dad is going to kill you!" Grace suddenly shouted as she leaned around the buttress. "As soon as he gets back, you'll be sorry!"

A gun went off and Grace slipped back into the shadows with another scream, a fraction of her t-shirt tearing as the bullet struck her. Holly screamed too, seeing a dark stain of blood rising to the surface of the material. She slammed a hand onto it, the pair of them ducking back into cover. Pax stared, at a loss for what to do.

"Clipped her," the second man said.

"All right," the first snarled. "Let's cave the place in."

Grace whimpered as Holly dabbed the wound with her torn t-shirt. The hole was clean, like a needle mark to the top of the teenager's shoulder. Bleeding but not severe. Watching them, this innocent mother and daughter, nothing to do with any of this, Pax shook her head. Not right. They shouldn't be here. She shouted down the tunnel, "They don't know anything! All Barton ever wanted was to protect them from it!"

While the fairies paused, Pax took out her phone and rushed through the numbers. She rapidly wrote a text: *In the Sunken City. Fae on us.* Clicked Send.

"Send them out," one of the men replied. "Promise they can go, unharmed."

"They'll kill us," Holly stated, simply. Pax nodded. She looked at the phone again. The message blinked with a cross. Failed to send.

"No signal," Pax said.

One hand on her wound, Grace stood uneasily, Holly helping her. She looked at the phone and suggested, with a pained voice, "You've got one bar. Use the GPS." Pax gave her a confused look and Grace insisted, "Share your location!"

Pax nodded and did as she was told, bringing up the contact.

"It'll show us at home, what use is that?" Holly said.

"They'll be ready for your husband no matter what," Pax warned, "but there's someone else who can help." She clicked Send, sharing her location, and the phone pinged. Success.

"I'm coming in," the rougher fairy shouted. "You know what that means?"

"He's going to shoot us!" Grace cried. Holly held her close, looking desperately at Pax, but Pax was shaking her head.

"No. They can't follow us down here. It'd just . . ." She stopped. She knew exactly what it meant. As one of them descended into the tunnel, the sound of fluttering wings getting closer, something groaned loudly, far away in the tunnels.

The weary squeak of an ancient pipe brought to life.

Grace whimpered. "What is that?"

"You got a choice," the fairy said, closer still. "Come to us, or stay here with them. I can at least promise to make it quick."

"You were with Letty, weren't you?" Pax shouted.

The fluttering paused, but when his voice came it was even more fierce. "Don't even say her name. You goddamned animal. She was a thousand times better than you. I oughta cut your hamstrings and make sure you suffer."

Pax went quiet. They didn't know. She said, "I didn't hurt her. She's *alive*."

The fairy hesitated again.

Another groan. Louder, not so far away.

"You're a liar," the fairy decided, then fired a shot in their direction to end the conversation. The bullet twanged into the brickwork. Pax wanted to argue, to make them see sense, but the fluttering wings retreated. She leant out and saw the blur of the fairy speeding towards the tunnel opening.

"Letty's alive!" Pax shouted. The fairy flew through the crack in the manhole, out of view. "We were helping each other! We tried to find you, at the betting shop!"

There was silence above.

If the fairies had any response to make, it was cut off by the rumbling of monsters. The pipe groan was met by an intense, high-pitched clicking, and Grace's whimpering picked up volume as Holly offered comforting words. Pax looked at the ladder, their only way out, guarded by the fairies, and considered making a break for it.

The higher-pitched one said, "All right, say she's alive. Come back up here and we can talk it through."

Not even halfway convincing. Pax cursed, pushing an angry hand against the wall, and turned to the endless dark of the tunnel ahead.

"Pax?" Holly said, voice strained as she struggled to keep strong. "What are those sounds?"

Pax listened. The tunnel started shaking as though a train was passing by. The clicking noise came again, closer than before. Another groan. Maybe all from one direction.

"What is it?" Grace sobbed.

"This isn't a sewer," Pax said, keeping her voice as steady as she could. "And those sounds aren't natural. We have to move, this way."

"What do you –" Holly started to question, and Pax shoved her, shedding her calm voice. It wasn't going to work.

"There's no time! Run!"

16

"I don't know how she did it," Casaria said loudly, finding it difficult to keep his voice level in the face of Deputy Director Mathers' nonchalance. "But this changes everything. This is a Fae weapon. It could be *the* Fae weapon. You know what it means as well as I."

Mathers was staring at the device on his desk, like he was unsure exactly what it was or where it had come from. He had the same vacant expression as Landon. Another moron who didn't get it. Casaria was sure, though: his instincts had told him the moment he set eyes on it, and a closer look had all but confirmed it. The metal was too intricately crafted to be of human origin. It made sense of everything: Rufaizu hadn't been running a con. He had the weapon all along, the same thing Apothel had been killed for. Something that could do serious harm to the Sunken City. No wonder the Fae had attacked him.

"It could be anything," Mathers mumbled. "Could be a factory part."

"Could be a water filtration system," Gumg offered from his corner.

"No one's killing people to stop them talking about a damned water filtration system!" Casaria said. He took a breath, brushed his hair back into place and shot Gumg an insincere smile. "Sir, I'd like to request that this waste of space be banned from speaking."

Mathers eyed Casaria, then Gumg, unimpressed. He sat back in his leather chair, netting his fingers behind his head. "We'll send it to the lab and have it tested. Then turn it over to the IS Relations Initiative."

"What for?" Casaria exclaimed, voice coming out higher than he'd intended. The mention of Ward's team was like ice down his neck. He made every effort to sound calm. "With all due respect, sir, Sam Ward's diplomats are the last people you want dealing with this. They'll want to talk it over – they'll give the Fae a chance to cover it up, or replace it – or worse."

"The FTC have always denied something like this existed, I don't –"

"Exactly!" Casaria caught himself again. After a pause, he continued, "Either they've been lying all this time, or they didn't know it was still out there. Either way, they want it back now."

"That's for the Initiative to decide."

"You know where we can find the FTC, don't you? Give me a team of ten men to block off all the exits to their hole and we can gas them once and for all."

"No one is entertaining that thought," Mathers replied blandly. "If there *was* a case to be made for exterminating the Fae, it would still rely on an IS analysis, and would require at least four levels of approval beyond that. And that's *if* a case could be made."

"Oh my God…" Casaria dragged out each word. "Don't give me ten men – give me a canister of gas and give me *permission*. I'll do it myself!"

"Why is it so important to you?" Landon grunted. Casaria shot him a look that warned him to be quiet or face violence, but the heavyset agent continued. "What've you got against the Fae? They stay out of our way, we stay out of theirs."

"You ignorant whale!" Casaria surged towards him. "They take advantage of us – because of apologists like Sam who want to *talk* to them. They shot at me! They're murderers and thieves who'd do anything to wipe us out, given the chance."

"No," Mathers said.

Casaria paused, a foot from Landon, and let his fists drop. "Excuse me?"

"I said no."

"No what?"

Mathers tapped the desk near the metallic device, face blank.

"No they wouldn't," he said. "If this weapon is what you think it is, they didn't use it when they made it. They have never claimed to have a weapon that could damage the *praelucente*, but they have made claims of equally important things. The truth is they choose not to use such technology. If it even works."

"The weapon was stolen!" Casaria protested. "That gypsy took it. They've been hunting for it ever since! We thought he was working with them, but he genuinely tried to screw them!"

Mathers' expression finally shifted, looking uncomfortable.

"That really is an ugly word, Casaria. We can't have representatives of Her Majesty's Services referring to people as *gypsies*. It wouldn't do."

Casaria froze, mouth open in surprise. It was all he could do not to explode.

Mathers continued. "Now, as for this, it's a matter for diplomacy, Casaria. Civilised discussion. It's not a case of everyone wanting to kill each other, is it? The Fae speak English, for heaven's sake. The IS Relations Initiative has made excellent inroads with their representatives."

"The Fae speak English," Casaria repeated with disbelief.

"Of course. And we have enjoyed mutual existence for a long time, now."

The deputy director said it as though this was obvious, but Landon and Gumg joined Casaria by frowning at the idea that diplomacy between their species had been so successful. Fae crimes had declined since the Initiative had started, but the thought of them actively working with the MEE was unheard of.

"What exactly are you saying?" Casaria said.

Mathers pointed to Landon and Gumg. "You two, give us a moment."

Gumg wanted to protest but Landon shook his head at him, gesturing to the door. As the pair left, Casaria stood rigid, unblinking, as he glowered at Mathers.

"I'll telling you this because you need to stop," the deputy director said. "You're a night watchman, Casaria. We value your work, you're an effective agent, but know your boundaries. What goes on in the Sunken City at night, and with rogue Fae agents, is not the same as what goes on in the management of the Ministry during the day. There are trade talks, negotiations, politics. Now, I know what it meant to you when Ms Ward was moved up, but it was because she understood all that. You never have. Perhaps it would be best if you talked to her again, I know she'd –"

"This isn't about her," Casaria answered through gritted teeth. "Everything I do down there is to protect our work. For the good of this city – does no one else see that? Seriously?"

"It's for the good of this city," Mathers continued, keeping impossibly calm, "that we don't rock the boat. We don't want to hurt the Fae and they don't want to hurt the *praelucente*."

"You *cannot* trust them. Whatever they tell you –"

Mathers waved a hand for silence. "Calm down. You couldn't understand, not from your position. Let me make this plain for you. Stop this maverick nonsense. We cannot have you assaulting your colleagues and members of the public. Talking about inciting violence, consorting with civilians without proper clearance."

"This was a special –"

"Casaria," Mathers said, more firmly. "Not another word. I want you to stop, right now, or you'll leave me no choice but to suspend you."

"Are you completely stupid –"

"Casaria," Mathers snapped. "That's enough. I'm suspending you for a week. I know you've had a tough few days, so be thankful it's not worse. You're not to set foot in the Sunken City, or anywhere near its entrances, until further notice. Hand in all your weapons and relinquish your vehicle."

"You're making a mistake."

Mathers stood, fastening the buttons on his jacket. He wasn't going anywhere; it was just his signal for Casaria to leave. "I think not."

"Sir." Casaria held his gaze, his passion subsiding as the deputy director's sincerity sank in. He fought the urge to beg. He squeezed his lips shut and asked in a muffled tone, "What about the device?"

"IS will look into it. You have done well and there will be results, don't worry."

"And the girl?"

"She'll be brought in. You will have nothing to do with it."

Casaria left the building flushed with anger, desperate to punch someone. It took all his willpower not to throw Gumg's satisfied face through a window as he passed him on the way out. He stormed onto the street and paced back and forth. They didn't deserve him. They were patsies to the fairies, after all. Sycophants, company men, cowards, bastards. And Sam Ward was their chief agent. It was his biggest mistake, bringing her in.

He'd go through St Alphege's and find someone to take his anger out on. Maybe two or three of them. Maybe he'd track down Mr Monroe and ask for a rematch with his men, they'd be game. Those big bastards could put up a fight. He needed it.

Pumping up, he walked briskly down the road.

He'd use the Tube. For the first time in God-knows-how-many years. It might tire him out slightly, and he was already running on steam from the night before, but a little more tiredness wasn't going to hurt. Why not flirt with the monsters, what difference did it make now. He'd go to the warehouse district and ask for Mr Monroe, that was as good a place to start as any. Then he'd figure out a plan. Get to those fairies, do it for himself, if they weren't willing to take action for the country.

As he marched towards the Underground, his phone beeped. The message stopped him cold.

PAX KURANES has shared her location.

17

The three women hurried down the tunnel, tripping over themselves as they reached out in front of them. The sounds were drawing in, becoming more horrific and unnatural the closer they got. Grace couldn't help but cry more loudly, panic overcoming her. Pax drew alongside her, felt her way to putting an arm around her and whispered, "Keep quiet, it's safer."

Grace choked back her next sob, and Pax felt her tensing in her grip, her head moving, nodding. Her next few breaths were strained, holding back whatever sound was ready to burst out. As they sped along, their footfalls splashing through puddles, a birdlike trill rolled past them.

"Use this wall!" Holly whispered, somewhere to the side.

Pax followed her voice, taking Grace with her, free hand reaching out until it touched brick. The wall curved upwards; it was a small tunnel, after all.

"Light," Grace said. She broke away and raised her voice. "There's a light! Look!"

Pax squinted. Was there something there, or just a trick of the darkness? It looked like a pale line. Grace's feet pattered ahead. Holly started running, too. As Pax got closer the line got bigger. It was definitely a light, a fluorescent one. She slowed down, recalling when that electric force had chased her before.

"Wait, wait!" she shouted, but Grace and Holly were moving away.

"It's another tunnel!" Grace shouted. "Lit up!"

Pax stopped, the light silhouetting the other two as they rushed towards it. It wasn't flickering. It was a clear, solid beam. She took a deep breath and committed, sprinted.

The trio turned into the next tunnel together, finding a long, empty corridor stretching into the distance, lit by occasional luminescent bulbs. They took a moment to stop and stare. Far down the corridor, new bulbs were coming on, one by one, extending the view, as though the system was just booting up.

"There's a door," said Holly, pointing.

"Go for it," Pax said, and Holly and Grace ran ahead. She hesitated, though, looking back the way they had come, towards the approaching sounds. A light came on just above her, making her flinch. Another one came on further back, lighting part of the path they had followed, a wide floor with a film of shimmering water across its surface. Another light, further back, then another. Pax was transfixed, for a moment, by the gradual progression of the lights towards the sounds. Another light, and she gasped. A beast reeled back with a hiss as the light hit it, eyes flashing at her. The light barely stopped it, though. Slowly, inexorably, it dragged itself towards her, filling the tunnel.

Pax ran.

She followed Holly and Grace, who were quickly approaching the doorway. Her heart was swelling as her mind tried to conceive what it was she had seen.

There was another hiss from the tunnel behind, almost upon them.

Holly rattled the door, but it wouldn't move. "It's locked!"

"I can do it, I can do it!" Pax panted, pounding towards them and fumbling a hand into her jacket pocket. Pins, metal pins somewhere in there. Grace and Holly watched with terror, checking in the other direction. Pax made it to the human-sized entrance and its heavy metal door. It had an archaic lock that made her heart sink; there'd be no technique involved here, just trial and error. She started rifling through her picks, thrusting one then another into place, as Holly said, "We can keep moving, this goes on –"

"We get through here, it'll cut off half of what's following us," Pax said, trying another pick. It stuck, jamming in place as though connecting with something. The lock didn't move.

"They're getting closer!" Grace cried.

Pax fumbled, dropping one of the picks. Rather than pick it up she moved on to another one, trying to keep calm. Can't use force, need to feel it out. She shimmied, this way and that. Not working, try another.

Grace screamed and Pax dropped another pick. She looked down the tunnel. The beast had made it to the turning and was coming their way. This tunnel was smaller than the first, it seemed, and their pursuer fully filled it.

"Come on, Grace!" Holly said, pulling her daughter's arm.

"No!" Pax yelled, picking up her pick to try again. "It won't fit through here!"

Holly tried to move but Grace stood fast, staring horrified at the creature.

Pax gave it another glance.

It was a bulbous mass of pulsating flesh, its many folds sucking away the light. What was illuminated was wet with thick slime. Somewhere in its amorphous shape, claws occasionally protruded forwards, dragging it down the tunnel. Towards the centre of its mass, surrounded by blinking golden orbs of eyes, it had a circular maw, an open hole that blew out steam. It moved slowly, its mouth hissing and puffing, claws scraping against the brick, but it was approaching them nonetheless.

"Grace!" Holly shrieked, pulling her daughter again. Grace stumbled towards her, into motion, and the pair were about to move when the door clicked. Pax shot a hand up, dropping more of her picks to catch Grace's other wrist before she moved out of reach. She hauled the teenager towards her, the sudden motion catching Holly off guard and tripping her. As Holly let go, Pax thrust Grace through the doorway, then grabbed Holly under the arms and dragged her in too. She slammed the metal door behind them, just as a jet of steam shot past them.

Beyond the door, the sound of the monster's approach continued, the tunnel creaking under its weight. Behind it, the high-pitched trill and the clicking resumed.

Holly had fallen by the side, sat on the floor staring back at the door with eyes wide in alarm. Grace ran further into the tunnel, hand over her mouth to hold in more screams, as Pax stood dumbly, turning on the spot. The new tunnel descended a few steps into another empty passage, narrow and square this time, lit by smaller and less frequent lights.

The door shook behind them, the beast trying to move it. The hinges shifted, coughing mortar. Pax helped Holly to her feet. "The door won't hold. We need to keep moving."

"What was that?" Holly asked. "What was it, what was it?"

Pax didn't answer. It didn't warrant a name, and a witty response was not forthcoming.

18

Letty had flown ahead, moving as quickly as the artificial wing would carry her. As the central apartments and offices fell away below her, giving way to increasingly spread-out suburban houses, Barton's car trailed behind her. He was driving like a maniac, weaving between cars, swerving around oncoming traffic and running red lights, and she was put-putting through the air like a bloody mechanised blimp. Pathetic.

She was barely ahead of him when she reached his street and saw the mess Barton's home was in. The entrance was caked in soil and broken pottery, glass scattered across the path. Letty searched for signs of life and spotted the manhole cover askew in the middle of the road. Had this arsehole moved his family near one of the Sunken City entrances? She torpedoed down. As she reached the road, car brakes screeched nearby, Barton turning the last corner to get there. Daylight was fading, and his headlights bounced erratically over the street. Letty checked her surroundings: no sign of her fellow Fae.

"Where are you fuckers?" Letty shouted, but the sound of Barton's engine muted her efforts. His car skidded towards her, smoke erupting from under the tires. Barton jumped out, turning towards the devastation of his house, and Letty sprang into the air. "Take cover, you oaf!"

He ducked, dipping behind the car door.

Nothing happened.

Letty flew onto the tip of the door, searching the street. It was empty, the other humans quiet in their homes, a few lights on but no one looking. Barton watched her cautiously.

"Where are they?" he said. He stood away from the car, spotting the manhole cover. A man appeared in an upstairs window opposite them, but when Barton looked his way he ducked back inside. Barton was flicking glances between his home and the manhole cover, torn between them. Letty's eyes were drawn more to the Sunken City entrance.

"That's what I think it is, right?" she asked.

He grunted an affirmative.

Nothing good was coming from this, but the writing was on the wall.

"They're not here," Letty said.

Barton thumped over to the manhole and grabbed the cover with both hands. He gave it one short tug and sent it clanging onto the road. Letty saw the nosey neighbour had re-emerged to watch. Still no one else showing an interest.

Another engine approached, making Barton look up. His car was blocking the road, door open. Letty watched him carefully as he climbed into the hole, no hesitation there. He said, "Guess we part ways here. Do me a favour and piss off."

Letty didn't reply, turning from him to the other car. As Barton dropped out of view, a light flashed on her eyes, from the side, and she followed the glint to a muddle of tree branches. It flashed again, a red light, scanning across her eyes. A signal.

"Oh shit," she said. "Barton! It's a trap, don't –"

Too late.

With a blast and a thick puff of brick and mortar, the manhole collapsed. The road fell into the entrance, like a sinkhole, fissures spreading across the tarmac as the street shook. It had come down directly on top of Barton. He was gone beneath it, no sound as the dust settled. The approaching car skidded to a halt. The man in the house flapped his frightened hands and was joined at the window by an equally shocked woman.

"You fucking idiots!" Letty roared, buzzing towards the tree. She sped through the leaves, to where Fresko was drawing his rifle back up against his shoulder. As she got closer, his satisfied expression contorted to surprise, reading her anger. He stood. "It *is* you. We thought –"

She didn't let him finish, slamming into him. Fists balling over his shirt, she lifted him up off the branch, through the air, and drove him into the next branch up. She pinned him there with her full weight, wing flapping and artificial engine whirring, forearm shoved into his throat. "What the fuck were you thinking?"

Fresko's face flushed red, then blue, blood restricted. He struggled, but the initial impact had knocked him weak.

"You fucking idiot!" Letty shook him. "You fucking moron!"

She turned and shoved him back down. He landed on another

branch, a foot below, falling too quickly to catch himself. Winded, he tried to push himself up. Letty dropped down next to him, pointing at the road. "You know what you've done? Do you?"

"Val," Fresko wheezed, struggling to recover his breath. "Val's orders."

"Fuck Val!" Letty shouted. "We need him!"

Fresko rose onto his hands and knees. He stopped there to glare up at her without apology. Letty's arms shook with tension, ready to hit him again. She shot another glance to the road, the cloud around the hole dispersing to reveal the shattered mess the tunnel had left. The other car driver was approaching it. A house door opened nearby.

"Pax," Letty said. She spun back to Fresko. "Where's Pax? What did you do with her?"

"The girl?" Fresko said, sitting back onto his haunches. "The Ministry one?"

"Yes, the fucking girl!" Letty launched at him again, one fist raised as the other closed on his tie. He scrambled back, gagging, as she tightened the tie around his neck. "What did you do?"

"She must be dead!" Fresko flapped his hands weakly, failing to break free as Letty sat on top of him, pulling even tighter. Letty shoved him down, pressing his face into the branch.

"Must be? You don't know?"

"She went down there, didn't come back!" Fresko said. "We left them to it!"

Letty let go, turning to face the road. The driver was waving at the people across the road, his back to the tree. He was calming them down.

"How long ago?" she asked.

Fresko coughed, nursing his neck. "I don't know. Half an hour."

"Because Val told you to."

"Because I thought she killed you!" Fresko replied forcibly. "I heard her say it!"

Letty shot him a vicious look. "Where's Mix?"

"Gone to the nearest entrances," Fresko said. "To make sure they're not getting back out."

"You bloody idiots," Letty said. "I was gone for two days. Two days and you screw the whole thing up."

" . . . no, that's fine." The car driver's voice got louder as he went to the manhole cover. Taking charge of the situation. "You stay inside, there could be fumes."

Letty paused, pricking up her ears.

"Val said this was it," Fresko said. "We've got the weed. There's a crew going to the boy's hideout to collect the Dispenser. Barton, his family, they just needed to disappear. We're back in, Letty. We can put all this behind us."

"Val can burn," Letty told him quietly, her mind tracking away from the Fae situation towards what was happening below. The guy in the suit had stopped by the caved-in tunnel with his hands on his hips, but he wasn't surveying the damage. He was looking up towards the sky. "You sent Pax down there. You utter prick."

"Aren't you listening to me? We're back in. This ends it – we're done with the Dispenser."

"No." Letty shook her head. "I'm not done. *She* understood."

"That fucking human?" Fresko snapped, and she sparked into action again, kicking down at him. She caught him unawares, boot cracking into his chin, but he'd regained enough energy to react. He rolled aside, one hand to his face and the other whipping to his back, where he had a pistol holstered. He ended on his back with the gun aimed at Letty as she stood over him, aiming her pistol right back at him. "I won't let you screw us on this," he said.

"You did this, not me," Letty snarled. With her eyes locked on his, she raised her voice to shout sideways, "We're up here!"

Fresko's eyes widened, and he shot a look to the side, to the man in the road. He lost his focus in his surprise, the man in the suit looking up at them, and Letty quickly jumped aside, out of the firing line and up next to him. With Fresko's pistol still aimed forward, hers was at his neck. She growled, "All right, drop it."

"Pax's friends, I take it?" Casaria called up from the road.

"Something like that," Letty replied, staring Fresko in the eye. He was shaking his head, appalled. She said, "We're gonna make this right. And that starts with getting Pax back."

19

"Mum," Grace bleated. She hadn't stopped making little noises of suffering since the fairies' assault, and Holly and Pax had started to simply accept them. They must have travelled a mile through the featureless tunnels, through a handful of doors and around a number of turns that betrayed no logic. For the most part, they walked in silence, to conserve energy and avoid alerting any more lurking creatures, and though Grace had whimpered Pax was impressed at her attempts to keep quiet. Now that the horrible clicking had faded behind them, and the high-pitched trill hadn't sounded for a while, the teenager seemed ready to speak louder. "Mum. Mum?"

"What is it, dear?" Holly replied wearily. Fatigue had calmed her: she sounded as though she was busy reading a newspaper, not fleeing from hellish monsters. "Can it wait?"

"Mum, no." Grace came to a halt. Pax stopped and turned back. "My feet. I can't go on."

Pax frowned at Grace's dirt-encrusted feet, not having noticed before this moment that the girl had made the whole terrifying journey barefoot. She had never had a chance to put her shoes on when they raced out. Her soles were red around the edges, swollen and maybe bleeding. Holly stared without an answer. She looked to Pax for guidance.

"Here." Pax started undoing her laces. "Take my boots."

"They won't fit," Grace said.

"You can try," Pax said, but Grace was firm. "No, I can see. You've got tiny feet, and mine look like balloons. Can we just rest? Can we stop and rest, please? I'll be okay."

"Dear." Holly's lip trembled. She swung towards her and held her in a loving hug. Pax saw her eyes welling with emotion. "My brave little girl. My poor little thing, I'm so sorry."

"It's not your fault," Grace replied, but her voice caught with emotion too. "I should've told you where I was going. I should've stayed home. I'm so sorry I went to that park, Mum!"

"No no no." Holly rubbed her soothingly. "This isn't your fault."

Pax stared at them silently. She tried to steel herself. It was like watching a board pair against your flush, with all your money in the pot. You didn't give in to emotion, no matter how unfair or irrational or dangerous the world became. You couldn't betray signs of weakness. Crying could come later. She looked away, the mother and daughter hug shifting up a notch as they both started crying.

"Are we going to die, Mum?" Grace asked.

"No, of course not, it's okay," Holly said, but clearly didn't believe it herself.

"I think there's some steps ahead," Pax said. "We can sit down."

Her sober voice cut through their emotions, tearing their attention away from each other. There was a little shame in Holly's face. She nodded and guided Grace onward, towards the steps. Back the way they had come, something clicked, a sound like a bird pecking wood. Pax tried to ignore it, sure it was far worse than any bird.

The steps led up to a small enclosure. The trio climbed into an unlit room, only a few metres square, a secure hideaway. Grace shuffled into a shadowy corner and sat down. Pax joined her. Taking the load off, she realised now how depleted she was. There was barely any sensation left in her legs and her chest was tight with pain. The moment she slumped against the wall she wondered if it would even be possible to stand again.

"Why aren't there any exits?" Grace asked, with a child's curiosity.

"There are," Pax told her. "We just haven't found them yet."

"What else is down here?" Holly asked.

"A lot," Pax said. "But as long as we see them coming, we'll be okay." Even as she said it a voice in her head disagreed; if they saw a sickle coming, they wouldn't be able to outrun it.

"You're tired," Holly noted. Pax frowned. She'd done nothing to betray it, she thought. "And your leg's hurt. It looks safe here, you can rest. I can go on, I can find a way out."

"No." Pax shook her head. "We can't split up."

"You can't keep going, either of you. I can cover more ground alone."

Grace wasn't arguing, too worn down to talk. Her bright eyes stared hopefully at her mother. Pax hardly had the energy, either. She said, "You'll get lost." Holly had no answer, so Pax took out one of her lockpicks and scraped it against the wall. It was hard enough to leave a scratch. She held it up. "Take this. Mark your way."

Holly nodded. She hesitated in the entrance to the room and then jumped on Grace with a hug. "I love you. Don't forget that."

All Grace could muster in response was "Mum", and with that Holly ducked out of the room. Pax shifted closer to Grace and put an arm around her, awkwardly stiff. What the hell did she know about comforting people. She said, "She'll be fine. We're the ones in trouble, waiting here."

As she heard her own words, she knew it was both unhelpful and true.

She rested back against the wall and allowed herself a moment to reflect on how monumentally she had screwed up. In the space of a few days she had discovered terrible things about this terrible place no one was supposed to know existed, and rather than escape it all, or so much as lend a kidnapped young man a hand, she had got herself and an innocent mother and daughter trapped there, facing imminent demise at the hands, or claws or teeth, of the most ungodly things imaginable.

This, she told herself, was why she did what she did. Connecting with other people led to trouble. Arguments at a wedding, accusations of shoplifting, monsters in a tunnel – it was the same old story. You get involved, you suffer.

Holly's footsteps faded into the distance, leaving quiet in their little room. The sounds of the myriad creatures did not seem to be any closer, though they occasionally emitted unsettling chirps or groans from some unknown distance away. Grace had calmed down, at last, in her exhaustion, and snuggled up against Pax like a puppy searching for comfort. Pax held her stiffly, unsure what to do. She gave Grace a little pat on the head, then rested her hand on Grace's shoulder and sat uncomfortably still.

Pax and Grace sat listening to the drips and scratches, hoping for Holly to rush back with good news at any moment. Holly did not return, though. The minutes had stretched ever longer between the sounds of the Sunken City. Pax considered the worst. What if

Holly had run into something? What if she couldn't find her way back? What else could they do? They couldn't move, in case Holly was trying to find them. And what about Barton? Had he made it home yet?

What did it matter. The fairies would not let them out, however lucky they were in escaping the creatures. And even if they did, what then? The Ministry were out to get her, the Fae were out to get her, by this point Bees and his employer probably thought she had betrayed them, too.

Something scratched down the hall, much closer than the previous sounds, making Pax jolt upright. Grace stirred with a little murmur, seeming to wake from sleep. Pax put a hand over her mouth and listened. Another scratch. It was in the tunnel, moving nearer. It chirped, like wood tapping together.

Grace started with surprise. Pax held her tighter.

"Not a sound," Pax whispered. "Not a movement. They sense vibrations."

It scratched closer, claws dragging against the brick. They held their breath and watched the room's opening with unblinking eyes. Another tapping sound signalled it was just outside. Even though she knew what was coming, the sight of it made Pax cringe.

The sickle moved into view slowly, its smooth head twitching from side to side as its vertical jawline snapped open and shut with another chirp. One of its gangly claws traced along the wall with a chalkboard screech as its canine body moved into the open. Pax felt Grace swelling in fear, and could almost hear her eyes bulging.

The beast paused in the doorway, its claw dragging to find the entrance. It tapped with its clawed feet, feeling for the steps.

Keep going keep going keep going, Pax prayed.

The monster reached a claw in towards them. It ventured up the steps. In the tight space, with it closing in on them, there was zero chance it wouldn't feel them sitting there. Pax and Grace were rigid, as the ungodly animal rose into the shadow of their room, mantis arms reaching around them. The claws rose over their heads, scratching the wall above, just missing their hair. Its wrinkled face tilted towards them, jaw opening and closing as though tasting the air. It stopped and let out another chirp.

Something in the pause told Pax it had found them.

"Run!" she screamed, and as the sickle reeled onto its hind legs she followed her instincts, same as facing any late-night predator. She drove both her fists into the creature's groin. Grace scrambled past, rolling out of the way of a flailing claw, as Pax punched and clawed at what felt like some kind of thick genitalia towards the base of the beast's torso. Whatever she got a hold of, it had the desired effect, as the sickle let out an ear-splitting shriek and fell to the side, arms curling around its face.

Pax followed Grace through the doorway. The teenager was already running, headlong down the tunnel, the wrong way.

"Grace! Here!" Pax shouted after her, waving a hand. In the room behind them, the monster was quickly recovering, its claws tapping against every wall as it tried to steady itself. Pax took a few steps in the opposite direction to Grace, seeing Holly's first scratch on the wall, but Grace was pelting away, shrieking, "No! No no no!"

The sickle emerged into the tunnel, turning towards Grace's yells. Without thinking, seeing its back was turned to her, Pax jumped onto it before it could give chase. She brought it to the floor, its stumpy dog legs unable to hold her weight, and as she slammed a hand onto the back of its head she saw that its claw arms couldn't pivot to the rear. It scratched around her, slicing at the bricks and gnashing its teeth, but for all the strength of its splayed limbs and bucking torso it couldn't reach her. She held on tight, pinning it down, and rammed its head into the floor. With sheer animal drive, she shoved its head into the floor again, momentarily weakening it. It stopped bucking long enough for her to adjust her grip, and with both hands she clutched the thing's twitching skull.

Grace had stopped, far down the tunnel, and she turned back to watch. No helping it, Pax thought – let her see, as she cracked the beast's head open against the floor.

20

"Take out your phone," Letty instructed as she glided down in front of Casaria. He looked at her uncertainly. "Take our your fucking phone so these prats watching don't think you're talking to dragonflies." He reached into his pocket, but Letty waved her pistol. "Ah ah, slowly."

He slowed down but continued, lifting the phone to his ear before responding. He put on a smile but spoke with a hint of aggression. "You're the ones that shot at me, aren't you?"

He turned back towards the couple in the nearby house, back inside, looking worriedly out through the front window. Whatever they were seeing, it wasn't the little people he saw, else they'd be doing more than watching. That was how the Fae worked, wasn't it? Shrouding themselves from onlookers. Casaria was better than that, though. He saw. He gave the couple a friendly *everything's okay* wave.

"You're the one who tore off my fucking wing," Letty snarled. She looked over her shoulder to Fresko, lingering in the air nearby. "Amazing how much damage you've managed to do without harming this greaseball."

Fresko did not respond. Being stripped of his weapons had left him grumpy and mute.

"How'd you know to come here?" Letty asked.

"Pax messaged me," Casaria said. "I take it things didn't work out between you. No surprise."

"Seriously?" Letty shot another look to Fresko. "You let her bring the Ministry to you, too, you prick."

"What did you do to her?" Casaria asked.

"Not me." Letty shook her head and pointed at Fresko. "Him. She's down there. And you're going to help us get her out. Where are your goons?"

Casaria looked to his empty car. "I work better without them. They'll follow me soon enough, though. What direction did she go in?"

Letty paused, studying him. "I don't even need to persuade you, do I? You're so sweet on her, you've run off from work to find her."

Casaria's smiling eyes suggested there was truth in it, but he didn't admit it. "The situation's complicated. Let's say we've got unfinished business."

"Then you can help me out."

"Why would I do that?"

"My people put her down there," Letty told him. "And they're not gonna let her back out. I don't see you being much use against my people on your own."

"And you're not going down there to get her out yourself," Casaria said, completing her thought. "This won't end well for you, you realise that? Even putting our differences aside for the moment."

"Doesn't matter," Letty said. "It's the way it is."

Casaria nodded slowly. He gestured to his car. "There's something I want from you, first."

"This is hardly the time for a fucking negotiation – we –"

"It's important." He was already walking to the car. Letty shot Fresko an uncertain look, but he shrugged. The pair hovered above Casaria's head as he pointed through the passenger window to the device lying on the seat. The metal and glass canister was instantly recognisable to them.

"How the hell did you get that?" Fresko asked.

"Doesn't matter. I need you to tell me how it works. And why it's never been used."

"Spin on it," Letty said.

"Do you even know the answer?" Casaria said, patiently.

Letty met his eyes angrily, but resisted the urge to insult him as his words hit her. His smug, knowing expression. He wasn't saying it like *he* knew, though. Letty thought of Valoria and her indifferent attitude to the device, and realised that the question Casaria was asking was the same one she had. Not the what of the machine, but the why. There was confusion on both sides of the divide. Pax had said it, hadn't she? Talking to these assholes might fill in the bigger picture.

"That was designed to destroy the berserker," Letty said. "Do you know that much?" Fresko opened his mouth to protest, but she flapped a hand at him and continued, "Not a word. Apothel stole this thing. All we needed was some electric weed to fuel it, and he took it away."

"All you needed was some electric weed?" Casaria replied sceptically.

"What'd I just say, Agent Orange?"

"Right." Casaria was smiling again. This time genuinely pleased, as though everything had been answered. He moved to get in the car. "Let's deal with it after saving Pax, shall we?"

"What? What the fuck are you smiling for? You think this is funny?"

"No." Casaria's smile spread. "I just get the idea that your people have been about as honest with you as mine."

Letty and Fresko flew in silence above Casaria's car as he left Dalford for the heart of the city. The next entrances to the Sunken City, their only hope, were the ones to the south. If the girls headed north, where the population got sparser and the Sunken City less developed, the nearest exit was over three miles away. It would be impossible for them to find it, let alone reach it, before the monsters caught up to them. The exits to the south were a mile at best, three of them with a network of winding tunnels that rose up and down between them. Then, whatever direction they went in, it would be perfectly possible to go by all the exits without ever seeing one, continuing towards the caverns of central Ordshaw.

Passing into a more built-up area, Letty shot Fresko disappointed, angry glares. He was trying to avoid eye contact, but eventually he responded, raising his voice above the sound of the wind. "Why are you doing this?"

Letty gave him a look to say the question itself was insulting.

"You know as well as me," Fresko said, "that everything we've done, ever since Apothel, has been to mend this rift. Leave them down there, ice this fool and take the Dispenser back, and it's done. We're done. You wanna throw that away for some fucking human? What happened to you?"

"It's not about some fucking human," Letty said. She paused, thinking it wasn't *just* about some fucking human. "Something major is off with Val. She isn't interested in stopping the berserker."

"So what?"

Letty slowed down to give him a severe look. "*So what*?"

"It's not our job to care," Fresko said. "We're tying up loose ends. We were supposed to recover the Dispenser, not use it. Wasted all our damned time drawing the Citizen back into this, just to dot all the Is – if Val isn't interested then we wasted time, that's all."

"Well, shit." Letty spat at him. "Sounds like you're okay with the Fae Transitional City being transitional forever? Leave the whole Sunken City to the abominations?"

"Why not?" Fresko said. "They feed off the humans, not us. What do we need the Sunken City for? We're good as we are. Or were."

Letty glided closer to him and swiped out, cuffing a hand across the back of his neck. She kept close, face near his as he tried to move away. She shouted, "That human down there, she got it. You don't leave the world to rot when you can do something about it. And she's my friend, and she fucking matters, okay?"

Fresko's eyes were fixed with shock. "You've lost it, Letty. Listen to yourself. The Council, the Dispenser, the berserker – none of that's our problem. None of it was ever our problem, not until you made it our problem."

It was hopeless. Him and the rest of them.

Letty picked up speed, moving ahead, just to put some distance between them.

"Casaria."

"Where are you?" Landon demanded through the phone. Casaria checked his mirrors, in case he was being followed. Didn't look like it.

"I'm driving," he said. "Not the best time."

"Yeah, I can hear that," Landon said, actually sounding annoyed. Good for you, Casaria smiled, finally emoting. "You were supposed to hand in the car. And why am I hearing reports that you've turned the power on across the Dalford sector? I'm assuming it was you that breached the Dalford entrance?"

Casaria considered channelling Pax's spirit for the correct response of *fuck* and *you*. Resisting long enough to think of the task ahead, he decided there was a better way. "There's some civilians in the Sunken City. The Dalford entrance has been destroyed."

"What?" Landon gasped.

"It's the Fae, Landon," Casaria continued, almost singing the words in a delighted I-told-you-so. "They went after Darren Barton's family and dropped half the road on him. Now there's three people down there, four if Barton's alive. If *any* of them are alive, they're running from the *praelucente*."

"Jesus Christ."

"You want to know what you need to do?"

Landon said nothing for a moment. "Where are you?"

"I'm heading for the entrance on Pestfax Road. I've got a couple of fairies with me – Sam Ward would be happy to hear that. But there's likely to be some Fae ordinance on the other entrances, one of the Fae is going Rambo on them. You want to know what you need to do?"

Landon paused again. In a small voice, he answered, "What?"

"Send people to Dalford, see if you can dig out Barton. Send people to Old Fairbrook and Pointing Avenue, check if those entrances are safe. Watch out for Fae traps. Send people in if you can. I'll take care of Pestfax. In the meantime, get Mathers, tell him to get me some electric weed, whatever it takes, and ship it up to Pestfax Road. If it comes to it, I want to have a fighting chance."

More silence.

Casaria waited, then said, "Landon, you still with me?"

"Yeah."

"You gonna do all that?"

"Yeah."

The sun had ducked behind the buildings by the time Casaria pulled up near Pestfax Road. He left the car a block away and approached the entrance painfully unarmed. It had been easy enough to steal back his own car, activate power switches and take the Fae device under the guise of courier work, but there'd been no way to get his weapons back.

This entrance was at the back of a dive bar; a heavy door sunk four feet below the street, like a tunnel for deliveries. All the neighbours assumed it belonged to someone else. Casaria entered the alleyway, shining his torch along the walls that flanked it. The problem with this city, he reflected, was that there were countless places that a two-inch fairy could hide. Especially with the dusk light casting shadows. And it looked like he'd lost the pair that were supposed to be supporting him. Flakes.

He shone his torch up and down the cracks of the entrance, over the hinges, around the handle. It was an old door, metal mottled in places that had taken on too much water, green paint cracked all over. Infinite possibilities for a tiny trace of Fae explosives to be hidden.

"Back off," a rough voice said, somewhere above. Casaria turned to face the man. Of course, a miniature thug in the denim guise of a biker, sitting on the alley's rear fence. Mix had a pistol in each hand, pointed his way. "It's not meant for you."

"I'm guessing this isn't the only one you've rigged," Casaria said. "You realise the night patrols will be starting soon. Did you intend to warn *everyone* not to go in?"

"Consider yourself the lucky one. Walk away, Ministry man. Quickly and permanently."

Casaria didn't move. The gunman was too far away for him to do anything, but he was damned if he was going to back down and do what he was told.

Mix looked away, though, eyes or ears picking out something that Casaria had not sensed. The other Fae, somewhere in the sky. Casaria looked up too. It was too dark to make anything out. The buzz of that odd machine on Letty's back got closer, louder.

"Never had any goddamned sense, did you!" Letty shouted.

"Letty?" Mix said. "You're alive?"

She dropped down next to him, her pistols raised, and he understood the threat immediately. Mix jumped off the fence, wings carrying him up and along the wall. Casaria watched as the pair squared off, spinning through the air like tiny fighter planes.

"Take the explosives off the damned door!" Letty commanded.

"What for?" Mix shot back, spiralling above Casaria's head, keeping his distance.

"If she's hurt I'm gonna gut you!"

Mix made an angry noise from somewhere deep in his gut. "Soft on a human? You're a disgrace, Letty. Would've been better if you *had* died."

Letty opened fire without warning. Mix twirled to the side, the bullets missing, and he started firing back. The pair of them flitted from side to side, four pistols blazing as they avoided the shots. At about two metres apart, it seemed neither could get a good shot on the other in flight. Following them with his eyes, Casaria sidestepped to the bins against the opposite wall and took off a large circular lid. When the two fairies had gone through the first clip in their pistols, they each threw a weapon aside to reload the other, never slowing down. Mix flew into a wall and used his legs to spring back off it. Letty somersaulted through the air to avoid his counter-attack. They started shooting again, flying in zig-zags. The chase had reversed, Mix going after Letty now, and she led him down, skating towards the ground.

Mix flew head on into the bin lid, the force of the blow sending him slamming into the wall, pistol flying away. He slid to the floor, wings twitching, as Letty doubled back. She fired at his almost motionless body. The shots glanced off the concrete next to him and her gun clicked empty as she sped towards him. Reaching Mix, she skirted suddenly to the side. Stepping over them, Casaria saw he had drawn another pistol, which he fired straight up. Casaria dropped back as the bullet glanced off his chin, shooting up the full length of his face along the cheek and catching his eyebrow. Casaria yelled, clutching a hand to his face, as Letty jumped onto Mix and kicked the gun from this hand.

The fairies grappled on the floor, exchanging punches. With the height advantage, Letty used her wing to rise above Mix's flailing fists. Then she sank back down to punch his face, again and again, and he finally fell back. She grabbed a knife from his leg sheath and twisted it back to stab him.

Fresko pushed between them.

Letty was thrown sideways, spinning again. She stopped, furious. Fresko had Mix up under an arm. He growled, "You've lost it, Letty. He's one of *us*!"

Letty panted, looking back at him angrily, but the fight was over. With Mix barely conscious, Fresko was shaking his head, disappointed. He carried Mix's weight, beating his wings to propel himself up towards the darkening sky. He shouted, "Enjoy your life with the fucking humans, you've earnt it!"

Casaria edged away from the wall, one hand supporting himself and the other applying pressure to his bleeding wound. He watched the fairy glide down to retrieve her guns, apparently not interested in pursuing her colleagues. He said, "You should've killed them."

21

Barton's ankle was stuck under a chunk of concrete, his left arm hurt all the way up and the impact from the fall had potentially shattered something. He reflected that he had otherwise been fortunate. His ears were ringing and his head throbbed worse than a hangover, but the rest of his body was apparently unscathed, other than a few surface wounds. The bulk of the blood was coming from a reopened wound on his head. It had bled enough for one day without killing him – not worth worrying about.

Using the light of his phone, he searched for something to use as a lever. Roads and tunnels had iron bars and that crap sticking through them, didn't they? You always saw shards like that in the rubble. Not here, it seemed. He had to get his hands underneath the concrete block instead, and put his back into heaving upwards, knowing this stupid movement was going to haunt him for life. It didn't matter, though, just another pain to add to the collection. He groaned and tugged and shifted the weight just enough to wriggle out. He gave the busted ankle the briefest look. It was limp and thick with blood. Examining the damage wasn't going to help.

Barton clambered up, falling against the wall and taking his weight on his other foot. He shone his phone up the tunnel. The lights were working up ahead, that was something. He took out his hip flask and swigged what was left of the glo. Barely a mouthful. It would do, though, for a short while. He let the flask drop with a clatter. Dead weight.

He waited a minute, while his head partially cleared and his eyes started to refocus.

The trails began to appear in the air before him. The colours of the myriad beasts, hanging like slug paths. So many of them. He took a few limping steps along the wall and peered ahead, to where a thick purple line led up to a doorway. A tuckle had come through here. Tried to smash through the door.

As the glo took control, he saw the rest, too. Hounds and

sickles. A turnbold in the mix, with its multiple skeletal faces. A horde of creatures. And at its centre, the minotaur.

Pax was desperately trying to recall the floorplans of the Sunken City from Apothel's book, but even the sections she could picture seemed, in her recollection, to be random lines. Uneven, probably not to scale and completely useless. There were names of entrances, but it was no help to know that one of the tunnels came out near the Morricone Theatre. That might be a two-mile walk away, it might be five miles. And it might be in any direction.

She had given Grace her coat, which the teenager draped over her shoulders after a hug of gratitude. Pax let her believe it was a gift of kindness, not just because the murderous grapple with the sickle had unbearably raised her body temperature. Grace was still soldiering on barefoot, though, which worried Pax. How far could they go before she collapsed?

The noises were behind them but getting no further away. Occasional new chirps and clicks kept startling them. Whatever was out there, of which there seemed to be an awful lot, was still following them. Equally daunting was the fact that after the very first tunnel they had lost Holly's scratches on the walls. Maybe she hadn't made them clear enough, maybe she had simply given up on the idea, maybe something worse. Yet Pax told Grace they were going the right way, with nothing whatsoever to base that on, and the girl seemed to believe her.

Eventually the tunnels got wider and more complex. One or two expanded to the width of a narrow street, with platforms at the edges, like walkways. Some resembled railway tunnels in size and shape, though without any of the fixtures to suggest rails had ever been laid there. It was remarkable, and Pax started to get an idea of the magnitude of this place – and how much vaster and more incredible it would seem to the Fae. These tunnels led to even wider rooms, with one large enough to house a truck, its ceiling over twenty feet high. It had four exits, one on each wall. They chose one that was up a small flight of steps. The lights were less reliable in these greater expanses. Some of the rooms were too large for the small lights to reach their corners; others, including whole corridors, did not have their lights activated. Pax assured Grace that there was nothing in the shadows, well aware it was nonsense.

When it was starting to seem like they would never encounter another living being in this nightmare maze, and would be doomed to walk its halls forever, a movement cut across the tunnel ahead. Another human. Pax and Grace stopped dead.

"Mum?" Grace asked hopefully.

Am I a bad mother? Am I a bad wife?

The two questions kept circling around Holly's mind as she picked her way through the tunnels. She had left what she thought was an admirable trail of scratches along the wall, but she was grimly aware that she had also left her only daughter behind her with a miscreant poker player, in an underground system teeming with monsters. She was also grimly aware that her husband had been dealing with all this for many years and had never once thought she could handle the truth of it.

Am I *that* hard to talk to that he couldn't trust me with this?

She had travelled through what seemed like a dozen narrow tunnels without getting anywhere, finding two doors that were locked and one set of stairs that led up to what seemed to be an exit, but turned out to be an impassable brick wall. She could swear that she had walked down some of these tunnels before, but her scratches were not on the walls. Whoever built the place must have produced an awful lot of identical mundane passages.

At least the sounds of the creatures were dying down. The birdlike noises and the caustic barks had been starting to grate on her. She kept calm by convincing herself that even here there must be some pathetic little man at the top of it all who could be told off. That would make her feel better when she got out. Locate the fool in charge and watch him shrivel up in the knowledge of his ineptitude.

If she could escape.

She turned a corner and finally saw a break in the monotony. The walls, for so long, had been nothing but tired concrete and brick; now, there was another texture, bumps in the shadows. Roots. Plant life. Something was growing out of the corner of a wall at the far end of the long corridor. It gave her hope. She hurried towards it, finding renewed energy to pick up her speed.

It was about the height and thickness of a sunflower, with large green roots tangling around its base and snaking up one wall.

As she got closer, she slowed down. Something about the plant wasn't right. There was a strange smell in the air, something she couldn't quite place but that made her nostrils wrinkle. A few more steps and it became too noxious for her to continue, a vile smell. She covered her nose and mouth and studied the plant. It was moving. The head on its thick green stalk swayed from side to side, while its centre, a broad brown circle, bubbled with a gooey liquid. Around its roots she noticed more liquid. The thing was secreting slime. One bubble expanded and then popped; with it came a rush of gas. Holly gagged and covered her face. She quickly backtracked, disgusted.

Reaching a corner, looking back down a tunnel she knew she recognised, Holly froze. The wall was bare. She looked closer, ran a hand over the brickwork. Her scratch had gone.

"Oh no," Holly gasped. "Why . . ."

She scanned the walls, searching for any blue patches. There was nothing there, but she knew in her gut what had happened. She ran back down the tunnel, tracing her fingers along the wall, searching for her markings.

They were all gone.

She took the lockpick and hurriedly carved into the wall: *Why?*

She stood back and waited, looking up and down.

It appeared, rising from the floor, the flat shape of a blue screen. The blue rectangle moved over her words and rested there. The brick distorted, the indentations turning in on themselves, healing before her eyes.

A moment of inactivity, then new letters formed, carving themselves into the brick.

Ugly.

Holly stared at the letters, shocked. She put her full indignation into a one-word response. "*Wow.*"

The word slowly faded again.

She thought for a moment, then scraped into the blue rectangle: *Way out?*

Her words faded and new letters appeared.

Myriads coming.

She put her hands on her hips and relented at the useless nature of this communication. How had Barton let whoever was hiding behind these flat squares tell him what to do for so long? She listened, though, and the sounds of the creatures were indeed getting nearer. There was another groan, like the movements of a pipe they had heard when they first came down here. Making a quick decision, she turned away from the antagonistic blue thing and took an alternative route into the next tunnel, away from the flower.

Pax and Grace hurried after the shape, turning a corner and seeing whoever it was disappear into another doorway. Grace shouted, "Mum! It's us! Wait!"

Pax grabbed Grace's arm and pulled her back. Grace tried to break free but Pax held her fast. "I don't think it's your mum."

"Who else would be down here?" Grace replied hotly.

"Grace, wait," Pax said forcibly, pulling her still. "That might not even be a person."

"Get off me! You're not helping!" Grace shoved Pax and turned towards the shape. She shouted again, running down the tunnel. "Mum!"

Pax watched her, thinking of the unthinkable act she had already done in protecting this girl from that dog demon. She could leave her, save herself. Grace was stumbling like a drunk goat, her feet barely functioning. She was so skinny and clueless, she wouldn't stand a chance against anything down there. Pax's mind ran back to her diminutive fairy friend, her ability to let all this go. Friend. That was rich. She was better than Letty, she'd already made that decision. Given the choice, she had to do the right thing. She charged after Grace. It took no time to catch up.

Pax skipped ahead of the hobbling girl and checked through the doorway into a cavernous expanse. As Grace drew up next to Pax, they both came to the same conclusion. There was no way Holly would have run into a room like that.

"The other way," Pax said gently, nodding back up the tunnel. "Whatever it was, we have to get away from it."

As she spoke, a light crept into the vast room, capturing their attention. On the far wall, a high-up doorway glowed faint blue. The light grew stronger, flowing like water, its source slowly moving into the room. Its growing flicker revealed a cathedral-like expanse with a domed ceiling. The pair were halfway up in their entrance, on the edge of a ring walkway that ran around an open centre, a drop of ten feet or so to the ground.

Pax had no name for the spectre they had followed, but she realised its purpose. It was designed to lead them to this place, and the thing that was entering it. A sound like a thunder crack came from the far tunnel.

"That way." Pax turned out of the room, but far down the corridor a shape had already appeared. Another canine centaur, its claws stretched ahead of it. It was searching the air, unaware that they were up ahead. Pax spun in the other direction. A dog was sniffing at the opposite end of the tunnel. Its flesh was smoking.

"Shit," Pax uttered under her breath. Grace moved close to her, more terrified than ever. They both looked back into the vast room, the brilliant blue growing ever brighter. Shards of electricity licked into the room from the distant doorway, like lizards' tongues. The room was otherwise empty, though, and there were at least two other doorways. Dark voids, but possibilities nonetheless.

They had been running from it since their arrival, but somehow they had arrived at the heart of their pursuer's domain. The myriad creatures surrounded it, but did not come close to it. Their best hope, Pax saw, was to get close. To go through the middle. No one understood it, after all. The Fae said they hated it but they hadn't gone through with stopping it. The Ministry wanted to protect it. There was a chance. The slightest chance that they might be able to brave it.

She took Grace's hand and looked her in the eye.

"I need you to trust me," she said, and pulled the teenager into the room.

22

Descending into the Sunken City, Casaria searched the walls with torchlight for any more fairy welcome presents. Down the steps and to the right, the lights were on. Letty was left watching from outside. Casaria turned back and said, half serious, "Not coming?"

"I got you in," Letty replied. "You get them out."

He nodded, creeping further into the tunnel. Unarmed. The fairy clearly had no idea that this was not what he usually did, but he felt naked without so much as a gun or a knife. All he had was the Fae device, which clearly had no fuel.

"Don't worry," Letty said. "I'll keep watch. In case my boys come back."

Casaria hummed. That wouldn't be much help if he ran into a griffix, would it?

He kept moving, into the featureless abyss of one of the Sunken City's anonymous tunnels. He took a breath. The Ministry would soon catch up to them with real weapons, but he'd be kept out. Likely as not, they'd have Sam Ward along, saying he was unfit for a sensitive rescue operation. But it had to be him down there, getting Pax out. Not them, not those glorified crossing guards.

Why? Why did it matter? He gave one final look back up to Letty. She was floating around at head-height, arms folded. He knew. It was the same reason that this ridiculous little creature had come to help.

Pax did not deserve to be down there, and for it all he could not bring himself to stop caring.

He pocketed his torch and waved the fairy off. "Just keep this door safe."

The pain in his ankle had all but subsided as Barton pressed on through the tunnels. He didn't think about the damage he might be doing to himself; the important thing was that he couldn't feel it. He picked up speed as the trail became clearer, the walls covered in claw marks. He was getting closer, but the horde was still moving, otherwise he would have caught up to it already. That was a good thing. If it was moving this quickly, it had to be still giving chase.

There were too many colours of creatures in the air for him to discern what he was going to come across first. Glogockles, turnbolds, sickles and perhaps another tuckle. They would be moving separately, different spokes of the minotaur's wheel, but they were close enough together that he might see one or all of them at any time.

It didn't matter.

Nothing mattered, he kept telling himself, other than getting Grace to safety.

The glo had given him strength. Bring on the beasts.

Pax and Grace sprinted through the domed room, in a low defensive crouch, for all the help it would afford them, as the electric arms of the berserker lashed into the room, lighting their way in a dazzling blue. The thing was moving into the open like a collection of lightning whips, swinging in and out through the doorway as the central body, still approaching, got brighter and brighter. The pair followed a slope down, below the tunnel that the thing was coming through, and they bolted for an arched opening on the opposite side, tucked under a concrete walkway.

As they reached the exit, one of the flashing limbs of the berserker crashed through the walkway, its tremendous power shattering the concrete. The pair staggered with a shared scream as the destructive limb rested there, pressing against the wall ahead. As it touched the bricks, sparking offshoots dug into the bricks like clawing fingers.

Pax pulled Grace towards the next doorway, glancing back at the tunnel. The monster was emerging, finally, its long electric limbs pulling the rest of it in like a kraken. Pax held up her hands to shield her eyes from it, the flash blinding as it came into view. As it revealed itself, though, the light faded, diluted by the size of the room. Grace was stone still, mouth wide open, and Pax had to shake her by the shoulders to get her moving.

"Look at it!" Grace gasped, but Pax was more interested in surviving. She shoved Grace ahead, towards the next opening. Grace tripped, distracted, and Pax heaved her back up. She pushed the girl into the tunnel, just as another electric limb cracked into the floor. A shockwave jolted through the ground and the walls, throwing Pax off balance. She fell into Grace and they tumbled down together, half-turning back. Multiple electric limbs were striking the floor behind them, pounding it like a stamping spider.

"There!" Grace pointed into their new tunnel. She scrambled out from under Pax and ran. Beyond the entrance Grace was going for, there was another small shape ahead, a low, sniffing creature. Two of them. Small smoking dogs. They looked up and bared their teeth. Twenty metres ahead, perhaps, beyond Grace's target door.

Pax jumped up and sprinted as Grace charged at the door fearlessly, seeming to not even see the dogs. The dogs started barking and Grace shrieked. That made them run; two hounds pounding towards her. Grace slammed into the door and rolled through, but the dogs were close, about to leap as Pax got there. They stopped, skidding to a halt with a whine just before her. Pax froze too. The dogs backed off, growling and snapping, puffs of smoke coming out of their mouths, and other orifices, and hovering over their fur. Pax turned a slow look over her shoulder. One of the electric limbs was snaking into the tunnel, still coming after them. Pax jumped through the doorway and slammed it shut as the dogs ran yelping in the other direction.

There was no light, but she could hear Grace nearby, panting and slapping the bricks, feeling for a way forward. She cried, "There's no exit! We're trapped!"

Pax turned back to the closed door. The light from the searching limb came through the edges of the door, giving the room a dull, eerie glow. Grace was right: it was an alcove with no exit, a tiny circular room built of brick, with a domed ceiling and no breaks in the walls. Pax leant against the door, out of options. She thought of Holly, somewhere out there, perhaps their only hope, and chose to deal with her distress through indignation.

"Why the hell did anyone even build this room?"

Barton was closing in on the sounds; he recognised the probing click of a sickle. Another twenty-metre tunnel and he was sure he would get to them. The clicking became frantic, though, and suddenly drew nearer. It was on the move. The pad of its claws across the floor was rapid, a pursuit he knew all too well. It had found a target. Had it somehow sensed him? He braced himself, spreading his arms, waiting for its approach.

The monstrous shape burst across the end of the tunnel and continued, gone in a flash.

Barton frowned as the sound of the monster died down. It was replaced by footsteps ahead, and the chatter of two men.

"Told you, just a sickle," one of them said.

"No, I've still got a reading. To the right."

Barton braced himself again; the two men stepped into view at the end of the tunnel. One of them had what looked like a radar dish out in front of him. The other, more tense in posture, had both hands on a pistol held at his side. One thick, one thin. The one with the scanner lowered it and waved towards Barton.

"There he is!" he said. "Hey, you there! We're here to help."

Barton looked back the way he'd come, then towards the men. They were approaching him.

"Christ, are you okay?" the thinner one asked, gawking at Barton's injuries.

The glo was fading. Barton's focus was growing weaker, the sounds less clear. Now that he'd been reminded of his state, and seen two ordinary people from the ordinary world above, all his strength and resolve seemed to be fading. He heard himself murmur, "My daughter . . ."

"Yeah, we're getting them all out, don't you worry," one of the men assured him.

Barton shook his head. They wanted to stop him. To take him out. He tried to move away from them but swayed. One of the men shouted something and he lashed out. Suddenly they were both on top of him, trying to hold him still. He threw a punch that connected, but it wasn't enough. They were swearing, flapping at him as he broke free. He made it two paces, maybe more, but the effort made his head spin. He fell to the side, hand on a wall to support himself. Then he slumped forward, crashing into the floor. As his consciousness faded, he heard one of them approaching. "Christ, we need a medic."

Holly heard a commotion somewhere ahead and paused. If those were shouts, her daughter might be in trouble. Or it might be something else, drawing her into danger. She started to skirt the sound, through tunnels that seemed to run parallel, without getting too close. She listened carefully for more.

At a doorway that ran towards the noise, she stopped and found a drop, a ledge looking over a brick courtyard below. There was a sound below like a pig sniffing for truffles. A large creature shuffling about. She leant into the room, looked down and immediately regretted the decision.

A creature that looked like a four-foot hairless man with spiky bones exposed along the length of his spine was crouched over something else; a heap of gore and fur that might once have been a creature but that was, in this instant, nothing more than a bloody mess. It was still moving. A pawed foot twitched and a round eye, part of what must have been its head, looked fearfully up towards her. The thing crouching over it was feeding, its snout rooting into flesh, splashing blood to the sides.

A hand clamped over Holly's face and pulled her back, held her tightly enough that her scream was muffled. A man's voice whispered, "Best not to disturb it, come."

He frog-marched her down the tunnel without removing his hand. She did as he bid, stiffly walking, eyes ahead. They reached a corner and he said, "I'm going to let you go. Can you be cool?"

She nodded.

He released her and she jumped away and turned back in one motion. Her index finger was up and pointing, ready to scold. Casaria's usual charm was somewhat diminished by the blood caking half his head and shirt. Still, when she saw his smile Holly found herself conflicted, halfway between fear and thankfulness.

"Where's Pax?" he asked.

Holly resisted answering, with questions of her own. "Who are you? What happened to you?"

"I'm here to help," he said, then repeated, "Where's Pax?"

Guilt suddenly rolled over Holly and she threw her hands up, despairing. "I don't know! I don't know where I am, or where anyone else is – I left my daughter, I wanted to help – but I left her, oh God, I'm a terrible person –"

"All right, all right." Casaria closed his eyes. "Let's get you out of here, at least. Christ."

He gestured for her to follow, with a dirtily bandaged hand, and walked ahead. She rushed to his heel as he continued without looking back, barely seeming to register her presence. He knew these corridors, she could see. She asked, "What are you doing down here?"

"Came to save you, didn't I?" he replied, though he hardly sounded happy about it. "When did you lose the others?"

"Ages ago. I left markings in the walls, but they disappeared."

Casaria hummed, not surprised.

"There are things down here," Holly told him. "Terrible things, lots of them. We need to be very careful."

"Sure. We don't have far to go."

"Thank God."

"Casaria?" A portly man in a tatty suit plodded into view, low on breath, unsurprisingly considering the state of him. A young fellow in a leather jacket appeared behind him, looking miserable. "You found another one!" The bigger man hurried towards them, waving his free hand; Holly saw he had a pistol in the other. She took a step behind Casaria for cover. The man huffed, looking at his gun, "Oh, don't mind this, ma'am, it's for your protection. Casaria, what were you thinking, coming down here?"

"Doing your job for you, evidently," Casaria said. "Now you can take her back to the surface and I can keep going."

"Absolutely not. You need to get out of here, now. You're in enough trouble as it is. What happened to your face?"

Holly frowned at Casaria, not liking where this was going. She reflected that the filthy bandaged hand and bloody face might have been clues as to him being bad news.

"Worry about it later," Casaria said. "Did you bring the weed, Landon?"

Holly was about to exclaim in shock; none of them looked like pot-heads. Maybe the younger one. But Landon thrust his hands onto his hips, puffing himself up, and said, "You're out of your mind if you thought Mathers would even entertain the idea."

Casaria gaped at him. "They're in the heart of the thing. And I have something that can help. You want them to just outrun it?"

"You couldn't have seriously thought it was an option," the leather jacket sneered. "Even if we knew what the machine did, why would we risk damaging the *praelucente*?"

"Because we need to!" Casaria snapped, marching towards him with his finger stiffly pointing. The young man retreated, fumbling for his gun, a moment from lifting it.

Landon stepped between them. "You need to *leave*."

"So you can do what? Create a distraction by wobbling your lard?"

"We already found a man, we're pulling him out. Given his

state, I'd say it's a big gamble that the others are even still alive."

"They are!" Holly blurted out. "My daughter – and the girl. You have to find them!"

All three men turned to her. Their expressions said her desperation was clear.

"This is a mess," Landon said.

"Take her out of here," Casaria said, "and give me your gun."

Landon eyed him. His hesitation was enough for Casaria to take charge. He ripped the pistol from Landon's hands and turned back the way he had come. Landon watched and didn't protest. He turned to the young man and, in an attempt to save face, snapped, "Go with him, I'll take care of the others."

The leather jacket hesitated, too, but rushed after Casaria.

"This way, ma'am," Landon said, holding a thick arm up. She followed, with one final look back towards Casaria. Landon's laboured breath got heavier as he walked, from discomfort, it seemed, as well as poor health.

"Will they be okay?" Holly asked. He did not reply.

They turned a corner to where Barton was lying. Landon started, "You can help me –"

Holly shot ahead with a cry, running to her husband's side. "Diz!"

23

Pax and Grace pressed themselves up against the far wall as more light seeped through the cracks around the door. Something thumped against it, like an enormous beast knocking to get in.

"What are we going to do?" Grace whispered.

Pax was out of ideas. The monstrous electric creature was filling the tunnel beyond their only exit. Even if they could get past it, there were creatures surrounding the whole thing. Had they been in its inner circle ever since she killed the sickle? Had they run the wrong way, and cut a path towards the inevitable ever since?

The door banged again, shaking on its hinges. Sparks of electricity flickered through.

"It's not going to hold," Grace said.

"It'll hold," Pax told her. "It has to."

She knew it wouldn't, staring at the shaking door. And no one was coming to save them. The only option was for one of them to save the other.

A plaintive howl rolled past Casaria and Gumg.

"We've saved two people, isn't that enough?" Gumg said, struggling to keep pace as Casaria strode ahead. Casaria did not reply. "We can get all the information we need from her, leave the others down here, deal with the aftermath when the horde has moved on."

Casaria kept his eyes ahead, only walking faster.

Gumg broke into a trot to catch up. "He had this on him, might interest you." Casaria gave Gumg a look as the younger man pulled a bag from his pocket. They stopped. Casaria stared at the glowing sack of mud. He reached, but Gumg dropped back, keeping it out of range. "Government property, now. You want to see what this is capable of, we take it back to the Ministry."

"You're raising your own bar in stupidity. We need that right now," Casaria said. "Where did you even get it? *Who* had it?"

"The other one we found. Barton, I guess. Don't know what he was up to but if you'd seen the state of him. Man, you're not using your head. This girl isn't worth losing your job over. Or worse." Casaria raised a fist, but Gumg was ready. His pistol was up, and though he took a fearful step back, he was resolute. "I'm doing you a favour. Think about it. You're not following protocol, breaking half a dozen rules with no upside for the Ministry. With this, with that machine, you can actually get ahead. Just play ball. What's this girl worth?"

Casaria turned away again; there was no time to argue. "We need to keep moving."

The sounds of the myriad creatures were getting closer.

"I oughta leave you down here with them!" Gumg called out. He could not, though, and Casaria knew it. The younger man rushed after him, but was not giving up. He said, "We can go as far as the break line. Hit a few of the creatures and give you an idea of how bad this is. But that's it. Then you have to admit it's over, turn back. Even if we *could* get them out, what'd be the point? The Ministry won't let them walk away."

Casaria gave him a sideways look. He wasn't sure, now, if he had an answer himself. Gumg was right. Saving Pax, and trying to free her, could spell the end of his career. It would lead to questioning and imprisonment, at best. In all likelihood, she would have to disappear. The thought of her ever joining the Ministry, after what she'd already done, was impossible. And even if she escaped their wrath, what then? She'd betrayed him from the start, and she was dangerous to the Sunken City. What use was she? Why did he care?

He shook the thoughts from his head. He cared precisely because she didn't. She'd defied the Ministry. And she'd reached out to him for help. He cared because this was his domain, and he was the sheriff down here. He wasn't going to let these monsters, or Ministry bullshit, get in the way of him doing his job and saving her. He'd figure the rest out later.

Turning another corner, they were both struck momentarily still by a tremendous fluttering, as though a cluster of bats had just taken flight. The noise grew louder, rapidly approaching.

"What is that?" Gumg asked.

"You should know," Casaria replied, readying both hands on the pistol.

Gumg cleared his throat before venturing a guess. "Wormbirds."

They flew into the tunnel, a flock of skeletal creatures with jagged, leathery wings. They fanned out across the ceiling, knocking into each other, ferociously swarming towards the men. Their curved bone-like beaks snapped with a war cry sharper than a pack of dogs barking.

Casaria stood his ground and started shooting, the pistol erupting in electric blasts that disappeared into the flock with explosions of feather and bone. Gumg looked over his shoulder, ready to run. Casaria shouted, "Stand your ground!"

Gumg did as he was told and started shooting too.

There were dozens of them, spread too wide for each shot to catch more than one or two at a time. As they got closer, the dark flock's detail became more apparent, white eyes flashing and tendrils dangling from their bellies, their noise roaring into a din. Gumg let out his own escalating shout of defiance. When the flock flapped within a few metres of them, Casaria saw Gumg's foot shift, the young man ready to run. Casaria turned his gun. One quick blast to the younger man's knee.

Gumg looked up in disbelief, more shocked by the betrayal than the pain. His leg was all but severed below the knee as he crumpled to the floor, mouth dumbly open, asking *why*? Casaria snatched at his pocket to take the bag of electric weed and leapt out of the way as the birds descended.

Gumg screamed under the attack. The wormbirds covered him, in a formidable cluster, too many for Gumg's final few shots and flapping hands to fend off. Their wings enveloped him, beaks pecking him into submission with sharp jabs. As their talons gripped his flesh and they settled, the belly tendrils stretched towards him. More and more piled onto Gumg, until he was completely hidden under the writhing mass. The whole flock was united, their flapping wings cloaking the egg-laying taking place underneath.

Casaria adjusted the setting on his gun and aimed down at the mass. They were all so concentrated now, the task was easy. Three shots of the wider, short-range charge and the mass was obliterated.

The pile of bodies smouldered on the floor, the stench of burnt flesh filling the tunnel. A few wings flapped up and down for a moment, and one or two of the birds fled back down the tunnel, having survived the final scorching.

Casaria stepped over the mangled remains and continued, giving the carnage no more than a cursory glance. As he walked, he threaded the pistol through his belt and lifted the Fae device, looking for a way to open it and fit the weed inside.

Holly's heart lifted as they broke free of the noxious underground, with Barton dragged between her and Landon. The fresh air filled her lungs as Landon needlessly helped her up the steps, out into a grotty back alley. They laid Barton down, groaning, on the concrete. Holly took in the surroundings. There was no one else there. An army of police cars and ambulances would have been nice. Fire trucks even, blaring red and blue lights and horns. Instead she had a man who looked like an overweight office worker with a beat-up saloon car parked beyond some overflowing steel bins.

"Where's the help?" Holly demanded. "My daughter is still down there, my husband is in" – she threw a frantic arm towards the bloodied, swollen mess of Barton – "*this* state. And you're all we have?"

"We'll take you back to the office," Landon mumbled, putting even less effort into talking than he had into carrying Barton. "He'll get the attention he needs. Help me lift him."

"He'll get help in an *office*?" Holly said, incredulous. Landon didn't appear to listen, puffing over to the vehicle and opening a door. "And the others? Are you going back down there?"

"It's under control," he said.

Holly stomped a foot. "My daughter is trapped down there. With monsters chasing her. *Chasing* her. If this is your department then you *must* go down there and help. Understood?"

Landon scratched the back of his head. "I can't leave you."

"I'm fine, as you can very well see. And I can keep myself more than occupied by trying to tackle whatever horror has befallen my husband. You, however, can help below, can't you?"

Landon grunted, then nodded. "Okay. Yes. Of course. After we get him into the car."

She watched him as though searching his face for some guarantee that he would help, and in return he gave her a weak smile. She sighed and did as she was asked. Together, they lifted

Barton and heaved him, with all their combined strength, up onto the back seat. As Holly got in and dragged her husband further in, his blood smearing across the leather upholstery, she fussed, "This is highly unorthodox. An ambulance would be more appropriate."

"We've got the best doctors in the city," Landon assured her. He closed the door behind them. Holly took Barton's head on her lap and scanned him up and down, as Landon took something from the trunk of the car. Some of Barton's wounds, Holly could see, had already been treated, with stitches and dirty bandages covering them. Many were fresh, though; cuts and bruises over his upper body. His unthinkably distorted ankle. She tore a length of her t-shirt off and tried to reach the ghastly thing. At least tying it off might help. She paused and looked through the window. Landon moved as slowly as physically possible, back into the maze entrance, a long gun hanging by his side now.

She was still staring when a tiny lady dropped onto the window in front of her. Holly fell back in surprise, then scrambled for the other door. She grabbed at the handle but it wouldn't open. There was no button to unlock it. She looked to the front. A grid of metal separated her from the driver's area, like the rear of a police car. Spinning back desperately, she found the tiny lady waving, her voice barely audible through the window. "I'm taking out the glass!"

A small firecrack sounded: a pistol blast that shattered the glass in front of the fairy. Holly froze in fear and awe as she watched Letty hover into the car, pistol in her hand. Her heart pounding in her ears, it took Holly a moment to acknowledge the fairy's words.

"We need to get you out of here."

Holly stared at her untrustingly, her hand probing behind her for the door handle. She subtly, quietly, tried again. Definitely not moving. From one world of monsters to another. She put on a brave face and turned back to the fairy. "Get away from me, you little devil!"

"Where's Pax?" Letty asked, ignoring the threat.

Holly steeled herself, gritting her teeth. She said, "Safe from you, at least."

"I'm trying to help," the fairy snarled, fluttering closer and making Holly flinch. "I heard you before. You said the things were following you. What things?"

"The worst! A whole army of them. Isn't that what you wanted?"

"Not me," Letty said. She looked at Barton. "Is he gonna make it?"

Holly hesitated. Was this thing asking so she could kill him? It sounded like concern, though. "I – I think he's okay – just his leg –"

"Okay. I need you to listen to me. It's not safe for you here. The guys who forced you down there – *not* me – they'll be back. The guys who helped you out, they're no better. I'm gonna unlock this car and get it ready for you to hightail it out of here, you got me?"

Holly shook her head. "My daughter – I can't just –"

"Don't worry. We're not going anywhere till the others get out."

"All right," a man's voice interrupted them. They snapped their attention back to the tunnel entrance. Landon was back, shotgun raised and aimed at the car. "Knew I shouldn't leave you."

Letty met Holly's gaze, dropping down into the car. The fairy whispered, "Don't let him know I'm here."

24

The electricity bled through the bricks around the doorway, though the monster's limbs could not seem to penetrate the door. It was trying to suck energy from their room, the same way it sucked energy from the city above. The mortar between the bricks lit up luminescent blue, which spread along the walls and slowly crept closer.

"What do we do?" Grace cried, tightening her grip on Pax.

Pax hesitated, deciding on her final plan. She'd spent all her life running from responsibility but she was better than that. She was not like the fairies or the Ministry. And this time she'd do something before it was too late. She closed her eyes and said, "I'll draw its attention. You run for another exit."

"What?" Grace yelped. "No – you can't –"

Pax moved Grace away from the rear wall, as the threat snaked through the brickwork and along the floor towards their feet. She said, "On three, I'm leaving. You go the opposite way. Stop for nothing. You understand?"

Trembling uncontrollably, Grace nodded, eyes fixed on the blue light.

"One . . . two . . ." Pax grabbed the door handle, braced herself. "Three!"

As the door opened, the blinding light flooded in. Pax ran headlong into it. She met no resistance, only the warmth of this creature, crackling from all directions. Thrusting her hands over her ears, Pax aimed for the large room, ducking under the centre of the beast of light. She screamed, "Go, Grace! Go!"

The blue light retreated from the walls, from the room, as Grace flashed through it. Pax rolled out into the massive room and the full force of the lightning creature followed her, its electric limbs licking over the walls and slamming into supportive positions. Pax scrambled across the floor, away from it, but one of the limbs dropped onto her, pinning her down. Her breath was punched out of her as she shouted to Grace, "Get out of here!"

Grace had stalled in the middle of the room, staring horrified at Pax. The shout triggered her, though, and she sprinted for a set of steps, the monster ignoring her. Pax twisted back to face it, as shards of electricity wrapped around her like a hundred fingers. The light surged, another blinding flash, and her whole body convulsed. The energy pulsed out of her again, preparing for another surge, and she slumped.

Pax watched the light shift above her, the beast settling with its tentacles of light rooted in the walls. Where the limbs touched the walls, they spread out, flowing into large rectangles of light. More limbs extended above, an array of reaching arms clambering into the roof, pressing towards the city above. As it jolted through her again, with the force of an electric shock, the whole thing began to pulse. It was feeding. As it was draining her, it was pumping energy down from above, too, all surging into its core, making it brighter. But it didn't stop there. The energy kept going, flowing through the lower limbs, back into the walls. Back into the rectangles where it was connecting.

The pulse slowed again, leaving Pax gasping for air.

As Pax lay helplessly, two horrible truths gripped her. First, the beast looked nothing like a minotaur. Barton and Apothel and the rest had been completely duped. Second, whatever energy was draining from her was not fuelling the beast. It was being siphoned elsewhere. Towards whatever it was that had supposedly been helping them.

There had to be a way out. Pax had to tell them. Had to tell someone. They were wrong about it, all of them. None of them really understood what this thing was, or what it was doing. She had to get out.

The monster waxed in luminescence once more, the glow signalling its next surge. Pax gritted her teeth in anticipation of what might be the final shock.

Casaria slammed into Grace as she ran out of a doorway and almost knocked him down. He pushed her against a wall as she shrieked. Aware of the blue glow ahead, he shouted, "Is she in there?"

"Yes!" Grace cried back. "She saved me!"

"Stay here!" Casaria ordered, and turned to the domed room, hefting the Fae device up. He entered on a high walkway, the *praelucente* below, filling the space in its full electric glory, limbs spread to the walls and above, all glowing a dazzling blue, near white. He had to shield his eyes from the brightness, spying movement below. It was on top of her, her limbs flapping amid the chaotic sparking.

Propping the Fae device against his hip, the thing now filled with dirt, Casaria spun the cogs that would spin and pressed a finger to the only button that he was confident would actually do anything. The weapon seemed to be reacting to the movements ahead, vibrating with a magnetic pull, emitting its own contrasting glow.

Pax screamed. He saw her face, writhing out from the chaos, and was shocked still. In her agony she caught Casaria's eye. Then it moved, a sudden shift, and Casaria let out an involuntary sound as he saw the central shape of the creature turning his way.

"Shoot it!" Pax gasped up to him, barely able to form the words.

He didn't think, couldn't think, merely clung to the sound of her voice and did as he was told. He pressed the button, and the monster's blinding light met with an even stronger flash from the Fae device. A terrific roar shook the walls and ceiling. The crackling and groaning and clicking of the monsters was overtaken by its sound, the world filled with light.

Then the beast retreated.

Quick as a spider, it sucked its tentacles back into the furthest exit, the room dipping into instant darkness. The roar decreased in volume as the creature moved further away, leaving behind a gentle rain of dust and mortar, a terrific ringing in the ears, and the vile smell of burnt flesh.

25

The trio made their way back through the tunnels without talking. Pax and Grace had no energy left for conversation. It was all Pax could do to use Casaria as a crutch and carry herself out. Casaria clearly knew the way and the creatures were gone, the horrible sounds of the Sunken City silenced. There was nothing else to discuss. They made no comments, not even when they passed the charred corridor of mangled bird corpses, with its steaming pile of bones and feathers that seemed, somewhere underneath, to contain human remains.

When they reached the surface, there was no sound of beasts pursuing them. It seemed, as they took gasps of the air above, that they had all been holding their breath. The moment they exited onto the alley, Grace crumpled and started sobbing. Pax followed her quickly, touching her shoulder and wanting to tell her it was okay, they were safe now. She didn't manage to say anything, just groaned.

"I know," Grace wept, tears streaming. The emotion flowed out of her, the despair she had been pushing down throughout the ordeal. Pax fixed Casaria with an accusing stare. She wasn't sure exactly how or why, but she needed him to know this young lady's suffering was his fault. He hardly looked bothered, regarding the pair of them, instead, with a quizzical eye. Pax must have looked frazzled, hair singed and clothes charred. Casaria gave her a shrug as he ran a hand through his slick hair and took out a cigarette. As he lit it, he looked around the alley, up to the windows and roofs.

"You still here?" he called out. The answer he got surprised him.

"Of course," Landon said, drawing all eyes to the alley entrance. He was next to a car, the rear window smashed, a shotgun in his hands, aimed in at Holly. Sat in the car, she looked petrified. In their elation at getting out, none of them had heard Holly's attempt to call to her daughter, or the agent's snarl for her to be quiet and stay put.

"Good to see you're with us, Landon," Casaria said flatly. "Don't know what we'd do without you."

"Where's Gant?" Landon said.

Casaria held the cigarette in his mouth for a still moment. Landon's former nonchalance was gone, his mouth tight with focus. He didn't need to voice the obvious conclusion.

"I need all of you over here," Landon said. "Join the parents."

As Pax stood up, Grace stopped crying, unable to comprehend who this newcomer was or what he wanted with them. She met Holly's worried gaze and her mother gave her a smile filled with relief. Grace struggled upright too, as Holly nodded to inside the car. Something for Grace to see. The bulk of her father was lying across the back seat with her.

No one moved towards Landon. Grace looked to Pax for guidance. She, in turn, looked to Casaria. He had set off the Fae device, and he and Landon hardly seemed to be on the best terms. Casaria kept smoking. He said, "Did you see where the horde went?"

"Gone," Landon said. "They came this way, but moved off. Quickly. Your doing?"

Casaria held up the weapon he'd set off.

"You maniac," Landon said. "What have you done?" He didn't wait for an answer. "We'll figure it out at the office. All of you, to the car."

It was time to test Casaria. Pax said, "I'd rather walk, if it's all the same to you." She nodded to the broken window. "Doesn't look safe."

"It's not all the same to me," Landon said irritably. "You'll all give full statements. And you'll need to fill in a W6-DPe, Casaria. Explaining *exactly* what happened to Gant."

"I've had a long day," Casaria said. "The forms can wait."

Landon turned the shotgun from Holly towards them. "It's not a choice."

"What's wrong with you?" Grace's voice quietly interrupted. Landon's face softened slightly at the sight of her. Her face dirty and bare feet black with blood, her round eyes shining in the encroaching dusk, pleading for everything to simply be okay. "After what we've been through. How can you point a gun at us? How could you point a gun at my *mum*?"

"Good question." Casaria tossed his cigarette butt aside.

"How's that necessary?"

"She was trying to get away," Landon said, glancing to his vehicle.

"The glass was smashed from the outside," Pax pointed out, frowning.

"Look –" Landon started, but stopped as Casaria took a step towards him.

Pax put a hand on Casaria's arm, brushing close to him. "Don't."

"It's okay," Casaria told her, determination in his eyes.

Exactly what she needed.

"You're being an idiot, Casaria!" Landon said, bumping into the car as he raised the shotgun. He did not fire. Casaria closed the distance between them and pushed the gun to the side. He threw a punch square into Landon's jaw. The bigger man smacked into the car but didn't go down. He was stunned for a moment, unbelieving. Then he fought back. He swung the gun at Casaria, and Casaria grabbed hold of it. They grappled away from the car.

Pax took Grace's hand. "Come on!"

"Here, here!" Holly called, bursting out of the car but immediately dropping into the driver's seat. Pax and Grace rushed around her, the sound of the men's struggles rising from strangled grunts to a flurry of thumps and flapping jackets. They broke away from each other and started swinging punches. Pax shoved Grace into the back of Landon's car, then scrambled for the passenger seat as Holly shoved the door open.

The slamming car doors and the starting engine drew Casaria's attention away from his fight. He let out a "Hey!", enough distraction for Landon to recoup, and took a punch to the gut.

Holly hit the accelerator hard and they lurched forwards, out onto the street and almost straight into another car. She swerved, and they were away. Pax twisted back to see Casaria thrusting Landon across the alley, taking control once more. He turned away from his stumbling adversary and ran after them. When he reached his own car, he stalled as he patted down his pockets. Pax held up his car keys for him to see, and smirked at his bemused face, just before they turned a corner.

"Oh thank God you're okay," Holly said quickly, clutching the steering wheel tight. "Thank God thank God thank God."

Grace clambered forward to hug her mother as they sped down

a main road. Pax sank into her own seat. She rolled her head to one side, impressed. "You stole his keys, too?"

"No," a familiar voice said from above. Pax's eyes widened at Letty, perched on the rear-view mirror. "I did."

26

Interrupted by the theft of his car and the continuing betrayal at the hands of Pax Kuranes, Cano Casaria's passion for defying the Ministry and pummelling the sense out of Landon left him. Landon had pulled himself to his feet and recovered the shotgun by the time Casaria returned to the alleyway, but he, too, was uninterested in continuing their fight. He used the gun to support himself as he gave Casaria an *I-told-you-so* sneer. They waited for a Ministry pick-up then drove back to the office together. Casaria considered, on the way, that it might be best to tell the whole Ministry where to shove their regulations, but he was weary and had done enough damage for one evening. That could wait until the next day, when he had more time and sense to weigh up his options.

When he stopped to think about it, Casaria realised that he had lost blood from the Fae gunshot and had taken a few blows from Landon, who was heavy, if poorly trained. He had also suffered some kind of impact from enduring the blast of the Fae device. Put it all together and he should receive some sort of medal, if he could make the story sound heroic enough for the powers that be. Never mind that Gumg (Gant?) had died and he'd had a hostile encounter with Landon; he had come face-to-face with the *praelucente* itself, and any divergent behaviour could, perhaps, be explained by that. People simply did not survive getting close to that thing.

By the time they reached the Ministry building, he had slipped in a brief apology to Landon, with a winning smile, saying he was not sure what had come over him and perhaps he had simply gone too deep into the Sunken City. Landon had no choice but to accept the apology; Casaria knew, after all, that his fellow agent had hardly shone in the crisis himself.

There was, indeed, a furious meeting with Mathers, who promised extended suspension without pay, but for all his bluster the deputy director could not hide his curiosity about the encounter with the *praelucente*. And he had to admit at least a little responsibility for neglecting the Fae threat. Casaria had warned them it would happen. He did not go into detail about exactly how the *praelucente* encounter had played out, though. Casaria started to warn Mathers about the apparent effect it had had on Pax, but Mathers shut him down. He didn't want the burden of that particular truth. Not at this juncture.

Casaria would give a full debrief in the next few days, to a council organised by the IS Relations Initiative. Just what he needed; a grilling from Sam Ward over his conduct in the field. The suspension was nothing in the face of that worse punishment. And before going home and taking his unpaid leave, Casaria had the added wound of needing to fill in a mountain of forms.

An R42, to give a general account of how Pax Kuranes originally came into contact with the Sunken City. Likewise, R42s accounting for Grace and Holly Barton's knowledge of the Sunken City. One wasn't necessary for Darren Barton, as his was already on file, but an R46b was needed to explain why he had resurfaced after a nine-year hiatus.

A series of F67s, one to record each encounter with the Fae.

A D7-PR for each and every civilian involved, including any notable encounters in the West Farling incident and the apprehension of Rufaizu. These would be supplemented with a D7-PRe each for Pax, Grace and Holly, to be shared with local and national law enforcement agencies who would be on the lookout for them as persons of interest.

A D7-X to notify local law enforcement of the stolen Ministry equipment, one car. Even though that should've been Landon's to write up.

A W4-SoI, describing the circumstances that had led to the civilians entering the Sunken City. Followed by a W4-SoE for each notable event within the Sunken City.

Then of course there was also the W6-DPe, explaining the exact circumstances and nature of Gumg's death, and a series of W4-GIs and MC12s that would explain anything else that had happened or been encountered over the course of this madness. The W6-DPe was particularly frustrating, as Casaria was well aware he would need to fill it in a second time after spelling Gumg's name wrong.

These forms were a living hell about one rung below the thought of repeating this information to Sam Ward in person, with each minute that Casaria spent writing seeming to stretch for an hour. Still, the more he wrote, the more he appreciated the situation, and the easier he imagined it would be to throw his successes in Ward's face. For all the trouble she had caused, Pax Kuranes was exactly the breath of fresh air he had hoped for. She had brought the fairies out of hiding and she had delivered Fae technology to the Ministry. With the destruction of a Sunken City entrance, one of their own agents dead and confirmed Fae shots fired at him, Casaria saw an unavoidable conflict on the near horizon, with Ward's Initiative in tatters.

It made him smile. There were precious few soldiers in the Ministry's ranks; they would need him when the Fae came. They needed him a lot more than he needed them. He concluded one document with every intention of being provocative, not caring how close to the truth he was:

The weapon that has fallen into our hands is what they are willing to cross the line and kill humans for. It cannot be questioned that it has the potential to harm the praelucente and change our world. It is the opinion of this agent that this is the first real evidence of the bigger plans of the Fae population. Their interests in the Sunken City are not, as MEE canon dictates, historical – these interests are current and dangerous.

Casaria left the office shortly after midnight, satisfied that some clerk would be suitably frightened into encouraging a superior officer to do something. He walked the short distance home, enjoying the night air and imagining the future. He would see the Fae and the Ministry clash, he would see blood in the tunnels of the Sunken City and he would be given permission to lead a force against the Fae Transitional City. His own initiative.

And he would see Pax Kuranes again.

They would argue and fight, and she would insult him and he would laugh, and they would be forced to join forces and he would channel her passion towards his own agenda. Maybe they would sleep together, he hadn't decided on that, yet. The more he saw of her the more tempted he became, despite himself. Maybe, he decided, she was more an 8 than a 7.

Beaming at his imagined future, Casaria approached his apartment block and stopped across the street. His smile disappeared as he felt, all in an instant, the trepidation and urge to run that he must have so frequently bestowed on others. He let it pass, forcing his smile back onto his face and walking towards the entrance.

The two large men he had fought in the afternoon were waiting with metal bats in their hands. There was no shame in their stance, even though they were loitering by the door of a wealthy apartment block in one of central Ordshaw's most prestigious neighbourhoods. Between them stood a shorter man, more discreet but menacing in a different way. He was round at his waist and cut a contrast to his goons in their labouring overalls, with his brown woollen suit – something he had clearly chosen with an eye to personal preference, rather than style. As Casaria approached, the man stepped forward.

"Mr Casaria." He had a rough west Ordshaw accent, the sort that intimidated people from out of town. "My name's Stacy Monroe. I believe you had a disagreement with my men today."

"I thought we'd settled that," Casaria replied.

"No. We're about to."

Casaria scanned all three men, particularly focusing on the bats. They were making a statement, bringing bats instead of guns. And he had already established that at least one of them was no pushover. Tired and injured as he was, it was unlikely he could take on all three of them. He kept smiling, though, thinking it was still worth a try.

27

Pax got out of the car for some air, finally clear of the centre of town and, apparently, not being followed. Letty flew out to settle on the car roof next to her. Pax rested an arm on the car, with barely the energy to keep standing.

"You got a new wing," Pax observed tiredly, mustering the strength to smile.

"Of sorts. You got all beat up."

"Kind of," Pax said, nodding.

"Reeling with regrets?"

Pax looked into the car, at Grace hunched exhausted across her defeated father's slowly breathing chest. She scanned over to Holly, who was stretching her legs, staring out at the city skyline. On this hillside road, the view was spectacular, all the skyscrapers and low houses coming together in a chain of yellow windows reflected in the calm river. Pax said, "Nah. You?"

Letty followed her gaze to the skyline. She took a breath. "Not especially."

"I hoped you'd come back," Pax told her.

"Yeah? *I* hoped you'd get yourself killed." Pax reached out to poke her, her finger all but knocking the fairy down, and Letty batted back at her. "Oi. I'll tear it off."

Holly turned back to them, no humour in her face. She had developed lines of exhaustion over the space of the past few hours. She gave Letty an odd look, still unsure quite how to reconcile the existence of such a small person. Rather than dwell on it, she turned to Pax. "Where do we go? I have a sister in Manchester."

"I'm not sure that's safe," Pax said. "I wish you hadn't become involved yourselves."

Holly nodded. "All this . . . it's unnatural. Not for normal people."

"I've got some people that we might contact. They're not normal." Pax pictured Bees' warehouse. He might still be there at this hour. Even if he wasn't, they could hide inside, it wouldn't be difficult to find a way in. Though given that Casaria had turned up with the device instead of them, and her phone was fried so she couldn't call ahead, that avenue looked hazy.

"My husband has a friend, near Long Culdon I believe," Holly said. "The inventor. She knows what we're dealing with, at least. And she's kept herself hidden from it, all these years, somehow. I think she could help him, if we can't go to a hospital."

Pax considered it, thinking out loud. "Mad scientist versus possible gangsters. Some choice."

"That settles it, then," Holly said firmly. "You didn't mention your friends were criminals."

"Ah." Pax lifted a finger, about to protest, but realised there was no point. "Okay." Holly nodded and went to get back in the car. Pax said, "Mrs Barton. You did well."

Holly gave her a short nod. "Thank you for keeping my daughter safe."

She sat back down in the car and turned to her family, whispering assurances to them.

Letty lolled onto her elbows and let out a big sigh. She said, "So you great lummox, what now? Now that there ain't no one wants to resolve this thing but us."

"Whatever that thing is down there," Pax said, "it's doing more damage than I think even your people realise. Or care about. And it's more complicated than you realise. It was feeding the thing that I think was giving Apothel orders."

"His Blue Angel?"

"Yeah. Its screens can do way more than communicate messages. Whoever or whatever's behind them, I think it's *their* monster. Why did they make Apothel jump through those hoops? Why did they encourage him to get your device if it could harm this thing that they're somehow connected to?"

"To remove it from the equation?" Letty replied. "Apothel *died*, remember."

Pax frowned. She drummed her fingers on the car. "Whatever he was doing, it wasn't what he thought it was. Right?"

"Yeah." Letty yawned. "I need a fucking drink. So do you."

Pax nodded. She imagined going back to the Sticky Tap, and putting a full stop in the craziest weekend of her life. Have a drink, pat herself on the back. They'd all got away more or less safely, at least. But that only reminded her of Rufaizu. He must've known what Apothel went through, having come back from wherever he'd been. And she hadn't done a thing for him, even as she'd risked everything to save this family. Hadn't done a thing for him *yet*, she told herself. She said, "We can figure this out, Letty. We want the same thing, don't we?"

Letty stared at her, like she was studying her anew. The fairy said, "Close enough."

"That'll do," Pax said. She laid her hand down for Letty to hop on, and the fairy regarded it oddly. She didn't need the help any more. But she shrugged and stepped up anyway. As Pax lifted Letty and moved to get back in the car, she said, "We've still got a few days until the WPT. Think we can save the city by then?"

Enjoyed reading?

It'd be an awful shame to stop there, wouldn't it? If you enjoyed *Under Ordshaw*, rest assured there's plenty more to come, starting with what happens on Monday…

In the meantime, I would be incredibly grateful if you could take a few minutes to leave a review online (even if it's short – to be concise is a virtue, after all). I am an independent author who relies on fans like you, as word of mouth does more to draw attention to my books than any advertising can.

To be the first to hear news of the upcoming sequel, and for some free reads and other great book offers, be sure to join my mailing list; you can find it via the various addresses below.

www.phil-williams.co.uk

You can also connect with Phil through:
Facebook: **www.facebook.com/philwilliamsauthor**
Twitter: **www.twitter.com/fantasticphil**
Email: **phil@phil-williams.co.uk**

About the Author

Phil Williams is the author of the Estalia, Ordshaw and Faergrowe series. Living in Sussex, UK with his wife, he also writes screenplays and spends a great deal of time walking his impossibly fluffy dog, Herbert.

ACKNOWLEDGEMENTS

This book would not have been possible without the input of many inspiring people. Some of the first seeds were sown when I visited New York, so thanks to Fran and Chris, whose companionship helped shine a light on the minotaur lurking under the city. Thanks are also due to everyone who read and gave encouragement to the screenplay of *Penguins and Seahorses* (even those that wanted the story completely changed). The project never manifested, but this novel is much richer for it.

Thanks, as always, to my excellent editor Carrie O'Grady, who helped me make sense of a labyrinthine story, and polished it up to boot. Thanks, too, to my readers who have offered words of support in the run-up to its release.

Above all, thanks to my wife, Marta, who I must emphasise has always been informed and supportive of my own forays into dark underworlds.

ALSO BY PHIL WILLIAMS

Wixon's Day (Estalia Series)

He just wanted to see what was left of the world. He never meant to join the war to save it.

Marquos drifts through the cloud-concealed Empire of Estalia, searching for hope of a better future as he scavenges to survive. In the Deadland of the North, they say the sky is clear, and the stars shine. Marquos believes there is beauty there.

With rebels plaguing the canals, and the authoritarian Guards pursuing Marquos for his attempts to liberate a child, the route north is wrought with peril. The militant rulers and the ragged resistance fighters vie for the boatman's support, drawing Marquos into a war many don't realise exists, and revealing secrets about the world that threaten to wipe out what little is left.

Aftan Whispers (Estalia Series)

As the days grow darker in the Estalian Empire, young Tyler stays positive by helping others. But when he meets a girl on the run with enemies in the highest places, Tyler's life gets complicated fast. Deni isn't afraid to kill, and she's got a secret that could tear apart the sky.

In a mortal chase that takes them from a besieged city across the war-torn countryside, Tyler soon discovers that the Empire's guardians are their most dangerous foe. Worse still, Deni is faced with a terrible choice: remain hidden and save herself – or expose herself to prevent the oncoming darkness.

Balfair's Confinement (Estalia Series)

The novella that started Deni's journey.

Isolated in the derelict estate of the engineer Balfair, with only a miserable fellow slave for company, Deni dreams of changing her arduous life. When her master drags something new from the swamp and excludes her from his secretive project, she finally sees her chance. Deni will do whatever it takes to break free – even if it means bringing the full weight of the war-mongering Guard down on Balfair.

The results may be devastating, but they will notice her at last – and she will be free.

28231665R00179

Printed in Poland
by Amazon Fulfillment
Poland Sp. z o.o., Wrocław